The Vineyards of Calanetti

Saying "I do" under the Tuscan sun…

Deep in the Tuscan countryside nestles the picturesque village of Monte Calanetti. Famed for its world-renowned vineyards, the village is also home to the crumbling but beautiful Palazzo di Comparino. Empty for months, rumors of a new owner are spreading like wildfire...and that's before the village is chosen as the setting for the royal wedding of the year!

It's going to be a roller coaster of a year, but will wedding bells ring out in Monte Calanetti for anyone else?

Find out in this fabulously heartwarming, uplifting and thrillingly romantic new eight-book continuity from the Mills & Boon® Cherish™ series!

A Bride for the Italian Boss by Susan Meier

Return of the Italian Tycoon by Jennifer Faye

Reunited by a Baby Secret by Michelle Douglas

***Soldier, Hero...Husband?* by Cara Colter**
Available October 2015

His Lost-and-Found Bride by Scarlet Wilson

The Best

His *Princ* … ers

Saved b

REUNITED BY A BABY SECRET

BY
MICHELLE DOUGLAS

Published in Great Britain 2015
by Mills & Boon, an imprint of Harlequin (UK) Limited,
Eton House, 18-24 Paradise Road, Richmond, Surrey, TW9 1SR

Special thanks and acknowledgement are given to Michelle Douglas for her contribution to The Vineyards of Calanetti series.

ISBN: 978-0-263-25165-4

23-0915

Harlequin (UK) Limited's policy is to use papers that are natural, renewable and recyclable products and made from wood grown in sustainable forests. The logging and manufacturing processes conform to the legal environmental regulations of the country of origin.

Printed and bound in Spain
by CPI, Barcelona

Michelle Douglas has been writing for Mills & Boon since 2007 and believes she has the best job in the world. She lives in a leafy suburb of Newcastle, on Australia's east coast, with her own romantic hero, a house full of dust and books, and an eclectic collection of '60s and '70s vinyl. She loves to hear from readers and can be contacted via her website, www.michelle-douglas.com.

With thanks to my fellow Romance authors for creating
such a strong and supportive community.
I can't begin to tell you how much
I appreciate it.

CHAPTER ONE

MARIANNA AMATUCCI STARED at the door of the Grande Plaza Hotel's Executive Suite and swallowed. With her heart pounding in her throat, she backed up to lean against the wall opposite. A glance up and down the corridor confirmed she was alone. Up here at the very top of the hotel all was free from bustle, the very air hushed.

She patted her roiling stomach. *You will behave.* Usually by mid-morning her nausea had eased.

It wasn't morning sickness that had her stomach rebelling, though. It was nerves. She stared at the door opposite and her skin broke out in a cool sheen of perspiration. She twisted her hands together. She had nothing to fear. This was Ryan—blond-haired, blue-eyed, tanned surfer boy Ryan.

An image of his long-limbed beauty and sexy smile rose in her mind and her heart started to flutter in an altogether different fashion. She pressed one hand to her abdomen. *Mia topolino, your papà is utterly lovely.*

She moistened her lips. No, she had nothing to fear. Her news would startle him of course. Heavens, the shock of it still reverberated through her own being. But he'd smile that slow, easy smile, pull her into his arms and tell her it'd all be okay…and she'd believe him. He'd come to see that a child would be a blessing.

Wouldn't he?

The corridor swam. She blinked hard and chafed her arms, the chill of the air-conditioning seeping into her bones. She stared at the door and pressed steepled hands to her mouth? It was just…what on earth was Ryan doing in the *Executive Suite*? She couldn't square that with the man she'd met on a Thai beach two months ago. A man more at home in board shorts and flip-flops and his own naked skin than a swish hotel that catered to Rome's elite.

Stupid girl! What do you really know of this man?

That was Angelo's voice sounding in her head. Not that he'd uttered the words out loud, of course. But she'd read them in his eyes in the same way she'd read the disappointment in Nico's. As usual, her brothers had a point.

What *did* she know of Ryan? She moistened her lips. She knew he made love as if he had all the time in the world. He'd made love to her with such a mixture of passion and tenderness he'd elicited a response from her that had delighted and frightened her simultaneously. She'd *never* forget their lovemaking. The week of their holiday fling had been one of the best weeks of her life, and while they'd made no plans to see each other again—too complicated with her in Italy and him in Australia—but…her head lifted. Maybe this was fate?

Or maybe being pregnant has addled your brain?

And standing here wondering why on earth Ryan was currently ensconced in the Executive Suite wouldn't provide her with an answer. Fortune smiled on men like Ryan—men that oozed easy-going good humour and warmth. The check-in clerk could simply have taken a shine to him and upgraded him, or a friend of a friend might've owed him a favour or…something. There'd be a logical explanation. Standing out here tying herself in knots was crazy, a delaying tactic.

She was no coward!

Marianna pushed away from the wall, wiped her palms down her skirt and straightened her shirt before lifting her hand and finally knocking. A thrill coursed through her. She and Ryan might not have made plans to see each other again, but he'd never been far from her thoughts during the last two months and maybe—

The door opened and Marianna's breath caught and held, suspended between hard pounds of her heart. The haze in front of her eyes slowly dissolved, and in sluggish bewilderment her brain registered that the stranger standing in front of her dressed in a bespoke suit and a crisp cotton business shirt and tie was—

She blinked and peered up at him. 'Ryan?'

He leaned towards her and then frowned. 'Marianna?'

The stranger *was* Ryan! Her pulse jumped as she took in the dark blond hair, the blue-green eyes, and the sensual curve of his lips. Lips that had started to lift, but were suddenly pressed together into a grim straight line.

She stared at that mouth, at the cool light in his eyes. How different he seemed. Her stomach started to churn with a seriousness that forced her to concentrate on her breathing for a moment.

'What are you doing here?'

That was uttered in a voice she barely recognised. She dug her fingernails into her palms. *Smile. Please. Please just smile.*

Her inner pleading did no good. If anything, his frown deepened. She stared at him, unable to push a word out of a throat that had started to cramp. *Keep breathing. Do not throw up on his feet!*

He glanced away and then back at her, and finally down at his watch. 'I have a meeting shortly.'

A chill chased itself down her spine as her nausea receded. Why would he not smile?

'I wish you'd called.'

She reached out to steady herself against the doorjamb. He was giving her the brush-off?

He lifted his wrist to glance at his watch again. 'I'm sorry, but—'

'I'm pregnant!'

The words blurted out of her with no forethought, without any real volition, and with the force of one of Thailand's summer storms. Her common sense put its head in its hands and wept.

He stilled, every muscle growing hard and rigid, and then his eyes froze to chips of blue ice. 'I see.' He opened the door wider, but the expression on his face told her he'd have rather slammed it in her face. 'You'd better come in.'

She strode into the room with her back ramrod straight. Inside, though, everything trembled. This wasn't how it was supposed to go. She'd meant to broach the subject of her pregnancy gently, not slap him over the head with it.

She stopped in the middle of the enormous living room with its plush sofas and ornate tables and furnishings and pulled in a deep breath. Right. Take two. She touched a hand to her stomach. *Mia topolino, I will fix this.*

Setting her shoulders, she turned to face him, but her words dried on her lips when she met the closed expression on his face. It became suddenly evident that he wasn't going to smile and hug her. She did her best not to wobble. Couldn't he at least take her hand and ask her if she was okay?

Except...why would he smile at her when she stood here glaring at him as if he were the enemy? She closed her eyes and did what she could to collect herself, to find a smile and a quip that would help her unearth the man she'd met two months ago. 'I know this must come as a shock—'

'I take it then that you're claiming the child is mine?'

She took a step back, her poor excuse for a smile dying on her lips, unable to reconcile this cold, hard stranger with the laid-back man she'd met in Thailand. Fear had lived inside her ever since she'd discovered she was pregnant—and she was tired of it. Seizing hold of that fear now, she turned it into anger. 'Of course it's yours! Are you attempting to make some slur on my character?'

She didn't believe in slut-shaming. If *that* was what he was trying to do she'd tear his eyes out.

'Don't be ridiculous!'

Oh, so now she was ridiculous, was she? She could feel her eyes narrowing and her fingers curving into claws. 'I'm just over two months pregnant. Two months ago I was—'

'On a beach in Thailand!' He whirled away from her, paced across the room and back again. His pallor made her swallow. He thrust a finger at her, his eyes blazing. 'Pregnancy wasn't part of the plan.'

'There was a plan?' She lifted her hands towards the ceiling and let loose a disbelieving laugh. 'Nobody told me about any plan.'

'Don't be so obtuse!'

Ridiculous? Obtuse? Her hands balled to fists.

'We were supposed to…to just have fun! No strings! Enjoy the moment, live in the moment, before sailing off into the sunset.' He set his legs and stabbed another finger at her. 'That's what we agreed.'

'You think…' Her breath caught. She choked it back. 'You think I planned this?'

If anything the chill in his eyes only intensified.

Her brothers might think her an immature, irresponsible piece of fluff, but it knocked the stuffing out of her to find Ryan did too.

Maybe they're all right.

And maybe they were not! She slammed her hands to her hips. 'Look, I know this has come as a shock and I know it wasn't planned, but the salient fact is that I'm pregnant and you're the biological father of the child I'm carrying.'

Her words seemed to bow him although as far as she could tell not a single one of his muscles moved. She pressed a fist to her mouth before pulling it down and pressing both hands together. She had to think of the baby.

What Ryan thought of her didn't matter. 'It…it took me a little while to get my head around it too, but now…'

She trailed off. How could she tell him that she now saw the baby as a blessing—that it had become a source of excitement and delight to her—when he stared at her like that? The tentative excitement rose up through her anew. 'Oh, Ryan!' She took a step towards him. 'Is this news really so dreadful to you?'

'Yes.'

The single word left him without hesitation and she found herself flinching away from him, her hands raised as if to ward him off, grateful her baby was too young to understand its father's words.

Ryan's chest rose and fell too hard and too fast. His face had become an immobile mask, but the pounding at the base of his jaw told her he wasn't as controlled as he might like her to think.

It was all the encouragement she needed. She raced over to him and seized him by the lapels of his expensive suit and shook him. She wanted some reaction that would help her recognise him, some real emotion. 'We're going to have a baby, Ryan! It's not the end of the world. We can work something out.' He stood there like a stone and panic rose up through her. She couldn't do this on her own. 'For heaven's sake.' She battled a sob. 'Say something useful!'

He merely detached her hands and stepped back, releasing her. 'I don't know what you expect from me.'

That was when some stupid fantasy she hadn't even realised she'd harboured came crashing down around her.

You are such an idiot, Marianna.

A breath juddered out of her. 'You really don't want this baby, do you?'

'No.'

'The bathroom?' she whispered.

He pointed and she fled, locking the door behind her

before throwing up the crackers she'd managed for breakfast. Flushing the toilet, she lowered the lid and sat down, blotting her face with toilet paper until the heat and flush had subsided. When she was certain her legs would support her again, she stood and rinsed her mouth at the sink.

She stared at her reflection in the mirror. *Screw-up!* The accusation screamed around and around in her mind.

She didn't know that man out there. A week on a beach hadn't given her any insight into his character at all. She'd let her hormones and her romantic notions rule her…as she always did. And now she'd humiliated herself by throwing up in the Executive Suite of the Grande Plaza Hotel. It was all she could do not to scream.

With a superhuman effort, she pushed her shoulders back. She might be impulsive and occasionally headstrong, she might be having trouble reining in her emotions at the moment, but the one thing she could do was save face. Her baby deserved far more than that man out there had to give.

She rinsed her mouth one more time, and dried her hands before pinching colour back into her cheeks. With a nod at her reflection, she turned and flung the bathroom door open…and almost careened straight into Ryan standing on the other side, with his hand raised as if to knock.

She might not recognise him, but the familiarity of those lean, strong hands on her shoulders as he steadied her made her ache.

'Are you okay?' His words shot out short and clipped.

She gave a curt nod. He let her go then as if she had some infectious disease he might catch. It took a concerted effort not to snap out, *Pregnancy isn't contagious, you know?*

He stalked back out into the main room and she followed him. 'Can I order something for you? Food, tea…iced water?'

'No, thank you.' All she wanted to do now was get out of here. The sooner she left, the better. 'I—'

'The fact that you're here tells me you've decided to go ahead with the pregnancy.'

'That's correct.'

He shoved his hands into his pockets, his lips pursed. 'Did you consider alternatives like abortion or adoption?'

She had, so it made no sense why anger should rattle through her with so much force she started to shake. 'That's the male answer to everything, isn't it? Get rid of it…make the problem go away.'

He spun to her. 'We were *so* careful!'

They had been. They'd not had unprotected sex once. Her pill prescription had run out a month before she was due to return to Italy, though, and she'd decided to wait until she'd got home before renewing it. They'd used condoms, but condoms, obviously, weren't infallible.

Her heart burned, but she ignored it and straightened. Not that her five feet two inches made any impact when compared to Ryan's lean, broad six feet. 'I made a mistake coming here. I thought…'

What had she thought?

Anger suddenly bubbled back up through her. 'What's this all about?' She gestured to his suit and tie, his Italian leather shoes, angry with him for his stupid clothes and herself for her overall general stupidity. 'I thought you were…'

His lips twisted into the mockery of a smile. 'You thought me a beach bum.'

She'd thought him a wanderer who went wherever whim and the wind blew him. She'd envied him that. 'You had many opportunities to correct my assumption.'

He dragged a hand down his face. 'That week in Thailand…' He shook his head, pulling his hand away. 'It was an aberration.'

'Aberration?' She started to shake with even more force. 'As I said, I made a mistake in coming here.'

'Why didn't you ring?'

She tossed her head and glared. 'I did. A couple of days ago. I hung up before I could be put through…*to the Executive Suite*. It didn't seem the kind of news one should give over the phone.' It obviously wasn't the kind of news she should've shared with him at all. This trip had been an entirely wasted effort. *I'm sorry,* topolino. She lifted her chin. 'I thought you would like to know that I was pregnant. I thought telling you was the right thing to do. I can see, though, that a child is the last thing you want.'

'And you do?'

His incredulity didn't sting. The answer still surprised her as much as it did him. She moved to cover her stomach with her hand. His gaze tracked the movement. 'Ryan, let's forget we ever had this conversation. Forget I ever came here. In fact, forget that you ever spent a week on a beach with me.' *Aberration that it was!*

She turned to leave. She'd go home to Monte Calanetti and she'd build a wonderful life for herself and her child and it'd be fine. Just…fine.

'I don't know what you want from me!'

His words sounded like a cry from the heart. She paused with her hand outstretched for the door, but when she turned his coldness and impassivity hit her like a slap in the face. The room swam. She blinked hard. 'Now? Nothing.'

He planted his feet. 'What were you *hoping* for?'

She'd swung away from him and her hand rested on the cold metal of the door handle. 'I wanted you to hug me and tell me we'd sort something out.' What a wild fantasy that now seemed. She turned and fixed him with a glare. 'But I'd have settled for you taking my hand and asking me if I was all right. That all seems a bit stupid now, doesn't it?'

Anger suddenly screamed up through her, scalding her throat and her tongue. 'Now I don't even think you're any kind of proper person! What I want from you *now* is to forget you ever knew me. Forget all of it!' *Aberration?* Of all the—

'You think I can do that? You think it's just that easy?'

'Oh, I think *you'll* find it incredibly easy!'

She seized the vase on the table by the door and hurled it at him with all of her might. The last thing she saw before she slammed out of the room was the shock on his face as he ducked.

Ryan stared at the broken vase and the scattered flowers, and then at the now-closed door. *Whoa!* Had that crazy spitfire been the sweet and carefree Marianna? The girl who'd featured in his dreams for the last two months? The girl who'd shown up on the beach in Thailand and had blown him away with her laughter and sensuality?

No way!

He bent to retrieve the flowers and broken pieces of the vase. *Pregnant?* He tossed the debris into the wastepaper basket and stumbled across to the sofa. *Pregnant?* He dropped his head to his hands as wave after wave of shock rolled over him.

In the next moment he leapt up and paced the room in an attempt to control the fury coursing through him. She couldn't be! A child did not figure in his future.

Ever.

Him a father? The very idea was laughable. Not to mention an utter disaster. No, no, this couldn't be happening to him. He rested his hands on his knees and breathed in deeply until the panic unclamped his chest.

You can walk away.

He lurched back to the sofa. What kind of man would that make him?

A wise one?

He slumped, head in hands. What on earth could he offer a child? Given his background…

Money?

He straightened, recalling Marianna's shock at finding him ensconced in the Executive Suite wearing a suit and tie. A groan rose up through him, but he ground it back. He'd played out a fantasy that week on the beach. He'd played at being the kind of man he could never be in the real world.

One thing was sure. Marianna hadn't deliberately got pregnant in an attempt to go after his money. She hadn't known he had any!

Did she, though? Have money? Enough to support a baby?

Why hadn't he thought to check?

He passed a hand across his eyes. When he'd opened the door to find her standing on the other side, his heart had leapt with such force it had scared him witless. He'd retreated behind a veneer of professional remoteness, unsure how to handle the emotions pummelling him. He had no room for those kinds of emotions in his life. It was why he'd made sure they'd said their final farewells in Thailand. But…

Pregnant?

Think! He pressed his fingers to his forehead. She'd mentioned that her family owned a vineyard in Tuscany. It didn't mean she herself would have a lot of spare cash to splash out on a baby, though, did it?

He strode to the window that overlooked the gardens and rooftops of Rome with the dome of Saint Peter's Basilica in the distance, but he didn't notice the grandeur of the view. His hand balled to a fist. Had he really asked her if the baby was his? No wonder she'd lost her temper. It had been an inexcusable thing to say.

I'm pregnant.

She'd blurted it out with such brutal austerity. It had taken everything inside him to stay where he was rather than to turn and run. He'd wanted to do anything to make her words not be true. Who'd have thought such cowardice ran through his veins? It shouldn't be a surprise, though, considering whose genes he carried.

He dragged a hand down his face. When she'd stood there staring at him with big, wounded eyes, he'd had to fight the urge to drag her into his arms and promise her the world. That wasn't the answer. It wouldn't work. And he'd hurt her enough as it was.

He let loose a sudden litany of curses. He should've taken her hand and asked her how she was, though. He should've hugged her and offered her a measure of comfort. Shame hit him.

Now I don't even think you're any kind of proper person.

He didn't blame her. She might even have a point. He seized the room phone and punched in the number for Reception. 'Do you have a guest by the name of Marianna Amatucci staying here at the moment?'

'I'm sorry, Signor White, but no.'

Damn! With a curt thank-you, Ryan hung up. He flung open the door and started down the hallway, but his feet slowed before he reached the elevator. What did he think he was going to do? Walk the streets of Rome looking for Marianna? She'd be long gone. And if by some miracle he did catch up with her, what would he say?

He slammed back into his room to pace. With a start, he glanced at his watch. Damn it all to hell! Seizing his mobile, he ordered his PA to cancel his meetings for the rest of the morning.

He shook off his suit jacket, loosened his tie, feeling suffocated by the layers of clothing. His mind whirled, but one thought detached itself and slammed into him, making him flinch. *You're going to become a father.* He didn't want to become a father!

Too bad. Too late. The deed has been done.

He stilled. Marianna no longer expected his involvement. In fact, she'd told him she wanted him to forget they'd ever met. And she'd meant it. He ran a finger beneath his collar, perspiration prickling his scalp, his nape, his top lip. He could walk away.

Better still he could give her money, lots of money, and just...bow out.

His grandmother's face suddenly rose in his mind. It made his shoulders sag. She'd saved him—from his parents and from himself—but it hadn't stopped him from letting her down.

He fell onto the sofa. Why think of her now? He'd tried to make it up to her—had pulled himself back from the brink of delinquency. He'd buckled down and made something of himself. He glanced around at the opulence of the hotel room and knew he'd almost succeeded on that head. If he walked away now from Marianna and his child, though, instinct told him he'd be letting his grandmother down in a way he could never make up.

He'd vowed never to do that again.

You vowed to never have children...a family.

What kind of life would this child of his and Marianna's have? He moistened his lips. Would it be loved? Would it feel secure? Or...

Or would it always feel like an outsider? When parenthood became too much for Marianna would this child be shunted to one side and—?

No! He shot to his feet, shaking from the force of emotions he didn't understand. He would not let that happen. He didn't want to be a father, but he had a duty to this child. He would not abandon it to a life of careless neglect. He would not allow it to be overlooked, pushed to one side and ignored.

He swallowed, his heart pounding. He didn't have a clue about how to be a father—he didn't know the first thing about parenting, but… He knew what it was like to be a child and unwanted. He remembered his parents separating. He remembered them remarrying new partners, embracing their new families. He remembered there being no place for him in that new order. He hadn't fitted in and they'd resented this flaw in their otherwise perfect new lives. His lips twisted. His distrust and suspicion, his wariness and hostility, had been a constant reminder of the mistake their first marriage had been. They'd moved on, and it had been easier to leave him behind. *That* was his experience of family.

He would not let it be his child's.

He might not know what made a good father, but he knew what made a miserable childhood. No child of his was going to suffer that fate.

He slammed his hands to his hips. Right. He glanced at his watch and then rang his PA. 'I'd like you to organise a car for me. I'm going to Monte Calanetti tomorrow. I'll continue working remotely while I'm there so offer my clients new appointments via telephone conferencing or reschedule.'

'Yes, sir, would you like me to organise that for this afternoon's appointment as well?'

'No. I'll be meeting with Signor Conti as planned.' This afternoon he worked. He wasn't letting Marianna's bombshell prevent him from sealing the biggest deal of his career. He'd worked too hard to let the Conti contract slip from his fingers now. Clinching this deal would launch him into the stratosphere.

Conti Industries, one of Italy's leading car-parts manufacturers, were transitioning their company's IT presence to cloud computing. It meant they'd be able to access all points in their production chain from a single system. Every car-part manufacturing company in the world was watching, assessing, waiting to see if Conti Industries could make the transition smoothly. Which meant every car-part manufacturing company in the world had their eyes on him. If he pulled this off, then he could handpick all future assignments, and name whatever price he wanted. His name would be synonymous with success.

Finally he'd prove that his grandmother's faith in him hadn't been misplaced.

In the meantime… He fired up his laptop and searched for the village of Monte Calanetti.

CHAPTER TWO

RYAN GLANCED DOWN at the address he'd scrawled on the back of a Grande Plaza envelope and then at the driveway in front of him, stretching through an avenue of grapevines to a series of buildings in the distance. A signpost proudly proclaimed Vigneto Calanetti—the Amatucci vineyard. This was the place.

With a tightening of his lips, he eased the car forward, glancing from left to right as he made his way down the avenue. Grapevines stretched in every direction, up and down hillsides in neat ordered rows. They glowed green and golden in the spring sunshine and Ryan lowered the windows of the car to breathe in the fragrant air. The warm scents and even warmer breeze tormented him with a holiday indolence he had no hope of assuming.

Pulling the car to a halt at the end of the driveway, he stared. This was Marianna's home? Her heritage? All about him vines grew with ordered vigour. The outbuildings were all in good repair and the spick and span grounds gave off an air of quiet affluence. He turned his gaze to the villa with its welcoming charm and some of the tension drained from him.

Good. He pushed out of the car. He'd never doubted Marianna's assertion that she could stand on her own two feet, but to have all of this behind her would make things that much easier for her.

And he wanted things to be as easy for her as they could be.

A nearby worker saluted him and asked if he was wishing to sample the wines. Ryan cast a longing look at the cellar building, but shook his head. 'Can you tell me where

I might find Signorina Amatucci? Marianna Amatucci,' he added. She'd mentioned brothers, but for all he knew she might have sisters too.

The worker pointed towards the long, low-slung villa.

He nodded. *'Grazie.'* Every muscle tensed as he strode towards it. He had to make Marianna see sense. He had to convince her not to banish him from their child's life.

Once he reached the shade of the veranda, Ryan saw that the large wooden front door stood open as if to welcome all comers. He stared down the cool shade of the hallway and crossed his fingers, and then reached up and pulled the bell.

A few moments later a tall lean figure appeared. He walked down the hallway with the easy saunter of someone who belonged there. 'Can I help you?'

Ryan pulled himself up to his full height. 'I'm here to see Marianna Amatucci.'

The suntanned face darkened, the relaxed easiness disappearing in an instant. 'You're the swine who got her pregnant!'

He'd already deduced from the hair—dark, and wavy like Marianna's—that this must be one of her brothers. A protective brother too. More tension eased out of Ryan's shoulders. Marianna should be surrounded by people who'd love and support her.

A moment later he swallowed. Protective was all well and good, but this guy was also angry and aggressive.

The two men sized each other up. The other man was a couple of inches taller than Ryan and he looked strong, but Ryan didn't doubt his ability to hold his own against him if push came to shove.

Fighting would be far from sensible.

He knew that but, recalling the way Marianna had thrown the vase at him yesterday, her brother might have the same hot temper. It wouldn't hurt to remain on his guard. He planted his hands on his hips and stood his ground.

'So…you have nothing to say?' the other man mocked.

'I have plenty to say…to Marianna.'

The brother bared his teeth. 'You don't deny it, then?'

'I deny nothing. All you need to know is that I'm here to see Marianna.'

'Do you have an appointment?'

He debated the merits of lying, but decided against it. 'No.'

'What if she doesn't want to see you?'

'What if she does?'

'I—'

'And if she doesn't want to see me, then I want to hear it from her.' He shoved his shoulders back and glared. 'I mean to see her, one way or another. Don't you think it would be best for that to happen here under your roof?'

The other man stared at him hard. Ryan stared right back, refusing to let his gaze drop. The brother swore in Italian. Ryan was glad his own Italian wasn't fluent enough for him to translate it. With a grim expression, he gestured for Ryan to follow him, leading him to a room at the back of the house that was full of rugs and sofas—a warm, charming, lived-in room. Light spilled in from three sets of French doors that stood open to a paved terrace sporting an assortment of cast-iron outdoor furniture and a riot of colour from potted plants.

Home. The word hit Ryan in the centre of his chest. This place was a home. He hadn't had that sense from any place since the day his grandmother had died. His lungs started to cramp. He didn't belong here.

Another man strode through one of the French doors. 'Nico, I—' He pulled up short when he saw Ryan.

Brilliant. Brother number two.

Brother number one—evidently called Nico—jerked a thumb at Ryan. 'This is Paulo.'

He glanced from one to the other. Marianna had told them his name was Paulo?

The second brother started towards him, anger rolling off him in great waves. Brilliant. This one was even taller than the first. Ryan set himself. He could hold his own against one, but not the two of them. He readied himself for a blow—he refused to throw the first punch—but at the last moment Nico moved between them, his hand on his brother's chest halting him.

Ryan let out a breath and then nodded. 'No. This is good.'

'Good?' brother number two spat out, his face turning almost purple.

'That Marianna has brothers who look out for her.'

The anger in the dark eyes that surveyed him turned from outright hostility to a simmering tension. 'You made her cry, you…' A rash of what Ryan guessed must be Italian insults followed. Brother number two flung out his arm, strode away, and then swung back to stab a finger at him. 'She returned here yesterday, locked herself in her room and cried. That is your fault!'

Ryan's shoulders slumped. He rubbed a hand across his chest. 'Yesterday…it was…it didn't go so well and she—' He pushed his shoulders back. 'I'm here to make it right.'

'What do you mean to do?' Nico asked. His voice had become measured but not for a second did Ryan mistake it for a softening.

'I mean to do whatever Marianna wants me to do.' Within reason, but he didn't add that caveat out loud.

Brother number two thrust out his jaw. 'But are you going to do what she *needs* you to do?'

He thrust his jaw out too. 'I will not *force* her to do

anything. I refuse to believe I know better than she does about what she needs. She's a grown woman who knows her own mind.'

The brothers laughed—harsh, scornful laughter as if he had no idea what he was talking about.

Ryan's every muscle tensed and he could feel his eyes narrow to slits as a dangerous and alien recklessness seized him. 'Have the two of you been bullying her or pressuring her in any way?'

Had they been pressuring her to keep the baby due to some outdated form of conservatism? Or… Had they been pressuring her to give the baby up because of scandal and—?

'And what if we have, Paulo?' brother number two mocked. 'What then?'

'Then I will beat the crap out of you!'

It was stupid, reckless, juvenile, but he couldn't help it. Marianna was pregnant! She needed calm and peace. She needed to take care of her health. She didn't need to be worried into an early grave by two overprotective brothers.

The brothers stared at him. Neither smiled but their chins lowered. Nico pursed his lips. The other rolled his shoulders. Ryan stabbed a finger first at brother number one and then at brother number two. 'Let me make one thing crystal clear. *I am not abandoning my child.* Marianna and I have a lot we need to sort out and we're going to do it without interference from either one of you.'

Raised voices drifted out across the terrace as Marianna marched towards the villa. She rolled her eyes. What on earth were Angelo and Nico bickering about now? She stepped into the room…

And froze.

Ryan!

A shock of sweet delight pierced through the numbness she'd been carrying around with her all day, making her tingle all over.

No! She shook it off. She would *not* be delighted to see him. Of all the low-down—

His gaze speared to her and the insults lining up in her mind dissolved.

'Hello, Marianna.' His voice washed over her like warm, spiced mead and she couldn't utter a single sound. She dragged her gaze away to glance at her brothers. Angelo raised a derisive eyebrow. 'Look what the cat dragged in, Marianna.' He folded his arms. 'Paulo.'

Ryan ignored his mockery to stride across to her. He took her hand in his and lifted it to his lips. Her heart fluttered like a wild crazy thing. 'Are you okay?' He uttered the words gently, his eyes as warm as the morning sun on a Thai beach.

While it wasn't a hug and an 'it'll all be okay' there was no mistaking the sincerity of his effort. She hadn't expected to see him again. Ever. She'd thought he'd have run for the hills.

'Marianna?'

She loved the way he said her name. It made things inside her tight and warm and loose and aching all at once. His grip on her hand tightened and she shook herself. 'Yes, thank you.' But the sudden sexual need that gripped had her reefing her hand from his. They were no longer Ryan and Mari, free and easy holidaymakers. They were Ryan and Marianna, prospective parents. That put a very different spin on matters and the sooner she got her head around that, the better.

This wasn't about him and her. It was about him and the baby. Did he want to be involved with the baby? If he did, and if he was sincere, then they would have to sort something out…come to some kind of arrangement.

Shadows gathered in Ryan's eyes. She swallowed, recalling the way she'd thrown the vase at him. 'And you? Are you okay?'

She watched him as he let out a slow breath. 'As you haven't thrown anything at me yet, then yes—so far, so good.'

Behind him, Nico groaned. 'You threw something at him?' he said in Italian.

'He made me angry,' she returned in her native tongue, trying not to wince at how rash and impetuous it must make her sound.

With a sigh she glanced back at Ryan. 'Have you been formally introduced to my brothers?'

'I've not had that pleasure, no.'

His tone told her they'd been giving him a hard time, but he didn't seem too fazed by it. A man who could hold his own against her two overprotective brothers? Maybe there were hidden depths to Ryan she had yet to plumb. *Let's hope so,* mia topolino. She wanted her baby to have a father who would love it.

She couldn't get her hopes up on that head, though. She recalled all the things he'd said yesterday and her stomach started to churn. He might just be here to offer her some kind of financial arrangement—to buy her off.

Keep your cool until you know for sure.

She tossed her head. She meant to keep her cool regardless.

She pulled herself back to the here and now and gestured. 'This is my oldest brother, Angelo, and this is Nico. He manages our vineyard.' She couldn't keep a thread of pride from her voice. She adored both of her brothers. 'And this—' she went to touch Ryan's arm and then thought the better of it '—is Ryan White.'

The men didn't shake hands.

Angelo gave a mock salute. 'Paulo.'

Ryan glanced down at her with a frown in his eyes. She waved a dismissive hand through the air. 'It is a stupid joke of theirs. Don't pay them any mind.'

'Marianna's boyfriends don't last too long,' Nico said. A deliberate jab, no doubt, at what he saw as her flightiness. 'Angelo and I decided long ago it was pointless remembering names.'

Angelo folded his arms. 'How long do you think this one will last, Nico?'

'Six weeks.'

'I'll give him four. He doesn't look as if he has what it takes to keep Mari's interest.'

'True. I can't see that he has anything more to offer her than any of the others.'

A clash of gazes ensued between the men and in some dark, dishonourable place in her heart the silent interchange fascinated her.

She tried to shake herself from under its spell. *What is wrong with you?*

With a snort, Ryan turned back to her. 'May I take you out to lunch?'

She glanced at Nico, who told her in Italian to take the afternoon off. 'Give him a chance.'

'You owe it to him, *bella*,' Angelo added.

What on earth…? She pulled in a breath, grateful her brothers spoke in their native tongue. She recalled the raised voices she'd heard when she'd approached the villa. 'How good is your Italian?' she asked Ryan.

'Very poor.' He glanced at Angelo and Nico. 'Which is probably a blessing.'

She folded her arms and glared at her brothers, reverting back to Italian. 'Did you put him up to this?'

Nico shook his head. 'But if this man is the father of your baby, you need to speak with him.'

'I did that yesterday!'

His gaze skewered her. 'Did you? Or did you merely drop your bombshell, throw a temper tantrum and run?'

Her face started to burn. It took an effort of will not to press her hands to her cheeks to cool them. Nico had a point.

Another thought slid into her then and she stared at each man in turn. If Angelo and Nico saw her dealing with the father of her prospective child maturely and responsibly, then that would help them see her as a responsible adult who could be trusted to make sensible decisions about her life, right? Not to mention the life of her unborn child. Maybe this was one way she could prove to them that she wasn't a failure or a flake.

She glanced down at her hands. Ryan *was* the father of her child. If he wanted to be a part of their baby's life…

Lifting her chin, she turned back to Ryan and reverted to English. 'I need to talk to Nico about the vines for a few minutes and then we can go for lunch.'

He nodded and glanced around. 'What if I wait over there?' He pointed to a sofa on the other side of the room.

She pressed her hands together. 'Perfect.' She wasn't so sure how perfect it was when Angelo followed him and took the seat opposite.

'Is there anything wrong with the vines?' Nico said, his face suddenly alive and intent.

'The soil is perfect! You have done an admirable job, Nico.'

'You set the groundwork before you left.'

Did he really believe that? Did he really think her an asset to the vineyard? She shook the thought off. She would prove herself to him. And Angelo. She was good at her job. 'The grapes are maturing as they should, but if the long-range weather forecast is to be believed, then we need to consider irrigating the northern slopes sooner than usual.'

'You mentioned last week something about new irrigation methods you'd picked up in Australia?'

She and Nico moved to the dining table to go over her report, but all the time her mind was occupied with Ryan. She heard him try to make small talk about the vineyard, but Nico asked her a question and she didn't hear Angelo's reply.

The next time she had a chancc to glance up it was to see Ryan flicking a business card across to Angelo with the kind of mocking arrogance that would've done both of her brothers proud.

She dragged her attention back to Nico. 'From what I've seen so far, Nico, the vines are in great shape. I'll continue with my soil samples over the next week and checking the vines for any signs of pests or moulds, but…' she shrugged '…so far, so good. Seems to me we're on track for the fattest, juiciest grapes in the history of winemaking.'

It might've been an exaggeration, but it made her brother smile as it was supposed to. 'I'm glad you're home, Mari.'

Guilt slid in between her ribs at that. She'd been Irresponsible Marianna too long. She'd left Nico to run the vineyard on his own and now… She rubbed a hand across her chest. And now both of her brothers thought her an incompetent—a screw-up—that they needed to look after. They hadn't said as much, of course, but she knew.

'I'm not sure I like him.'

She glanced up to find Nico staring at Ryan.

She'd liked the man she'd met in Thailand. She'd liked him a lot. She hadn't liked the man she'd met at the Grande Plaza Hotel yesterday, though. Not one little bit. The man sitting on the sofa…she wasn't sure she knew *him* at all.

She touched Nico's arm. 'What matters is if I like him or not, I think, Nico.'

The faintest of smiles touched his lips. 'You always like them, Marianna…for a week or two.'

'This one is different.'

'Is he?'

Yes. He was the father of her unborn child.

CHAPTER THREE

'THE FOOD HERE is superb,' Marianna told Ryan, staring at the *arancini* balls the waitress set in front of her. Very carefully she drew the scent into her lungs and then gave up a silent thanks when her stomach didn't rebel.

It didn't mean she had an appetite, though. When Ryan didn't pick up his cutlery to sample his fettuccine, she figured he wasn't all that hungry either. She leaned back and folded her hands in her lap. 'So…it wasn't food you wanted after all.'

'I wanted to talk to you…privately.'

Daniella, the maître d', had taken one look at Marianna's face and seated them in the most secluded corner of the restaurant. Marianna was glad now that she had. 'Well…talk.'

He picked up his fork and tested each tine with his index finger. He made as if to stab at a mushroom, but he set the fork down again and shuffled back in his seat. Marianna had no interest in making the way easy for him, but his continuing silence started to stretch her nerves thin.

'I did an Internet search on you last night.'

His gaze speared to hers.

'I know you're some hotshot consultant who comes in and saves companies who are on the brink of bankruptcy. I know you're worth a lot of money.' She shook her head. Her idea of him being some free and easy gypsy type must've had him laughing up his sleeve. She suspected her hope that he would love their child would prove just as ridiculous. 'So let's clear this up right now. I do not want your money. I have no intention whatsoever of making any claim on it.

No doubt you've come prepared with papers you've had your lawyers draw up.'

The darkness in his eyes throbbed between them. Marianna swallowed. 'C'mon, then.' She beckoned with both hands. 'Pull them out and let me sign them. Then, perhaps, we can enjoy our meal before going our separate ways.'

'You think that's why I'm here?'

She arranged her serviette in her lap and then folded her hands on the table. 'Isn't it?'

He reached out as if to take her hand, but pulled back to rub his nape instead. Marianna pulled her hands into her lap and glanced away. Looking at him… It was too hard. It hurt all of the sore places inside her.

'I'm sorry I didn't react well yesterday. Your news blind-sided me. I was…stunned. In shock.'

That was one way of putting it.

'At the time I didn't consider how hard it must've been for you to deal with the news all on your own. I'm sorry.'

His apology surprised her.

She grimaced. She hadn't exactly broached the subject of her pregnancy gently, had she? She'd shot the news at him like a torpedo…and she'd expected him to deal with that with grace? Her brothers would blame it on her flair for the dramatic. The truth of the matter was she'd taken one look at the stranger who'd confronted her yesterday and had panicked.

He had another think coming, though, if he expected her to apologise for that! She seized her cutlery and sliced off a sliver of food, lifting it towards her mouth.

'What I'm trying to say, Marianna, is that I have no intention of abandoning my child.'

She dropped her knife and fork back to her plate, the morsel untouched. Her heart pounded. 'And what if you have no say in that?' He'd said he didn't want a baby. *Ever.* She wasn't letting a man like that anywhere near her child.

He turned grey. 'Please don't prevent me from being a part of my child's life. I know I behaved badly yesterday and I know I'm not what you thought I was, but then you're not what I thought you were either.'

That arrow found its mark.

He leaned towards her, his eyes ablaze. 'I know what it's like to feel unwanted by one's parents.'

Something inside her stilled, and then started to ache at the pain he tried to mask in the depths of his eyes.

'I have no intention of letting a child of mine feel rejected like that.'

Yesterday, before their unfortunate meeting, she'd expected him to be a part of their child's life…regardless of anything else that might or might not happen between them. She passed a hand across her eyes and tried to still the sudden pounding of her heart. 'How do you think this can work?'

He captured her hand and forced her to look at him. The sincerity in his face caught at her. 'Marianna, I will do anything you ask of me. Anything except…' He swallowed.

'Except?'

'Walk away from our child. Or…'

'Or?'

'Marry you.'

She reclaimed her hand and glared. 'Who mentioned anything about marriage?'

'I didn't say I thought that's what you wanted. I—'

'Good! Because I don't! We don't even know each other!' A fact that was becoming increasingly clear. 'What kind of antiquated notions do you think I harbour?'

'Don't fly off the handle.' He glared right back at her. 'I thought it wise to make myself and my intentions clear. Your brothers seem very traditional and—'

'They're protective, not stupid! They wouldn't want me marrying some man just because I'm pregnant. For heaven's sake, women get pregnant all the time—single women. No one expects them to get married any more. No one thinks it's shameful or a scandal.'

He leaned towards her, his eyes intent. 'So your brothers haven't been pressuring you about the baby?'

'What are you talking about?'

He eyed her warily. 'Don't fly off the handle again.'

Her hands clenched. 'Do *not* tell me what to do.'

His eyes narrowed, turning cold and hard, and Marianna had to suppress a shiver, but she held her ground. He folded his arms and eased back. 'I was concerned your brothers might've been pressuring you to keep the baby when you didn't want to. Or, alternatively, pressuring you to give it away when you wanted to keep it.'

'They've been nothing but supportive.' She'd screwed up, again, but she had their support. They might think her a total write-off, but she would always have their support.

But if they were pressuring her, had Ryan meant to intervene on her behalf? The idea intrigued her.

She moistened her lips. 'What do *you* mean to pressure me to do?'

'It seems to me I have very little say in the matter.' He picked up his fork again, put it down. 'It's your body and your life that will be most immediately impacted. I'll support you in whatever decisions you make. If there's anything practical I can do, I hope you'll let me know.'

He made her feel like a spoilt child.

'Correct me if I'm wrong, but yesterday I was under the impression that you meant to keep the baby.' He frowned, looking not altogether pleased. 'Have you changed your mind?'

She shook her head. An unplanned pregnancy hadn't been part of her life plan, but… She'd always intended to become a mother one day. She'd just thought she'd be married to the man of her dreams first. Still, the moment the pregnancy test had confirmed that she was, indeed, pregnant, she'd been gripped by such a fierce sense of protectiveness for the new life growing inside her that, while she'd considered all of the options available to her, the only one that had made any sense to her *emotionally* was to keep her baby. To love it. To give it a wonderful life. 'I'm going to have this baby and I'm going to raise it and love it.'

He nodded. 'I know I've made it clear that I'm a lone wolf—I never intend to marry—but I do mean to be a father to this child.'

She rubbed her temples, unable to look at him. She finally picked up her cutlery and ate a bite of food.

He honed in on her unease immediately. 'What's wrong with that? Why do you have a problem with that?'

'Lone wolves don't hang around to help raise the young, Ryan. They hotfoot it to pastures greener.' Nothing he said made sense. 'If you intend to never marry, that's your business. But I don't see how you can be both a lone wolf and any kind of decent father.'

She raised her hands, complete with cutlery, heavenwards. 'To be a good father you need to be connected to your child, involved with it. When it needs you to, you have to drop everything at a moment's notice. You have to…' She met his gaze across the table. 'You have to put its needs above your own…even when you're craving solitude and no strings.'

He swallowed.

'A baby is just about the *biggest strings* that you can ever have.' She leaned towards him. 'Ryan, you will be bound to this child for life. Are you prepared for that?'

He'd gone pale. He stared back at her with eyes the colour of a stormy sea.

'For a start, how do you mean to make it work? How…?' She rubbed a hand across her brow. 'I can tell you how I mean to make it work. I mean to stay here in Monte Calanetti where I have a good job, a family I love and a network of friends. My entire network of support is here. What do you mean to do—drop in for a few days here and there every few months when you're between assignments?'

'I…'

She massaged her temples. 'I don't know what your definition of a good father might be, but that's not mine.'

'Mine neither.' Hooded eyes surveyed her. 'You have to realise I've only had a day so far to try and think things through.'

He wanted her to cut him some slack, but…this was her child's life they were talking about.

'I did have a thought during the drive up here,' he said. The slight hesitancy in his voice coupled with the deep, whisky tones made the flutters start up in her stomach.

She swallowed. 'Okay, run it by me, then.'

'What if I buy a house for you and the baby, and whenever I can get back here I can stay and spend time with our child? I do mean to get back here as often as I can.'

He wanted what? She seized her fork and shoved lukewarm *arancini* into her mouth to stop from yelling at him. Yelling wouldn't be mature or adult. It wouldn't help their child. Her grip on her cutlery tightened. Oh, but it would be entirely understandable! Any innocent bystander would surely agree?

'You don't like the idea?'

She shook her head and chewed doggedly.

'But the house would be yours and—'

He broke off when she pushed a whole half of an *arancini* ball into her mouth.

He rubbed a hand across his jaw. 'Okay, what's wrong with that plan?'

It took her a moment of chewing and swallowing and

sipping of water before she could trust herself to answer with any equanimity. 'You don't ever mean to marry, no?'

His frown deepened. 'Right.'

'But it doesn't necessarily follow that I won't.'

He gazed at her blankly.

'The mother, her baby, her ex-lover and her husband,' she quipped. 'All under one roof? How cosy. *Not!*' She stabbed her fork at him. '*Not* going to happen.'

He dragged a hand down his face, before glancing back at her with eyes that throbbed.

'Ryan, I will organise my own life—my own house and furniture, not to mention my work. If you want contact with the baby, then that's fine. I have no intention of stopping you—but nor do I have any intention of being your glorified housekeeper while you do it. Buy a house in Monte Calanetti by all means. Feel free to hire a housekeeper and a nanny to help you with housework and the baby, but don't think you're going to cramp my life like that.'

'You mean to marry one day?'

Of all the things she'd just said, *that* was what he wanted to focus on? 'Of course I do.' And while they were on the topic… 'I mean to have more babies too.'

He paled. 'And do you think this future husband of yours will love our child?'

What kind of question was that? How on earth could he think it possible for her to fall in love with someone who wouldn't love her child too?

He sat back, his spine ramrod-rigid. 'My offer of a house wasn't meant to curtail your freedom. I can see now it was ill considered. You're right—it would never work. I'm sorry.'

Did he really want what was best for their baby? She recalled the way his eyes had flashed when he'd said he wouldn't let his child feel unloved or rejected. They were on the same side, but it didn't feel that way.

He pressed his lips together. 'We're going to have to learn to work together on this.'

'Yes.' At least they agreed about that.

He thrust a finger at her. 'And I can tell you now that I won't be foisting my child off onto some nanny.'

That scored him a few brownie points, but… 'What do you know about caring for a baby? Have you ever fed one and then burped it? Have you ever changed a diaper?'

He glanced away.

Marianna choked. 'Please tell me you've at least held one.'

He didn't answer, but his expression told its own story. Why on earth was he here? If he avoided children with the same ferocity he did marriage, why hadn't he run for the hills?

I know what it's like to feel unwanted.

Her heart suddenly burned for the small boy that was still buried deep in the man opposite her. He'd been hurt badly by his childhood, that much was evident, and he wanted to do better by his child. She couldn't help but applaud that.

'Hell, Marianna!' He swung back. 'I know nothing about babies or children. They're a complete mystery to me. But I can learn and I will love our child.'

For their baby's sake, she hoped he was right.

He'd gone so pale it frightened her. 'Can you teach me what I need to know?'

'Me?' The word squeaked out of her.

'There isn't anyone else I can ask.'

The implication of his lone-wolf ways hit her then and she gulped. It occurred to her that he might need this baby more than he realised. She gripped her hands together in her lap. Admittedly, she and he did have to learn to work together—that'd be in the best interests of their child. And seeing the two of them working things out together in a rational, *adult* way would put both Angelo's and Nico's minds at rest.

If Ryan really was willing to make an effort then…then their baby deserved to know him, to have him in its life. Her baby deserved to be loved by as many people as possible. And… She swallowed. And if Ryan did suddenly decide that he couldn't handle fatherhood, it'd be better to discover that now, before the baby was born.

You mean to test him to see if he's worthy?

Was that what she was doing?

Who's going to test you?

She closed her eyes.

'Is everything okay with your meals?'

Marianna's eyes sprang open to find Daniella frowning at their barely touched plates. 'The food is divine,' Marianna assured her.

The maître d' planted her hands on her hips. 'Would you like me to get Raffaele to prepare something else for you?'

'No, no, Daniella. Honestly, the food is wonderful. It's just…' Marianna pulled in a deep breath. 'Well, the fact of the matter is I'm pregnant, and food at the moment—any food—is a bit…iffy.'

Daniella stared, and then an enormous smile spread across her face. 'Marianna! What exciting news! Congratulations!'

She bent and hugged her and Marianna's throat thickened. 'I…thank you.'

The maître d' tapped a finger against her lips and then suddenly winked and wheeled away. Her smile speared straight into Marianna's heart. She swallowed and blinked hard. She stared down into her lap and fiddled with her napkin.

Ryan ducked his head and tried to catch her eye. 'Are you okay?'

'Uh-huh.' She nodded.

He brought a fist up to his mouth. 'Are you crying?'

Marianna lifted her napkin and buried her face in it for a moment, before drawing back and dabbing at her eyes.

Ryan stared at her as if he didn't have a clue what to do. He shuffled on his seat, but he didn't run. 'What's wrong?'

'Nothing's wrong. It's just...Daniella is the first person who's actually congratulated me and...and it was nice. The news of a baby should be celebrated.'

Ryan's face darkened. 'I thought you said your brothers had been supportive.'

'They have been, but...well, the pregnancy was obviously unplanned and...' They hadn't meant to make her feel as if she'd messed up. 'They've been worried about me.'

On the table, his hand clenched. 'And I acted like a damn jerk.'

She blew out a breath. She hadn't really given him much of a chance to act any other way.

Daniella returned with an enormous slice of chocolate cherry cake—Marianna's favourite. 'Compliments of the chef,' she said, setting it down with a flourish.

Darn it! Her throat went all thick again. Her emotions were see-sawing so much at the moment they were making her dizzy. 'Thank him for me,' she managed.

She promptly curved her spoon through it and brought it to her mouth, closing her eyes in ecstasy as the taste hit her. She opened them again to find Ryan staring at her as if mesmerised. A strange electricity started to hum through her blood.

They both glanced away at the same time.

Her heart pounded. Okay. In her mind she drew the word out. She and Ryan might be virtual strangers—in their real world incarnations—but they still generated heat. A lot of heat. She ate more cake. Ryan set to work on his fettuccine. They studiously avoided meeting each other's eyes.

If they were going to successfully co-parent, they were going to have to ignore that heat.

What a pity.

She choked when the unbidden voice sounded in her head. She was shameless!

'Everything okay?'

She pulled in a breath. 'If we want this to work, Ryan—'

'I for one *really* want it to.'

His vehemence made her feel less alone. She couldn't afford to trust it too deeply, to enjoy it too much, but…it was still kind of nice. 'Then we need to be really, *really* honest with each other, yes?'

He set his knife and fork down. 'Yes. Even when it proves difficult.'

'Probably especially when it proves difficult.' She pursed her lips. 'So, by definition, some of our conversations and discussions are going to be…difficult.'

The colour in his eyes deepened to a green that reminded her of a lagoon in Thailand where they'd spent a lazy afternoon. She swallowed and tried not to linger on what had happened after that swim when Ryan had taken her back to his beach hut.

'You want to hit me with whatever's on your mind?'

She dragged herself back.

The colour in his eyes intensified. 'I swear to you, Marianna, that I mean to do right by our baby. And by you too. I want to make things as easy for you as I can. I don't want you thinking you're in this alone.'

It was a nice sentiment but… She motioned to his plate. 'You can keep eating while I talk.'

The faintest of smiles touched his lips. 'If we're going

to have one of those difficult conversations it might be better if I don't. I wouldn't want to choke, now, would I?'

Her lips kicked up into a smile before she managed to pull herself back into line. 'I think there's an enormous difference between being a good father and being a man who holds the title of father.'

'I agree.'

'To be good at anything means working hard at it, don't you think?'

Again, he nodded. 'I'm not afraid of hard work, I promise you.' He met her gaze, his face pale but his eyes steady. 'What I'm afraid of is failure.'

His admission had her breaking out in gooseflesh as her own fears crowded about her. She chafed her arms. 'That's something I can definitely relate to.'

He shook his head. 'You're going to be a brilliant mother. You shouldn't doubt that for a moment. Already you're fighting for your baby's happiness—protecting it.'

But did it need protecting from Ryan?

'You will be a wonderful mother,' he repeated.

Her stomach screwed up tight. She hoped so.

His eyes suddenly narrowed. 'Are you afraid you won't be?'

'No,' she lied. 'Of course not.' She'd be just fine. She would! Besides, one of them feeling wobbly on the parent front was more than enough, thank you very much.

Ryan folded his arms. 'It hasn't been a terribly difficult discussion so far.'

Ah. Well. She could fix that. She pushed her cake to one side and pressed her hands together. 'Ryan, in Thailand I…' She faltered for a moment before finding her footing again. 'I was coming home to Italy after a year spent travelling and working through Australia. Thailand was my… last hurrah, so to speak. That holiday was about having no responsibilities, being young and free, and living in the moment before settling back into my real life.'

A furrow appeared on his brow. 'I understand that.'

'You are an incredibly attractive man.'

He blinked.

'But what we had in Thailand—all of that glorious sex…' He grinned as if in remembrance and it made her pulse skitter. 'It…it just doesn't belong here in my real world.'

He sobered as he caught her drift.

'If we're to successfully co-parent, then sex has no place in that. Friendship would be great if we can manage it. Sex would wreck that.'

'Too complicated,' he agreed.

She shook her head. 'It's actually incredibly simple. You never want to marry while I'd love to find the man of my dreams and settle down with him. If we make love here—in my real world—I would be in grave danger of falling in love with you.'

He shot back in his seat, his eyes filling with horror. The pulse in his throat pounded. 'I…' He gulped. 'That would be seriously unwise.'

She snorted. 'It'd be a disaster.' And if they were being honest… 'I doubt I'd make a particularly gracious jilted lover.'

He raised both hands. 'Point taken. We keep our hands to ourselves, keep things strictly platonic and…friendship.' He nodded vigorously. 'We focus on friendship.'

Ryan stared at Marianna, his heart doing its best to pound a way out of his chest. There couldn't be any sex between them. *Ever again.* She'd just presented him with his nightmare scenario and… Just, *no.* It would wreck everything.

He swallowed and tried to slow his pulse. If only he could forget the satin slide of her skin or the dancing delight of her fingertips as they travelled across his naked flesh, not to mention the sweet warm scent of her and the way he'd relished burying his face in her hair and breathing her in.

He stamped a lid on those memories and shoved them into a vault in his mind marked: *Never to be opened.*

Marianna lifted another spoonful of cake to her lips. He glanced at his fettuccine, but pushed the plate away, his stomach now too acid. Marianna had told him the food here was superb, world class, but it could've been sawdust for all he knew.

He glanced across the table and his gaze snagged hers. 'You really don't mean to make it difficult for me to see our child?'

Very slowly she shook her head. 'Not if you want to be involved.'

He wanted to be involved all right. He just didn't know what *involved* actually entailed. 'So…where do we go from here?'

She halted with a spoon of cake only centimetres from her mouth.

He tried not to focus on her mouth. 'I mean, what do we do next?'

She lowered her spoon. 'I don't really know. I…' She frowned and he went on immediate alert. It had to be better for her health and the baby's if she smiled rather than frowned.

Also, it had to be seriously bad for her health—her blood pressure—to go about hurling vases at people. He made a mental note to try and defuse all such high emotion in the future.

Her spoon clattered back to her plate and she gestured heavenwards with a dramatic flourish. 'It feels as if there must be a million things to do before the baby arrives!'

Were there? Asking what they were would only reveal the extent of his ignorance. He hadn't been able to shake off her horrified expression when she'd realised he'd never so much as held a baby. So, he didn't ask what needed doing. Instead he asked, 'What can I do?'

She folded her arms and surveyed him. She might only be a petite five feet two inches, but it took all of his strength to not fidget under that gaze.

'You really want to help?'

'Yes.' That was unequivocal. He *needed* to help.

'I plan to move out of the family home and into a cottage on the estate.'

He wondered if her brothers knew about this yet.

'It's solid and hardy, but I'd like to spruce up the inside with a new coat of paint and make everything lovely and fresh for the baby.'

It took a moment before he realised what she was asking of him. His heart started to thud. She'd told him that if he was serious about becoming a good father, his time would no longer be his own. His mouth dried. Could he do this?

He had to do this!

He reviewed his upcoming work schedule. He set his shoulders and rested both arms on the table. 'How would it be if I spent the next month—' *four whole weeks!* '—in Monte Calanetti? I can work remotely with maybe just the odd day trip back to Rome, and in my spare time I can help you get established in your cottage, help you set up a nursery…and in return you can tell me what you see as the duties and responsibilities of a good father?'

Her eyes widened, and he was suddenly fiercely glad he'd made the offer. 'You'd stay for a whole month?'

It wouldn't interfere with the Conti contract, and he didn't kid himself—he'd only have one chance to prove himself to the mother of his yet-to-be-born child, and he wasn't going to waste it. 'Consider it done,' he said.

CHAPTER FOUR

MARIANNA STARED AT him and Ryan found himself holding his breath, waiting for her answer…her verdict.

She folded her arms. 'That would help me out a lot.'

'And me,' he added, wanting her to remember that she'd just promised to tutor him in the arts of fatherhood.

She stared down at her cake and bit her lip. Her hair fell around her shoulders in a riot of dark waves, and it suddenly struck him how young she looked. He pushed his plate further away and glanced at her again. 'How old are you, Marianna?'

'Twenty-four.'

She was so young!

'And you?'

'Twenty-nine.' It was one of the many pieces of information they hadn't exchanged during their week in Thailand.

'If you researched me on the Internet, then you know what I do for a living.' As a specialist freelance consultant brought in, usually at the last moment, to turn the fortunes of ailing companies around, he enjoyed the adrenaline surge, the high-stakes pressure, and the tight deadlines. He shifted on his seat. 'What about you? What's your role at the vineyard? Are you a winemaker?'

She shook her head and those glorious curls performed a gentle dance around her face and shoulders. 'Nico is the vintner. I'm a viticulturist. I grow the grapes, look after the health of the vines.' She pushed a lock of hair behind her ear. 'The art of grape growing is a science.'

He knew she had a brain. It shouldn't surprise him that she used it. 'Sounds…technical.'

'I grew up on the vineyard. It's in my blood.'

The smile she sent him tightened his skin. He tried to ignore the pulse of sexual awareness coursing through him. That was *not* going to happen. No matter how much he might want her, he wasn't messing with her emotions.

'What?' she said.

He shook himself. 'So your job is stable? Financially you're…secure?'

He could've groaned when her face turned stormy.

He raised both hands. 'No offence meant. Difficult conversations, remember?'

She blew out a breath and slumped back, offered him a tiny smile that speared straight into the centre of him. 'I feel as if you're quizzing me to make sure I'm suitable mother material.'

'*Not* what I'm doing.' He'd be the least qualified person on earth to do that.

She kinked an eyebrow. 'No?'

He shook his head. 'When I said I wanted to make things easier for you, I meant in every way.'

He saw the moment his meaning reached her. The hand she rested on the table—small like the rest of her—clenched. He waited with an internal grimace and a kind of fatalistic inevitability for her to throw something at him.

In amazement he watched as her hand unclenched again. 'I keep forgetting that you don't really know me.'

He knew the shape of her legs, the dip of her waist and the curves of her breasts. He knew the feel of her skin and how she tasted. Hunger rushed through him. He closed his eyes. He had to stop this.

'One thing you ought to know is that I do have my pride.' She pulled in a breath and let it out slowly. 'I have both the means and the wherewithal to take care of myself and—' her hand moved to cover her still-flat stomach '—whoever else comes along. I have a share in Vigneto Calanetti, I'm a qualified viticulturist, I work hard and I draw a good salary. It may not be in the same league as what you earn, Ryan, but it's more than sufficient for both my and the baby's needs. I think you ought to know that if you were to offer me money it would seriously offend me.'

Right. That *was* good to know, but… 'What if I weren't offering it to you, but to the baby?'

She frowned and gestured to his plate. 'Are you finished?' At his nod she glanced across the room and caught the maître d's eye, wordlessly asking for the bill.

He let her distract herself with these things, but this money issue wasn't something he'd let her ignore indefinitely. He had a financial responsibility to this child—a responsibility he was determined to meet. He left a generous tip and followed Marianna to the cobbled street outside. He glanced at her and then glanced around. 'Your village is charming.'

It did what it was supposed to do—it cleared the frown from her face and perked her up. 'This was a stronghold back in medieval times. Many of the stones from the wall have since been used to build the houses that came after, but sections of the wall still stand. Would you like to walk for a bit?'

'I'd like that a lot. If you're not feeling too tired.'

She scoffed at that and set about leading him through cool cobbled streets that wound through the town with a grace that seemed to belong to a bygone age. He found himself entranced with houses made from stone that had mellowed to every shade of rose and gold, with archways leading down quaint alleys that curved intriguingly out of view. There were walled gardens, quirky turrets and fountains in the oddest places. And all the while Marianna pointed out architectural curiosities and regaled him with stories from local folklore. Her skill on the subject surprised him.

It shouldn't. Her quick wit and keen intelligence had been evident from their very first meeting.

Her enthusiasm for her subject made her eyes shine. She gestured with her hands as if they were an extension of her mind. His gut tightened as he watched her. Hunger roared through him…

He wrenched his gaze heavenwards. *For heaven's sake, can't you get your mind off sex for just ten minutes?*

'I'm boring you.'

He swung back to her. 'On the contrary, I'm finding all of this fascinating.' He refused to notice the shape of her lips. 'You obviously love your town.'

'It's my home,' she said simply. 'I love it. I missed it when I was in Australia.' She frowned up at him. 'Don't you love your home?'

Something inside him froze.

Her frown deepened. 'Where *is* your home, Ryan?'

'Have you heard the saying "Wherever I lay my hat, that's my home"? That pretty much sums me up.'

She halted, hands on her hips. 'But you have to live somewhere when you're between assignments. I mean, where do you keep your belongings?'

'I have office facilities in Sydney and London, and staff who work for me in both locations, but…' He shrugged.

Her eyes grew round. 'What? Are you telling me that you just live out of hotel rooms?'

'Suites,' he corrected.

'But—' She frowned. 'What about your car? Where do you keep that?'

'Whenever I need a car, I hire one.'

'Then what about the gifts people give you, your books and CDs, photographs, art you've gathered and… Oh, I don't know. The myriad things we collect?'

'I travel light. All I need is a suitcase and my laptop.'

She eased away from him, those dark eyes surveying

him. 'I wasn't so wrong about you after all,' she finally said. 'You are a kind of gypsy.'

She didn't look too pleased with her discovery. He shrugged. 'While we're on the subject of accommodation, perhaps you could recommend somewhere for me to stay while I'm in Monte Calanetti?'

She folded her arms and frowned at him for a long moment and then tossed her head, eyes flashing. 'Oh, that's easy.' She swung away and led him down an avenue that opened out into a town square. 'If you're going to help me get the cottage shipshape then you can stay there.'

His heart stuttered. 'With you?'

Some of his horror must've seeped into his voice because she swung back with narrowed eyes. 'Do you have a problem with that?'

'Not at all,' he assured her hastily. *Hell, yes!* How on earth was he going to avoid temptation when he was living with her? He rolled his shoulders. Not that he could ask the question out loud. Not when she stood glaring at him like that.

She turned and moved off, sending him a knowing glance over her shoulder. 'Considering the circumstances of our *acquaintance*, local traditions of hospitality demand I offer you a place to stay.'

What on earth was she talking about?

'If you don't stay at the vineyard, Ryan, tongues will wag.'

Ah. He didn't want to make things here in the village uncomfortable for her.

Her lips suddenly twitched. 'Of course, you could always stay in the main house with Angelo and Nico if you prefer.'

'No, no, the cottage will be great.'

She waved to a group of men on the other side of the square before leading Ryan to a bench bathed in warm spring sunshine. The square rose up around them in stone that glowed gold and pink. In the middle of the square stood a stone fountain—a nymph holding aloft a clamshell. It sent a glittering sparkle of water cascading, the fine mist making rainbows in the air. The nearby scent of sautéing onion, garlic and bacon tantalised his nose, reminding him of lunch and the abandoned conversation that he hadn't forgotten.

'In my country, Marianna, it's the law for a man to pay child maintenance to help look after his children. I expect it's the law here too. I *will* be giving you money. It's only right and fair that I contribute financially.'

Her mouth opened but he rushed on before she could speak. 'This is non-negotiable. I insist on contributing to my child's upkeep. I have my pride too.' She tried to butt in but he held up a hand. 'The money is not for you, it's for the baby.'

She folded her arms and slumped back against the bench, dark eyes staring towards the centre of the square. He couldn't help feeling he'd wounded her in some way. It didn't mean he wanted to unsay it. He had every intention of being financially accountable in this situation, but…

'None of that is to say that I believe for a single moment that you're not capable of looking after the baby on your own. Of course you are.'

Those dark eyes met his and he didn't understand the turmoil in their depths. 'Imagine for a moment I was one of your brothers. Wouldn't they want to contribute to the care of their child?'

Very slowly her chin and her shoulders unhitched. 'I suppose you're right.'

He let out a breath he hadn't known he'd been holding. Being around this woman was like negotiating a minefield. He didn't know from one moment to the next what would set her off. He dragged a hand back through his hair. What on earth had happened to the sweet sunny girl he'd met in Thailand?

She still had the same sweet curves, and when she smiled—

Stop it!

'So…' She pursed those luscious lips of hers and Ryan had to drag his gaze away. 'We've discussed the fact that you want to be involved in the baby's life, that you want to be a good father. We've talked about money, and settled that you're going to stay here in Monte Calanetti for the next month. We've organised where you're going to stay during that time. Is there anything else we need to tackle today?'

The dark circles beneath her eyes beat at him. He'd put them there. She'd returned here yesterday after their dreadful interview and cried. She'd probably barely slept a wink for worry. *His fault.*

'Maybe we should return to the vineyard. You can put your feet up and relax for a bit and—'

'Oh, for heaven's sake, Ryan, I'm pregnant not an invalid!'

Whoa. Okay. 'I, um…well, maybe I can put my feet up. I'm kind of beat after the drive from Rome.'

She swung to him, her eyes filling with tears. 'Oh, I'm sorry. Of course you're tired. What a dreadful hostess I'm proving to be.'

He prayed her tears wouldn't fall. He didn't want to deal with a sobbing woman. 'You, uh…you don't have to assume any role on my account.' If they were going to make this work then they had to drop pretences.

And he *had* to make it work. He had to learn how to be a good father to this child so that when Marianna found her true love and had more babies, he'd be there when she no longer had time for the cuckoo in the nest.

There was no doubt in his mind that when she did marry

and start a new family, this child could be cast aside. She wasn't as young as his mother had been when she'd become pregnant with Ryan, but she was still young. Marianna mightn't see it at the moment, but raising another man's baby would throw a pall over any life she tried to build with a new man. And Ryan vowed to be there for his child when that happened.

Marianna directed Ryan to park his car beneath the carport standing to one side of the villa—the villa that was her family home. He switched off the ignition and turned to her. 'Have you told your brothers about your plan to move?'

His tone told her he thought she'd have a fight on her hands. She bit back a sigh. Tell her something she didn't know. 'Not yet.'

'Would you like me there when you do?'

'No, thank you.' His earlier non-negotiable 'I'm paying for my child' still stung. Did he think her completely helpless? Did he think her utterly incapable of looking after her baby?

'When are you planning to move in?'

She lifted her chin. 'Tomorrow.' And nobody was going to stop her. But…

Pushing out of the car, she bit back a curse. What on earth had possessed her to offer him a room at the cottage? How relaxing was that going to be? *Not.*

She passed a hand across her forehead. It was just… She'd been utterly horrified when she'd learned how he lived his life. How could someone have no home? What kind of upbringing had this man had to have him still shunning the idea of a home?

If he wanted to co-parent he would need to create a home for their child, and she wanted him to experience at least a little of the welcoming atmosphere of a real home.

If he helped her to create that warm environment perhaps he could emulate it.

Unless he had his heart set on sticking to hotel rooms. *Suites.* Would a baby mind…or even notice? Heavens, a toddler would have a field day!

When she turned back to face him, however, it wasn't their child's welfare that occupied her thoughts. It was his. Her heart burned for him and she couldn't explain why, but for as long as he stayed here in Monte Calanetti she wanted to wipe away the memories of all of those impersonal anonymous hotel rooms and replace them with warmth and belonging.

Which, of course, made no sense at all.

Think with your head, not your heart.

You're too impulsive.

Those were the voices of her brothers.

She reached up to scratch between her shoulder blades. Maybe it was simply pregnancy hormones making her feel maternal early or something.

Speaking of hormones… She thought back to some of her reactions during lunch and grimaced. She wasn't exactly doing a great job at holding her emotions in check at the moment, was she?

Do you really think you can blame that on pregnancy hormones?

She flinched. Maybe she was as immature and irresponsible as her brothers seemed to think. Maybe she had no right becoming a mother. Maybe she'd be a terrible mother—

'What's wrong?'

She blinked to find Ryan right beside her. How had he known anything was wrong? She hadn't even been facing him. How could he be so attuned to her when he didn't really know her?

But he does know you. He knows every inch of your body intimately.

She gulped. *Don't think about that now.*

'Marianna.' He smoothed her hair back from her face before clasping her shoulders. 'If you're afraid of your brothers, then let me inform them of your intentions. I'll do anything you need me to.'

Except marry me.

That had her jerking out of his grip. She *didn't* want to marry him. 'I'm not afraid of Angelo and Nico, Ryan. It's just…I…' She spun away, swore and spun back. 'I feel as if I have constant PMS—as if some alien has taken over my mind and is making me behave irrationally. And it's taken over my body too. My breasts hurt. If I cross my arms, it hurts. If I reach up to get something from a shelf, it hurts. Putting a seat belt on is an exercise in agony, and I'm not even going to talk about the torture of putting on a bra. I…it's making me tetchy. And then I feel like I'm some kind of immature loser who can't deal with a bit of breast tenderness and some whacky hormones, and who's creating a whole lot of trouble for everyone else.'

She paused, running out of breath and Ryan's jaw dropped. 'Why didn't you say something earlier?'

'Because—' she ground her teeth together '—I should be bigger than it.'

'Garbage!' He reached out and cupped her face. 'I would hug you only I don't want to hurt you.' The sweet sincerity in his eyes melted something inside her. 'But let me tell you now that you're not a loser. You're warm and beautiful and brave.'

He thought her beautiful?

So that's the bit—out of all that he just said—that you latch onto, is it? Very mature.

She tried to ignore that critical inner voice.

'I don't feel brave,' she murmured. She didn't feel beautiful either, but she left that unsaid.

'I think you're wonderfully brave. I also think it understandable for you to be worried about the future. You shouldn't beat yourself up about that.'

'Okay,' she whispered.

With that, he drew away. She missed his touch, the brief connection they'd seemed to share. She shook it off and made herself smile. 'C'mon, I'll show you the cottage.'

'You want to do what?' Angelo shouted from where he set the table.

She bit back a sigh. The moment she'd informed her brothers that Ryan was coming to dinner, Angelo had cancelled his date with Kayla, and Nico had returned earlier than normal from the vineyard with a martial light in his eye. She'd figured, *In for a penny...*

'That's ridiculous!' Angelo slammed down the last knife and fork. 'Nico, talk sense into the girl.'

Marianna doggedly tossed the salad from her post at the kitchen bench.

'Mari—' Nico swung from where he turned steaks on the grill. '*This* is your home. *This* is where you belong.'

She turned at that. 'No, Nico, this is *your* home.' One day he'd fill it with a wife and children of his own, but his head rocked back at her words and he turned white. Her head bled a little for him. 'Turn the steaks,' she ordered and he did as she bid. 'I don't mean that as some kind of denial or as an indication that I don't feel welcome here. This is my childhood home. It will always be a haven for me. If I need it. Currently, though, I don't need a haven.'

'But—'

'No!' She spun back to Angelo. 'Do *you* feel as if this is your home? When you marry your beautiful Kayla, do *you* mean to settle in this house?'

He rolled his shoulders. 'That's different.'

'Why?' she fired back at him. 'Because you're a man?'

'Because I haven't lived here in years! I've built a different life for myself.'

'And what's wrong with me building a different life for myself?'

'Marianna,' Nico spluttered. 'You *do* belong here! You play a key role at Vigneto Calanetti—'

'But it doesn't mean I have to live under this roof. I'll still be living on the estate.'

Both brothers started remonstrating again. Marianna tossed the salad for all she was worth while she waited for them to wear themselves out. It had always been this way. She'd make a bid for independence, they'd rail at her, telling her why it was a bad idea and forbidding her to do it—whatever *it* might be—they'd eventually calm down, and then she'd go ahead and do it anyway.

Their overprotectiveness was a sign of their love for her. She knew that. They'd had more of a hand in raising her than their parents. But there was no denying that they could get suffocating at times.

'Enough!'

The voice came from the French doors. *Ryan.* She glanced around to find him framed in the doorway—all broad and bristling and commanding. Her blood did a cha-cha-cha. She swallowed and waved him inside, hoping no one noticed how her hand shook. 'You're right on time.'

He strode up to her side. 'Leave Marianna be. The one thing she doesn't need is to be bullied by the pair of you.'

'Bullied?' Nico spluttered.

'Who are you to tell us what to do?' Angelo said in a deceptively soft voice.

Ryan turned his gaze on her eldest brother—a determined intense glare that made her heart beat harder. 'I'm the father of her unborn child, that's who. And I'm telling you now that she doesn't need all of this…high drama.'

Her brothers blinked and she had to bite back a laugh. Normally it was she who was accused of the high drama.

It was her turn to blink when he took her shoulders in his hands and propelled her around the kitchen bench into the nearest chair at the dining table. 'Oh, but I was tossing the salad!'

He glanced at the bowl and his lips twitched. 'Believe me, that salad is well and truly tossed.' But he brought the bowl over and set it on the table in front of her.

Angelo glanced into the bowl and grimaced. 'You trying to mangle it?'

She bit her lip. Perhaps she had been a little enthusiastic on the tossing front.

'It looks great,' Ryan assured her.

The fibber! But it made her feel better all the same.

Angelo shook himself up into 'protective big brother' mode. 'Are you supporting my sister in this crazy scheme of hers to move out of the family home?'

'I'm supporting Marianna's right to assert her independence, to live wherever she chooses and to build the home she wants to for her child.'

'And *your* child,' Nico said, bringing the steaks across to the table.

'And my child,' Ryan agreed, not waiting to be told where to sit, but planting himself firmly in the seat beside Marianna.

'Are you planning to marry?'

Ryan glared at both of her brothers. 'You want Marianna to marry a man she doesn't love?'

Both Angelo and Nico glanced away.

Her shoulders started to slump. Why wouldn't they believe she could take care of herself? Maybe if she didn't have such a dreadful dating track record…?

She shook herself upright again, took the platter of steaks and placed a portion on each of their plates. She then handed the bowl of salad to Ryan, as their guest, to serve himself first. He didn't, though. He served out the salad to her plate first, and then his own before passing the bowl across the table to Nico. He seized the basket of bread and held it out for her to select one of the warmed rolls.

Her brothers noted all of this through narrowed eyes. Marianna lifted her chin. 'Ryan is going to stay here for a bit while we sort out how we mean to arrange things.'

Nico's eyes narrowed even further. He glared at Ryan. 'Where precisely will you be staying?'

Marianna rounded on him. 'Don't speak to him like that! Ryan is my guest. For as long as he's in Monte Calanetti he'll be staying at the cottage with me.'

Her brothers' eyes flashed.

Ryan drew himself up to his full seated height. 'Marianna and I might have decided against marriage, but I have an enormous amount of respect for your sister. I…' He shrugged. 'I like her.'

She blinked. Really? But… He barely knew her.

Still, if he could claim to like her after she'd thrown a vase of flowers at his head, and sound as if he meant it, then…who knew? Maybe he did like her.

'We're friends.'

'Pshaw!' Angelo slashed a disgusted hand through the air. 'If Mari hadn't become pregnant you'd have never clapped eyes on her again. That's not my idea of friendship.'

'But she is pregnant. I *am* the father of her child. We're now a team.'

Marianna speared a piece of cucumber and brought it to her mouth. A team? That sounded nice. 'Please, guys, will you eat before your steaks get cold?'

The three men picked up their cutlery.

'Still,' Nico grumbled. 'This is a fine pickle the two of you have landed in.'

Ryan halted from slicing into his steak. 'This is not a pickle. Granted, Marianna's pregnancy wasn't planned, but she's having a baby. She's bringing a new life into the world. That is a cause for celebration and joy, *not* recriminations.'

Her eyes filled as he repeated her sentiment from earlier in the day.

Ryan took her hand. 'Do you think your sister won't be a wonderful mother?'

'She'll be a fabulous mother, of course,' Nico said.

'Do you not think it'll be a joyous thing to have a nephew or niece?'

'Naturally, when Marianna's *bambino* arrives, it will be cause for great celebration.' Angelo rolled his shoulders and then a smile touched his lips. 'I am looking forward to teaching my nephew how to play catch.'

'No, no, Angelo, we will have to teach him how to kick a ball so he can go on to play for Fiorentina.'

She rolled her eyes at Nico's mention of his and Angelo's favourite football team.

'What will you teach him?' Angelo challenged.

'Cricket.' Ryan thrust out his jaw. 'I'm going to teach him how to play cricket like a champion.'

'Cricket! That's a stupid sport. I—'

'And what if my *bambino* is a girl?' Marianna said, breaking into the male posturing, but she too found herself gripped with the sudden excitement of having a child. Her brothers would make wonderful uncles. They'd dote on her child and if she weren't careful they'd spoil it rotten.

'A girl can play soccer,' Nico said.

'And cricket,' Ryan added.

'She might like a pony,' Angelo piped in.

Her jaw dropped. 'You wouldn't let *me* get a pony when I wanted one.'

'I was afraid you'd try and jump the first fence you came across and break your neck.' Angelo shook his head. 'Mari, it was hard enough keeping up with you when you were powered by your own steam. It would've been explosive to add anything additional to the mix.' His eyes danced for a moment. 'Besides, if you do have a daughter and if she does get a pony, it'll be your responsibility to keep up with her. Something you'll manage on your ear, no doubt.'

She found herself suddenly beaming. Nico laughed and it hit her then that Ryan had accomplished this. He'd made her brothers—and her—excited at the prospect of their new arrival. He'd channelled their fear and worry into this—a new focus on the positive.

Reaching beneath the table, she squeezed his hand in thanks. He gazed at her blankly and she realised that he hadn't a clue what he'd done. She released him again with a sigh.

'Okay, Paulo,' Angelo said grudgingly. 'You're at least saying the right things. Still, in my book actions speak louder than words. I'll be watching you.'

Marianna rolled her eyes. Ryan shrugged as if completely unaffected by the latent threat lacing her brother's words. He glanced across at Nico. 'Anything you'd like to add?'

Nico stared at him with his dark steady eyes. 'I will abide by Marianna's wishes. You can stay. But I don't trust you.'

Marianna's stomach screwed up tight then and started to churn. She didn't know if she could trust him or not either.

Ryan's mobile phone chose that moment to ring. He pulled it from his pocket and glanced at the display. 'I'm sorry, but I have to take this.'

But…but…he was supposed to be making a good impression on her brothers!

With barely a glance of apology, he rose and strode out to the terrace, phone pressed to his ear.

He was supposed to be learning how to be a good father!

Lone wolf. The words went round and round in her mind. Was this how the next month would go? Ryan claiming he was invested and committed to their child, but leaping into work mode every time his phone rang? Her brothers stared at her with hard eyes. 'Excuse me.' Pressing a hand to her mouth, she fled for the bathroom.

CHAPTER FIVE

For the next three days, Ryan kept himself busy alternating between conference calls and prepping the inside walls of the three-bedroom stone cottage that Marianna had her heart set on calling home. In her parents' time, apparently, it had been used as a guesthouse and before that it had been the head vintner's cottage. For the last few years, however, the cottage had stood empty.

Ryan had insisted on cleaning everything first—mopping and vacuuming—before Marianna moved in. She'd grumbled something about being more than capable of wielding a mop, but he'd ordered her off the premises. Cleaning seemed the least he could do, even if it had delayed her move for an additional day. He'd claimed the smallest of the three bedrooms as his for the next month.

As Marianna had spent what he assumed was a long day tending grapevines and whatever else it was that she did, Ryan cooked dinner.

She walked in, found him stir-frying vegetables, and folded her arms. 'Do you also think me incapable of cooking dinner?'

He thought women were supposed to like men who cooked and cleaned. Not that he wanted her to like him. At least, not like *that*. 'Of course not, but I don't expect you to do all the cooking while I'm here. I thought we could take it turn about. You can cook tomorrow night.'

She grumbled something in Italian that he was glad he didn't understand. Throwing herself down on the sofa, she rifled through the stack of magazines on the coffee table and settled back with one without another word.

He stared at the previously *neat* stack. He itched to

march over there to tidy them back up, but a glance at Marianna warned him to stay right where he was.

Dinner was a strained affair. 'Bad day at work?' he asked.

'I've had better.'

Something inside him tightened. Had her brothers been hassling her again? He opened his mouth, but the tired lines around her eyes had him closing it again. His hands clenched and unclenched in his lap. What he should do was wash the dishes and then retreat to his room to do some work. Work was something he could do—something he had a handle on and was good at. He glanced at Marianna, grimaced at the way her mouth drooped, and with a silent curse pulled his laptop towards him. 'I thought maybe you could choose the colours for the walls.' He clicked on the screen, bringing up a colour chart.

The entire cottage oozed quaint cosy charm. The main living-dining area was a single room—long and low—with the kitchen tucked in one corner, sectioned off from the rest of the room by a breakfast nook. The ceiling was low-beamed, which should've made the room dark, but a set of French doors off the dining area, opening to a small walled garden, flooded the room with light. The garden was completely overgrown, of course, but if a body had a mind to they could create a great herb garden out there.

'Colour charts?' Marianna perked up, pushing her plate aside. 'That sounds like fun.'

Colour charts fun? That was a new one, but he'd go with it if it put a bit of colour back into her cheeks. He removed their plates as unobtrusively as he could. Hesitating on his way back from the kitchen, he detoured past the coffee table and swooped down to straighten the stack of magazines before easing into the seat beside Marianna at the dining table again.

She moved the laptop so he could see it too. 'That one.'

She pointed to a particularly vivid yellow. 'I've always wanted a yellow kitchen.'

He glanced at the screen and then at her. Did she really want a yellow so intense it glowed neon? 'That one's really bright.'

'I know. Gorgeous, isn't it?'

'Um… I'm thinking it might be a tad brighter on your walls than you realise.'

'Or it could be perfect.'

He didn't doubt for a moment she'd hate the colour once it was on her walls, but a colour scheme wasn't worth arguing about—especially if she was feeling a bit testy and—his gaze dropped momentarily to her breasts—sore. He reefed his gaze back to the computer screen. He'd paint her walls pink and purple stripes if she wanted. Pulling in a breath, he reconciled himself to the fact he'd be repainting said wall at some stage in the future. 'Butter Ball, right.' He made a note.

He'd started to twig to the fact that there were two Mariannas. There was the sunny, sassy Marianna he partially recognised from his holiday in Thailand. And then there was 'crazy pregnant lady' Marianna. She swung between these extremes with no rhyme or reason—sunny one moment and all snark and growl the next.

It kept a man on his toes.

'You mentioned you wanted some sort of green in the living and dining areas.' He glanced around. At the moment they were a nice inoffensive cream. With a shake of his head, he clicked to bring up a green palette. Heaven only knew what hideous colour she'd sentence him to using next.

She leaned in closer to peer at the screen, drenching him in the scent of…frangipani? Whatever it was, it was sweet and flowery and so fresh it took all his strength not to lean over and breathe her in all the more deeply.

'It'll have a name like olive or sage or something,' she said. 'Hmm…that one.'

He forced his attention back to the screen. 'Sea foam,' he read. It was a lot better than he'd been expecting.

'Does *it* pass muster?'

He didn't like the martial light in her eye. *Deflect the snark.* 'It's perfect.'

She blinked. Her shoulders slumped and he had to fight the urge to give her a hug. 'How are your breasts?'

She stiffened and then shot away from him with a glare. '*I beg your pardon?* What have my breasts to do with *you*?'

Heat crept up his neck. 'I didn't mean it in a salacious, pervy kind of way. It's just…the other day you said they were sore and…and I was just hoping that…that it had settled down.'

'Why should you care?' she all but yelled at him, leaping up to pace around the table and then the length of the room. She flung out an arm. 'You're probably happy! I've inconvenienced you so I expect you're secretly pleased to see me suffer.'

He stood too. 'Then you'd be spectacularly wrong! I have absolutely no desire to see you suffer. Ideally, what I want is you happy and healthy.'

She stopped dead in the middle of the room and stared at him, her hands pressed together at her waist. Ryan pulled in a breath. 'It's obvious, though, that at the moment you're not happy.'

Where did that leave him and her?

Where did it leave the baby? If she were having second thoughts about keeping the child…

She swallowed. Her bottom lip wobbled for a fraction of a sentence. Her vulnerability tugged at him. 'If I'm the cause of that, if my living here in your cottage, and invading your space, is adding to your stress, then I can easily move into the village. It wouldn't be a big deal and—'

He broke off when she backed up to drop down onto the sofa, covered her face with her hands and burst into tears.

He brought his fist to his mouth. Hell! He hadn't meant to make her cry. He shifted his weight from one foot to the other before kicking himself into action and lurching over to the sofa to put an arm around her. 'I'm sorry, Mari. I didn't mean to upset you. I'm a clumsy oaf—no finesse.'

At his words she turned her face into his chest and sobbed harder. He wrapped both arms around her, smoothed a hand up and down her back in an attempt to soothe her. Protectiveness rose up through him and all but tried to crush him. He fought back an overwhelming sense of suffocation. At the moment he had to focus on making Marianna feel better. His discomfiture had no bearing on anything. Her health and the baby's health, they were what mattered.

Eventually her sobs eased. She rested against him and he could feel the exhaustion pounding through her. So far this week all his suggestions that she rest had been met with scorn, sarcasm and a flood of vindictive Italian. Now he kept his mouth firmly closed on the subject.

'I'm sorry,' she whispered.

She eased away from him and her pallor made him wince.

'I can't believe I said something so mean to you, Ryan. I didn't mean it. It was dreadfully unfair. I know you don't want to see me suffer.'

'It's okay. It doesn't matter.'

'It's *not* okay. And it *does* matter.' Her voice, though vehement, was pitched low. 'I don't know what's happening to me. I'm being so awful to everyone. Today at work when I was lifting a bag of supplies, Tobias came rushing over to take it from me.'

She was heavy lifting at work!

'I mean, I know he meant well, but I just let fly at him

in the most awful way. I apologised later, of course, but Tobias has worked for my family for twenty years. He deserves nothing from me except respect and courtesy. And now I'm going out of my way to be extra nice to him to try and make amends and…this is terrible to admit, but it's exhausting.'

He could imagine, but… *She was heavy lifting at work?*

'And then I come home here and you've been working on my lovely cottage and am I grateful? No, not a bit of it!' She stiffened and then swung to him. 'I mean, I *am* grateful. Truly I am. But how on earth are you to know that when I keep acting like a shrew?'

Her earnestness made him smile. 'I know you are.'

She shook her head, her wild curls fizzing up all around her. 'How can you possibly know that when all I do is yell and say cruel things? I'm so sorry, Ryan. Even as I'm saying them a part of me is utterly appalled, but I can't seem to make myself stop. I just…' She swallowed. 'I don't know what's wrong with me.'

'I do.'

She stared at him. She folded her arms. 'You do?'

He tried not to let her incredulity sting. 'It's not that there's anything wrong with you. It's just your body is being flooded with pregnancy hormones. What you're feeling is natural. I read about it on the Net.'

She straightened. 'I should be able to deal with hormones. I should be able to get the better of them and not let them rule me.'

'Why? When your breasts are feeling sore, can you magically wish that soreness away just by concentrating hard?'

'Well, of course not, but that's different.'

'It's exactly the same,' he countered. 'It's a physical symptom, just like morning sickness.' From what he could tell, pregnancy put a woman's body completely through the wringer. He wished he could share some of the load with her, or carry it completely, to spare her the upheaval it was causing.

'So…' She moistened her lips. 'It'll pass?'

'Yep.'

'When?'

Ah, that was a little more difficult to nail down. She groaned as if reading that answer in his face. 'What am I going to do? If I keep going on like this I'm not going to have any friends left.'

It was an exaggeration, but it probably felt like gospel truth to her. He aimed for light. 'I could lock you up here in the cottage until it passes.'

Her lips twitched. 'It's one solution,' she agreed. 'My brothers, though, might take issue with that approach.' A moment later she bit back a sigh that speared straight into his gut. 'I guess I'm just going to have to ride it out.'

He stood, lifted her feet so that she lay lengthwise on the sofa, and moved across to grab his laptop. 'There're a couple of things we can try.' He came back and crouched down next to the coffee table. 'Meditation is supposed to help.'

She rose up on her elbows. 'Meditation?'

He gestured for her to lie back down. 'I downloaded a couple of guided meditations in case you wanted to try one to see if you thought it might help.'

'Oh.' She lay back down. 'Okay.'

He clicked play and trickling water and birdcalls started to sound. He moved back towards the dining table.

'Ryan?'

He swung back.

'Thank you.'

'You're welcome.'

She shook her head. 'I mean for everything. For understanding and not holding my horridness against me. You're really lovely, you know that?'

His throat thickened.

'I don't want you to move into the village, okay? It's nice to have…a friend here.'

A low melodic voice from his computer instructed her to close her eyes and she did, not waiting for his reply. Which was just as well because he wasn't sure he could utter a single word if his life depended on it.

He moved to sit at the dining table and suddenly realised that with his laptop already in use, he had nothing to do—couldn't lose himself in work as he'd meant to do. Pursing his lips, he glanced around. He'd start the dishes except he didn't want the clattering to disturb her.

Biting back a sigh, he pulled a magazine towards him—some kind of interior decorating magazine that Marianna must've picked up at some point…and left lying around the place. Instead of focusing on the magazine, though, he found his attention returning again and again to the woman on the sofa. He clocked the exact moment she fell asleep. He tiptoed across to cover her with a throw blanket, before moving straight back to his seat at the table where he wouldn't be in danger of reaching out to trace a finger down the softness of her cheek.

No touching. She'd said it was nice having a friend. He had to work on being that friend. Just a friend.

She slept for an hour. He registered the exact moment she woke too. 'How are you feeling?' he asked when she turned her head in his direction.

She stretched her arms back behind her head. 'Good. Really good.'

She sat up and smiled and he knew he had sunny Marianna back for the moment. He gestured. 'I've been looking through your magazines at the pictures you have marked.'

She leapt up, grabbed a jug of water from the fridge and poured them both a glass before moving across to where he sat. She left the jug on the bench top. He forced himself to stay in his seat and to not go and put it back in the fridge.

'Do you like any of them?'

He dragged his gaze from the offending jug and nodded. She had great taste. If one discounted that awful yellow she'd chosen for the kitchen walls.

She moistened her lips, not meeting his eye. 'Did you look at the pictures of the nurseries?'

Those were the ones he was looking at now. He angled the magazine so she could see. Her eyes went soft. 'They're lovely, aren't they?'

His heart started to hammer in his chest. Never in a million years had he thought he'd be looking at pictures of nurseries. He ran a finger around the collar of his T-shirt. 'Have you decided what kind of style and colour scheme you want in there yet?'

'I can't make up my mind between a nice calm colour that'll aid sleep or something vibrant that'll stimulate the imagination. I've been researching articles on the topic.'

Her enthusiasm made him smile. 'You're putting a lot of thought into this.'

She pushed her hair behind her ears. 'It's important and…'

'And?'

'I want my—our—baby to be happy. I want to give it every possible advantage I can.'

He stared at her. How long would their baby's welfare be important to her, though?

'Do you have any thoughts?'

Her question pulled him back. 'Personally I'd go for a calm colour because that's what I'd like best. I don't know what a baby would prefer.' He frowned. 'You could go with a calm colour on the walls and brighten the room up with a striking decal and a colourful mobile and…and accessories, couldn't you?'

'Hmm…' she mused. 'The best of both worlds perhaps?'

It warmed something inside him that she took his suggestion seriously. Still… What did he know? He knew nothing about this parenthood caper. 'It seems to me one needs a lot of equipment for a baby.'

'Ooh, yes, I know.' She rubbed her hands together, her eyes dancing. 'Shopping for the baby is going to be so much fun.'

Shopping in his experience was a necessary evil, not fun. Speaking of which… 'Marianna, where will I find the closest hardware store?'

'Ah.' She nodded.

He didn't point out that *Ah* wasn't an answer. He wanted Sunny Marianna hanging around for as long as possible.

'What do you have planned for Saturday?' she asked.

That was the day after tomorrow. He considered his work schedule. He had two video-conferencing calls tomorrow plus a detailed report to write by the end of next week. Saturday he'd planned… He glanced back at Marianna and gestured to the cottage. 'I was hoping to be painting by then.'

'Have you ever been to Siena?'

He shook his head. If that was where the nearest hardware store was, then he hoped it wasn't too far away.

'It's only an hour away. Write up a list of things that we need and we'll make a day of it.'

'Right.' Shopping. Yay.

Her smile slowly dissolved. She stared at him, twisting her hands together for a bit and he hoped he hadn't let his lack of enthusiasm show. He found a smile. 'Sounds good.'

Her fingers moved to worry at the collar of her shirt. She half grimaced, half squinted at him. 'Ryan, do you want to be present at the birth?'

He froze. Um…

'There's an information evening about…stuff coming up soon.'

How on earth had they gone from shopping to the birth? 'What stuff?'

'Like birthing classes.'

He didn't know what to say.

'I'm going to need a birthing partner.'

It became suddenly hard to breathe. 'Are you asking me to be your birthing partner?' What kind of time commitment would that demand?

Her eyes narrowed. 'No. I'm asking you to attend an information evening so we'll have all the available facts and can then make an informed decision about birthing classes and who I might want present at the labour.'

He thought about it. It didn't seem like much to ask. 'Right.' He nodded.

Her hands went to her hips. 'Is that a yes or a no?'

'It's a—yes I'll attend the information evening. When is it?'

'This Monday. Six-thirty.'

He pulled out his phone and put it in his electronic diary. He slotted the phone back into his pocket. 'Got it.'

'The town centre is heritage-listed,' Marianna said, gesturing around the Piazza del Campo. This was the real reason she'd brought Ryan to Siena—to have him experience something spectacular in an effort to make up for all he'd had to put up with from her for the last few days. So much for her resolve to give him a homey, welcoming environment. She'd been acting like a temperamental diva. He'd been incredibly patient and *adult* in the face of it.

Not to mention controlled. She bit back a sigh. If only she could channel some of that control.

Now, though, she had the satisfaction of seeing his eyes widen as he completed a slow circle on the spot to take in the full beauty and splendour of the town square. 'It's amazing.'

'Would you like to see the *duomo*?' Siena Cathedral. 'It's a three-minute walk away.'

At his nod, she led him across the Piazza del Campo and down one of the shady avenues on the other side, detailing a little of the history of the city for him, before eventually leading him to the cathedral.

They gazed at the medieval façade for a long moment, neither saying a word. Eventually Marianna led him through one of the smaller side doors and had the satisfaction of hearing his swift intake of breath. White and greenish-black marble stripes alternated on the walls and columns, creating a magnificent backdrop for the cool and hushed interior. She watched him as he studied everything with a concentrated interest that reminded her of the way he'd explored the underwater wonders of Thailand on their scuba-diving expeditions. It reminded her of the way he'd explored her body during those warm fragrant evenings afterwards.

Something inside her shifted.

Catching her breath, she tried to hitch it back into place. Over and over in her mind she silently recited: *Do not fall for him. Do not fall for him.*

She couldn't fall for Ryan. It had the potential to ruin everything. It had the potential to ruin her child's relationship with him and she couldn't risk that.

She lifted her chin. She *wouldn't* risk that. It'd be selfish, wilful and wrong. What she could do, though, was give Ryan a taste of home and hearth, a sense of how family worked. That was what would be best for their baby.

She turned to look at him and snorted. Fall for him? Not likely. She could never fall for someone so controlled, someone so cold.

He wasn't like that in Thailand.

Maybe not, but that was an aberration, remember?

'What's wrong?'

She snapped to, to find him staring at her. She dredged up a smile, reminding herself she wanted today to be a treat for him. 'Nothing, it's just…' She glanced around the medieval church. 'I've been here many times, but it amazes me all over again each time I come back.'

The smile he sent her warmed her to her very toes. 'I can see why.'

They spent two and a half hours wandering around the city and exploring its sights, and Marianna did her best to be cordial and friendly…and nothing more. After a leisurely lunch, though, Ryan reverted to the colder, more distant version of himself. 'We do need to get supplies at some stage today.'

She bit back a sigh. 'There's a hardware store not too far from where we parked the car.'

'Have you chosen what colour you want for the nursery yet?' he asked when they walked into the store a little while later.

She shook her head. She hadn't settled on anything to do with the nursery. In fact, she found herself strangely reluctant to decorate said nursery with Ryan.

'What?' he said.

She realised she was staring at him. 'I…I'm wondering if I shouldn't leave it and wait until I've had my scan.' She glanced around and then headed down an aisle.

He followed hot on her heels. 'Scan?'

'Hmm… If I find out whether I'm having a boy or a girl maybe that will make it easier to personalise the room.'

He didn't say anything and when she turned to gaze up at him she couldn't read a single emotion in his face. It worried her, though she couldn't have said why.

'You mean to find out the gender of the baby?'

She couldn't work out if that was censure or curiosity

in his voice. 'I…I, uh, hadn't made a decision about that yet. There's no denying it'd make things like decorating and buying clothes easier.'

'You don't want it to be a surprise?'

She peered down her nose at him. 'Ryan, don't you think there's been enough of a surprise factor surrounding this pregnancy already?'

He laughed and it eased something inside her. 'Perhaps you're right.'

'If you don't want to know the sex of the baby, then I can keep it a secret.'

He cocked an eyebrow. 'You think that's going to work?'

A chill hand wrapped around her heart. Did he think he could read her so easily?

Her heart started to thump. Maybe he could. She had a tendency to wear her heart on her sleeve while he—he could be utterly inscrutable.

'If I'm doing the majority of the decorating, don't you think your choice of colour schemes is going to give the game away?'

The hand clutching her heart relaxed. 'I could decorate the nursery on my own.'

'You're pregnant. You should be taking it easy.'

She loved that excuse when it came to ducking out of the dishes, but… 'Slapping on a coat of paint can't be that hard.'

One broad shoulder lifted and a little thrill shot through her at its breadth, its latent strength…its utter maleness. Her mouth started to water. *No thrills!*

'But you may as well make use of me while you have me.'

With an abrupt movement, she turned and marched across to an aisle full of decorative decals. It would be unwise to forget that he was only here for a month. And that he hadn't promised her anything more than help decorating her house. She ground her teeth together. If she could just get her darn hormones under control…

She pulled in a breath and willed the tightness from her body. 'If you wish to remain in suspense as to our baby's sex we best go with something neutral.'

'I didn't say that I didn't want to know.'

She left off staring at teddy bear decals to swing around to him, planting her hands on her hips. 'Well, do you or don't you?'

'I, um…I don't know.'

Helpful. *Not.* She didn't say that out loud, though. She'd been doing her best to aim for pleasant and rational and she had no intention of failing now.

'I…I kind of feel you've sprung this on me. Not your fault,' he added hastily, as if he thought his admission would have her losing her temper and hurling something at him. 'Can I think about it?'

She shrugged. 'Sure.' She could hardly blame him for feeling all at sea. This was uncharted territory and she felt exactly the same way. She pulled out one of the rolls. 'This is nice, isn't it?'

He took it from her and frowned. 'You can't use this in a boy's room.'

'Why on earth not? It has teddy bears. Teddy bears aren't gender specific. And it's not pink.' It gleamed in the most beautiful shades of ochre and gold.

'It has unicorns.'

'And…?'

He put the roll back on the shelf. 'Believe me, unicorns are a girl thing.' He picked up a different decal displaying jungle animals. 'What about this?'

She pointed. 'The tiger looks a bit fierce. I don't want to give the baby nightmares.'

He put it back and she found she didn't want to talk about nurseries any more, though if pressed she couldn't have said why. She'd been so excited at the prospect yesterday, but…

Before he could reach for another roll she said, 'Can I spring something else on you?'

He halted and then very slowly turned to face her. 'What?'

'I'm having that scan next week. Would you like to come along?'

'I've a few meetings next week.' His face closed up. 'I may even need to spend a day back in Rome, but if I'm free I'll be more than happy to drive you anywhere you need to go.'

'That's not what I meant, Ryan. I have a car. I can drive myself. What I'm asking is if you'd like to be present during the scan.'

He took a step back. 'I don't think…' He looked as if he wanted to turn and flee, but he set himself as if readying for a blow. 'What do you need me to do? What would you like me to do?'

She had to swallow back the ache that rose in her throat. 'It doesn't matter.' But it did. It mattered a lot.

'Then I'll just hang out in the waiting room until you're done.'

He didn't want to see the first pictures of his child, didn't want to hear its heartbeat? She turned from him to run her fingers along the decals, but she didn't see them. 'Ryan, do you love this baby yet?'

She glanced around at his quick intake of breath. He regarded her as if trying to work out what she wanted to hear and she shook her head. 'Honesty, remember? We promised to be honest with each other.'

His shoulders slumped a fraction. A passer-by wouldn't have noticed, but Marianna did. 'It still doesn't feel real to me,' he finally admitted.

She already loved this baby with a fierce protectiveness that took her completely off guard.

'You do.'

His words weren't a question, but a statement. She nodded. 'I expect it's different for a woman. The baby is growing inside of me—it's affecting me physically. That makes it feel very real.' Her stomach constricted at his stricken expression. 'I've also had more time to get used to the idea than you have, Ryan. There was no right or wrong answer to my question.' Just as long as he loved their baby once it arrived. That was all she asked.

He would, wouldn't he? It wouldn't just be a duty?

She reached up to scratch between her shoulder blades. 'How about we shelve the nursery for another day and focus on the things we need for the rest of the cottage?'

'Right.' He nodded. But he was quiet the entire time they bought paint, brushes, drop sheets and all the other associated paraphernalia one needed for painting. Marianna kept glancing at him, but she couldn't read his mood. While his expression remained neutral, she sensed turmoil churning beneath the surface.

'What next?' he asked when they'd stowed their purchases in the car.

'Soft furnishings.'

She waited for him to make an excuse to go and do something else and arrange to meet up again in an hour. He didn't. He said, 'Lead the way.'

Wow. Okay.

He didn't huff out so much as a single exaggerated sigh while endlessly shifting and fidgeting either. He didn't overtly quell yawns meant to inform her of his boredom, as her brothers would've done. He simply stacked the items she chose into the trolley he pushed, giving his opinion when she asked for it.

He had good taste too.

They moved from bedding to cushions and tablecloths and finally to curtains. 'They're just not right!' she finally said, tossing a set of curtains back to the shelf.

'What are you looking for?'

'Kitchen curtains. You know, the ones with the bit at the top and then…' She made vague hand gestures.

'Café curtains?'

She stared at him. 'Um…'

He rifled through the selections. 'Like these?'

'That style yes, but the print is hideous.'

'What kind of material are you after?'

She marched over to the store's fabric section and pulled out a roll with a print of orange and lime daisies. 'This is perfect.' A sudden thought struck her. 'Ooh, I wonder if I could find somebody to make them for me? I—'

'I can.'

'And then I—' She stopped dead. She moistened her lips and glanced around at him. 'Did you just say…' no, she couldn't have heard him right '…that you could make me a pair of curtains?'

'That's right.'

'You can sew?'

He nodded.

'How? Why?'

'I had a grandmother who loved to sew.'

He shuffled his feet and glanced away. She did her best to remake her expression into one of friendly interest rather than outright shock. 'She taught you to sew?'

He rolled his shoulders, glancing back at her with hooded eyes. 'Her eyesight started to fail and so…I used to help her out.'

She reached behind to support herself against a shelf. Of course he would love their baby. How could she have doubted it? A man who took the time to help an elderly lady sew because that was what she loved to do…because he loved her…

She swallowed and blinked hard. 'You'd make curtains for me?'

'Sure I will.' He suddenly frowned. 'Do you have a sewing machine?'

'My grandmother's will be rattling around somewhere.'

He shrugged again. 'Then no problem.'

Her eyes filled. He backed up a step, rubbed a fist across his mouth. 'Uh, Marianna…you're not going to cry, are you?'

She fanned her eyes. 'Pregnancy hormones,' she whispered.

He moved in close and took her shoulders in his hands. 'Okay, remember the drill. Close your eyes and take a deep breath.' As he counted to six she pulled in a long, slow breath. 'Hold.' She held. 'Now let it out to the count of six.'

They repeated that three times. When they were finished and she'd opened her eyes, he stepped back, letting his hands drop to his sides. 'Better?'

'Yes, thank you.'

'It's the silliest things, isn't it, that set you off?'

'Uh-huh.'

He snorted. 'It's just a pair of curtains.'

Oh, no, it wasn't. She spun around and pretended to consider the other rolls of fabric arrayed in front of them. These weren't just curtains. They were proof of his commitment to their baby. That wasn't nothing. It was huge… and she had to remember moments like this when he turned all cold and distant and unreadable. He was here for the baby. And he was here for her.

Who was there for him?

She swung back to him. 'You've been incredibly patient with me, Ryan. You haven't hassled me once yet about keeping up my end of our bargain.'

'You haven't been feeling well. Plus you've been working hard on the estate. I've no desire to add to your stress levels.'

He might be cool and controlled but he had a kind heart. 'I've done enough mooching and mood swinging.' From here on in she meant to help him as much as he helped her. 'I need to make another stop before we call it a day.'

'No problem.'

She couldn't help it. She reached up on tiptoe and kissed him.

CHAPTER SIX

'You said you wanted to learn about babies, right?'

Ryan eased back from where he taped the kitchen windows, to find Marianna setting a pile of bags onto the dining table. His pulse rate kicked up a notch, though he couldn't explain why. 'That's right.' He *needed* to learn about babies if he had any hope of making a halfway decent father.

She sent him a smile that carried the same warmth as the lavender-scented air drifting in from the French doors. It reminded him of how she'd smiled at him yesterday when he'd told her he'd make those stupid curtains she wanted.

It reminded him of the way she'd *kissed* him yesterday.

And just like that his skin tightened and he had to fight the rush of blood through his body—a rush that urged him to recklessness. He ground his teeth against it. Recklessness would wreck everything.

Marianna hadn't kissed him as a come-on or an invitation. She'd reached up on tiptoe and had pressed her warm, laughing lips to his in a moment of gratitude and high spirits. It wasn't the kind of kiss that should rock a man's world. It wasn't the kind of kiss that should keep a man up all night.

And yet hunger, need and desire had been gnawing away at him with a cruel persistence ever since. And now Marianna stood there smiling at him, eyes dancing, bouncing as if she could barely contain the energy coursing through her petite frame, and it was all he could do to bite back a groan.

Her smile wavered and she bit her lip. 'You don't have

other plans do you? Earlier you said you didn't mean to start painting in here until tomorrow.'

He wanted the smile back on her face. 'No plans.' Today he was prepping the walls for painting…and then getting to work on that report. He set the roll of tape to the kitchen bench and moved straight over to the table. 'I don't want the paint fumes making you feel sick. I thought that if I paint while you're at work…'

'The worst of it will have passed?' She wrinkled her nose—her darn gorgeous nose.

Don't notice her nose. Don't notice her mouth. Don't notice anything below her neck!

He shoved his hands into the pockets of his jeans. 'I'll air the house as well as I can. I bought an extractor fan, so…' He held out crossed fingers before shoving his hand into his pocket again where it was firmly out of temptation's way.

'Have I said thank you yet?'

Dear God in heaven, he couldn't risk her kissing him again. 'You have.' To distract her from further displays of gratitude, he nodded towards the bags. 'What have you got there?'

'A lesson.'

He tried to pull his mind to the task in hand. *Pay attention.* He had to learn how to take care of a baby.

She reached into the nearest bag and, with a flourish, pulled out a…

He blinked and backed up a step. "Uh, Marianna, that's a doll.' He scratched the back of his neck and glared at her from beneath a lock of hair that had fallen forward on his forehead. He really should get it cut. 'Don't you think we're a little old to be playing with dolls?'

She stared at that lock of hair and for a tension-fraught moment he thought she meant to lean across and push it out of his eyes. Hastily, he ran a hand back through his hair himself. She blinked and then shook herself. He let out a breath, his heart thumping.

She, however, seemed completely oblivious to his state. She dangled the doll—a life-sized version from what he could make out—from its foot, and smirked at him. 'Ooh, is the big strong man frightened of the itty-bitty dolly?'

He scowled. 'Don't be ridiculous.'

A laugh bubbled out of her and she sashayed around the table still dangling that stupid doll by its foot. 'Is your super-duper masculinity threatened by a little dolly?'

He snaked a hand around her head and drew her face in close to his. 'Tread carefully, Marianna.'

Her curls, all silk and sass, tickled his hand. 'I'm holding on by a thread here. My so-called masculinity is telling me to throw caution to the wind. It's telling me to kiss you, to take you to my bed and make love with you until you can barely stand.' And then he told her in the most straightforward, vivid language at his command exactly what he craved to do.

Her eyes darkened until they were nearly black. Her lips parted and she stared at his mouth as if she were parched. The pulse in her throat pounded. If he touched his lips to that spot they'd both be lost.

He hauled in a breath. With a super-human effort he let her go. She made a tiny sound halfway between an out-breath and a whimper that arrowed straight to his groin. He closed his eyes and gritted his teeth. 'You told me that if I do that—here in your real world—that I will hurt you, break your heart. I don't want to do that.'

He cracked open his eyes to find her nodding and smoothing a hand across her chest. She gripped the doll by its leg as if it were a hammer. He reached out and plucked it from her. 'There's no need to hurt poor dolly, though, is there?'

He said it to make her smile. It didn't work. She moved

back around the other side of the table, her movements jerky and uncoordinated. It hurt him somehow. It hurt to think he'd caused her even momentarily to lose her natural grace and bounce. Her gaze darted to him and away again. 'I'm sorry. I didn't mean for that to come across as any kind of…teasing.'

'I know. It's just…I'm…' He was teetering. He bit back a curse. 'I shouldn't have said anything. I—'

'No, no! It's best that I know.'

Not if it made her feel awkward. He shoved his hands as deep into his pockets as he could. 'It will pass, you know?'

'Oh, I know.' She nodded vigorously. 'It always does.'

He frowned then, recalling her brothers' taunting, *Paulo*. 'That sounds like the voice of experience.'

Her head snapped up. 'So what if it is?'

He blinked, but he had to admit that she had a point.

'It's okay for you to feel that way, but not me? It's okay for you to have had a lot of lovers, but not for me?'

'Not what I meant,' he growled. 'But if you do have experience in this…area, maybe you can hand out a tip or two about how to make it pass quickly.'

'Oh.' Her shoulders sagged. She lifted her hands and let them drop. 'In the past I haven't always had what's considered a good…attention span where men are concerned. I meet a new guy and it's all exciting and fun for a couple of weeks and then…'

Curiosity inched through him. 'And then?'

She wrinkled that cute nose. 'I don't know. It becomes dull, a bit boring and tedious.'

'This happens to you a lot?'

She shrugged, not meeting his eye.

'Which is why your brothers came up with the Paulo moniker.'

Her chin lifted. 'I believe in true love, okay? I don't believe there's anything wrong with looking for it.' Her chin hitched up higher. 'And I don't believe one should settle for anything less.'

'So… When a guy doesn't come up to scratch you what—dump him?'

She glared at him. 'What am I supposed to do? String him along and let him think I'm in love with him?'

'Of course not! I just—'

'I'd hate for any man to do that to me.' She folded her arms. 'I don't believe anyone should settle for anything less than true love.'

He couldn't have found a woman more unlike him if he'd tried!

'So what if I have high expectations of the man I mean to spend the rest of my life with? I'm more than happy for him to have high expectations of me too.'

Right…wow. 'So, you're happy to kiss a lot of frogs in this search for your Prince Charming?'

'Just because a man isn't my Prince Charming doesn't make him a frog, Ryan.'

Right.

She glanced at him. 'Isn't it like that for you—things becoming a bit boring and tedious after a while?'

He shook his head. 'One-night stands, that's what I do. No promises, no complications…and no time for them to become boring.' At her raised eyebrow he shuffled his feet. 'And once in a blue moon I might indulge in a holiday fling. A week is a long-term commitment in my book.'

'I should be flattered,' she said, her lips twisting in a wry humour that had a grin tugging at the corners of his mouth. She pulled out a chair and plonked down on it. 'What a pair.'

Cautiously he eased into the chair opposite.

She brightened, turning to him. 'All you need to do is start boring me.'

'I've been trying that with the colour charts.'

Her face fell. 'But I don't find them boring.' She tapped a finger to her chin. 'I could try nagging you,' she offered.

His lips twitched. A laugh shot out of her. 'Are you calling me a nag?'

'I wouldn't dream of it.'

She slapped her hands to the table, her eyes dancing. 'You're a bore and I'm a nag!'

Laughter spilled from her then—contagious, infectious—and Ryan found his entire body suddenly convulsing with it, every muscle juddering, a rush of warmth shooting through him. Belly-deep roars of laughter blasted out of him and he was helpless to quieten them even when he developed a stitch in his side.

Marianna laughed just as hard, her legs bouncing up and down, her curls dancing and tears that she tried to stem with her palms pouring down her cheeks. Every time he started to get himself back under control, Marianna would let loose with another giggle or snort and they'd both set off shrieking again. It was a complete overreaction, but the release in tension was irresistible.

'What on earth…?' Nico slid into the room, breathing hard. 'It sounds as if someone is being murdered in here!'

An utterance that only made Marianna laugh harder. Ryan choked back another burst of mirth. 'I'm thinking if I told you that I'm a bore and Marianna is a nag, that you wouldn't get the joke.'

'You'd be right.' But Nico's face softened when he glanced at his sister. He said something to her in Italian. She slowly sobered, although she retained an obscenely wide smile, and nodded.

It was stupid to feel excluded, but he did.

Marianna shot upright and clapped her hands. 'Ryan, will the painting be finished in here—' she gestured around the living, dining and kitchen areas '—by Saturday?'

He shrugged. 'Sure.' That was nearly a week away.

'Nico, are you busy next Saturday night? I want to invite you and Angelo for dinner—a housewarming dinner in my new home.'

Nico's face darkened. 'Are you sure you wouldn't prefer to live up at the villa?'

'Positive.' She tossed her glorious head of hair. 'Now say you'll come to dinner.'

He stared at her for a moment longer and finally smiled. 'I'd be delighted to.' He glanced at Ryan. 'I'll bring the wine.'

Ryan had a feeling that was meant to be some kind of subtle set down, but before he could form a response Nico's gaze lit on the doll. His mouth hooked up. *'You're playing dolls with my sister?'*

He squirmed and ran a finger around the collar of his shirt.

'We're learning to change a diaper,' Marianna announced.

Ah, so that had been her plan.

She raced around the table and dragged her brother across to the doll. 'You're going to want to play with *mia topolino* when it is born, yes?'

'Naturally.'

'"Mia topolino"?' Ryan asked.

'My little mouse,' she translated for him and his gut clenched. She had a pet name for their baby?

She turned back to Nico. 'You're going to want to babysit, yes?'

'Of course.'

'Then you need to know how to change a diaper.'

'I can already do so.'

Ryan stared at the other man. He could?

Marianna, however, refused to take Nico at his word.

She shoved the doll at him and then reached into another bag and brandished a disposable nappy. Ryan had never seen one before. With a supreme lack of self-consciousness, Nico quickly and deftly placed said nappy on the baby…uh, doll. Ryan frowned. That didn't look too hard.

He caught the doll when Nico tossed it to him with a mocking, 'Your turn.'

His stomach screwed up tight, but he refused to back down from the challenge. How hard could it be? He held out a hand to Marianna like a doctor waiting for a scalpel. 'Nappy.' She blinked. 'Diaper,' he amended. 'We call them nappies in Australia.'

She passed one across to him. He stared at it, turned it over. Why didn't these things come with Front and Back labels? And instructions? Gingerly he rested the baby on the table. *Doll, not baby.*

Nico's hands rested on his hips. 'You need to keep a hand on the baby to make sure it doesn't roll off the table.'

Marianna shushed her brother. Ryan tried to keep hold of the doll with one hand while unfolding the nappy with the other. Nico snickered. Damn it! He was all thumbs.

Ryan blocked his audience out as he tried to decipher the puzzle in front of him. Slipping what he hoped was the rear of the nappy beneath the baby, he brought the front up, and secured the sticky tabs at the sides. There, that hadn't been too hard, and for a first attempt it didn't look too bad. He lifted the baby under the arms prepared to crow at his performance, but the nappy slid off and fell to the floor with a soft thud. Damn!

Nico snorted. 'And you call yourself a father?'

Marianna opened her mouth, her eyes flashing, but Ryan touched her arm and she closed it again. He glared at Nico. 'I call myself a father-to-be.' He tossed the doll back. 'Show me how you did it again.' He would master this!

Twenty minutes later Ryan finally lifted the doll and

this time his effort at least stayed in place. Discarded diapers littered the table and the floor. He shook the doll.

'You're not—'

Ryan held up a finger to the man opposite. 'I know you're not supposed to shake babies, but this is a doll, in case you hadn't noticed. I've already killed it multiple times by letting it roll off the table, smothering it beneath a sea of nappies, and it's probably concussed from where I accidentally cracked its head on the back of the chair.'

Thank heavens Marianna had the foresight to give him a doll to practise on.

'I know it's probably peed on me—' that discussion had proved particularly enlightening '—puked on me and probably bitten me, but…' he shook the doll again '…that nappy isn't going anywhere.'

He felt a ludicrous sense of achievement. He could change a nappy!

'Don't get too cocky. Wait until you have to change a dirty diaper. One that smells so bad it's like a kick in the gut and—'

'Enough, Nico,' Marianna said. 'My turn now.'

She took the doll, and, with her tongue caught between her teeth, repeated the process of putting the diaper on. Ryan moved in closer to check her handiwork. 'That looks pretty good.'

She shook her head and frowned. 'I did what you did. I didn't make it tight enough.' She slid several fingers between the diaper and the doll to prove her point. 'It's just… I don't want to cut the poor baby's circulation off.' She glanced across at her brother. 'Are you going to say something cutting about my prospective mothering abilities?'

Nico shuffled his feet and glowered at the floor. 'Of course not.'

A surge of affection swamped Ryan then. She'd just risked criticism and scorn from her brother to show solidarity with him. Nobody had done anything like that for him before, and he was fairly certain he didn't deserve it now, but…to not feel cut off, adrift, alone. To feel connected and part of a team, it was… He rolled his shoulders. It was kind of nice.

Nico pointed a finger at Marianna. 'You've changed diapers before. You must have at harvest time. We have so many workers then. Many of them with children,' he added for Ryan's benefit.

'I did, but I was never particularly good at it and…well, people stopped asking me.' Her shoulders had started inching up towards her ears. In the next moment she tossed her head. 'I was really good at keeping the children entertained, cajoling them out of tears and bad tempers.'

For the first time it struck him that Marianna might be feeling as intimidated and overwhelmed as he did about their impending parenthood.

'And what's more, dearest brother of mine, if you mean to continue standing there criticising us, then be warned that I'll tell Ryan how you used to play Barbie dolls with me when I was a little girl.'

Nico backed up a step and pointed behind him. 'I'll, uh, leave you to it. I have work to do.' He turned and fled.

Ryan stared after him. Had he really played dolls with his little sister? He glanced at Marianna, who was having a second attempt at getting the nappy on, and then at the door again. The guy couldn't be all bad.

'Ryan?'

He turned to face her more fully. 'Yes?'

'I'm sorry about my brother.'

'No apology needed. And thank you.' He gestured to the table, the doll and the pile of nappies. 'This was a great idea. I'm going to have to start practising.' He was going to be the best damn nappy changer the Amatucci clan had ever seen.

* * *

Marianna watched Ryan put, oh, yet another diaper on the doll, his face a mask of determination, and something inside her softened. He was trying so hard. 'You're getting better,' she offered.

'We're going to run out of diapers soon.'

It was sweet too that he called them diapers now, probably for her benefit. 'We can get more.'

He glanced at her; his eyes danced for a moment, bringing out the deep blue in their depths that so intrigued her. 'I'll make a deal with you, Mari…'

The easy shortening of her name and the familiarity it implied made her break out in delicious gooseflesh. *It's a lie—an illusion.* She couldn't forget that. 'A deal?'

'I'll be the main diaper changer if you take on the role of dealing with Junior's tears and temper.'

'We'd need to be co-parenting together full-time for that kind of deal to work.' It was starting to hit her how difficult single parenthood was going to be. Sure, Ryan wanted to be involved, but they both knew the bulk of the baby's care would fall to her.

Unless Ryan moved to Monte Calanetti and they agreed to a fifty-fifty child custody arrangement. She bit her lip. She didn't like that thought. She wanted the baby with her full-time. She rolled her lip between her teeth. Okay, she was honest enough to admit that she might want the occasional night off, but nothing more. She didn't want the baby spending half its time away from her. She glanced at Ryan to find he'd gone deathly pale. What on earth…?

She went back over their conversation and then rolled her eyes. 'Get over yourself! I'm not angling for a marriage proposal. We decided against that, remember?'

He searched her face, and slowly his colour returned. He nodded and dragged a hand down his face.

'I haven't forgotten. You're commitment-shy and a lone wolf.'

'While you have a short attention span when it comes to men.'

She folded her arms and stared at him for a long moment. 'You're different from the other men I've known, though. This is different—us…we're different.' Why was that? 'But it doesn't mean I want to marry you.' She couldn't fool herself that it meant anything or that it would lead anywhere. 'I've never stayed friends with any of my previous lovers.' That probably had something to do with it.

'Me neither.'

'And I've certainly never had a baby with anyone before.'

He raised both hands. 'Nor I.'

'So obviously this is going to be different from any other experience we've had before, right?'

'Absolutely.'

She glanced at him but it wasn't relief that trickled through her. The itch she couldn't reach, the one right in the middle of her back between her shoulder blades, pricked with a renewed ferocity that made her grit her teeth. Her skin prickled, her stomach clenched, and a roaring hunger bellowed through her with so much ferocity it was all she could do not to scream. Sleeping with Ryan would sate that itch and need, soothe the burn and bite. Sleeping with Ryan would quieten the fears racing through her and—

'Don't look at me like that, Marianna!'

She started, the hunger in his eyes making her sway towards him, but he shook his head and took a step back. Instinct told her that if she continued to stare at him so boldly, so…lustfully, he'd seize her in his arms, kiss her and they probably wouldn't even make it to her bedroom.

She craved that like a drug. She craved it more than she'd ever craved anything. To fall into Ryan's arms and lose herself in a world of sensation and physical gratification, what a dream! But… What she felt for Ryan was different from what she'd felt for anyone. The intensity of it frightened her. She didn't want this man breaking her heart. That'd be a disaster. Through their child, they'd be tied to each other for the rest of their lives. It'd leave her no room to get over him.

She gripped the back of a chair and dragged her gaze from his. Pulling the chair out, she fell into it. 'I really, *really* can't wait for the time when you become boring. I…I have things to do.' With that she leapt up and strode away, and all the while her fickle heart urged her to turn back and throw herself into Ryan's arms, to throw caution to the wind.

Ryan pounced on his phone the moment it rang. 'Ryan White.'

'It's confirmed. Conti Industries are getting cold feet,' his assistant in Rome said without preamble. She knew his impatience with small talk and had learned long ago to get straight to the point. Time was money.

'Why?' Was someone conducting a smear campaign, attempting to discredit him?

'It appears the fact that you're not personally in Rome at the moment has them questioning your commitment.'

Damn it! He wheeled away, raking a hand back through his hair. He'd been afraid this would happen—that Conti Industries would develop cold feet. Why on earth had he promised to stay in Monte Calanetti for a whole month? He needed his head read!

He straightened, moving immediately into damage control. 'Can you arrange a meeting?'

'I already have.'

He let out a breath. 'That's the reason I pay you the big bucks.' Face-to-face with the Conti Industries' executive committee he'd be able to turn things around, prove their former faith in him wasn't a mistake.

'But it's this afternoon. You need to get down here *pronto*.'

Today!

'I tried making it for tomorrow, but they insisted. They're viewing this meeting as, quote, "a validation of your commitment to their project and your ability to deliver". They've left me in no doubt that agreeing to meet is an unprecedented demonstration of faith. I don't need to tell you what'll happen if you miss this meeting.'

He pressed his lips together. No, she didn't. If he weren't in Rome this afternoon, the whole deal would go down the gurgler. He thrust out his jaw. He wasn't letting that happen. Not without a fight.

'I'll be there,' he said, bringing the call to an abrupt end.

He glanced through his electronic diary as he hauled on a suit. The only thing he had slotted in was Marianna's information session this evening. He let out a breath. He'd be able to catch up on that another time. He slipped a tie around his collar and tied a perfect Windsor knot. He'd ring her later to let her know he couldn't make it.

As he drove away from the vineyard a short time later the rush of chasing the big deal sped through him, filling him with adrenaline and fire. He'd missed that cut-and-thrust this past week. This was the world where he belonged, not decorating nurseries. Drumming his fingers against the car's steering wheel, he wondered if he could cut his time at Marianna's vineyard a week or two short.

Marianna glanced at her watch and paced the length of her living room before whirling back. It was ten past six.

Where was Ryan? The information session at the clinic started in twenty minutes!

She'd reminded him about it this morning. He'd told her he hadn't forgotten, that it was in his diary, that he'd drive them. So where was he?

She glanced at her watch again. Eleven minutes past six. With a growl, she dialled his mobile number and pressed her phone to her ear. It went straight to voicemail. Brilliant. 'Where are you? The session starts in nineteen minutes! I can't wait any longer. I'll meet you at the clinic.'

Seizing her car keys, she stormed out and drove herself to the town's medical clinic. She'd just parked when her phone buzzed in her handbag. A text. From Ryan.

Something came up. In Rome. Won't be back till tomorrow. Sorry, couldn't be helped. Meeting very important. Will make next info session.

He couldn't even be bothered to ring her?

She stared at the screen. Blinking hard, she shoved the phone back into her bag. Right, well, she knew exactly where she and the baby stood in the list of Ryan's priorities—right at the very bottom.

How on earth did either one of them think this was going to work?

'Don't even think about it!'

Marianna spun around, clutching her chest, to find Ryan—with hands on his hips—silhouetted in the large cellar door. As he was backlit by the sun she couldn't see his face, but she had a fair inkling that he was glaring at her. She gestured to the barrel, her heart pounding. 'It's empty.'

He moved forward and effortlessly lifted it onto her trolley.

She swallowed and tried to smile. 'See? Not heavy.'

He stabbed a finger at her. 'You shouldn't be lifting anything. You should be looking after yourself.'

She batted his finger away. 'Stop being such a mother hen. I'm used to this kind of manual labour. It won't hurt the baby.'

'But why take the risk?' He gestured to the barrel. 'You must have staff here who can take care of these things for you?'

Of course they did, but she didn't want anyone thinking she couldn't do her job. She didn't want anyone thinking she was using her pregnancy as an excuse to slacken off. She wanted everyone to see how steady and professional she'd become since returning from Australia. She wanted everyone to see how she'd developed her potential, wanted them to say what a talent she was, what an asset for Vigneto Calanetti.

'I don't want to lose my fitness or my strength, Ryan. I'll need them for when I return to work after my maternity leave.'

He blinked.

'I'm going to need both for the labour too.' The information evening had brought that home to her with stunning—and awful—clarity. The information evening he *hadn't* attended so what right did he think he had ordering her around like this now?

He frowned. 'You're active—always on the go. I don't think you need to worry on that head.'

Ha! If he, Nico and Angelo had any say in the matter she wouldn't lift a finger for the next six and a half months. Well, at dinner on Saturday night she'd show her brothers how accomplished and capable she'd become. She'd wow them with her new house, a superb dinner and marvellous conversation. They'd realise she was a woman in charge of her own destiny—they'd stop worrying she'd screwed up her life and…and they'd all move forward from there.

'Are you worried about the labour?'

'Not a bit of it,' she lied. She straightened. 'How was your meeting in Rome?'

'Yes, I'm so sorry about that. It really couldn't be helped.'

Why wasn't he asking about the info session? She tried to keep the disapproving tone out of her voice. 'Did you come looking especially for me? Was there something you needed?'

'Just a break from painting for a bit.' He grimaced. 'The smell can become a little overwhelming.'

'I'm sorry. I didn't think about—'

'I'm enjoying it. Don't apologise. It's just…I found myself curious about what you do all day and—' he gestured around '—this place.'

So he was interested in her work, but not their baby. She had to remind herself that the idea of a baby was still very new to him, and that at least he was trying. And she couldn't wholly blame him—to her mind vineyards and wineries were fascinating.

He rolled his shoulders. 'I mean, you leave at the crack of dawn each day.'

She suddenly laughed. 'Ryan, I'm not leaving early to avoid you. I've always been a lark and I love checking the vines in the early morning when everything is fresh and drenched in dew. It means I can have the afternoons free if I want.' At his look she added, 'At the moment there's a certain amount of work that needs to be done, but it doesn't really matter when I do it.'

'The convenience of being your own boss.'

'Don't you believe it. Nico is the boss here. Don't let his easy-going mildness fool you. He has a killer work ethic.'

'Easy-going?' he choked. 'Mild?'

She laughed at his disbelief and led him out of the door and gestured to the row upon row of vines marching up the hill, all starting to flower. Those flowers might not be considered pretty, but she thought them beautiful. And if each of them were properly pollinated they'd become a glorious luscious grape. 'Beautiful, isn't it?'

He blew out a long breath and nodded.

'I can offer our child a good home, Ryan. A good life.'

'I know that.'

She hoped he did. 'Would you like a tour of our facilities here?'

'I'd love that.' He suddenly frowned. 'But only because I'm curious, not because I doubt you.'

She wasn't so convinced, but she showed him everything. She showed him what she looked for in a grape and what she was working towards. She took him to see the presses, the fermentation vats and the aging vessels. She even took him into the bottling room. She ended the tour at the cellar door where she had him try several of their more renowned wines.

'Things are relatively quiet at the moment, but at harvest time it becomes crazy here. In September, we eat, breathe and sleep grapes.' She glanced up at him. 'You should try and make it back then to experience it. It's frenetic but fun.'

'I'll see what I can do.' But he already knew he'd be tied up working the Conti contract. He glanced beyond her and nodded. 'Nico.'

She turned to find Nico with their new neighbour Louisa standing behind her. She straightened, hoping Nico didn't think she was skiving off. 'I was just showing Ryan around. Hello, Louisa.'

The other woman smiled and it somehow helped to ease the tension between the two men. 'I understand congratulations are in order,' the other woman said. 'News of your pregnancy has spread like wildfire through the village.'

She could barely contain her grin. *A baby!* 'Thank you.' Beside her, Ryan shifted and she came back to herself. 'Louisa, this is Ryan White. He's staying with me for a bit. Ryan, this is Louisa Harrison. She recently inherited the vineyard and glorious *palazzo* next door. Speaking of which, how are the renovations coming along?'

Louisa lifted a shoulder. 'No sooner did the architect arrive than it seemed the renovations to the chapel started. There are workers swarming all over the *palazzo*! The schedule is to have it completed by the end of July. But… it's such a big job.'

Marianna nodded. The *palazzo* was glorious and the family chapel absolutely exquisite, but it'd been neglected for a long time. It'd be wonderful to see it restored to its former glory.

'The architect is based in Rome and has a very good reputation,' Louisa continued. 'He used to holiday here as a child apparently. It seemed sensible to choose a firm that had connections to the area.'

'What's his name?' Marianna asked.

'Logan Cascini.'

'I remember him! He and Angelo were a similar age, I think. I'm sure they hung out together.'

Nico nodded. 'They did.'

'It'll be lovely to see him again. Is he married?' Was there a new woman in town who needed befriending? 'Any *bambinos*?' She bit back a smile. It wasn't as if she had babies on the brain or anything.

Louisa shook her head.

Beside her, Ryan shifted again and she glanced up at him, puzzled at the sudden tension that coursed through him. He glared at Nico. 'While you're here, perhaps you can talk some sense into your sister and tell her heavy lifting is off the agenda until after the baby is born.'

Oh, brilliant. She and Nico had already had words on this head.

Nico stiffened. 'Marianna?'

'I caught her lifting a barrel.'

She sent Ryan an exasperated glare. The big fat tale teller! 'It was an *empty* barrel.'

Nico let forth with a torrent of Italian curses that made her wince. Finally he stabbed a finger at her. 'Why can you not get this through your thick skull?'

She started to shrivel inside.

'No more lifting. One more time, Mari, and I'm firing you!'

Her jaw dropped. 'You can't!' This was her job, her work, her home!

'I can and I will!'

He would too. She battled the lump in her throat.

'No more lifting! You hear me?'

All she could manage was a nod. *Screw-up. Useless. Failure.* The accusations went around and around in her head. So much for proving her worth.

'Why have you not been keeping a better eye on her?' Nico shot at Ryan.

'Me? You're her employer!'

She closed her eyes. She opened them again when Louisa touched her arm. 'How have you been feeling? Have you had much morning sickness?'

She could've hugged her for changing the subject and bringing Ryan and Nico's finger-pointing to a halt. 'A little. And the morning part of that is a lie. It can happen at any time of the day.' She sucked her bottom lip into her mouth. 'I probably shouldn't have announced my pregnancy until after my scan.' What if something went wrong? Everybody would know and—

'But you were excited.'

Louisa smiled her understanding, and it helped Marianna to straighten and push her shoulders back. This incident might've been a backward step as far as Nico's view of her went, but she was going to be a mother, and she was determined to be a good one.

'Speaking of which,' Nico said, 'I believe you said your scan is tomorrow, yes?'

Ryan stiffened and then swung to her. 'Tomorrow?'

Nico's eyes narrowed and she could see his view of her maturity take another nosedive. *Damn it!*

She waved an airy hand in the air. 'Don't tell me you've forgotten? You did say you'd take me.'

To Ryan's credit, he adjusted swiftly and smoothly. 'Of course. Just as we planned.'

Damn it again! She hadn't wanted him to take her. What use would she have for a man who had no interest in hearing his baby's heartbeat?

CHAPTER SEVEN

MARIANNA THREW HERSELF down on a bench in the garden, slapping a palm to her forehead. 'Well done, you…doofus!' she muttered. To think she'd been making progress where Angelo and Nico were concerned, to think—

She leaned to the side until her head rested on the arm of the bench and did what she could to halt the flood of recriminations pounding through her. She tried the breathing technique that Ryan had taught her, but in this instance it didn't work. All it did was bring to mind the light in his eyes when he'd returned to the cottage to paint her walls. It'd told her that the subject of her scan—of her not telling him the actual date of said scan—would be the topic of conversation the moment she returned.

Yay. More talking. Which, of course, was why she was hiding out in the garden like a coward.

Very adult of you, Marianna.

Heat pricked the backs of her eyes and a lump swelled in her throat. What if they were right? What if she were making a hash of everything? She pressed a hand to her stomach. What if she made a mess of her baby's life?

'It's all a mess!'

For a moment she thought Nico's voice sounded in her own mind. When Louisa answered with, 'What do you mean?' Marianna realised that her brother and their neighbour passed close by on the other side of the hedge. The hedge's shade and its new spring growth shielded her from view. She shrank back against the bench, not wanting Nico to see her so upset.

'I don't trust this latest man of Marianna's.'

Marianna wanted to cover her ears. Ryan wasn't hers.

'Can I give you a word of advice, Nico?'

Her brother must've nodded because Louisa continued. 'You don't have to like Ryan, but if Marianna has decided that he's to be a part of her baby's life, then you're going to have to accept that. He's going to be a part of your niece or nephew's life for evermore—in effect, a part of your extended family. You don't have to like him, but if Marianna has asked that you respect her decision, then you're going to have to find a way to get along with him…for both Marianna and the baby's sake.'

'But—'

'No buts, Nico. You know, if you eased up on him for a bit, you might even find yourself liking Ryan.'

Her brother snorted. 'You think?'

'You never know.'

Marianna remained where she was, barely moving, until the voices drifted out of earshot. She hadn't meant to overhear. She hadn't meant to throw everyone into chaos with her baby news either. She forced herself off the bench and set off for the cottage.

The smell of paint hit her the moment she entered. She paused on the threshold, but her stomach remained calm and quiet and with a relieved breath she continued down the hallway to the living area.

She pulled to an immediate halt with a delighted, 'Oh!' Clutching her hands beneath her chin, she gazed around in wonder at the transformation a coat of deliciously tranquil 'sea foam'-coloured paint had created. Ryan must've worked his socks off!

She completed a slow circle. 'Oh, Ryan, it's perfect. Thank you.' She ached to lie on the sofa and revel in the calm, draw it into her soul.

'You weren't going to tell me that your appointment is tomorrow, were you?'

She bit back a sigh. The calm was only an illusion. In

the same way her and Ryan's *friendship* was an illusion. She turned towards the dining table where he sat. He rose and she wished herself back outside in her shady glen. 'Tea?' She stumbled into the kitchen and filled the kettle.

'Marianna?'

She didn't like the growl in his voice or the latent possessiveness rippling beneath it. 'No.' She turned and faced him, hands on her hips. 'You have that correct. I wasn't going to tell you about tomorrow's appointment.'

'Why not?'

She pulled two cups towards her and tossed teabags into them. 'Because you have no interest in being there.' Just as he'd had no interest in attending the information session.

'I said I would drive you.'

'And I told you I don't need a taxi service!'

His head reared back as if she'd slapped him. 'But… we're a team.'

Were they? Wasn't that just a polite fiction? 'If you don't want to be present at the scan, Ryan, then you're more use to me here fixing up the cottage.'

She spoke as baldly and bluntly as she could to remind herself that what they had here was a deal, an arrangement, and not a relationship.

He dragged a hand across his jaw, his eyes troubled. 'Then why the pretence in front of Nico?'

She pulled in a breath, held it to the count of three and let it out again. 'Because I don't want him to think badly of you…and I don't want him to think badly of me.'

'Why would he think badly of you? He worships the ground you walk on.'

She snorted and he frowned. She swung away to pour boiling water into their mugs. 'I'm his pesky little sister who's always getting into scrapes.'

'He adores you, Mari. He'd die for you.'

'I know.' He spoke nothing less than the truth.

'So would Angelo.'

That was the truth too. But sometimes she felt the weight of their love would suffocate her.

She started. 'Oh! I made you a chamomile tea. Should I—?'

'You should've asked me to make the tea! You've been on your feet all day.'

She nodded at the walls. 'And you haven't?' Not only was he painting her house, he was working on some new company report or other, taking endless calls on his mobile phone and making video calls on his laptop. If anyone were the slacker around here it'd be her.

He came around and took the mug from her. 'This will be fine, thank you.' When he gestured for her to take a seat on the sofa, she submitted. If they had to *talk*, then they might as well be comfortable while they did so.

'Look, I know you love your brothers.' He sat in the armchair opposite. 'I know you would die for them too.'

She would. In a heartbeat. She blinked, frowned. Did her love ever suffocate them?

'I understand it's important to you that I get along with them.'

He took a sip of his tea and grimaced.

She couldn't help grimacing too. In sympathy. 'You don't have to drink that, you know? Chamomile is an acquired taste.'

'You went to the trouble of making it, therefore I mean to drink it.'

What an enigma this man was proving to be. She slumped back. 'Getting on with my brothers isn't entirely in your control, Ryan. It's up to them too.'

His eyes had turned a stormy green that she was starting to recognise as a mixture of confusion and frustration. 'The fact you lied to Nico—'

'Lied is a bit harsh!'

'Well, let him believe I was included in tomorrow's appointment, then.'

Not that it'd worked. Nico had seen through her deception.

'Leads me to believe,' Ryan continued, 'that being present at this scan is something a *good* father would do.'

She leapt to her feet, setting her mug to the coffee table before she could spill it. 'Oh! You think?' How could this man be so clueless?

No, no, he couldn't be this clueless. It was just that whole stupid lone-wolf thing he had going and—

'Oh!' She stopped dead before racing across to the kitchen again. 'You made the kitchen curtains.' She ran her hands down the material. How had she not noticed them earlier? 'They're...*exactly* what I wanted.' They would look wonderful against the vibrant yellow of the walls once Ryan had painted in here—a nook of colour amidst the calm.

His voice came from behind her. 'You like them?'

She loved them. A lump blocked her throat and all she could do was nod. They were perfect. She glanced around the cottage at the new paint on the living and dining room walls, the kitchen primed and ready for its first coat of paint tomorrow, and at those darn curtains. Ryan was doing everything she asked of him without a murmur of complaint. He was doing everything he could to help her create the perfect home for their baby.

She moved across to the dining table and picked up the doll lying there—a doll sporting a perfect diaper and a ridiculous smile. She clutched the doll to her chest and swung to face him. 'Ryan, how can you not want to see the first pictures of our baby? How can you not want to hear its heartbeat?'

He dragged a hand across his jaw, not meeting her gaze. 'I have work to do.'

She dropped the doll back to the table. 'Work that's more important than your own child?'

Tension shot through him. With an oath, he started to pace. 'The truth?' he shot at her.

'The truth,' she demanded.

'Fine, then!' He swung back. 'Attending the ultrasound with you seems…'

'Seems what?' she pushed.

He skewered her to the spot with the ruthless light in his eyes. 'Too intimate.'

She rocked back on her heels, his words shocking her. 'It's not as intimate as the deed that's led us to this point in time.'

'True.' He nodded, his gaze not softening. 'But making love with you—our holiday fling…absolutely nothing out of character for me there.'

Except it'd lasted for a whole week rather than a single night. She left that observation unsaid.

'Attending an ultrasound with a woman…now that's utterly out of character. Can't see what use I'm going to be to you in that scenario, Marianna.'

Her chest cramped up so tight it became an effort to even breathe. Finally she managed a curt nod. 'If you want to become a halfway decent father, Ryan, you're going to have to get over this kind of squeamishness.'

His eyes bugged. 'Squeamishness?'

'Squeamishness about doing family things, feeling able to step up to the plate for another person, being relied upon.'

He swung away. 'I'm supposed to be in Rome tomorrow afternoon.'

'And just for the record, this isn't about you stepping up to the plate for me. It's not about you—' how had he put it? '—being of any use to me. This isn't about you and me.' There was no him and her. 'This is about you and the baby.'

His mouth thinned. 'This is all because I missed that damn info session, isn't it?'

"It's becoming obvious that your work is more important to you than our baby."

"Correction. That particular meeting was more important than attending an info session I can catch again at another time."

"And in the years to come a different important meeting will have you missing your child's second birthday, others will have you missing the school concert, a soccer grand final. You'll cancel promised outings and holidays because something important has come up at work. I want more than that for my child, Ryan. And you should too."

They stared at each other, both breathing hard. She swallowed and shrugged. 'The ultrasound is early—nine-thirty a.m.' He could attend the scan and still make an afternoon appointment in Rome. 'I'm driving myself. If you wish to attend, a flyer for the clinic with its address is on the fridge. I don't want to discuss this any more. I'm tired and I don't feel like fighting.' With that she walked back over to the sofa and picked up her chamomile tea.

He was quiet for a moment. 'I didn't mean to upset you.'

She waved that away.

He strode back and threw himself down into his chair. He leaned towards her suddenly, frowning. 'Are you worried about tomorrow's scan?'

She stared down into her tea. 'Of course not,' she lied.

But… What if she'd somehow hurt their baby? Her fingers tightened about her mug. For the best part of two months she hadn't even realised she was pregnant. She'd been drinking wine and coffee—not copious amounts, but still… She should've been taking special vitamins. If she'd planned this baby, she wouldn't have these worries. She'd have done everything right from the start.

She swallowed. She might be an irresponsible fool and

if the scan showed a problem tomorrow she'd have nobody to blame but herself. And now she wouldn't even have the comfort of Ryan's hand to cling to.

Marianna readied herself for the sensation of cold gel on her tummy when the technician's assistant tapped on the door and then popped her head around the curtain that screened Marianna. 'Sorry to disturb, but there's a Mr White out here who claims he's the baby's father.'

Marianna couldn't help it, her heart leapt.

'Shall I send him in?'

Marianna nodded. 'Yes, please.'

A moment later Ryan hovered awkwardly on the other side of the curtain, his face appearing in the gap. 'Sorry, I'm late.'

Marianna ached to hold her hand out to him, but she resisted the urge. She had no intention of making this all seem too *intimate*. 'I wasn't sure you'd make it.' She gestured to the equipment. 'Come on over and watch the show.'

He moved to stand beside her, but he didn't take her hand.

Marianna tried to ignore his warmth and scent, focusing on the monitor as the radiologist moved the sensor across her stomach and pointed out the baby's arms and legs, feet and fingers. She pronounced the baby to be in the best of health and Marianna let out the breath she'd been holding, her eyes still glued to the screen. *Thank you!*

Her heart started to pound, wonder filling her from the inside out, and she couldn't stop from reaching a hand towards the image on the monitor. She couldn't remember a more amazing moment in her life. Her baby!

Their baby.

She turned to Ryan and her heart stilled at the expression that spread across his face. She watched as his amazement turned to awe. He blinked hard several times, and a fist seized her heart. He swallowed and leaned towards the monitor…and she watched him fall in love with their baby.

That was the moment her chest cracked open. She felt as if she were falling and falling—as if there were no end in sight, no bottom to bring her up short—and then Ryan seized her hand, a breath whooshed out of her, and the world righted itself again.

He squeezed her hand, not taking his eyes from the screen. 'That's really something, isn't it?'

'Utterly amazing,' she breathed, not taking her eyes from his face.

But then he suddenly shot back, shaking his fingers free from hers, the colour leaching from him.

'Ryan?'

He glanced at his watch. 'I'm sorry, but if I don't get a move on I won't make my appointment this afternoon in Rome. I won't be back till tomorrow.'

With that he spun on his heel and left the room. Marianna turned back to the monitor and the image of her baby. Her temples started to throb.

Ryan stared around the chaos of the kitchen and grimaced. He rubbed the back of his head. 'What can I do?'

'Nothing!'

He glanced at his watch. Angelo and Nico weren't due to arrive for at least another hour, but…

The house was spick and span with not a single item out of place. Marianna had slaved over it all day. Ryan valued neatness and utility, but this was…*so* neat. Then again, maybe the kitchen made up for it. He turned to view it again and had to blink. The yellow on the walls was…bright.

He spun back to the rest of the room. It wasn't as if the neatness made things sterile, like a hotel room. Marianna's new scatter cushions and strategically draped throw rugs brightened the sofa, making it look like an inviting oasis to rest one's weary bones. But…

He shuffled his feet. 'Marianna—'

'No, no, don't talk to me! I have to concentrate. This recipe is complicated.'

He touched her arm. 'It's just your brothers. They won't care if you ring out for pizza.'

'Ring out?' Her mouth dropped open, her hair fizzing about her face in outrage.

He stared at that mouth and tension coiled up through him.

'I'm not ringing out! This dinner is going to be perfect!'

Why? Not because of him, he hoped. He didn't want her putting this kind of pressure on herself on his behalf.

He tapped a clenched fist against his mouth. It'd be pointless trying to reason with her when she was in this mood, though. Mind you, she'd been distant—wary—ever since he'd returned from Rome yesterday.

He winced anew when he recalled the way he'd bolted from the clinic during the ultrasound. The moment had been… He rubbed his nape. Well, it'd been perfect for a bit…before he'd started to feel as if he were drowning. Emotions he'd had no name for had pummelled him, trying to drag him under, and he'd needed to get away—needed time to breathe and pull himself back together.

It was all of those happy family vibes flying about the room. They'd tried to wrestle him into a straitjacket and put a noose around his neck. Worse still, for a moment he'd wanted to let them.

He didn't do happy families. He'd be the best father he could be to this child, but he wasn't marrying Marianna. He dragged a hand down his face. *That* would be a disaster.

He'd calmed down. Eventually. He had his head together again.

Now all he had to do was get through this evening.

He glanced at Marianna again. Her jerky movements and the way she muttered under her breath told him how much importance she'd placed on this meal. He made a mental note to do all he could to get along with her brothers tonight.

'There's nothing you can do. Go sit on the sofa and enjoy doing nothing for a change.'

He didn't. When she became absorbed again in some complicated manoeuvre involving flour, butter and potato, he slid in behind her and made a start on washing up the tower of dishes that was in danger of toppling over and burying her.

The scent of her earlier preparations—sautéed onion, garlic and bacon—rose up around him, making his mouth water. He managed to clear one entire sink of dishes without her yelling at him to get out from under her feet or accusing him once of being a neat freak. He even managed to dry and put them away, sliding out of her way whenever she spun around to seize another dish or wooden spoon or ingredient.

He was just starting on a second sink full of dishes—how could anyone use so many dishes to make one meal?—when a commotion sounded at the front door and Angelo and Nico marched in. Angelo carried an armful of flowers in one hand and a gift-wrapped vase under his arm. Nico bore a brightly wrapped gift. 'Happy housewarming!' they bellowed.

Marianna glared at them and pointed to the clock on the wall. 'You're early!'

'We couldn't wait to see you, *bella sorella*,' Angelo said, dropping an arm to her shoulders and easing her away from the stove and towards the living area. In one smooth movement Nico slid into her place and took over the cooking. 'Besides, we come bearing gifts.'

It was masterfully done and if he hadn't had wet hands Ryan would've applauded.

Marianna glanced at the flowers and clasped her hands beneath her chin. 'Oh! They're beautiful.'

Without a word, Ryan took the vase Angelo handed across the breakfast bar and filled it with water.

Marianna spun around to point a finger at Nico. 'I know exactly what the two of you are doing!'

Angelo took the now-filled vase and placed it on the coffee table. 'Should I just dump the flowers in?'

Marianna immediately swung back. 'No, you should not!' And set about arranging the flowers. 'But it doesn't change the fact that I know what the two of you are doing. You still don't think I can cook gnocchi.'

'You can't,' Nico said with a grin. 'And we knew it's what you'd try to make tonight.'

She shrugged. 'It's your favourite.' She straightened. 'And I'll have you know I've become very adept at the dish.'

'No, you haven't,' Angelo said with a grin. 'You're a brilliant tosser of salads, Mari, you make masterful pizzas, and your omelettes are to die for, but gnocchi isn't your thing. In the same way that Nico can't master a good sauterne.'

'Pah!' She waved that away. 'We don't grow the right grapes for sauterne.'

'And yet he keeps trying,' Angelo said with a teasing grin at his brother.

'Ooh, says you.' Marianna rolled her eyes. 'You keep telling me you have a green thumb, but who keeps killing my African violets?'

Ryan watched the three of them tease each other, boss each other, and a chasm of longing suddenly cracked open in his chest. He didn't understand it. He tried to shake it off. He told himself he was glad his child would have this family. And he was…but when Marianna eventually married *the man of her dreams* would their child feel an outsider amidst all of this belonging? As he did.

'You've done a good job in here, Ryan,' Nico said in an undertone. 'How on earth did you make it into the kitchen without having something thrown at you?'

'Subterfuge…and a quick two-step shuffle to get out of her way whenever she was reaching for something.'

Her brothers obviously knew her well. And then it hit him. Nico had just called him Ryan, not Paulo. Did that mean Marianna's brothers had decided on a temporary ceasefire? He put the last dried dish away. 'Anything I can do?'

'Know anything about gnocchi?'

'Nope.'

'Know anything about wine?'

Ryan glanced at the bottle Nico had placed on the bench earlier. 'I know how to pour it.'

'Then pour away.'

He poured three glasses of wine and then filled a fourth with mineral water, three ice cubes and a slice of lime—the exact way Marianna liked it. When he took their drinks to them, though, Marianna pursed her lips, glanced over at Nico, and started to rise. Nico chose that moment to move out from behind the breakfast bar with his glass of wine and handed her the wrapped package, ensuring she remained ensconced on the sofa. 'It's not a housewarming present,' he warned. 'It's a…' He shrugged. 'Open and see.'

Ryan watched in interest, his breath catching in his chest when Marianna pulled forth the most exquisite teddy bear he'd ever seen. Her eyes filled with tears and she hugged it. 'Oh, Angelo and Nico, it's perfect. Just perfect!'

His heart thudded. Why hadn't he thought to buy a toy for their baby? Since the scan all he could think about was the baby—the tiny life growing inside Marianna. The moment he'd been able to make out the baby's image on the monitor a love so powerful and protective had surged through him that, even now, just thinking about it left him reeling. He craved to be the best father he could be. He didn't want this child to doubt for a single second that it was loved.

His hands clenched. Could he really bear to be away from Monte Calanetti once the baby was born? Could he really envisage spending months at a time away from his child?

Nico turned with a wry grin. 'Want to put a diaper on teddy to match the one on dolly?'

He forced a smile to lips that didn't want to work. 'You might be surprised to find yourself with serious competition in the diaper-changing stakes.'

As one, he and Nico turned to Angelo with raised eyebrows. The other man raised his hands. 'No way.'

Ryan took a sip of wine. 'Has Mari showed you the ultrasound pictures yet? Our baby is beautiful.'

Mari's mouth slackened as she turned those big brown eyes of hers to him. They filled and his chest cramped—*please don't cry,* he silently begged—and then they shone. 'Our baby is perfect!' She leapt up to seize the scan photos for her brothers to admire.

Ryan found it hard to believe, but he enjoyed the meal. He didn't doubt that the other two men were reserving their judgement for the time being, but they'd put their overt hostility to one side.

Why?

The answer became increasingly clear as the meal progressed. They adored Marianna and they wanted her to be happy. How could they not love her? She bossed them outrageously, she said deliberately preposterous things to make them laugh, she'd touch their arms in ways that spoke of silent communications he had no knowledge of, but he could see how both men blossomed under her attention, how they relished and treasured it.

In return, she looked up to them so much and loved them so hard that an ache started up deep inside him.

He gripped his cutlery until it bit into him. He wanted her to look up to him like that. He wanted to win her respect. He wanted…

Not love. Never that.

His heart throbbed. Would she love their baby with the same fierceness that she loved her brothers? If she did, then…then this baby didn't need him.

When the children of *another man* took up her heart and her time, though, would her love lose its strength?

A hard rock of resentment lodged in his gut.

If you don't like the idea, pal, marry her yourself.

He shot back in his seat. As if that'd work! Couples shouldn't marry just because they were expecting a baby. It made things ten times worse when they broke up. His parents were proof positive of that. No. He wouldn't be party to making Marianna resent their child more than she inevitably would.

He glanced up to find all eyes at the table on him. He straightened and cleared his throat. He had no idea what question had just been shot his way, but… 'There's something I've been meaning to raise.'

Marianna stared at him and her eyes suddenly narrowed. Nico gestured for him to continue.

'I understand that harvest time is pretty busy?'

Nico nodded. 'Flat out.'

Ryan glanced first at Marianna and then her brothers. 'Please tell me Marianna won't be working sixty-to eighty-hour weeks.'

'She'll be on maternity leave from August,' Angelo said. 'Nico and I have already discussed it.'

He let out a breath. Good.

'I beg your pardon?' Marianna's eyes flashed and she folded her arms. 'You haven't discussed this with me.'

He stared at her folded arms, at the way her fingers clenched and unclenched, recalled the way she'd flung that vase at him and reached out and took the bowl containing the remainder of the fruit salad they'd had for dessert, pretending to help himself to more before placing it out of her reach. Just to be on the safe side.

'I'll have you know that come harvest I'll still be more than capable of pulling my weight.'

'I need you to monitor the grapes until the end of July,' Nico said. 'But after that I take over.'

'But—'

'No buts.'

Ryan reached a hand towards her, but she ignored it. He soldiered on anyway. 'You're going to be in the last few weeks of your pregnancy. You're going to have a sore back and aching legs.' He wished he could bear those things for her.

'It doesn't make me incapable of doing my job.'

'No one is saying it is,' Angelo said.

She made a wild flourish in the air. 'You cannot exclude me from this!'

Nico seized her hand. 'We're not excluding you, but your health and your *bambino's* health is precious to us. You can sit in a chair in the shade and direct proceedings.'

'You mean I can sit and watch you all work while I put my feet up!'

'You'll still be a part of it.'

She pulled her hand free from Nico's. 'That's bunk and you know it.'

Ryan folded his arms. 'You're going to have to keep an eye on her.'

Nico met Ryan's gaze with a challenge in his own. 'You

could always come back for harvest and keep an eye on her yourself.'

It took an effort not to run a finger around the collar of his shirt. If things went to plan, he'd be neck deep in his assignment for Conti Industries. He might be able to get away for the odd day, but a week, let alone a whole month, would be out of the question. 'I'll see what I can do.' But he already knew he wouldn't be back for the harvest.

'Oh, and now they think I need a babysitter! Fabulous!"

Marianna stalked away to throw herself down on the sofa, where she glowered at them all. Ryan pushed his chair back a tad so he could still include her in the conversation. 'Marianna gave me a tour of the winery the other day.'

'And?' Angelo said.

'You two know what I do, right? That I get called in to turn ailing companies around?'

Nico glared. 'My vineyard is not ailing.'

From the corner of his eye he saw Marianna straighten and turn towards them. 'It's not,' Ryan agreed.

Nico's glare abated but Angelo's interest had been piqued. 'But?'

'You have bottling facilities that stand idle for much of the year. Did you know that further down the valley there's a brewery that specialises in boutique vinegars? It's an outfit that doesn't have its own bottling facilities. Currently they're sending their stock to Florence for bottling.'

'You're suggesting we could bottle their vinegar?'

Ryan shrugged.

Angelo pursed his lips and glanced at Nico. 'They'd be interested. It'd reduce their transportation costs. And it'd bring additional money into the vineyard with very little effort on our part.'

Nico tapped a finger to the table. 'It'd create more jobs too.'

Angelo and Nico started talking at each other in a rush.

Ryan glanced across at Marianna to find her frowning at him, consternation and something else he couldn't identify in the depths of her eyes.

She started when she realised he watched her. Seizing a magazine, she buried her nose in it. But he couldn't help noticing that she didn't turn a single page.

Ryan turned back to the other men. 'I figured it was worth mentioning.' If they were interested in expanding their operations here, it'd be a good place to start.

'How'd you know about this?' Angelo asked.

'It's my job to know.' Old habits died hard. 'I was called in a couple of years ago to overhaul a vineyard in the Barossa Valley. It's one of the things we did to improve their bottom line.'

'And did you save it?'

He shrugged. 'Of course.'

Nico and Angelo started talking ten to the dozen. Marianna came back to the table and joined the debate. Ryan sat back and watched, and hoped he'd proved himself in some small way, hoped he'd eased Marianna's mind and shown her that he and her brothers could get on.

CHAPTER EIGHT

MARIANNA GAVE UP all pretence of conviviality the moment her brothers' broad figures disappeared into the warm darkness of the spring night. Trudging back into the living room, she slumped onto the sofa and stared at the beautiful teddy bear they'd bought for their prospective niece or nephew.

Her eyes filled. Oh, how she loved them!

Ryan clattered about, taking their now-empty coffee cups and wine glasses into the kitchen. 'The evening seemed to go well, don't you think?'

A happy lilt she hadn't heard since Thailand threaded through his voice. She slumped further into the sofa. Of course he'd be happy. *He'd* had a chance to prove his worth and show off his expertise to her brothers.

He started to run hot water into the sink. 'Leave them.' She didn't shout, though it took an effort not to. Who'd have thought he'd have turned out to be such a neat freak? 'I'll do them in the morning.' At least washing dishes was something she *could* do.

Even though she didn't turn around, she sensed his hesitation before he turned the taps off. He moved across to the living area and she could feel him as he drew closer, as if some invisible cord attached her to him. All nonsense!

He picked up the teddy bear, tweaked its ear. 'I think perhaps your brothers are starting to see that I'm not the villain they first thought me.'

No, now they saw him as some kind of super-duper business guru.

He is a business guru.

She ignored that. She could practically see what her

brothers now thought. *Poor Ryan—Mari's latest victim who's headed for heartbreak because she's too erratic to settle down.*

She wasn't the one who couldn't settle down. Not that they'd see that. What they'd see was that she'd caught Ryan in her snares—the poor schmuck—and that he was paying a hefty price for it. And…and they'd *admire* him for making the best out of a bad situation.

Having a baby wasn't a bad situation!

'Marianna?'

She started. Had Ryan been talking to her this entire time? She hadn't heard a word of it beyond the fact her brothers didn't hate him any more. His eyes narrowed on her face. 'You didn't enjoy this evening.'

It was a statement, not a question, so she didn't feel the need to respond.

He eased down into the chair opposite, his frown deepening. 'But I thought you wanted me to get along with your brothers.'

She had. She did! But not at the expense of their opinion of her.

He leaned forward, his expression intent, and something in her chest turned over. She wasn't the one who couldn't settle down. She *ached* to settle down. Not necessarily with Ryan, but… She'd never planned to have a baby on her own. What she'd wanted was to fall in love, get married and then start a family. That sure as heck wasn't going to happen with Ryan. So now she was going to have a baby on her own and it scared her witless.

'This has nothing to do with pregnancy hormones, does it?'

How could he tell? How could he be so attuned to her and yet so far out of her reach?

'No,' she finally said, figuring some kind of response would eventually be expected.

'Do you want to tell me about it?'

She opened her mouth to say no, but the word refused to emerge. Did she want to talk about it? She blinked when she realised the answer to that question was a rather loud yes.

She moistened her lips and risked another glance into Ryan's face. She'd never spoken to anyone about this before. It seemed too…personal. Besides, all the people she could talk about it with knew Angelo and Nico too.

Ryan knows them now as well.

True, but he'd still be on her side.

Would he? She waved a hand in front of her face. This wasn't about sides. She fixed him with a glare. 'Do you want to know even if it's something you can't fix?'

His eyes didn't leave her face. 'Yes.'

'And if I tell you I don't want you to do anything to try and fix it, because I expect that would only make matters worse, and I don't think I could bear that.'

Slowly he nodded. 'Okay.'

'I meant for tonight to impress Angelo and Nico. I wanted them to recognise my maturity. I wanted to wow them with my graciousness as a hostess. I wanted to prove to them that I'm not an irresponsible idiot or a screw-up!' Her voice had started to rise and she forced it back down. 'But that's certainly not something I managed to accomplish this evening, is it?' She flung out an arm. 'They didn't even trust me to cook the meal properly!'

Ryan's jaw dropped and she leapt up to pace. 'And then you had to go and bring up the whole "Marianna can't work during harvest" thing and all that garbage.' She spun around to glare at him. 'Thank you very much for making me look even worse!'

He shot to his feet and the sheer beauty of his body beat at her. 'The harvest thing? That's because we're all concerned about you.'

She gave up trying to moderate her voice. 'Because none of you think I can look after myself!'

'It's not that at all!'

She folded her arms and kinked a disbelieving eyebrow.

'It's because—' he stabbed a finger at her '—we all want to…' He trailed off, shuffling his feet and looking mildly embarrassed. 'We all want to pamper you,' he mumbled.

It was her jaw that dropped this time. 'I beg your pardon?'

'You're the one who's doing all of the hard work where the baby is concerned. You're the one who has morning sickness, and has had to give up coffee and wine. You're the one who's growing the baby inside you, which probably means you'll get a sore back and sore legs. And then you're the one who's going to have to give birth.'

Ugh. Don't remind her.

'While we—' he slashed a hand through the air '—we're utterly useless! You should know by now that men hate feeling like that. So, while we can't do anything for the baby, we can do things for you—to try and make things easier and nicer for you.'

Ryan felt useless?

'I just…' He grimaced. 'It didn't occur to me that in the process we might be making you feel useless too.'

His explanation put a whole new complexion on the matter. How could she begrudge him—or her brothers—for wanting to help where they could with the baby? She moved a step closer and peered up into his face. 'So…you don't think I'm stupid or that I'm acting irresponsibly?'

'Of course not! I…'

She swung away. 'Of course there's a but.'

'All I was going to say is that I think, in your determination to prove to us all how capable you are, you could be in danger of overdoing it.'

He was talking about that incident with the barrel.

'I did hear you, though—your concern about losing your fitness.'

He had? She turned back.

'I've been trying to find a good time to raise the subject.'

Why? Because she was so touchy she was liable to fly off the handle without warning? She closed her eyes, conceding he might have a point there.

'So I picked up one of these for you.'

She opened her eyes to find him holding out a flyer towards her. She took it. Yoga classes. With an instructor who specialised in yoga for pregnant women. A lump lodged in her throat.

'I just thought you might...' More feet shuffling ensued. 'I mean, if you're not interested, if it's not your thing, then no problem.'

She swallowed the lump. 'No, it's great. I'd have never thought of it, but...it's perfect.'

He didn't smile. He continued to stare at her with a frown in his eyes. 'Mari, your brothers love you. They don't consider you a screw-up.'

Tension shot back through her. 'Those two statements are not mutually exclusive.' She speared the flyer to the fridge with a magnet, before grabbing a glass of water and downing it in one. 'I know my brothers love me.' *That* was why it was so important that she prove herself to them.

Weariness overtook her then. She turned to move back to the sofa, to collapse onto it—to put her feet up and close her eyes—but Ryan blocked her way, anger blazing from the cool depths of his eyes. She backed up a step. 'What?'

'If you believe your brothers think you a screw-up then you're a complete idiot!'

She blinked.

'They adore you!'

'Adoring someone, loving someone,' she found herself yelling back, 'has nothing to do with thinking them capable or adult or believing they're making good decisions about their life!' It didn't mean they thought she'd make a good mother.

'I don't know your brothers very well, but even I can see that's not what they think.'

'Oh, really?' She poked him in the chest. 'What makes you such an expert on the subject? They certainly thought my taking a year off to tour around Australia irresponsible.' Maybe it had been. It'd certainly been indulgent, but she'd needed to spread her wings or go mad. 'And you should've seen the looks on their faces when I told them I was expecting a baby. They definitely thought that an irresponsible mistake of *monumental* proportions.'

She slammed the glass she still held to the bench and pushed past Ryan's intriguing bulk and bristling maleness. His heat and his scent reached around her, making her feel too much, stoking her anger even more. 'So did you!'

'I was wrong! I want this baby. I love this baby!'

She fell onto the sofa, rubbing her temples. Ryan strode across and seized the teddy bear, shook it at her. 'And your brothers love this baby too.'

'You think I don't know that?' She pulled in a breath. 'But I'm not married. This baby wasn't planned.' That last was irresponsible. 'It doesn't mean they don't think I've made a mistake with my life.' And what if they were right? She touched a hand to her stomach. *I'm sorry,* mia topolino.

Ryan sat on the coffee table, knee to knee with her, crowding her. 'So what if they do?'

That was her cue to toss her head and say that it didn't matter, except she didn't have the heart for the lie. She lifted her chin. 'I love them. Their opinions matter to me.'

And what if they were right?

'In this day and age, being a single mother isn't scandalous.'

'I know that, but I live in a conservative part of the world.'

'Your brothers' shock is merely proof of their concern for you, their concern that you'd have no support with the baby—that you would have to do it alone.'

She did have to do it alone. Ryan wanted to be a part of the baby's life, but he didn't want to be part of a family. Ninety per cent of the baby's care would fall to her.

'For heaven's sake, Mari, they don't see you as incapable or a screw-up. Can't you see that? Haven't you worked it out yet? You're the glue that holds this family together.'

He stared at her with such seriousness her heart stopped for a beat. It kicked back in with renewed vigour a moment later. 'What on earth are you talking about?'

'Angelo and Nico obviously have their differences. They want different things from life.'

She snorted. He could say that again.

'Do you think they see each other as inadequate or incompetent?'

She stilled, suddenly seeing where he was going with this.

He leaned over and took her chin in his hand. 'The one thing they can bond over is you. Their love for you, their worry for you and their joy in you—that strengthens their bond and makes you a family.'

He paused. His index finger moved back and forth across her cheek and all Marianna wanted to do was lean into it and purr…to lean into him. An ache started up deep in the centre of her. An ache she knew from experience that Ryan could assuage.

He frowned, his attention elsewhere, and Marianna told herself she was glad he hadn't read her thoughts. 'I don't know what the deal with your parents is, but I've picked up enough to know that you act as a bridge between them and your brothers.'

That was true, but she could only acknowledge it dimly. Ryan continued to frown, but his gaze had caught on her lips and such a roaring hunger stretched through his eyes it made her breath catch and her lips part. His nostrils flared, time stilled. And then he reefed his hand away and shot back.

Not that there was really anywhere he could move back to—they still sat knee to knee. If she leaned forward, she could run a hand up his leg with seductive intent, a silent invitation that she was almost certain he wouldn't rebuff. Her thigh muscles squeezed in delight at the thought. Deep in the back of her mind, though, a caution sounded. She found herself hovering, caught between a course of action that felt as if it had the potential to change her life.

Sleeping with Ryan will not make him fall in love with you.

Of course it wouldn't. Yet she didn't move away.

'Tell me you've heard all that I've just said.'

She started at his voice.

'About your brothers,' he continued inexorably. 'That you can see they don't think of you as any kind of a failure. They may not agree with every decision you make about your life, just as you may not agree with every decision they make about theirs, but it doesn't mean any of you believe one of the others is a loser or a write-off. It doesn't mean that you don't respect each other.'

Her heart started to pound. 'You truly believe that?'

'I do.' He eased forward again, resting his elbows on his knees. 'Where is this coming from, Mari? Why haven't you spoken to Angelo or Nico about it?'

She glanced down at her hands. 'They've looked after me since I was a tiny thing. They've spoiled me rotten, indulged me and…I felt as if I'd disappointed them, that I hadn't honoured the faith they'd put in me.' She lifted one shoulder. 'I wanted to prove to them that I was up to the task—that I could do a really good job here at the vineyard *and* be a wonderful mother. But it seemed the harder I tried, the worse I came off. Working so hard suddenly became not looking after myself, or the baby. It seemed to me that everything I did was reinforcing their view of me being incompetent and needing to be looked after.'

'Crazy woman,' he murmured.

'And I didn't feel I should confide all of that in them. They've given me so much—they're the best brothers a girl could ever ask for—and it didn't seem fair to ask more from them, to ask them for assurances.'

'They'd have given them gladly.'

She swallowed. 'A part of me couldn't help feeling they were right.'

His jaw dropped.

She rubbed a hand across her chest. 'How could I take them to task for their reaction to my baby news when my own initial reaction wasn't much better? Oh, Ryan, joy and excitement weren't my first emotions when I found out I was pregnant. I was frightened…and angry with myself. I wanted it all to go away. I wanted the news to not be true. How dreadful is that?'

He reached out and took her hand 'It's not dreadful. It's human.'

She'd have said exactly the same thing to any one of her girlfriends who found themselves in a similar predicament. She knew that, but…

'Mari, you have to forgive yourself for that. And you have to forgive your brothers for their initial reaction too. And me.' He paused. 'You made a brave decision—an exciting decision—and I can't tell you how grateful I now am for that.'

She could tell he meant every word. And just like that a weight lifted from her.

'You should be proud of yourself.'

Proud?

'You're having a baby. It's exciting. It feels like a miracle.'

Her heart all but stopped. He was right!

She gave up trying to fight temptation then. She leaned forward, took his face in her hands and pressed her lips to his. He froze, but a surge of electricity passed between them, making her tingle all over. She eased back, her heart thumping. 'Thank you.'

He swallowed and nodded. The pulse at the base of his throat pounded and she could feel its rhythm reach right down into the depths of her. Her breath started to come in short sharp spurts. She'd never wanted a man or physical release with such intensity.

Ever.

Maybe it was a pregnancy-hormone thing?

Whatever it was, it was becoming increasingly clear that attempting to explain it, understand it, did nothing to ease its ferocity. She glanced at Ryan, and glanced away again biting her lip. They were both adults. They knew sex didn't mean forever. She tossed her head. If they chose to, they could give each other pleasure in the here and now.

Without giving herself time to think, Marianna slid forward to straddle Ryan's lap.

'What on—?'

Her fingers against his mouth halted his words. 'I want you, Ryan, and I know you want me. I don't really see the point in denying ourselves. Do you?'

She trailed her hand down his chest, relishing the firm feel of him beneath the cotton of his shirt. He slammed his hand over it, trapping it above the hard thudding of his heart. 'You said if I made love with you here in your real world, that I would break your heart.'

She lifted one shoulder and then let it drop. 'What do I know? Ten minutes ago I was convinced my brothers thought me an incompetent little fool. It appears I was wrong about that.'

For a moment the strength seemed to go out of him. She took advantage of the moment to slide her hands around his shoulders to caress the hair at his nape in a way that she knew drove him wild.

He reached up to remove her hands. 'Mari, I—'

She covered his mouth with her own—open mouth, hot, questing tongue, and a hunger she refused to temper. The taste of him, his heat, drove her wild. With a moan, she sank her teeth into his bottom lip and then laved it with her tongue. Ryan groaned, his hand at the back of her head drawing her closer. His mouth, his lips and his tongue controlled her effortlessly, taming her to his tempo and pace. He drank her in like a starving man and she could only respond with a silent, inarticulate plea that he not stop, that he give her what she needed.

She opened her thighs wider to slide more fully against him and he broke off the kiss to drag in a breath, his chest rising and falling as if he'd run a race.

'We can't do this,' he groaned.

'No?' Marianna peeled off her shirt and threw it to the floor. Her bra followed. She lifted his hands to her breasts, revelling in the way he swallowed, the way he stared at her as if she were the most beautiful woman in the world. 'I understand that you don't want to hurt me, and that's earned you a lot of brownie points, believe me. But at the moment I don't want you honourable. I want you naked and your hands on me, driving me to distraction.'

She moved against his hands. He sucked in a breath. 'Mari…'

She cupped his face, staring into his eyes. 'Just once I want to make love with the father of my child with joy at the knowledge of what we've created.'

He stilled. She swallowed. If he rejected her now she wasn't sure she could bear it. 'It seems to me,' she whispered, 'that would be a good thing to do.'

'Mari…'

She pressed a finger to his lips. 'No promises. I know that. Just pleasure…and joy. That's all I'm asking.'

She saw the moment he decided to stop fighting it and her heart soared. His eyes gleamed. 'Pleasure, huh?' He ran his hands down her sides, thumbs brushing her breasts and making her bite her lip. 'How much pleasure?'

'I'm greedy,' she whispered.

His hands cupped her buttocks, his fingers digging into her flesh through the thin cotton of her skirt.

She clutched his shoulders, swallowing back a whimper. 'I want a lot of pleasure.'

'A lot, huh?'

His fingers raked down her thighs with deliberate slowness…and with a latent promise of where they would go when he raked them back up again. Marianna started to tremble. Despite the weakness flooding her she managed to toss her head. 'As much as you have to give.'

His eyes darkened with wolfish hunger. 'Whatever the lady wants.' He eased forward to draw her nipple into his mouth and Marianna lost herself in the pleasure.

And the newfound joy that gripped her and seemed to bathe her entire being in sunlight.

The sound of Ryan's mobile phone ringing woke her. Through half-closed eyes, Marianna watched him reach for it, the long, lean line of his back making her mouth water.

He glanced back towards her and she smiled, sent him a little wave to let him know she was awake and that he didn't need to be extra quiet or leave the room. One side of his mouth kinked up, his eyes darkening as he took in her naked form beneath the sheet. She stretched cheekily, letting the sheet fall to her waist and his grin widened. It made her heart turn over and over. And over.

He finally punched a button on his phone and turned away to concentrate on his call.

A tumbling heart?

Very slowly Marianna sat up, a tight fist squeezing her chest as she continued to stare at Ryan. Her mouth went dry. She drew the sheet back over her. It took all her strength not to pull it right over her head. What on earth had she gone and done?

She didn't want to let this man go. *Ever.*

Her hands fisted. When had it happened? *How* had it happened? Why…?

She swallowed. What did any of that matter? What mattered was that she wanted Ryan to stay here with her forever and be a true partner. She wanted him to share in the day-to-day rearing of their child. She wanted to see him last thing at night and again first thing in the morning.

She *loved* Ryan.

He doesn't want that!

She bit down on her lip to stop from crying out, rubbing a hand across her chest to ease the ache there.

You should never have slept with him.

She waved that away with an impatient movement. Sex had nothing to do with it. Sex wasn't the reason she'd fallen in love with him. His determination to become a good father, his care and consideration of her, the effort he'd put into making a good impression on her brothers, the fact he wanted her to be happy—they were the reasons she'd fallen in love with him. She passed a hand across her eyes. It seemed for the last week she'd been doing her best to hide from that fact.

What good was hiding, though?

And yet, what good was facing the truth? He loved his work more than he'd ever love her.

'I'll be there as soon as I can!'

She snapped to at Ryan's words. 'What's wrong?' she demanded, pushing her own concerns aside at his grim expression and the greyness that hovered in the lines around his mouth.

'My mother has been taken ill. I need to return to Sydney as soon as I can.'

He had a mother?

She hadn't realised she'd said that out loud until he said, 'And a father. They divorced when I was young. They both have new families now.'

Which meant he had siblings. And yet…amidst this big family Ryan managed to be a lone wolf?

She surged out of bed, pulling on her dressing gown to race into the spare bedroom after him where he'd set about throwing clothes into his suitcase. She wanted to hold him, chase that haggard look from his face. 'What can I do?'

He stilled from hauling on a clean pair of suit trousers. He zipped them up and then moved to touch her face with one hand. 'I just want you to look after yourself and the baby.'

If he left now she'd have lost him forever. She'd never get the opportunity to win his love.

It could be for the best—a quick, clean break.

But…

Lone wolf.

If something terrible happened—if he received dreadful news or, heaven forbid, if his mother died—who would be there to comfort him, to offer him support and anything else he needed?

She moistened her lips, pulling the dressing gown about her all the more tightly. 'Can I come with you?'

* * *

Ryan froze at Marianna's request. He turned. 'Why would you want to do that?'

She pushed a strand of gloriously mussed hair behind her ears. 'I didn't know you had a family.'

He didn't. *They* were a family and *he* was an outsider. They were simply people he happened to be related to by blood.

So why is your heart pounding nineteen to the dozen at the thought of your mother lying in a hospital bed?

He pushed that thought away and focused on Marianna again. She swallowed. 'I'd like to meet them. They'll be a part of our baby's life and—'

'A small part,' he said. 'A *very* small part.'

She thrust out her chin and he found himself having to fight the urge to kiss her. 'You've met my family.'

'Not your parents.'

'But you will,' she promised. 'Just as soon as I can arrange it.'

How could she so easily make him feel part of something—like her family—when there was no place for him in it? It had to be an illusion.

'I don't mean to be gone long, Marianna. I need to be back in Rome in two weeks at the latest—' preferably sooner '—to settle the contract I've been working on.'

One of her shoulders lifted and then she surged forward to grip his hand. 'Ryan, we're friends, right?'

Were they? It was what he'd been striving for, but the word didn't seem right somehow.

Because you slept with her, you idiot.

He shook that off. He couldn't regret last night if he tried his hardest. He'd only regret it if it'd hurt Marianna.

He stared down into her eyes—their warmth and generosity caught at him. Her gaze held his, steadily. Neither pain nor regret reached out to squeeze his heart dry, only concern. Concern for him. He swallowed. Friendship might not be the right word, but it didn't mean he couldn't continue to strive for exactly that.

'Ryan, I'd like to be there for you if you receive bad news.'

It took an effort to lock his knees against the weakness that shook through him when he realised the kind of bad news she referred to. It didn't make sense. He was barely a part of his mother's life. Or his father's. Family made no sense to him at all.

But it made sense to Marianna. That might come in handy. She might be able to help him to navigate the tricky waters ahead.

She attempted a smile. 'I might even be able to make myself useful.'

He wanted her to come with him. The thought shocked him.

It didn't mean anything. It *couldn't* mean anything.

He pulled in a breath. He supposed he'd have to tell them all at some point that he was going to become a father. That would be easier with Marianna by his side.

Finally he nodded. 'Okay, but I want to be on the first available flight out of Rome for Sydney.'

She raced back towards her bedroom. 'I'll be ready!'

CHAPTER NINE

'TELL ME ABOUT your family.'

Ryan fought a grimace as he shifted on his seat—a generous business class seat that would recline full length when he wanted to sleep. Sleep was the furthest thing from his mind at the moment, though. He wished planes had on-board gyms. 'What do you want to know?'

'Do both of your parents live in Sydney?'

In stark contrast to him, Marianna looked cool and comfortable and *very* delectable. He tried to tamp down on the ache that rose up through him. 'Yes.'

She stared as if waiting for more. He lifted a hand. 'What?'

'Sydney is a big city, Ryan.'

Right. 'They live in the eastern suburbs. In adjoining suburbs, would you believe? It's where they grew up.'

She pursed her lips and he waited for her next question with a kind of fatalistic resignation. He supposed it'd help pass the time.

'You said they divorced when you were young. How old were you?'

'Four.'

'And…and did they share custody?'

Her questions started to make sense. He shook his head. 'I went to live with my maternal grandmother.'

She smiled and he couldn't explain why, but it bathed him in warmth. It made him very glad to have her sitting beside him. 'The grandmother who taught you to make curtains?'

'The very one.'

'Where were your parents? What were they doing?'

'They went their separate ways to "find" themselves.' He couldn't stop himself from making mocking inverted commas in the air.

She turned more fully in her seat to face him, crossing her legs in the process, and her skirt rode up higher on her thigh. He stared at the perfectly respectable amount of flesh on display, remembering how he'd run his hands up her thighs last night…and how he'd followed with his mouth. He wished he could do that right now—lose himself in the pleasure of being in her arms, give himself over to the generous delights of her body.

'That makes them sound very young. How old were they?'

He pulled himself back. He had to stop thinking about making love with Marianna. It couldn't happen again. Already it was starting to feel too concentrated, too…intimate. Like an affair. He didn't do affairs. He did one-night stands. He did ships passing in the night. He did short-term dalliances. Somehow, from the wreck of his and Marianna's entanglement, he had to fashion a friendship that would endure the coming years.

Boring.

He stiffened. It was the responsible route. The *essential* route. And like everything else he'd turned his hand to, if he worked at it hard enough he would achieve it.

'Ryan?'

He shook himself, dragged a hand down his face. 'They were eighteen when they had me.'

'Eighteen?' Her eyes widened. 'I'm twenty-four and most days I don't feel ready for parenthood. But eighteen? Just…wow.'

He'd started to realise that parenthood frightened her as much as it frightened him. It was why he had to remain close and keep things pleasant between them. When motherhood and the responsibility of raising a child overwhelmed Marianna, when it lost its gloss, he'd be there to take over.

'How long did you live with your grandmother?'

'Until I was nineteen.'

Her jaw dropped. She shuffled a little closer, drenching him with her sweet scent. 'You never lived with your parents again?'

He stared at the back of the seat in front of him. 'I visited with them.' But he'd never fitted in. It had always been a relief to return home to his grandmother. He'd only kept up the visits because his grandmother had insisted. For her he'd have done anything.

'So, you and your parents, you're not what one would call…close?'

'Not close at all.'

'But…'

He turned and met her gaze.

'You've dropped everything to go to your mother.'

'That's not a mystery.' He turned back to the front. 'I'm the one with the money, and money talks. I can make things happen.'

'Like?'

'Get in the best doctors, fly in the top specialists, fast-track test results—that kind of thing.' He'd do that—make sure everything was in place for his mother—and then he'd hightail it back to Italy to wrap up the Conti contract.

Marianna blinked and then frowned. 'That's terrible!'

It took an effort of will to stop his lips from twisting. 'It's the way the world works.'

She was silent for a moment. 'I meant it's terrible that's the way you feel, that that's the role you see for yourself in your family.'

Maybe he should've taken the time to pretty it all up for her, except she'd see it all for herself soon enough.

'You have siblings?'

Tiredness washed through him. 'Yes.' He didn't give her the time to ask how many. 'My father is onto marriage number three. He has a daughter to wife number two and two boys with wife number three. My mother has one of each with her second husband. The eldest of them is twenty-two—my mother's daughter who has a toddler of her own. The youngest is my father's son who is thirteen.'

'Wow. Where do you spend Christmas?'

'*Not* in Australia.'

She nodded, but the sadness in her eyes pierced him, making his chest throb. 'Why don't you get some sleep?' he suggested. She must be bone-tired. 'You didn't get a whole lot of rest last night.'

The sudden wicked grin she flashed him kicked up his pulse, making his blood pump faster. 'I wish I was getting next to no sleep tonight for exactly the same reason.'

So did he. Except… *No affairs.* He knew she'd said no promises, but… 'Do we need to talk about last night?' Did they need to double-check that they were still on the same page?

She smiled a smile so slow and seductive he had to bite back a groan. 'We can if you like,' she all but purred. 'There was a manoeuvre of yours that I particularly relished. It was when you—'

He pressed a finger to her lips, his heart pounding so hard the sound of it filled his ears. 'Stop it!' But a laugh shot out of him at the same time. 'You're incorrigible. Give me some peace, woman, and go to sleep.'

'On one condition.'

'Anything!'

'Kiss me first.'

Her eyes darkened with an unmistakable challenge. He leaned towards her. 'Do you think I won't?'

She leaned in closer still. 'I'm very much hoping you will.'

He seized her lips in a fierce kiss, not questioning the hunger that roared through him. He didn't gather her close. He didn't even cup her face. She didn't reach out a hand to touch him either, but a kiss he'd thought would be all fire and sass changed when her lips parted and softened and moved beneath his with a warmth and a relish that shifted something inside him. He went to move away, but her lips followed and he found himself unable to stop; he surged forward again to plunder and explore that softness and warmth, to pull it into himself. The kiss went on and on…and on, as if she had an endless supply of something he desperately needed.

Eventually they drew apart. 'Mmm…yum.' Her tongue ran across her bottom lip as if savouring the taste of him there.

He had no words. All he could do was stare at her. She reclined her seat. She reached out a hand to his knee; her touch… He couldn't find the right word for it—comforting, reassuring? 'Put your seat back and keep me company.'

He covered her with a blanket first and then did as she bid.

'Close your eyes,' she murmured, not even opening hers to see if he obeyed.

After a moment, he did. He could feel sleep coming to claim him and suddenly realised that Marianna's kiss had stolen some of the sting from his soul. He had no idea what it meant. He breathed air into lungs that didn't feel quite so cramped and drifted off to sleep, promising himself he'd work it out later.

He slept for three hours. Not just dozed, but slept. He woke and stretched, feeling strangely refreshed. He checked his phone, but there weren't any messages.

Half an hour later, Marianna stirred. 'Sleep well?' he asked when she opened her eyes.

'Perfectly,' she declared, sitting up. 'You?'

He nodded.

She sent him a grin that made his blood sizzle. 'Wanna kiss me again in a little while when I'm ready for another snooze?'

He laughed, but shook his head—trying to ignore the ache that surged through him. 'We can't keep doing that.'

She reached for the bottle of water the stewardess had left for her. 'I expect you're right, but I mean to enjoy it while it lasts.'

How long would it last? More to the point, how long did he want it to last? Could they maybe make love one more time without Marianna's heart becoming entangled? Twice more? He'd give up a lot to have another week like they had in Thailand.

But not at the expense of screwing up friendship and fatherhood.

His seat suddenly felt as hard and unyielding as a boulder. He excused himself and bolted to the rest room to dash cold water onto his face, to stare at himself in the mirror and order himself to keep his hands and lips to himself.

When he couldn't remain in there any longer without exciting comment, he forced himself back to his seat. 'Why don't you tell me about your parents?' he suggested, hoping conversation would keep his raging hormones in check. 'It seems that you and your brothers have different opinions on the subject.'

She nodded. 'Mamma and Papà have a very…tempestuous relationship. They're both very passionate people.'

Sounded like a recipe for disaster to him.

'When we were growing up there were a lot of…um… rather loud discussions.'

'Fights.'

She wrinkled her nose. 'A bit of shouting…a bit of door-slamming.'

He recalled the way she'd thrown that vase at him.

Uh-huh, utter nightmare. He thanked the stewardess when she brought him the drink he'd requested.

'They divorced once. And then they remarried.'

He choked on his drink. 'But…why?'

She lifted one slim shoulder. 'It's the same now. They're currently in America, but their relationship is as fiery as it ever was. They're forever threatening to leave each other, storming out for a few days before coming back. On again off again.' She gave a low laugh. 'They can't live without each other. It's wildly romantic.'

He stared at her. 'Romantic? Are you serious? It sounds like a nightmare.'

She leaned back, her gaze narrowing. 'Maybe it's a male thing. You seem to have jumped to the same conclusion as Angelo and Nico.'

They were obviously men of sense. 'You say they can't live without each other. Seems to me they can't live *with* each other.'

She shook her head. He tried not to let her dancing curls distract him. 'The intensity of their love drives them to distraction. So, yes, I think that romantic. Boredom is death to a relationship and while you can say a lot of things about my parents the one thing you can't accuse them of is being bored…or boring.'

Was that the kind of relationship she wanted? Did she mean to marry a man and raise Ryan's child in a battleground? 'Boredom?' he spat. 'I'd take it over never being able to relax or wind down. What on earth is wrong with contentment?'

Her face wrinkled up as if she'd just sucked on a lemon. 'Oh, yay, that sounds like fun.'

'The way your parents act, it's immature. Sounds as if neither one of them has the ability to compromise and I don't see what's particularly loving or romantic about that.'

She glared at him. 'I'm starting to think you wouldn't know love if it jumped up and bit you on the nose. You avoid love and connection as if it's some kind of plague, so you'll have to excuse me if I don't take you as an expert on the topic.'

She had a point, but… 'You'd really prefer to have the kind of screaming match that leaves you shaken and in tears than…than smiles and easiness and happiness?'

'It's not an either-or situation.' She folded her arms. 'Besides, I hear that make-up sex is the best.'

'Is it all about sex with you?'

'Oh, excuse me while I roll my eyes out loud! I like sex.' She thrust out her chin. 'And I have no intention of apologising for that.'

'You'd have that kind of crazy, outrageous relationship even if it made the people around you miserable?'

'My parents' relationship didn't make *me* miserable.'

'I expect that's because Angelo and Nico shielded you from the worst of it. It certainly made them miserable. What if it makes our child miserable?'

Her eyes flashed. 'Oh, no, you don't! You are not going to control me or my future romantic liaisons by means of some kind of twisted maternal guilt you feel you have the right to impose on me. I will marry whomever I choose, Ryan, and it will have nothing to do with you.' With that she grabbed a magazine and promptly set about ignoring him.

He had absolutely no right to tell her who she should or shouldn't marry but…

Why couldn't she just remain single?

With a groan, he dragged both hands back through his hair. Why on earth hadn't he simply forgone the small talk and kissed her again?

Marianna stood the moment Ryan returned to the waiting room, twisting her hands together and searching his face.

All they'd known prior to arriving at the hospital was that Stacey, Ryan's mother, had snapped a tendon in her calf playing squash and that a blood clot had formed at the site of the injury. The doctors were doing everything they could to dissolve the clot, but so far it hadn't responded. If the clot—or any part of it—moved and made its way to her heart or brain…

Marianna suppressed a shudder, and made a vow to never play squash again. 'How is she?'

Ryan didn't answer. His pallor squeezed her heart. She reached out and wrapped her arm through his. 'The doctors are doing everything they can.'

He nodded and swallowed and her heart bled for him. He might not be close to his family, but he loved his mother. That much was evident.

'She'd like to see you.'

She eased away to stare up into his face. 'Me?'

'The doctor said that's fine, but she's only allowed one visitor at a time and she's not to get excited or upset.'

No excitement and no upsetting the woman. Right. She pressed a hand to her stomach. 'Did you tell her about the baby?'

He nodded. 'That's why she wants to meet you.'

She moistened her lips. 'In my experience, news about a baby definitely falls under the heading of exciting.' And depending on the situation and the person being told, fraught with the possibility of distress and worry.

'She's fine with it.' He pushed her towards the door of his mother's room. 'Go and introduce yourself and then we can get the hell out of here.'

She didn't remonstrate with him. For pity's sake, she'd done enough of that on the plane! Not a smart move when trying to make oneself an attractive long-term romantic prospect. But behind his impatience and assumed insensitivity she recognised his fear. She wished she could do something to allay it.

He frowned. 'You don't want to meet her?'

She shook herself. 'I do, yes, very much.' She straightened her shirt and smoothed down her skirt, wishing she'd had an opportunity to at least shower before meeting Ryan's mother. Ryan collapsed onto a chair and rested back, his eyes closed. He must be exhausted. As soon as she'd visited a little with Stacey she'd get him to a hotel somewhere where he could rest up.

Pulling in a breath, she padded down the hallway and tapped on Stacey's door before entering. 'Mrs White, um, sorry…Mrs Pickering?'

'You must be Marianna. Do come in and, please, call me Stacey.'

Ryan had Stacey's colouring, and her eyes. For some reason it put Marianna at ease. 'It's lovely to meet you.' She took the hand Stacey held out to her, pressed it warmly, before taking a seat at the side of the bed. 'I've been ordered to not wear you out.'

Stacey sighed. 'It seems a whole lot of fuss and bother for nothing.'

That sounded like Ryan too. Marianna glanced down her nose and lifted an eyebrow.

Stacey laughed. 'I know, I know. It's not nothing, but the fact of the matter is I'm not even in that much pain and all of this sitting around is driving me mad.'

She sounded *a lot* like Ryan.

'You're having a baby.'

Straight to the heart of the matter. 'Yes.'

'That's lovely news.' The other woman nodded. 'A baby… That's exactly what Ryan needs.'

Marianna didn't know what to say.

'You care about my son?'

She didn't bother dissembling. Stacey was Ryan's mother and her baby's grandmother. 'Yes, I do.'

Their eyes met and held. They both knew that her *caring* about Ryan could end in heartbreak.

'I made a grave mistake when I separated from my then husband and left Ryan with his grandmother. She loved Ryan to bits, but I only ever meant to leave him with her for a couple of weeks.'

Marianna opened her mouth to ask why she hadn't gone back for him—how had two weeks turned into fifteen years—but she closed it again.

'My heart was broken,' Stacey continued, 'and it took me a long time to recover.'

Marianna could understand that, but she still wouldn't have given up her child.

Stacey met Marianna's gaze. 'I was crippled with self-doubt and a lack of confidence. I felt I'd made a mess of everything. I'd hurt Ryan's father. I'd disappointed my mother. I thought I must be a bad person and I convinced myself that I'd ruin Ryan's life. That is the single biggest regret I have.'

Marianna understood self-doubt all too well, and Stacey would've been even younger than Marianna was now. She reached out and touched Stacey's arm. 'You were young. It was all such a long time ago. It's in the past—'

'No, it's not.' Her gaze didn't drop. 'It's there between us every time I see him. He's not trusted me since. He's never forgiven me.'

Her heart burned for the both of them. But… What did Stacey want her to do—to reconcile Ryan with his past? She could try, but—

'I'm telling you this to help you understand my son a little better, Marianna. Since his grandmother died I'm not sure he's trusted anyone, but I think he might trust you. At least a little.'

She hoped he did.

'Maybe you'll be able to find it in your heart to make allowances for him when he doesn't act as emotionally invested as you'd like.'

Therein lay the rub. She wanted—needed—Ryan's wholehearted involvement, his complete commitment. She wasn't a masochist. She couldn't settle for anything less.

Ryan liked everyone to see him as cool and controlled, but she knew the passion that lurked beneath the impassive veneer. She lifted her chin. She and Ryan, they didn't have to end in heartbreak. She could win his love yet. The first step, though, would be to reconcile him with his family. It wouldn't be easy, of course. But it couldn't be impossible, could it?

'I still don't see why we have to stay at Rebecca's,' Ryan muttered.

'Because she asked us,' Marianna returned.

He opened his mouth.

'And because she's going to be our child's aunt. It's natural she should want to get to know me, and I'd like to get to know her.'

Yesterday, Marianna had walked out of Stacey's hospital room to find a large portion of Ryan's family in the waiting room—his stepfather, as well as his sister, her husband and their little girl. When Rebecca, Ryan's sister, had invited them to stay with her, Marianna had jumped at the invitation.

'What if I don't want these people to be part of my child's life?'

'Lulu, honey, don't put that in your mouth.' Marianna jumped up from her seat on the park bench to take the stick from the toddler's hand and to wipe her mouth, before distracting her with a bright red toy truck, helping her to push it through the sand.

She'd dragged Ryan out to the little park across the road from Rebecca's house on the pretext of taking his niece, Lulu, for a little outing.

In reality, though, she'd just wanted to get Ryan out of the house before he exploded—to give them all a bit of a breather. She took her seat on the bench again. 'I like your sister.'

'So that settles it, does it? I hate to point this out to you, but you might find it difficult to become best buds with my sister when she lives here and you live in Monte Calanetti.'

She swung to him, loathing the tone he'd assumed. 'And I hate to point out that it's not Rebecca's fault that your parents separated and left you with your grandmother.'

His eyes turned to chips of ice. 'Very mature.'

'My point exactly! Rebecca is making every effort to forge a relationship with you and you're freezing her out. Why?'

He dragged a hand down his face and she suddenly wished she'd spat those home truths out with a little more kindness. 'I have never felt a part of these people's lives.'

'I know,' she whispered. 'Life gets messy and people don't always know the right way to deal with things. But you're an adult now, Ryan. You can choose to become a part of this family.'

He stared at her. His lips twisted in mockery, but she recognised pain in the hidden depths of his eyes. 'What's the point?'

She couldn't speak for a moment. She turned away to check on Lulu. 'Belonging is its own reward,' she finally managed.

He shook his head. 'Lone wolf.'

'Family is a gift you can give our baby.' Couldn't he see that? 'The more people who love it, the better.'

'You mean the more people there will then be in the world with the potential to hurt it, let it down…betray it.'

She shot to her feet. He could *not* be serious. She started to shake. 'I will not let you turn our child into an emotional cripple…into an emotional coward.'

He turned those cold eyes to her. 'And I won't let you turn it into an emotion junkie.'

That was what he thought of her? She turned away to check again on Lulu, who was perfectly content crawling in the sand with her toy truck. Marianna pulled in a breath and closed her eyes. This wasn't about her. It was about Ryan. She could tell how much he hated being here—in Australia, at Rebecca's—but…

He'd organised a top specialist for his mother at his own expense. Rebecca had told her that her husband owed his job in a top-flying computer graphics company to Ryan's machinations. Rebecca owed her university education to him. They admired him, respected him, and looked up to him. He looked out for them—made sure they had everything they needed—yet he continued to hold himself aloof from them.

He might not want to acknowledge it, but he loved this family that he kept at arm's length.

She sat again. 'Rebecca loves you.'

He stiffened.

'And treating her the way you do…' She used his earlier words against him. 'It hurts her, lets her down, betrays her.'

He stood, his eyes wild. 'That's not true!'

'Yes, it is. Now sit back down and don't frighten the baby.'

He sat. His hands clenched. 'I don't mean to hurt anyone.'

The coldness had melted from him. It took all her strength not to take him in her arms. 'Rebecca would never hurt our child,' she said instead. 'She'd love it, protect it, support it.'

Lulu came over and pulled herself upright using Ryan's

trouser leg. She grinned up at him, slapping her hand to his knee in time to her garbled, 'Ga, ga, ga!'

'I, uh…' He glanced at Marianna, who kept her mouth firmly shut. He glanced back at the toddler, lifted a shoulder. 'Ga, ga, ga?' he said back.

Lulu chortled as if he were the funniest man alive. Just for a moment he grinned and it reached right down inside her. This man deserved to be surrounded by a big, loving family.

Lulu wobbled and then fell down onto her diaper-clad bottom. Her face crumpled and she started to cry.

His hands fluttered. 'Uh, what do I do?'

Was he talking about Lulu or Rebecca? Either way, the advice would be almost the same. 'You pick her up and cuddle her. Cuddles make most things better.'

Gingerly he picked Lulu up, sat her on his knee and patted her back, jiggling his knee up and down. She gave him a watery smile and Marianna's chest cramped as she watched him melt. She crossed her fingers and silently ordered Lulu to keep working her magic.

CHAPTER TEN

MARIANNA GLANCED UP from slicing salad vegetables when Ryan strode into the kitchen.

'Hey, Ryan,' Rebecca said from her spot by the grill where she turned marinated chicken breasts.

Ryan stole a cherry tomato from the salad bowl. 'Is there anything I can do?'

Marianna would've smacked his hand except she sensed the effort it took him to appear casual and relaxed.

'Not much to do,' his sister said. 'I think we have it all under control.'

He reached into the salad bowl again, and this time she slapped the back of his hand with the flat of her knife.

'Ow!'

'You can stop eating all the salad, for one thing.'

His gaze speared to hers. He visibly relaxed at her smile. He turned back to Rebecca. 'I kind of figured there'd be nothing useful I could do in here so I went out and bought this.'

He handed her a bottle of wine. Her eyes widened when she saw the label. 'Ooh, you really shouldn't have, but… nice!'

He shoved his hands in his pockets. 'I thought you deserved a treat after everything you've done—dealing with Mum, putting us up.'

Rebecca's chin came up. 'We're family, Ryan.'

He took the bottle of wine from her and poured out two glasses. He handed her one. He raised his own. 'Yes, we are.' Her eyes widened, a smile trembled on her lips, and then she touched her glass to his.

After his first sip, he set his glass down and poured

Marianna a big glass of mineral water, complete with lemon slice and ice. With his hands on her shoulders, he shepherded her around the kitchen bench and into a chair at the kitchen table, before taking over the slicing of a cucumber.

Marianna didn't make a single peep about not feeling useful. Instead, she held her breath as she watched Ryan begin to forge a relationship with his sister.

He glanced around. 'Where's my…ahem…where's Lulu?'

Rebecca laughed. 'Your niece is having a much-needed nap. And you are *not* disturbing her.'

'Wouldn't dream of it.'

'She has you wrapped around her little finger.'

'Can't deny that I've taken to the little tyke.' He paused, pursed his lips. 'You know, Lulu's going to be less than three years older than her yet-to-be-born cousin. They could—you know—' he lifted a shoulder '—become great mates.'

Rebecca stilled and Marianna saw her blink hard. She wanted to jump up and down, cheer, dance around the kitchen.

Rebecca simply nodded. 'Wouldn't that be great?'

Ryan focused doubly hard on slicing a red capsicum, and nodded.

A moment later his mobile rang. He fished it out, listened intently, murmured a few words and then shoved it back into his pocket. 'That was the hospital. The clot has started to dissolve and if all goes as the specialist hopes, Mum will be released in a couple of days.'

Rebecca clapped a hand to her chest and closed her eyes. 'Thank heaven.'

Ryan let out a long, slow breath and then lifted his glass. 'To the prognosis being correct.'

They drank. When he set his glass down, Ryan rolled

his shoulders. 'Do you think you could keep an eye out for a suitable property for me?'

Marianna stilled with her glass of mineral water halted halfway to her mouth. Had she just heard him right?

'Sure.' Rebecca—a real estate agent—nodded. 'What kind of property did you have in mind?'

Marianna's heart started to thud. Did Ryan mean to give up his anonymous hotel rooms for a real home?

'Here in Sydney?' Rebecca asked.

Ryan nodded.

'Preferred suburbs?'

Marianna waited for him to request some swish apartment overlooking Sydney harbour.

He threw the freshly cut capsicum into the salad bowl. 'The eastern suburbs are finc by me.'

'Apartment? Villa? Town house?' Rebecca shot each option at him.

'I want a house,' he said. 'With a yard.'

Marianna choked and had to thump her chest to get herself back under control.

He glanced at her. 'A child needs a yard, right? A place to run around and play?'

She nodded.

He frowned. 'You won't mind me bringing the baby to visit?'

She suspected she kind of would, but… 'Of course not.' She wanted their baby to know his family. 'You might have to wait until he or she is weaned first, though.'

'You could come too.'

If she had her way, that was exactly what would happen—the three of them coming here as a family. She dabbed her napkin to her mouth. When Ryan decided to do something—like become an involved father or build bridges with his sister—he certainly did it with gusto. If possible, it only made her love him more.

* * *

'Are you planning on going to the hospital today?' Marianna asked Ryan the next morning.

He didn't glance up from his newspaper. 'I don't think so.'

She bit her tongue to stop from asking, *Why not?*

They'd slept late—probably due to jet lag—and currently had the house to themselves. Rebecca's note had said she'd gone up to the hospital. Marianna took a sip of her decaffeinated coffee. Setting her mug back to the table, she ran her finger around its rim. 'Your grandmother lived close to here?'

'On the other side of the main street.' One shoulder lifted. 'Probably a ten-or fifteen-minute walk from here.'

'A walk would be nice. So would a big fat piece of cake.'

He glanced up. 'You want to see where my grandmother lived?'

'I want to see where *you* lived.'

'Why?'

She wanted each and every insight into him that she could get. She wanted to understand why he'd exiled himself from his family. She wanted every weapon she could lay her hands on to make sure he didn't exile himself from her.

Or their baby.

No. Their baby already had his heart.

But she didn't. Not yet.

And she couldn't simply blurt out, *I've fallen deeply and completely in love with you and I want to understand you so that I can work out how to make you fall in love with me.*

She imagined the look on his face if she did, and it almost made her laugh.

And then she imagined the fallout from such an admission and she wanted to throw up.

Ryan's frown deepened. 'You looked for a moment as if you might laugh and now you look as if you want to cry.'

Oops. 'Pregnancy hormones.'

'Breathing exercises,' he ordered.

She feigned doing breathing exercises until she had herself back under control. 'I'd like to see where you grew up. You've seen my world and now I'd like to see yours.' A sudden thought occurred to her. 'But if you'd rather not revisit your past then that's okay too.' She didn't mean to raise demons for him. 'I just…' She wrinkled her nose. 'It's probably a bit selfish of me, but knowing all this stuff—your life here in Australia—it'll make it easier for me when our child does come out here for visits.'

His face softened. 'You're frightened by how much you'll miss it?'

She nodded.

'Me too. I mean, how much I'll miss it when I'm away with work.'

Did that mean…? 'Are you planning on buying a home in Monte Calanetti too?'

He nodded and it occurred to her that she could use this baby as leverage, to convince him that marriage would be the best thing, but… She didn't want him to marry her for any other reason than that he couldn't live without her.

'You could come on the visits to Australia too if you wanted, Mari. You'd be very welcome. My family adores you.'

It was his adoration she craved, not his family's—as much as she liked them. 'You forget that I have a job.'

'I'll pay you so much child support you'll never have to work again.'

'You forget that I like my job.'

He stared at her for a long moment. With a curse he seized their mugs and took them to the sink. 'Don't worry.

I haven't forgotten that you don't want me cramping your style.'

A thrill shot through her at his scowl. If the thought of her with another man made him look like that, then… She left the thought unfinished, but in her lap she crossed her fingers. 'So, are you going to show me your grandmother's house or not?'

'I expect if I want any peace I'll have to,' he grumbled.

'And buy me a piece of cake on the way home?'

He battled a smile. 'And what do I get in return?'

She didn't bother hiding her grin. 'Peace.'

'Deal!'

This time he laughed and it lifted her heart. She could make him laugh. She could drive him wild in bed. She'd helped him make peace with his sister. *And* she was going to have his baby. Surely it was just a matter of time before he fell in love with her?

She crossed her fingers harder.

Ryan pulled to a halt and gestured to the simple brick bungalow. 'There it is.' The house he'd grown up in. He watched a myriad expressions cross Marianna's face. It was easier looking at her than looking at the house and experiencing the gut-wrenching loss of his grandmother all over again.

Avid curiosity transformed into a genuine smile. 'It's tiny!'

He glanced up and down the street. 'Once upon a time this entire suburb was composed of these two-bedroom miners' cottages.' Most had long since been knocked down, replaced with large, sprawling, modern homes.

'It's charming! It looks like a proper home…just like my cottage.'

He glanced back and waited for pain to hit him. It did, but it didn't crush him. He let out a careful breath.

Marianna swung to him. 'Don't you agree?'

She was right. Gran's house did remind him of her cottage.

'Was the garden this tidy when you were growing up?'

'Keeping this garden tidy was how I earned my pocket money.' That and stacking shelves at the local supermarket.

A teasing smile lit her lips and it tugged at his heart. 'So...were you a tearaway? A handful? Did you turn your grandmother's hair prematurely grey?'

He pressed his lips together as the old regrets rose up to bite him. 'Definitely a handful.' She didn't look at him, too interested in the house and garden, and he was glad for it. 'I was...rebellious.'

A laugh tinkled out of her. 'Surely not.'

He wanted to close his eyes, but he set his shoulders instead. Marianna ought to know the truth. 'As a teenager I fell in with a bad crowd. I was expelled from school.'

She spun around. Her mouth opened and closed, but no sound came out. He didn't blame her. 'My grandmother was a saint.'

'Expelled?'

He nodded.

'From school?'

'That's right.'

'But look at you now!' She suddenly seemed to realise that her shock might be making him uncomfortable. She tutored her face to something he figured she hoped was more polite. 'You, uh...certainly turned your life around.'

Not soon enough for his grandmother to have seen it.

She glanced back at the house and swallowed. 'I wish I could've met her.'

He hesitated for a moment before pulling his wallet from his pocket and removing a photo. Silently he handed it across to her.

She stared at it for a long moment, ran a finger across the face. 'You have her smile.'

He did?

She smiled at the photo before handing it back. 'I hope our baby has that smile.'

He hoped their child had Marianna's love of life, her exuberance, and her generosity.

He blinked, his head rearing back. Where had that come from? He put the photo away. Those things were all well and good as long as the child also had his logical thinking and the ability to read a situation quickly and accurately.

'Your grandmother helped you find your way again?'

Heaviness settled across his chest. 'In a manner of speaking. When she died, I realised I hadn't honoured her enough in life.'

She pressed a hand to her chest, her eyes filling. 'Oh!'

After a couple of moments she slid her arm through his and rested her head against his shoulder. It wasn't a sexy move but a companionable one and it immediately made him feel a little less alone.

'So you decided to honour her memory?'

He nodded.

'That was a good thing to do,' she whispered. 'I think she'd be proud of you.'

He hoped so. 'She always claimed I had a quick mind that I shouldn't waste.'

She eased away from him. 'I meant I think she'd be pleased with the way you're accepting your responsibilities as a prospective father.'

He swallowed.

'And with the way you're building a relationship with Rebecca.'

That would definitely have eased her heart. 'I…' He shrugged and then glanced at her helplessly. 'That thing you said yesterday about my distance hurting Rebecca, I…'

He dragged a hand back through his hair, that heaviness settling all the more firmly over him. He stared at the front door of his grandmother's old house and wished with everything he had that he could walk in there and talk with her one last time.

'You didn't know you were hurting her. It wasn't something you were doing on purpose.'

'But now that I do know I can't just…' He turned to face her fully. 'I can't ignore it. I can't keep hurting her.'

She reached up to touch his cheek. 'You're a good man, you know that?'

She made him feel like a good man. Rebecca's smile yesterday when they'd clinked wine glasses had made him feel like a good man too. Mari's hand against his cheek, her softness, made his heart start to pound, alerted all of his senses until they were dredged with the scent of her. It took all of his strength not to turn his mouth and press a kiss into the palm of her hand.

Kissing her would not be a good thing to do.

It'd be glorious.

He tried to shut that thought off.

She kept her hand there a beat and a half longer than she should've and it near killed him to resist her silent invitation. When she moved back a step, though, he had to grind back a groan of frustration.

'Thank you.'

He moistened suddenly dry lips. 'For what?'

'For showing me this.' She gestured to the house. 'For giving me a little insight into your background.'

She stared at him as if he were… As if he were a hero! His stomach lurched. He was no hero. And the last thing he needed was Marianna getting starry-eyed. *You should never have slept with her.* For the rest of their lives they'd be inextricably linked through their child. It only seemed right they should know each other, but… An ache stretched behind his eyes. He had to bring a halt to this right now. 'Friends, right?'

Her smile slipped a little and it was like a knife sliding in between his ribs.

He soldiered on. 'This sharing of confidences, it's what friends do, isn't it?' He hoped to God he wasn't leading her on.

She pursed her lips and then straightened with a nod. 'I've shared things with you I've never told another living soul.'

It made him feel privileged, honoured. It made him feel insanely suffocated too.

Lines of strain fanned around her mouth. He'd caused those. He took her arm, his chest burning. 'It must be time for that cake.' Cake would buck her up. She'd eventually realise that this—that friendship—would be for the best.

They found a funky bustling café on the main street and ordered tea and cake. When the waitress brought their order over, Marianna glanced at Ryan from beneath her lashes before fiddling with her teaspoon. 'You really don't mean to visit your mother today?'

Her too casual tone had him immediately on guard. 'Why is that so hard for you to believe?'

Her shoulder lifted. 'It's just that you've flown all this way…'

He'd done what he'd come here to do. His mother was recovering. As far as he was concerned, the sooner they left now, the better.

She stirred two packets of sugar into her tea, not meeting his eye. 'You never asked me what your mother and I spoke about that first day.'

He pulled his tea towards him. 'Is it relevant to anything?'

She sent him an exasperated glare.

He sipped his tea. He tried to get comfortable on his

chair. In the end he gave up. 'Fine! What did you and Stacey talk about?'

'You.'

He blinked. Not the baby?

'She told me the biggest regret of her life was leaving you with your grandmother.'

A ball of lead settled in the pit of Ryan's stomach. He moistened suddenly dry lips. He'd been doing everything he could to avoid being alone with his mother. He set his mug down with more force than necessary. 'No doubt she was just making excuses.'

'Oh, it wasn't anything like that.'

He suddenly frowned. 'If she made you feel uncomfortable, I'm very sorry.'

Her head shot up. 'It was nothing like that!'

A breath eased out of him. Good.

'I mean, I'm sure your mother likes me and everything, but, frankly, I doubt what I think of her matters to her one jot.'

He raised his hands, at a loss. 'So…'

'It was my opinion of you that mattered to her. She wanted to defend those…lone-wolf tendencies of yours.'

She'd what!

'And your opinion—what you think of her—that's what really mattered to her.'

He stared at her, unable to utter a word. If what Marianna said was true, and she had no reason to lie, then… then that meant Stacey cared for him. *That* was what Marianna was saying, whether she realised it or not. His breath jammed in his chest. On one level he knew Stacey must, but it had never been the kind of caring he'd been able to rely on, to trust in or to give himself over to.

For pity's sake, he didn't need the same family ties that Marianna did! He'd spent a lifetime guarding his privacy, his…isolation. He sat back. 'You want me to go and see her, don't you?' He glared. 'You want me to give her the opportunity to tell me what she told you?'

Marianna seemed impervious to his glare. She forked a piece of cake into her mouth and shrugged. 'What would it hurt?' she finally said.

What would it hurt? It'd… He suddenly frowned. What would it hurt?

'You want to bring our child to Australia to visit, yes?'

'Yes.'

'You'll be introducing our child to Stacey, yes?'

'Yes.'

'Don't you think the…tension between the two of you could be…awkward for our child?'

A tiny part of his heart clenched. 'You'd prefer it if I didn't let Stacey see our child?'

She huffed out a sigh and shook her head. 'No, Ryan, that's *not* what I'm saying.'

His heart started to thump, the blood thundering through his body. It hit him then that if he wanted to be the best father he could be, then making peace with his family would be necessary. He couldn't project his own issues with his mother onto his child. That would be patently unfair and potentially harmful to the child. He wanted to protect his son or daughter, help it grow up healthy in body and mind, not turn it into a neurotic mess.

Nausea surged through him. How did one go about fixing a relationship like his and Stacey's?

He glanced at the woman opposite. She'd tell him to listen to what Stacey had to say. She'd tell him to listen with an open heart. He passed a hand across his face. How did one unlock something that had been sealed shut for so long? It was a crazy idea. It—

Do it for the baby.

He stilled. If he wanted to do better than his parents had, he wouldn't run away when the going got tough. He pushed his shoulders back. It was time to man up and face his demons. It was time to lay them to rest.

'Fine.'

Marianna glanced up from her cake. 'Fine what?'

'I'll go and see Stacey.' Though, he had no idea what on earth he was going to say to her.

'You will?' she breathed.

There it was again, that look in her eye. He should never have brought her with him to Australia. *What had he been thinking?* He hadn't been thinking…at least, not with his head. He leaned towards her. 'Mari, even if I do patch up every rift between me and my family, that doesn't change things between us.'

She blinked.

He tried to choose his words carefully. 'It won't make me a family man. I'm never going to be the kind of man who can make you happy. You understand that, don't you?'

She tossed her head. 'Of course.'

His heart shrivelled to the size of a pea. He knew her too well, could see through her deceptions. She didn't believe him. She thought she could change him. She thought he'd offer her love, marriage, the works. If he didn't offer her those things would she keep his child from him?

A noose tightened about his throat, squeezing the air from his body. Marrying for the sake of their child would be a mistake—one that would destroy all of them. Anger slashed through him then. He should never have slept with her! And why couldn't she have kept her word? She'd sworn, *No promises!*

He shot to his feet. 'I'm going.'

'What, now?'

She started to rise too, but he shook his head. 'Stay and finish your cake.' He didn't give her time to reply, but turned on his heel and strode away.

* * *

Ryan tapped on the door to his mother's room, surprised to find her alone.

'You just missed Rebecca and Lulu,' she told him.

A stuffed cat with ludicrously long skinny legs had fallen behind the chair and he picked it up and stared at it, rather than at Stacey.

'Oh, dear.' Stacey sat up a little straighter in bed. 'You better take that home with you when you leave. It's Lulu's favourite. She'll be beside herself if she can't find Kitty Cat.'

That was why it looked familiar. He nodded. 'Right.'

'Colin should be along any minute. He promised to bring me a custard tart for afternoon tea.'

What was it with women and cake?

'Should I text and tell him to pick one up for you too?'

He shook his head and then realised he had barely said a word since walking into her room. 'No, thank you.' Eating custard tarts with his mother and her husband didn't fill him with a huge amount of enthusiasm. 'I…uh…how are you feeling?'

'Very well, thank you. The doctors are very happy with my progress.'

'That's good news.'

'The man you called in—the specialist—is a real wizard apparently. The rest of the staff have been whispering what an honour it is to see him in action.'

'Excellent.'

They glanced at each other and then quickly away again. An awkward silence descended. Ryan moved to stare out of the window.

'How is your Marianna doing?'

It wasn't so much the words as the tone that had an imaginary rope tightening around his neck and coiling down his body, binding him with suffocating tightness. He made an impatient movement to try and dispel the sense of constriction. 'She's not *my* Marianna.' And he wasn't *her* Ryan. The sooner everyone understood that, the better.

'Oh.'

He grimaced, wondering if he'd been too forceful.

'She's a lovely young woman.'

'She is.' But how on earth had he let her talk him into coming to see Stacey like this? 'We walked around to Gran's house this morning.'

'Ah.'

Ah? What the hell was that supposed to mean?

'Marianna encouraged you to come and see me today, didn't she?'

He halted his pacing to glance around at her. 'I don't think it was such a good idea.' He started for the door. 'I don't see the point in raking over the past.'

'Sit down, Ryan.'

His mother's voice held a note of command that made him falter. He turned and folded his arms, the stupid Kitty Cat still dangling from his hand.

'Please.'

He stared at the stuffed toy. He thought about Marianna. He knew how disappointed she'd be if he left now. He didn't want to disappoint her. At least, not on that head. He sat down.

'I want to tell you what I told Marianna when I first met her.'

He pulled in a breath. 'Which was?'

'That the biggest regret of my life was leaving you with your grandmother.'

He couldn't look at her, afraid his face would betray his disbelief and bitterness.

From the corner of his eye he saw her lean towards him. 'Will you listen? I mean *really* listen?'

With an effort he unclenched his hands from around the stuffed toy. 'Sure.'

She didn't speak for a long moment, but still he refused to look at her.

'It's hard to know where to start precisely, but we may as well start with the breakdown of my marriage to your father. You see, I thought it all my fault.'

That made him glance up and he tried not to wince at her pallor or the way she pleated and unpleated the bed sheet. 'Are you're sure you're up to this? Maybe we should wait until you've been sent home with a clean bill of health.'

'No!' She gave a short laugh. 'I'm under no illusion that I'll ever get another shot at this.'

He could just walk out, but Marianna's face rose in his mind. He cast another quick glance in his mother's direction. Walking out now might cause her more distress. He forced himself to remain in his seat and nod. 'Fine.'

'Ryan, I only meant to leave you with your grandmother for a couple of weeks. I needed to find a new place to live.'

'But Andrew—' his father '—had gone. There was no need for you to move out of the house as well.'

'I couldn't afford the rent on my own.'

'He would've had to pay you child maintenance. That would've helped.'

'I…I refused it.'

His head rocked back.

'As I said, I blamed myself for our split and it didn't seem right to me at the time to take his money.'

'You thought *that* in my best interests?'

'I thought that if I could just get a job…find a cheap place to rent, that I could make things perfect for us and…' She lifted a hand and then let it drop again. 'Getting a job proved harder than I expected. Eventually I managed to find one in the kitchen of a cruise ship, but it meant being away for months on end.'

Ryan folded his arms. 'You were gone for three years!'

'I know,' she whispered. 'I'm sorry. I saved every dollar I could and came home to make a life with you and—'

He leapt up to pace the room again. 'Let's not pretty it up. You met Colin on that cruise liner, got pregnant, and came back here to start a family with him.' *With Colin not with Ryan.*

'But you were part of our plans. We wanted you to live with us. It's just…when I came back it was as if you hated me.'

'I was seven years old. I barely knew you!'

'I cried for a week.'

'Poor you.'

She flinched and he knew he should feel ashamed of himself, but all he felt was a deep, abiding anger. 'From memory I don't recall you expending a whole lot of energy in an effort to win me over.'

'You brought all of my hidden insecurities to the surface,' she whispered. 'I told myself I deserved your anger and resentment. I didn't want to wreck things with Colin…and I had a new baby. I had to consider them. You were happy with your grandmother. It seemed best to leave you with her for a bit longer.'

A bit longer, though, had become forever.

He spun around and glared. 'Never once did you put my needs first.'

She paled. 'I didn't mean it to happen that way. I was crippled by guilt, a lack of confidence and low self-esteem. I never realised, though, that you would be the one to pay the price for those things.'

His lips twisted. In other words things had got tough and she hadn't been able to deal with them. But something in her face caught at him, tugged at some part of him that still wanted to believe in her.

Idiot!

He tried to smother the confusion that converged on him with anger.

'You're never going to forgive me, are you?'

'It's not about forgiveness.' His voice sounded cold even to his own ears. 'It's about trust. I don't trust you to ever put me and mine first. I don't trust you to ever have my back.'

She pressed both hands to her chest, her eyes filling. 'Heavens, your father and I really did a job on you, didn't we?'

'You taught me at a very young age how the world works. It's a lesson I haven't forgotten.'

'Son, please…'

He resented her use of the word.

'Tell me that you at least trust Marianna, that you don't keep her at arm's length.'

He gave a harsh bark of laughter. He wanted to trust Marianna. He couldn't deny it, but nor could he trust the impulse. An ache rose up through him—an ache for all of those things he could never have, all of those things Marianna wanted from him that he was unable to give. *Impossible!* The best way to deal with such delusions, the smartest, most logical course of action, was to deliver them a swift mortal blow.

He whirled back to Stacey. 'Trust? What you taught me, *Mother*, was the frailties and weaknesses of women. I'm ready for that. When motherhood and the responsibility of raising a child become too much for Marianna, I'll be there for my child. *I* won't abandon it.'

A gasp in the doorway had him spinning around. Marianna stood there pale and shaking, her eyes dark and bruised. Without another word, she turned on her heel and spun away.

CHAPTER ELEVEN

THE EXPRESSION IN Marianna's eyes pushed all thought from Ryan's mind. He surged forward and caught her wrist, bringing her to a halt. 'Wait, Mari—'

She swung back, her eyes savage. 'Don't call me that!'

He swallowed back a howl. 'You have to let me explain.'

'Explain? No explanation is necessary! You made yourself perfectly clear, and I have to say it was most enlightening to find what you really think of me and our current situation.'

It hit him then how badly he'd hurt her and it felt as if he'd thrust a knife deep into his own heart. He let her go and staggered back a step, wondering what on earth was happening to him, searching his mind for a way to make things right—to stop her from looking at him as if he were a monster.

'To think I thought… And all this time you've been thinking I would *abandon* our child?'

The jagged edges of her laugh sliced into him. Marianna might be impulsive, passionate and headstrong, but she was also full of love and loyalty. He need look no further than her relationships with her brothers for proof of that. The truth that had been growing inside him, the truth he'd been hiding from, slammed into him now, bowing his shoulders and making him fall back a step. She would never abandon her child. *Never.*

What right did he have to thrust his worst-case scenario onto her? How could he have been so stupid? So…*blind*?

His chest cramped. He'd held on to that mistaken belief as an excuse to justify remaining close to her. Because he'd wanted to be close to her.

She reached out and stabbed a finger to his chest. 'Stay away from me,' she rasped, her eyes bright with unshed tears. 'I will let you know when the baby is born, but you can't ask anything else of me.'

She wheeled away from him, making for the door. *He couldn't let her go!* He started after her, not sure what he could say but unable to bear losing sight of her. Rebecca, holding Lulu, stepped in front of him, bringing him up short. He couldn't thrust her aside, not when she was holding the baby. He made to go around her, but she laid a hand on his chest. 'You can't go after her when you look like that. You can't go after her without a plan.'

He lurched over to the chair and fell into it. A plan? He'd need a miracle!

'So it's true.' His mother's words broke into the darkness surrounding him. 'You're in love with her.'

He lifted his head and looked at her. In love with Marianna? Yes. The knowledge should surprise him more than it did. 'What do I do?' The words broke from him.

She didn't flinch from his gaze. 'We play to your strengths.' He could hardly believe she was still talking to him after all he'd just flung at her.

'You're a logical man. What does Marianna want?'

'Passion, an undying love, to never be bored.' The words left him without hesitation.

'Can you give her those things?'

He recalled the way her brothers had taunted him with their stupid Paulo joke. The fact, though, was there was a thread of truth running beneath that. What if, a month down the track, Marianna dumped him?

Darkness speared into him. For a moment it hurt to even breathe.

No! He shoved his shoulders back. He wouldn't give her the opportunity to get bored. He wouldn't let their life and relationship become dull. He loved her—heart and soul—

and if she'd just give him the chance he'd give her all the passion and intensity that her generous heart yearned for. He set his mouth—he'd make it his life's work.

He met his mother's gaze. 'I can give her those things.'

'You'll need to give a hundred per cent of yourself. Everything,' she warned.

Fine.

'I'm talking about your *time* here, Ryan.'

He frowned—what was she talking about?

'You're going to need to focus all your efforts on Marianna if you want to win her back.'

It hit him then—the Conti contract! If he signed on the dotted line, they'd need him on board from the week after next. He'd be working sixty-hour weeks for at least a month.

He swore. He scratched a hand through his hair. If he managed to smooth things over in the coming week with Marianna, maybe she'd let him off the hook for the following month and—

Fat chance! She'd demand all of him. Damn it! Why did she have to be so demanding? Why so unreasonable?

Suck it up, buddy. After the way you just acted, Marianna deserves to have any demand met, deserves proof of your sincerity.

Acid burned his throat. Panic rolled through him. What if he didn't succeed in smoothing things over?

What if she never forgave him?

He shot to his feet, paced the length of the room before flinging himself back into the chair. If she never forgave him he'd have lost both her and the Conti contract. Where was the sense in that?

He couldn't throw away all of that hard work. He couldn't just dismiss months' worth of nail-biting preparation. This was the contract that would set him up long term, would guarantee his livelihood for the rest of his working life and cement him as one of the business's leading lights. The Conti contract would prove once and for all that his grandmother's faith in him had been justified! He *couldn't* walk away.

Darkness descended over him, swallowing him whole. A moment later a single light pierced the darkness, making him lift his head. But what if he did win Marianna's forgiveness? What if she did agree to marry him, build a family with him…to love him? A yearning stronger than anything he'd ever experienced gripped him now. Wasn't winning Marianna's love worth any risk?

His heart pounded so hard he thought he'd crack a rib. No contract meant anything without Marianna and his child by his side. The knowledge filtered through him, scaring him senseless, but he refused to turn away from it. There'd be no point to any of his success—small or large—if he couldn't share it with Marianna and their child. He lifted his head. 'For Marianna, I'll make the time.'

Marianna stumbled into her cottage, clicking on all the lights in an attempt to push back the darkness, but it didn't work—not when the darkness was inside her. Forty hours of travel clung to her like a haze of grit. All she wanted to do was shower and fall into bed. The exhaustion, though, was worth not having had to clap eyes on Ryan again.

She halted in the doorway to her bedroom—the bed unmade, the sheets dishevelled from her and Ryan's love-making.

She dropped her bags and with a growl she pulled the sheets from the bed, resisting the urge to bury her face in them to see if they still carried a trace of Ryan's scent. She dumped them straight into the washing machine, set it going and then, leaving her clothes where they fell, she pushed herself under the stinging hot spray of the shower, doing what she could to rub the effects of travel and heartbreak from her body. She succeeded with the former, but it gave her little comfort.

Like a robot she dressed, remade the bed and forced herself to eat scrambled eggs. She didn't think she'd ever feel hungry again, but she had to keep eating for the baby's sake.

In the next moment she shot to her feet, the utter tidiness of the room setting her teeth on edge. With a growl, she pushed over the stack of magazines on the coffee table so they fell in an untidy sprawl. She messed up the cushions on the sofa, threw a dishtowel across the back of a dining chair—haphazardly. She didn't push her chair in at the table, and she slammed her plate and cutlery on the sink, but didn't wash them. She shoved the tea, coffee and sugar canisters on the kitchen bench out of perfect alignment.

None of it made her feel any better.

A tap on the door accompanied with a 'Marianna?' pulled her up short.

Nico. She swallowed. 'Come on through,' she called out.

He sauntered into the room. 'I saw the lights on and thought you must be home. You should've let us know to expect you. I'd have collected you from the airport.'

He pulled up short and took her in at a single glance. He'd always managed to do that, but she lifted her chin. She didn't want to talk about it.

'Alone?' he finally ventured.

She moved to fill the kettle. 'Yes.'

He was silent for a moment. 'How's Ryan's mother?'

'Out of danger and recovering beautifully.' She'd ring Stacey tomorrow to double-check that the scene in her hospital room hadn't had any detrimental effects on her recovery. And to assure her that she wouldn't prevent any of them from seeing the baby once it was born.

'That's good news.'

'It is.'

He paused again. 'How are you?'

She met his gaze and his expression gentled. 'Oh, Mari.'

She couldn't keep it together then. She walked into his arms and burst into tears, her heart shredding afresh with every sob. *Why couldn't Ryan love her?*

She refused to let the words fall from her lips, though, and she did what she could to pull herself together. She moved away, scrubbing the tears from her cheeks. 'I'm sorry. I'm tired.'

'You have nothing to apologise for.'

Was that true?

'I take it we shouldn't expect Ryan any time soon?'

Her brother deserved some form of explanation. 'I told him I'd let him know when the baby was born.'

Nico's eyes darkened in concern.

'It's okay.' She could see he didn't believe her and she didn't blame him. It wasn't okay, but there was nothing she could do about it. She just had to get on with it the best she could. 'We…we just messed up, that's all. And I find that I can't be…friends with him.'

He swore softly in Italian.

She managed a smile. 'It's okay, Nico. I'm a big girl. I will never denigrate him to my child. When we meet I will be polite and calm. That's what will be best for my darling *topolino*.'

He took her hand. 'But what's best for you?'

She could never tell him and Angelo all that had passed between her and Ryan. They'd have to find a way to be polite to him too. She didn't want to make that more difficult for them than it had to be. 'The baby has to come first. That's what matters to me.'

He swore again and his grip on her hand tightened. 'He's broken your heart!'

She moistened her lips and dredged up another smile.

'Some would say it's no less than I deserve for that trail of Paulos I've left in my wake.'

'I wouldn't agree.'

'I know that,' she whispered back, managing a genuine smile this time. Ryan might be a complete and utter idiot, but he had eased her fears about her brothers.

Time to change the subject. 'Where's Angelo?'

'Out with Kayla.'

'Naturally.'

They grinned at each other. 'We've missed you, Mari.'

She gave him a quick hug. 'I've missed you too.'

She made tea and they settled on the sofa. 'Now catch me up on all the news.'

Ryan turned the hire car in at the gates of Vigneto Calanetti and made his way down the long drive. He'd been away less than three weeks, but he swore the grapevines were lusher and greener. The sky was blue and the day was warm, and inside his chest his heart pounded like a jackhammer.

Would she see him?

Please, God, let her spare him ten minutes. Please give him at least ten minutes to make his mark, to try and win her love.

He parked the hire car out at the front of Nico's villa. He wanted to race straight across to Marianna's cottage, but instinct warned him to check in with her brothers first. He wanted to do things right—by the book. He didn't want to make things worse for Marianna than he already had.

He recalled the last look she'd sent him, filled with pain and utter betrayal, and his gut clenched. *Please, God, let her be okay. Please let her and the baby be in good health.*

He knocked on the villa's wide-open door and tried to control the pounding of his heart. If Marianna should appear now…

He stared down the hallway, willing it to happen. A figure did appear. A male figure. It was what he'd expected, but he had to lock his knees against the disappointment. 'Nico,' he said in greeting as the other man strode down the hallway.

'Ryan.'

They stared at each other for a long moment. Nico bit back a sigh. 'She's not going to want to see you.'

'I can't say as though I blame her. I messed up.' Ryan pulled in a breath. 'I messed up badly. I won't retaliate if you want to take a swing at me.' He wouldn't even block the blow.

'I'm not going to hit you, but…whatever it is you want to say, can't you put it in an email?'

He moistened suddenly dry lips. 'I want to ask her to marry me.'

'For the sake of the baby?'

He shook his head. 'Not for the baby.'

'I see.'

Ryan suspected he did.

'I suppose I better take you to her.'

Ryan followed him through the house, out the French doors and across the terrace towards the outbuildings. 'You think I need an escort? I have no intention of harming a single hair on Mari's head.'

'I realise that, but my loyalty lies with my sister.' He cast a sidelong glance at Ryan. 'My one consolation is that you look in even worse shape than she does.'

Ryan seized Nico by the shoulders and dragged him to a halt, fear cramping his chest. 'She isn't well?' he croaked.

'Physically she's fine. She's taking very good care of her health.'

He released Nico, dragged a hand down his face and then continued to plant one foot in front of the other, his blood pounding a furious tempo through his body. 'That's…that's something.'

'It is.'

They walked through the shadowed cool of the vineyard's cellar door, skirting a group of tourists wine tasting, and out the back to where the great barrels of wine were stored, and then beyond that to the fermentation vats. That was when he saw her. He pulled up short and drank her in like a starving man.

In the soft light her hair fizzed about her face. He watched her direct a team of three workers to move barrels from one location to another and she then checked the gauges on the nearest vat. Her slim, vigorous form so familiar to him it made his arms ache with the need to hold her.

And then she turned and saw him. She froze. Her every muscle tightened and a bitter taste rose in his mouth. He did that to her. He made her tense and unhappy.

He thought she'd simply turn around and walk away. After several fraught moments, however, she lifted her chin and moved towards them. But her body that had once moved with such freedom and grace was now held tight and rigid. He had to bite back a protest. *How could he have done that to her?*

'I don't want you here, Ryan. Please go.'

Her pallor and the dark circles beneath her eyes beat at him. 'I can't say that I blame you.' He stared down at his hands and then back at her. 'I came to apologise. What I said—'

'Pah!' She slashed a hand through the air.

He tried to take her hand, but she snapped back a step, her eyes flashing.

He swallowed and nodded. 'What I said…I was wrong. I know you will love our child with your whole heart. I know you will never abandon it. And just because that's what I experienced in my family…' He shook his head. 'I had no right tarring you with the same brush. It was an excuse I was hiding behind. It let me justify to myself the amount of time I was spending with you. It helped me keep my distance. I…I didn't realise I'd been lying to myself, though, until you walked out of Mum's hospital room.'

She folded her arms and glanced away, tapped a foot. 'How is your mother?'

'Excellent. She sends her love. So does Rebecca.'

She finally glanced back. 'I accept your apology, Ryan, but I'm afraid you and I are never going to be friends.'

'I don't want to be friends.'

She paled and eased back another step. 'I'm glad we have that sorted.' Spinning on her heel, she stalked away.

'Damn it, Marianna!' Had she wilfully misunderstood him? 'I want a whole lot more than friendship,' he hollered to her back. 'I want it all—love, marriage, babies…a family.' He punctuated each word with a stab in the air, but she didn't turn around. *'With you!'*

She didn't so much as falter. He shook off Nico's restraining hand and set off after her, muttering a curse under his breath. He waited, though, until she'd reached her stone cottage before catching her up.

She wheeled on him. 'Get out of my house!'

'I'll leave once you hear me out.'

'I've heard enough!'

'You've only heard what you want to hear!'

'Mari?' Nico stood in the doorway, one eyebrow raised.

Ryan planted his feet all the more solidly. No one was kicking him off the premises until he'd done what he'd come here to do.

Marianna's eyes flashed as if she'd read that intention in his face. She glanced at her watch. 'If his car is still here in ten minutes, come back with Angelo.'

With a nod, Nico left.

She was going to give him ten minutes?

He couldn't speak for a moment. He had to fight the urge to haul her into his arms and kiss her. If he did any such thing he'd deserve to be thrown out.

She remained where she stood, bathed in the sunlight that poured in at the kitchen windows, tapping her foot. She glanced at her watch as if counting down every second of his allotted ten minutes.

He missed her smile and her teasing. He even missed her untidiness and her temper. He'd rather she threw something at him than this *nothingness*.

'Since you left,' he started, 'I've been in a misery of guilt, a misery of mortification at my stupidity, and a misery of loss.'

'Good.' She lifted her chin. 'Why should you be exempt? I've been miserable on my baby's behalf that its father is such a jerk.'

His head throbbed. What was he doing here other than making a fool of himself? He should turn around and leave. She loathed him and he couldn't blame her. She was going to laugh at him; throw his love back in his face.

It's no less than you deserve.

He pulled in a breath and steeled himself. 'I love you, Mari.' He had to say what he'd come here to say.

Her eyes narrowed. 'I told you not to call me that.'

He ground his teeth together, unclenched them to say, 'I love you, *Marianna*.'

She moved in to peer up into his face. 'Piffle.' She stalked past him to the dining table, but she didn't sit.

'I want to marry you.'

She turned at that and laughed. He rocked back, her expression running him through like a sword. He locked his knees. 'You think it funny?'

'Absolutely hilarious!' But her flashing eyes and fingers that curved into claws told a different story. 'You've lost whatever advantage you think you had. You believe I'm going to withhold your child from you and this is your way to try and claw back all you've lost. I'm sorry, Ryan, but it's not going to work.'

The last puff of hope eased out of him in a single breath.

'You needn't worry, though.' She tossed her hair. 'I'm not going to stop you from seeing our child, but the visitation arrangements will be on my terms.'

He moistened his lips. 'This isn't about the baby, Mari.'

She turned away with a shrug, not even bothering to correct him—as if it no longer mattered to her what he called her. She glanced at her watch.

This couldn't be it! Where would he find that strength to walk away from her?

Think! How could he win her heart? *What is it she wants?*

He pulled up short. Passion, an undying love, and to never be bored—those were the things Marianna wanted. *Could* he give them to her?

He pulled in a breath and channelled his inner thespian. 'You want to know what I've been doing for the last two weeks?' He roared the words and she started and turned around, her eyes wide.

He stalked over to where she stood and stabbed a finger at her. 'I've been working on my relationships with my family so I'd have something of worth to offer you! And you want to laugh in my face and act as if it's nothing when it's been one of the most difficult and…and frightening things I've ever done?'

She moistened her lips and edged away. 'I didn't intend to belittle your…um, efforts. I'm… I'm sure they've been very admirable.'

'My efforts!' He threw both hands in the air and then paced the length of the room. He prayed to God he wasn't frightening her. He hated yelling at her, but if that was what she needed as proof of his love, then he'd do it.

He swung back to find her biting her thumbnail and staring at him, a frown in her eyes.

'If I'm correct it's not my efforts being disparaged but my intentions!'

He glared at her as hard as he could. She pulled her hand away from her mouth and straightened. 'You come in here and say outlandish things and expect me to believe you?'

'Saying *I love you* is not outlandish!' How could he make her see that? His gaze landed on the vase her brothers had given her. He grabbed it and lifted it above his head. 'I can't live without you, Mari! How can I get that through your thick skull?'

Marianna's bottom lip started to wobble, though she did her best to stop it. 'You're…you're going to throw a vase at me?'

He stared at her, and then rolled his shoulder. 'Of course not.' He lowered the vase, grimaced. 'I was going to throw it on the floor as evidence of my…high emotion.'

She couldn't drag her gaze from him. It hurt her to look at him, but she had a feeling it'd hurt more to look away.

I can't live without you!

She swallowed. 'Please don't break the vase. I…it has sentimental value.' Whenever she looked at it, it reminded her of her and Ryan's dinner with her brothers here in this cottage, and the conversation she and Ryan had had afterwards…how kind he'd been…and gentle.

She much preferred that Ryan to the shouting, angry man who'd just raged at her. It occurred to her now that his calm and his control had given her a safe harbour—that was what she wanted, not a stormy sea.

Ryan set the vase back on the table just as her brothers

burst into the room—their bodies tense, fists clenched and eyes blazing. Had they heard him yelling at her?

Angelo seemed to grow in size. 'Nobody speaks to our sister like that!'

They moved towards Ryan with unmistakable intent. 'No!' she screeched. Ryan's time might be up, but… She did the only thing she could think of. She ran across the room and hurled herself into Ryan's arms. He caught her easily, as if she weighed nothing. He held her as if she were precious.

Her heart pounded and it was all she could do not to melt against him. 'Turn me around,' she murmured in his ear.

He turned so that she could face her brothers. They glared at her, hands on hips. 'Go away,' she ordered.

They didn't move.

She tightened her hold on Ryan's neck, loving the feel of all his hardness and strength pressed against her. 'I have things under control here.'

Nico raised an eyebrow. Angelo snorted.

She widened her eyes, made them big and pleading. 'Please?' she whispered.

Muttering, they left.

Two beats passed. Marianna swallowed. 'You can put me down now.'

'Do I have to?'

'Yes.'

The minute he set her feet back on the ground, she moved away from him—put the table between them. The flare of his nostrils told her that her caution hurt him. She didn't want to hurt him. She loved him with every fibre of her being, but she couldn't accept anything less than his whole heart in return.

The silence stretched, pulling her nerves taut. She wiped damp palms down her trousers. 'You have to understand that I find your declaration a little unbelievable.'

'Why?'

'Lone wolf,' she whispered.

He adjusted his stance. 'That was a lie I told myself to make me feel better. It doesn't matter what happens today, I'm never going to be a lone wolf again. That all changed when I thought I'd lost you.'

He strode around the table and to her utter amazement dropped to his knees in front of her. He seized her hands and held them to his lips, and then his brow. Her heart hammered so hard she thought it'd pound a path right out of her chest.

'I'm nothing without you, Mari.'

And there it was, the thrill she couldn't suppress whenever he said her name.

'What I feel for you is so encompassing, so overwhelming it makes the thought of living without you unbearable. It's why I'd been resisting it so long and why I fought against it so fiercely. But it's no use fighting it any more or hiding from the truth. Marianna, you make me want to be a better man.'

He glanced up at her and what she saw in his face pierced her to the very marrow.

'Knowing you has brought untold treasures to my life—a baby.'

She nodded. He would cherish their child.

'You've shown me the way back to my family.'

Had he really reconciled with his mother? What about his father and the rest of his siblings?

'You've given me a vision of what my life could be like.'

He hauled himself upright, kissed the tips of her fingers before releasing her hands and stepping back. 'I understand your hesitation. I understand that you might see me as a poor bet.' He glanced at his watch and his chest heaved. 'I've taken up enough of your time. I should give you the space to consider all that I've said.'

He turned to leave and it was the hunch in his shoulders, the way they drooped in utter defeat that did it—that blasted away the last of her doubts. She pressed a hand to her heart, her pulse leaping every which way. 'You really do love me.'

He swung back, hope alive in his face. She could feel her face crumple. 'But you yelled at me.'

And then she burst into tears.

Ryan swooped across and pulled her into his arms, holding her as if he never meant to let her go. 'I only yelled at you to prove that I really do love you, to prove I could give you the passion that you said you've always wanted.'

She eased back, scrubbed a hand across her face. 'I hated it! I'm an idiot forever thinking that's what I wanted.'

He swiped his thumbs across her cheeks. 'You're not an idiot.'

'I love you,' she whispered.

He nodded gravely. '*That* might make you an idiot.'

'Are you going to break my heart?'

He shook his head. 'I'm going to take the very best care of your heart. I'm going to do everything within my power to make you happy.' The tension in his shoulders eased a fraction. 'I'm going to be very relieved if not yelling at you is on that list, though.' He smoothed his hands down the sides of her face. 'I hated yelling at you. I'm sorry it upset you.'

She wound her arms around his neck. 'Then I'm not an idiot. I'm the luckiest woman in the world.'

Her smile started up in the centre of her and reached out to every extremity. 'You really love me?' It wasn't that she didn't believe him. She just wanted to hear him say it again.

'I really love you.' His grin was all the assurance she needed.

'I really love you too,' she said, just in case he needed to hear it again as well.

'Will you marry me?'

A lump promptly lodged in her throat, momentarily robbing her of the ability to speak.

'I meant to go down on one knee and propose properly.'

She swallowed the lump. 'Don't you dare let go of me yet.'

'That's what I was hoping you'd say.'

This tough loner of a man had really trusted his heart and happiness to her? She touched his face in wonder. He let out a ragged breath. Plastered as closely as she was to him, she could feel how tightly he held himself in check. 'That…and yes,' he rasped.

She came back to herself with a start, the uncertainty in his eyes catching at her. 'Yes.'

He blinked.

'Yes, I will marry you. Yes, I will keep your heart safe. Yes, we'll build a wonderful family together, and grow old together and be generous with our love to all who want and need it.'

'You mean that?'

She reached up on tiptoe to cup his face. 'I love you, Ryan. How could you possibly think I would want anything else?'

'Can I kiss you now?' he groaned.

'In just a moment.'

He groaned louder.

'I want you to tell me how you reconciled with your mother…and father?' He nodded at the question in her voice. 'How did that all come about? I mean, you were so angry with them.'

He lifted her in his arms and strode across to the sofa with her, settling her in his lap as if she belonged there, as if he had no intention of letting her go anywhere else for a very long time. It sent another delicious thrill racing through her. She pressed a kiss to his cheek. 'I'm not saying you weren't entitled to your anger.'

'But it was time to let it go.'

She let out a breath she hadn't realised she'd been holding.

'And I discovered that forgiveness is an act of hope.'

Her heart soared. 'Oh, Ryan, I'm so glad.'

'I'd made such a terrible mistake with you and the thought of not winning your forgiveness was a torment. The thought I might be putting my parents through a similar torment shook some sense into me.' He met her gaze. 'I couldn't live with that thought.'

Of course he couldn't. He had a heart that was too big and generous for that.

'When you left I was beside myself.'

He would've been. She could see that now.

'And they all rallied around me, so worried for me. It made me realise that they do all care for me.'

'They do.'

He touched her cheek. 'I'd have never realised if it wasn't for you.'

She ran her hands across his shoulders and down his arms, revelling in the sculpted strength of him. 'We're good for each other, Ryan. I've heard of people finding their soul mates, I knew that kind of love existed. I knew it couldn't be wrong to hold out for it.'

'My soul mate,' he said as if testing the idea on his tongue.

'Your rationality balances out my flights of fancy.'

'Your sense of fun balances out my seriousness.'

'Your control balances out my, uh...lack of restraint.'

He ran a finger down the V made by the collar of her shirt, making her shiver. 'I promise never to yell at you again.'

'But...' She lifted one shoulder. 'What if I'm testing

your patience beyond endurance, being stubborn and headstrong?'

He pressed a kiss to the tender spot behind her ear. 'I'll find a different way to get your attention.'

She arched against him. 'Mmm, I like the sound of that. I promise never to throw another vase at you.'

He eased back, a smile in his eyes. 'I don't know. That kind of thing keeps a man on his toes.' His eyes darkened. 'Mind you, I'll be doing my very best to not provoke you into throwing vases.'

'Ryan?'

'Yes?'

'You can kiss me now.'

His grin became teasing, wolfish, and a thrill shot through her. His mouth descended towards hers. He stopped millimetres short. 'Do you have to go back to work this afternoon?'

Her breath hitched. 'Not unless I want to.'

'You're really not going to want to,' he promised.

She tilted her chin, a smile building in the depths of her. 'Prove it.'

So he did.

* * * * *

"I'm sorry. That was wrong."

Lani blinked at him, trying to focus her fuzzy brain. "Why?"

"I'm an officer of the law. Using a position of power to take advantage of you is the very definition of sexual harassment. You have every right to be upset."

Upset? Lani wasn't the least bit upset. Russ had finally noticed her! He'd kissed her, and it had felt really, really good. She wanted him to notice her some more. "I'm not upset."

"Well, I wouldn't blame you if you added sexual harassment to that false imprisonment complaint."

"Why did you really stop?" She slid closer, until their thighs were touching and her arm brushed his. The heat of just that small contact threatened to make her go up in flames.

"I've sworn to uphold the law. There are rules." His voice was ragged and he was breathing hard.

So was she. And right this moment she didn't give a flying fig about rules.

* * *

Montana Mavericks:
What Happened at the Wedding?
A weekend Rust Creek Falls will never forget!

AN OFFICER AND A MAVERICK

BY

TERESA SOUTHWICK

Published in Great Britain 2015
by Mills & Boon, an imprint of Harlequin (UK) Limited,
Eton House, 18-24 Paradise Road, Richmond, Surrey, TW9 1SR

Special thanks and acknowledgement to Teresa Southwick for her
contribution to the Montana Mavericks: What Happened at the Wedding?
continuity

ISBN: 978-0-263-25165-4

23-0915

Harlequin (UK) Limited's policy is to use papers that are natural, renewable and recyclable products and made from wood grown in sustainable forests. The logging and manufacturing processes conform to the legal environmental regulations of the country of origin.

Printed and bound in Spain
by CPI, Barcelona

Teresa Southwick lives with her husband in Las Vegas, the city that reinvents itself every day. An avid fan of romance novels, she is delighted to be living out her dream of writing for Mills & Boon.

To my brothers—Jim, Mike, Dan and Chris.
Thanks for always being there. You're my heroes.
I love you guys!

Chapter One

Fourth of July

"I wouldn't be surprised if someone strips naked and jumps in the park fountain," Lani Dalton said out loud, to no one in particular.

And no one in particular paid any attention to her, what with all the partying going on around her at the wedding reception. Everyone was having a really good time. Braden Traub had married Jennifer MacCallum, and there was little that folks in Rust Creek Falls liked more than celebrating a happy occasion. And wow, were they celebrating!

It looked as if the colors of American independence had exploded all over Rust Creek Falls Park. Picnic tables were covered by red-and white-checkered oilcloth covers, while red and blue tarps had protected people from the afternoon sun, although it had gone down a while ago. Fireworks had been shot off but people were still hanging around, dancing, talking, laughing and drinking wedding punch.

She'd just finished two-stepping with her brother and figured there was something weird going on for that to have happened. Nothing said relationship loser like dancing with your brother. Anderson was her favorite, but still… After chug-a-lugging her fourth—or was it fifth?—cup of punch, she felt a little light-headed. Sitting down suddenly seemed like an awfully good idea.

Walking around and searching for an empty seat, she wasn't watching where she was going. As a result, she ran into what felt like a brick wall and was nearly knocked onto her backside.

Strong hands reached out and steadied her. "You okay?"

Lani was pretty sure that voice belonged to Russ Campbell, a detective from Kalispell who filled in sometimes to help out Sheriff Gage Christensen here in Rust Creek Falls. She felt a familiar quiver of attraction lick through her as she looked up to confirm her suspicion. "Detective Dreamy."

"Excuse me?"

"Lani Dalton." She pointed at herself. "I work part-time at the Ace in the Hole, the local bar and grill. You're Russ Campbell."

"I know."

"I know you know who you are." She giggled and that surprised her because she wasn't normally a giggler. "I meant that *I* know who you are and was introducing myself to you. Lani Dalton," she said again.

"Okay."

"Not much of a talker, are you?"

The sheriff was short a deputy and Russ filled in at least once or twice a week. That's about how often he came into the bar but he never really paid much attention to her. She, however, had definitely noticed *him*. He was tall and broad-shouldered with thick, wavy brown hair and hazel eyes that didn't miss a thing. Except her.

He was nice-looking, but if you happened to catch a glimpse of one of his rare grins, he was absolutely adorable. As far as she knew—and she'd asked about him—no female in Rust Creek Falls or anywhere else for that matter was on the receiving end of those smiles.

"Okay, then." He cleared his throat and continually scanned the crowd of people who were getting happier by the minute. "Well, if you'll excuse me, I have to keep moving."

After months of being ignored, Lani had finally struck up a conversation. Sort of. It was an opportunity, and she wanted it to go on.

"Are you here for the bride or groom?" she asked.

"What?"

"Are you a friend of the bride or groom?"

"Neither." He indicated the gold shield hooked to the belt at the waist of his worn jeans. "I'm working. Sheriff Christensen hired me to help with crowd control."

Looking way up at him, his features seemed to blur and she swayed a little. Again, his hands reached out to steady her. She couldn't help noticing his arms, where the sleeves of his black T-shirt stretched across impressive biceps. It was swoon-worthy—that must be why she was a little woozy.

"Wow, you're really strong. And your reflexes are really good." Did she just say that? It wasn't like her to say whatever popped into her head.

He was already frowning, but her words seemed to turn the frown into a scowl. "I think you should lay off the liquor."

"All I had was punch from the reception, and they said it was some concoction with sparkling wine. No hard alcohol allowed in the public park. You should know that. So I haven't had any liquor to speak of. I swear," she said, raising her hand, palm out. "That's the thing. I work at the bar but I hardly ever drink alcohol. Am I talking too much?"

"Uh-huh." His tone was unnecessarily sarcastic. "Let's find you a place to sober up."

"I'm not drunk. And I was looking for a place to sit when you ran into me."

"For the record, *you* ran into *me*," he said.

She shook her head—that was a big mistake. "I don't think so."

"Take my word for it." His mouth tightened as he scanned the tables and didn't spot an empty place. "Let's go over here."

She felt his fingers on her arm as he led her through a maze of people who moved for him as if he was Moses parting the Red Sea. "Where are you taking me?"

"To the park fountain. The edge is wide enough to sit on, and it's cooler there."

They were passing the last of the tables when she saw her older brother Travis chatting up a pretty blonde who Lani happened to know was dating a hot-tempered, jealous cowboy. She would have warned him off, but Detective Dreamy had her in a pretty tight grip. And she spotted her other brother Anderson moving in. He would make sure Travis didn't do anything stupid.

"Here you go," Russ said after they crossed the open grassy area then reached the fountain that was spewing water in the center. "Have a seat."

Lani did and set her flag-stamped cup beside her. "Thank you, Detective."

"Yes, ma'am."

Ma'am? She was a generic female who could be anywhere from nineteen to ninety-five? Seriously? She knew he was on duty, but it wouldn't hurt him to work on his people skills. Honestly, sometimes she wondered why she was attracted to him at all. Except he was pretty cute, and she'd seen him at the bar, chatting up other people and making them laugh. Apparently, he just wasn't that into *her*. Well, she wasn't into being called *ma'am*.

"You can call me Lani. I'm not crazy about sweetie, honey or babe. But please don't ever call me ma'am. It's like nails on a chalkboard."

"Understood."

Loud voices suddenly cut through the general celebratory hum of activity. They were coming from the direction where Anderson had just walked. Skip Webster, the jealous cowboy, was arguing with Travis, who was trying to back away. Then the cowboy took a swing when Travis wasn't looking. Instead of turning the other cheek, his fists came up to retaliate. Anderson stepped between them to defuse the situation. The other man punched him, and Anderson lashed out with a fist, a knee-jerk reaction.

Skip went down then started shouting for help. He spotted Russ and hollered for an immediate arrest.

"I have to go," Russ said.

Lani had a bad feeling. "What are you going to do?"

"Arrest that guy for assault and battery."

That guy would be her brother Anderson, and that wasn't good anytime, but he had a personal legal issue pending. An arrest wouldn't work in his favor considering he was going to try to get custody of a child he'd just learned he had. Detective Russ Campbell was headed toward that ruckus unless she did something to stop him. Whatever it was had to be loud and immediate.

She heard the water gushing from the middle of the fountain behind her and did the first thing that popped into her mind, which was clearly becoming a habit tonight. She jumped into the water then gasped at the cold liquid soaking the bottom of her skirt. Russ looked at her as if she was nuts then started toward the arguing men. She couldn't think how else to stop him, so she started belting out "Firework," her favorite Katy Perry song, which certainly made her more of a spectacle!

Well, good. Anything to help Anderson…

At the same time she smacked the water, sending a wave over the edge that hit Russ's back. When he turned, she added some dance moves to go with the song.

He walked over and stopped in front of her. "Please come out of there, *ma'am*."

Now she was just mad and used both hands to shower him with water. Satisfaction circled through her when he swiped a hand over his wet face, and she sang even louder. Surprisingly, she was enjoying herself.

"Okay, you've had your fun." Russ was using his I'm-the-law voice. "The show here is over."

But it seemed no one was listening to him. A few people were stopping to see what the disturbance was all about. Lani appreciated her fan club, especially because Russ kept glancing over at her brothers and Skip Webster, who was still demanding justice at the top of his lungs. Officer Campbell was clearly dying to give it to him—at the expense of her brother. She couldn't let that happen and had to up her game.

"Come on in, the water's fine." She waved to the few onlookers who seemed to like the idea of a dip in the fountain.

"Whoa," Russ said, putting his hands up to warn them off. He sent a glare in her direction. "That's inciting public disorderliness. If you don't come out of there voluntarily, I'm going to have to arrest you." He glanced over his shoulder again.

Lani didn't much like the idea of going to jail, but better her than Anderson. She didn't have any legal problems, although that could be about to change.

"I dare you to come in and get me, Detective Dreamy."

Russ reached out to grab her, and the frown on his face

deepened when she backed up and eluded him. “Come on, Lani. Out of the water.”

“You’re not the boss of me.”

“As it happens, I am. I told you already, Gage brought me in for crowd control, what with the wedding and Fourth of July celebrations going on at the same time.” He looked around at the happier-than-normal people scattered throughout the park. “And it was obviously the right call.”

“You look hot under the collar.” Although he wasn’t actually wearing a collared shirt, or technically a uniform. But there was something about his ensemble of choice. The black T-shirt, jeans and boots made him about as hot as a man could get.

“Doesn’t he look hot?” she said to the crowd around the fountain.

“Cool him off,” someone called out.

“Okay.” She sent walls of water at him as hard and fast as she could. Not much connected, though, on account of her keeping her distance so he couldn’t grab her. The physical effort had her staggering, and she almost slipped.

“That does it,” he said impatiently. “I’m arresting you for drunk and disorderly conduct.”

“That’s the nicest thing you’ve ever said to me, Detective.” Until a few minutes ago it was practically the only thing he’d ever said with the possible exception of *could you get me a beer.*

His expression went from grim to really grim as he stepped over the edge into the fountain. Lani winced at what the water would do to those leather boots. Well, it couldn’t be helped. This was for Anderson. She backed away from the advancing lawman while one person started chanting, “Lani! Lani!”

With the water choppy from their movements, it was hard to dodge him. He was bigger, stronger and faster, so she couldn't get away indefinitely. But the longer she could keep his attention focused on her, the better.

She backed up a step, and her sandal hit a slick spot on the bottom of the fountain. Down she went, not completely underwater, but enough to soak the top of her dress and ruin her hair. A second later Russ was right there in front of her, holding out a big hand to help her up. She wasn't sure where the idea came from but at this moment she didn't really care. After putting her hand in his palm, she yanked forward with all her strength. He was already off balance and fell on top of her.

"Damn it," he sputtered. "You're under arrest—"

"So you said." She brushed the hair out of her face.

He gripped her arm and tugged her up with him when he stood. "You have the right to remain silent but there's probably a snowball's chance in hell of that happening."

He finished with her rights then started walking her out of the fountain. When she slipped again, he swore under his breath before swinging her into his arms. Lani sincerely regretted that fate hadn't warned her about Russ Campbell picking her up, because she would have lost a few pounds in preparation. Points to him that he made her feel as if she weighed nothing.

After stepping out of the water, he set her down. When she wobbled a bit he asked, "Can you walk?"

"'Course. I've been doing it for years."

"Good." He curved his fingers around her upper arm and, without another word, started moving.

"Aren't you going to put the cuffs on me?" she asked sweetly.

His eyes narrowed as he looked down at her. "Are you going to resist arrest?"

"No."

"Okay, then." He kept walking and tugged her along with him.

Wow. She was going to the slammer.

For the first time since running into Russ she didn't say what popped into her head. She didn't think it would improve his mood if she started singing "Jailhouse Rock."

Russ Campbell walked Lani Dalton into the sheriff's office, his temper rising with every step. This was the last place he needed to be—and she was the last person he should be with.

Her eyes were wide, but she looked more curious than scared. "Wow, I've never been in the slammer before. This is kind of exciting."

Glancing around the room he tried to see the hub of Rust Creek Falls law enforcement through her eyes. It was a big room with a couple of desks, one where the dispatcher sat. The other was for the deputy, although Gage was short one right now. While the sheriff looked for a replacement, Russ filled in when he had time off from his detective job with the Kalispell Police Department. A room off to the right had a closing door, and that's where the sheriff worked. The place wasn't especially intimidating, but then again, he'd worked in Denver, where the department was bigger—and so were the problems.

"If you think this is cool, wait until you see the cell."

"Isn't there some law against false imprisonment?"

He took her arm and led her through a doorway, where there were two six-by-eight-foot cells. Either she was naturally sassy, putting on a front to hide her nerves, or she was still not sober enough for her situation to sink in. *Sink* wasn't the best choice of words after that surprise swim in the fountain. He couldn't believe he'd let his guard down and should have known better than to let her distract him. But Lani had been a distraction from the first time he saw her.

"This arrest is ridiculous. My father is a lawyer, and I'll be out of here before my dress dries."

He figured she was trying to look defiant but with those pretty big brown eyes of hers, she only managed to come across as innocent, and they both knew she wasn't. The drive over from the park was short, and she was still wet. He was having a devil of a time not staring at the way that bright yellow sundress clung to her small waist and curvy hips. And, dammit, the material was wet, which made it practically transparent. He didn't need her reminding him about that.

He curled his fingers around the smooth skin of her arm and tried not to think about the fact that he could use another dunking in the fountain to cool off. "Come on. I'll give you a guided tour of the slammer."

"I can see it just fine from here." She stood her ground and looked up at him, wobbling just a little. "Is it really necessary to lock me up?"

"Yes. Between the Fourth of July and that wedding reception, there's been way too much celebrating going on in this town. I've been looking the other way most of the night, but things are starting to get out of hand. My job is to not let that happen."

"So I'm the lucky one you decided to make an example of. But you don't really work here in Rust Creek Falls," she reminded him.

"That's funny. Gage Christensen pretty much said he was paying me to be on duty. Sounds like work to me." He gave her his detective glare, the one he used to intimidate people who broke the law. It came more naturally right now, since his jeans were heavy, and water squished in his boots. "Thanks to you, I'm really earning that paycheck tonight."

"The sheriff wouldn't have arrested me." Her tone was defiant. "But you're not from around here."

Not one of us, she was saying. That struck a nerve. Before he'd left the Denver Police Department everyone had been avoiding him as if he had the plague. He was treated like an outsider for blowing the whistle on a crooked cop then busted down to patrol. When his career went backward his fiancée dumped him. So much for loyalty—and love.

"I might not live in Rust Creek Falls, but I'm the one with the badge." He drilled her with a look. "You broke the law on my watch, Lani Dalton."

Her eyes widened a fraction. "Since when aren't you calling me *ma'am*?"

Not using her name was a way to keep his distance, and he'd been trying to do that since the first time he'd seen her. She had long brown hair and creamy skin that tempted a man to touch her. Resisting that temptation tested his willpower under normal circumstances, but nothing about this night was normal.

"Do you know who my father is?"

"You said he's an attorney, but right this minute I don't much care." He walked her through the doorway and into one of the cells then pulled the door shut behind them. The bolt clicked into place and echoed off the bare walls.

She flinched slightly "So, we're locked in."

"No," he said. "You're the one locked up, and I'm the cop who has the key in his pocket."

Her eyebrow rose. "You're sure?"

"Absolutely."

"You're very confident." Lani shrugged then walked over to the metal-framed bunk. She lifted the sheet covering the thin, plastic mattress. "Wow, five-star accommodations. That looks like a yoga mat."

"Let me know if it's comfortable. You're going to be here awhile." She wasn't as far gone as some he'd seen under the influence. In his opinion, she could be left alone, and that was a good thing. Russ didn't have time to babysit the princess. "It's nuts out there, and your stunt in the fountain took me away from where I need to be."

"Lighten up, Detective. Everyone's just having fun."

"I don't think the cowboy who got decked was having such a great time."

"Oh? I didn't notice." She put just a little too much innocence in those words.

"Then you're the only one in Rust Creek Falls who didn't. Now I have to go deal with the guy who decked him."

"You're not really going to arrest him?" Her bravado slipped for the first time since he'd politely suggested she exit the public fountain.

"Yeah, I am. On the upside, you'll have some company in here tonight."

"Seriously, you're going to leave me alone?"

Apparently, the reality of the situation was sinking in, because some of the spunk finally seemed to drain out of her.

"You'll be fine."

"I don't think so." She put a shaking hand up to her forehead and swayed on her feet, the color draining from her face. "I'm feeling a little dizzy. I think I might be sick."

In one stride he was beside her, sliding an arm around her waist. She collapsed against him, clingier than the wet dress. She was deadweight, and her hand clutched him, just below his belt, trying to hang on and keep from falling. He practically carried her to the bunk and settled her on it, sitting beside her.

"Take deep breaths. Put your head between your knees."

"I'll fall on my face." She sat stiffly on the thin, plastic mattress, hands clenched into fists on either side of her, and breathed deeply several times. "I think I'm feeling a little better."

Russ studied her face and noted the color was returning. "I'll get you some water."

"No." That was a little more emphatic than necessary. "What I mean is, I'm afraid it might come back up."

"After drinking too much, the best thing you can do is hydrate. And a couple of aspirin wouldn't hurt, either."

There was something about her that brought out his protective streak, but he chalked it up to doing his duty. The job he could handle, but being in this small space with Lani Dalton was trouble. There wasn't enough room for him to avoid the sweet scent of her skin. That made him want to lean in even closer and find out if that sassy, sarcastic mouth of hers would taste as good as he'd been imagining for months now.

Abruptly, he stood and turned his back on her.

"Is something wrong?" she asked.

Behind him there was the sound of the plastic mattress creaking as she shifted her weight. He turned, and the innocent expression he'd noted moments ago was back in place. She sat quietly looking at him, hands folded in her lap. Her dress was still wet, and the sight of the thin cotton clinging to her breasts ignited the familiar conflict inside him.

He was really attracted to her but knew that acting on it was a complication he just didn't need. Not now, not ever. His heart had taken a hit, through and through, and that experience made him determined not to be a fool again. His new philosophy was never trust anyone unless they gave you a reason to. So he'd decided not to get to know Lani Dalton better. And she'd done nothing tonight to make him regret the decision. Although that wet dress was giving his self-control a real workout.

"Okay, I have to go now. Looks like you're fine."

"I still feel nauseous. What if I have to throw up?"

"Do what you have to do." And he would do the same,

which meant getting out of here, away from her. "And right now I have to go make rounds and investigate that assault-and-battery incident. I'll be back before you even know I'm gone."

"Solitary will be an improvement." She folded her arms over her chest, trying to look bored.

"Be sure to put that on the customer satisfaction survey."

But Russ was sure some vulnerability was trickling out. And with that thought he knew it was past time to get the hell away from her. He moved the short distance to the barred door at the same time feeling his jeans pocket for the key. The familiar outline of the metal wasn't in the usual place so he dug deeper. It wasn't there. He checked his left pocket then the back ones.

Nothing.

"That's the damnedest thing."

"Is there a problem?" She didn't sound the least bit anxious.

"I don't have the key." He met her gaze, waiting for her to mock this turn of events.

Lani held her breath, waiting for Russ to figure out that she'd taken his keys and shoved them under the "yoga mat." She was feeling very bold for some reason and figured she had nothing to lose. The plan was conceived in desperation, and she didn't expect to get away with it, but couldn't think of any other way to stop him from arresting her brother.

"I guess you forgot to put the keys in your pocket. And that's understandable considering how crazy it is out there. It feels like a horror movie—night of the living party-animal apocalypse."

One corner of his mouth tilted up, and for a moment she thought he was going to give her one of his adorable smiles. But he seemed to catch himself then pulled his cell phone from a back pocket.

"I'll just give Gage a call." He pushed some keys and frowned. "Apparently, water and sensitive electronic devices are incompatible."

"I'm so sorry." And she really was. Ruining his phone hadn't crossed her mind when all she could think about was helping her brother. And the longer Russ was distracted with her, the better it would be for Anderson. So she was kind of glad he couldn't call the sheriff. "I'll pay for a new phone," she offered.

He glared at her. "I don't suppose you have one that works."

"I do. Because it's at home."

"A likely story."

"Seriously?" She glanced down at her dress and realized the still-damp cotton made her body half a step from being naked. She should be embarrassed, but that tendency toward boldness was still firing on all cylinders. "I rode to the park with my parents and left my purse at home. And really, if I had one on me, it would be as wet as yours. It would also have to be somewhere a gentleman wouldn't go looking for it."

"No one would accuse me of being a gentleman, but you're right about one thing. There's no point in searching even if you're lying."

"Well, that hurts my feelings."

"Which part?" he asked.

That she was a liar? Or her body was not interesting enough? "Both."

But what was that saying about poking an angry bear? Lani had lost count of all the times Russ Campbell had been at the Ace in the Hole with Gage Christensen and never talked to her. She'd asked Gage about him and knew Russ was a detective on the Kalispell Police Department and had moved back to Montana from Denver. No one knew why.

Now she was finally having a conversation with him, but it was about her being deceptive and lacking even a speck of sex appeal. That was disappointing and humiliating in equal parts. And, if that wasn't bad enough, now there was every reason to believe he really didn't like her. Well, he was pretty cute, but that didn't stop her from being a little annoyed with him right now, too.

He sighed. "I just meant that if you had a phone, yours wouldn't work, either."

"It's really not important," she finally said.

That all-seeing hazel gaze of his narrowed on her. "You're one cool customer, Lani Dalton."

"Oh?" Cool as in attractive, intriguing and alluring? Or cool as in nervy and annoying?

"Yeah. I've seen women fall apart over being stopped for a speeding ticket, and you don't seem the least bit upset about the fact that you've been arrested and locked up in jail."

"So are you," she reminded him.

"But I'm not in legal trouble."

Okay, he won that round. She wasn't too worried about the fountain dance, although after tonight probably a notice would be posted on it with a warning to keep out. But destroying his phone and helping herself to the jail cell keys could be a problem. Intellectually, she knew that, but her lovely buzz made it impossible to care.

"I'm not really worried. Ben Dalton is my father. You may have heard he has an excellent legal reputation."

"Ah." He nodded, but the tone and his expression hinted at a deep well of sarcasm.

"What does that mean?"

"That you're the little princess. Rules don't apply to you because daddy can find a loophole and make it all go away." He moved back until bumping up against the bars stopped him.

Lani was pretty sure he was staying as far away from her as he could get, and it bummed her more than a little.

"You don't know my father. Or me." She didn't much care about the angry defensiveness in her tone. Russ had gone out of his way *not* to know her. "He took an oath to uphold the law and wouldn't compromise his principles. Ever. Not even for one of his children."

That was the truth and probably why Anderson hadn't said anything to anyone else in the family about his legal trouble and made her swear not to, either. She'd caught her brother at a weak moment, and he apparently had been feeling the stress of carrying this burden alone. That's the only reason she knew.

Russ didn't say anything, but clearly he wasn't a happy camper. And who could blame him? Her cotton dress was drying faster than his jeans and T-shirt, and those boots were probably dead to him. She should offer to pay for those, too.

"Look, Russ—"

"I should be out there. Gage hired me to help him keep the peace with so much going on today, and now he's alone." He started pacing. "There's no telling when he'll check in. It might not be until morning what with half the town three sheets to the wind."

Guilt weighed on Lani. If only she knew that Anderson and Travis had walked away and not escalated the situation, she would confess her sins and take her punishment. But she didn't know and had to keep up her distraction as long as possible.

"Okay," she said, "we're stuck. When life gives you lemons, make lemonade. We should talk."

The look he sent in her direction was ironic. "I suppose it was too much to hope we wouldn't have to."

"Are you always this mean or do I just bring out the

worst in you?" She met his gaze and refused to look away. "We should get to know each other."

"That's really not a good idea—"

"It could be. You have an opinion of me. I have an opinion of you and maybe we're both wrong. Attitude is everything. Think of it as an opportunity to make a better impression." She refused to be put off by the stubborn, skeptical expression on his face. "Okay, I'll start."

Chapter Two

Russ stared long and hard at his prisoner. She was sitting on the bunk in a jail cell looking all wide-eyed and perky and pretty damned appealing. If she was the least bit intimidated by him or the situation, he couldn't see it. Although as she'd so helpfully pointed out, he was locked in, too, which kind of took the starch out of his intimidation factor.

How the hell could he have forgotten to put the keys in his pocket before walking her in here? That wasn't like him. The movement was automatic, muscle memory.

As much as he hated to admit it, she was probably right. It *had* been a crazy night, and there'd been a lot of calls to the sheriff's office. He'd been busy, distracted.

Now he was uncomfortably and undeniably distracted by his "roomie," who wanted to share personal information. Last time he'd checked, it wasn't a cop's job to spill his guts to a detainee.

"You want to join hands and sing 'Kumbaya' because

it's not bad enough that we're locked up together?" he asked.

"No." She shifted on the bunk and spread out the damp skirt of her sundress. "Look, the fact is that we're stuck in here, unless one of us can bend steel in their bare hands, and that sure isn't me."

"Superman. That's just great." He nodded grimly.

Doing the right thing had cost Russ his law enforcement career in Denver, but somehow that never seemed to happen to the legendary comic book superhero. And Lois Lane never dumped him when everyone else thought he was gum on the bottom of their shoe.

"Seriously, Russ, we don't know how long it might be before someone comes looking."

"I don't think it will be that long before Gage checks in." He hoped he was right about that, but the situation in the park hadn't been quieting down when he'd brought Lani in.

"That's just wishful thinking because obviously you don't like me very much."

"Arresting you wasn't personal." Russ figured it was best not to put a finer point on that statement by saying he didn't *want* to like her. There was a difference. "It's my job."

"Whatever." She met his gaze. "We could sit here in awkward silence. Or we can make conversation to help the time pass a little faster."

He hated to admit it, but she had a point. "Okay. But if you say anything about braiding each other's hair, I'm pretty sure my head will explode."

"If only." She gathered the stringy, drying strands of her long hair and lifted them off her neck. "I'd give anything to be able to brush this mess."

"You should have thought of that before dancing in the fountain—"

She held up a finger to stop his words. "I thought we had a truce."

"My bad."

"Okay, then. Have a seat." She patted the mattress next to her. "There's nowhere else to sit in here. I'll have to have a word with your decorator about what a conversation area should look like."

He didn't want to sit next to her but couldn't say so or he'd have to explain why. And he didn't quite understand that himself, other than the fact that he'd just arrested her. Since she occupied the center of the bunk and showed no inclination to move, he took the end, as far away from her as he could get.

Lani looked at him expectantly and when he didn't say anything, she cleared her throat. "I was born here in Rust Creek Falls twenty-six years ago, number five of six children."

"Braiding hair is starting to sound like a high-speed freeway pursuit." When she laughed, the merry sound burrowed inside him, landing like a gentle rain that softened rock-hard soil.

"Compared to what you do my life *is* boring, but I like it. And I love this town." She shrugged. "I live with my parents here in Rust Creek Falls and work on the family ranch, which is north of town. I do everything from mucking out stalls to riding fence and feeding stock."

"What about working at the Ace in the Hole?"

"That's part-time. Rosey Traven, the owner, is the best boss in the world."

Russ had been in his share of bars and seen how badly guys who drank too much behaved. A woman as beautiful as Lani would be a first-class target for come-ons and drunken passes. The thought of some jerk hitting on her made him almost as mad as the water in his boots. But all he said was, "It probably gets rough in there."

"It can sometimes. But Rosey's husband, Sam, was a

navy SEAL. He knows three hundred ways to immobilize a creep with a cocktail napkin."

That made Russ feel a little better, but not much. "What do you like about the job?"

Her shrug did mind-blowing things to what was under the top part of that sundress. The material was thin, still damp, and he could almost see her breasts. They looked just about perfect to him and made his hands ache to touch her and find out for sure. And this wasn't the first time he'd experienced that particular feeling around her, but he'd always made sure not to get too close.

"I'm a people person," she finally said. "I like chatting with the regulars, and almost everyone in Rust Creek Falls comes in to hang out at some point or other. You know, guys' nights, girls' night out, poker games…or people just coming in for a burger and a beer. I like hearing what's going on in their lives and apparently, that makes them want to talk to me."

He laughed, but there was no humor in the sound.

"What's funny?" she asked, a small frown marring the smooth skin of her forehead.

"My job is the polar opposite. I'm a detective for Kalispell PD, and no one wants to talk to me."

"I see what you mean." She smiled her happy, under-the-influence smile. "But can you blame them? It makes a difference when your job is selling drinks as opposed to interrogating a perp."

"I suppose."

She half turned toward him in her earnestness to make him understand. "I'm somewhere between a family counselor and confessor. People feel comfortable baring their heart and soul to me, and I take that as an obligation. I consider it part of my job description to offer sensible advice or sometimes to simply listen. Whatever the situation calls for."

"I had no idea the job was so demanding."

"Go ahead. Make fun." There was annoyance in the look she settled on him. "But I think people trust me."

"In what way?"

"Rust Creek Falls is a small town. Everyone knows everyone, and some people think that gives them the right to every last detail of a person's life. But some things shouldn't be spread around. I know the difference, and folks who know me know I'll keep that sort of information to myself."

"I know what you mean about a small town," he said.

"How? Kalispell is a pretty big city compared to Rust Creek."

"I grew up in Boulder Junction. It's a small town about halfway between here and Kalispell."

She nodded. "I know it. That's farming country, right?"

"Yeah. My family has one. Mainly they grow wheat, corn and hay. But they have smaller crops, too."

"Like what?"

"Apples. Potatoes. Barley."

"Sounds like a pretty big farm."

"Yeah." One of the biggest in Montana.

"Family, huh? Does that mean you weren't found under an arugula leaf?"

"It does." The corners of his mouth turned up a little in spite of his resolve to keep his distance. "I actually have parents and siblings."

"Plural?" she asked. "Boys? Girls?"

"Two brothers and a sister. I'm the oldest." He didn't usually talk this much, but there was something about Lani Dalton, something in her eyes that said she was sincerely interested. She was listening, and he didn't even have to buy a drink, just arrest her for drinking too much.

"So you grew up in a small town, too. Have you done any traveling?" she asked.

"Some."

"Lucky you. I've never really been anywhere." There was a wistful expression in her eyes. "Have you ever thought about leaving Montana?"

"No." Not since he'd come back from Colorado a couple years ago.

"Really?"

Russ had done enough interrogations to spot a technique for coaxing information out of someone who was reluctant to part with it. He wasn't inclined to do that. "Really."

She studied him for several moments then nodded, as if she knew the subject was closed. "Tell me about your brothers and sister. Anyone married? Do you have any nieces or nephews?"

"No to all of the above. What about you?"

"I have two sisters and three brothers. The oldest two were at Braden and Jennifer's wedding—"

"What?" he asked when she stopped talking.

"Nothing." But her body language changed. She sat up straighter and shook her head. There was something she didn't want to talk about. "My brother Caleb got married last year. My sister Paige took the plunge the year before that, and now she and her husband have a baby boy."

"Good for them."

"Yeah, they seem happy. But I'm not sure it would work for me."

On a night full of surprises, that might have been the biggest one yet. "Doesn't every girl dream of a long white dress and walking down the aisle?"

She laughed. "I'm not every girl. And in case you didn't get the memo, a woman doesn't need a man to be happy and fulfilled."

"Spoken like a woman who's been dumped." He was watching her and saw a slight tightening of her full lips, indicating he'd gotten that one right.

Irritated, she leaned in closer to make a point. "Is that observation based on crack investigative skill, Detective Campbell?"

"Nope. It's based more on gut instinct."

"Wow, who knew I was going to get locked up with Dr. Phil?"

"I have my moments." He could feel the heat from her body and her breath on his cheek. The sensations were taking him to a place he was trying very hard not to go. "You know, Lani, it's none of my business, but I don't think you should let one bad experience sour you on marriage."

"Why? Because you're married and highly recommend it?"

"No."

"Ever been married?"

"No."

"Then how are you qualified to endorse marriage?"

"There's a lot to be said for it." He hoped that didn't sound as lame as he thought, especially because it didn't really answer the question. He just kind of liked the way her eyes flashed when she was annoyed. It made the green and gold flecks stand out, warm colors that hinted at the fire inside.

"Like what?" she demanded.

"Well…" He thought for several moments. "Having someone waiting for you at the end of the day." He'd missed that when Alexis walked out on him. "Someone there to listen to you bellyache about the bad stuff. And celebrate the good."

"I have girlfriends for that." She slid a little closer, practically quivering with indignation. "Frankly, I don't get the appeal of being with one person for the rest of your life. Guys just stand you up. Make promises they don't intend to keep. I mean, seriously? The very expression—tying the knot. Sounds an awful lot like a noose around your neck."

"You said yourself that marriage is working for your brother and sister," he challenged.

"Yeah, well, those two always were the black sheep of the family. Who wants to be tied down? Take the plunge? Think about that. Every expression referring to wedded bliss has a negative connotation. And I don't think I'd like having to answer to someone else when I want to come and go."

If that's what she wanted, why should it bother him? And that, in a nutshell, was the damn problem. It did bother him. The idea of her playing the field seemed wrong. When confronted with right and wrong, wrong tweaked his temper every time.

"You know what?" he said. "Forget I mentioned it."

She rolled her eyes. "How come your badge is all bent out of shape? You brought it up."

"No, you did," he reminded her. "Asking about my family and telling me about yours."

"I thought most guys wanted to be bachelors, but you're the one pushing the perks of matrimony. I disagree with everything you said, and now you're crabby—" She stopped. "Make that *more* crabby."

She was full of intensity and obviously capable of strong feelings. More than his next breath he wanted to hold all that passion in his arms. And every rational part of his brain not drenched in testosterone was telling him to move as far away from her as he could get. The problem was the locked door meant he couldn't go anywhere. Shutting down this conversation was his only choice.

"You are absolutely right. Being on my own is good. I like being on my own." His face was only inches from hers. "The best thing about my life is not having any commitments."

"A girl could get a serious case of whiplash the way you

change your mind. Just what makes you so happy about not being committed?"

Before Russ even knew what was happening, he closed the small distance between them. "Because if I were committed, I couldn't do this."

He hadn't planned to kiss her, didn't know he was going to until his lips touched hers. But once it happened, he couldn't seem to stop. She had, without a doubt, the sweetest mouth he'd ever tasted. He cupped her smooth, soft cheek in his hand, ready to go wherever she would take him. Her sigh of contentment said she'd take him somewhere special, make him forget where they were.

That thought was like getting a bucket of ice water dumped over his head. They were in jail, dammit. With an effort, he pulled back and dropped his hand. "I'm sorry. That was wrong."

Lani blinked at him, trying to focus her fuzzy brain. "Why?"

"I'm an officer of the law. Using a position of power to take advantage of you is the very definition of sexual harassment. You have every right to be upset."

Upset? Lani wasn't the least bit upset. He'd finally noticed her! He'd kissed her and it felt really, really good. She wanted him to notice her some more. "I'm not upset."

"Well, I wouldn't blame you if you added sexual harassment to that false imprisonment complaint."

"Why did you really stop?" She slid closer, until their thighs were touching, and her arm brushed his. The heat of just that small contact threatened to make her go up in flames.

"I've sworn to uphold the law. There are rules." His voice was ragged, and he was breathing hard.

So was she. And right this moment she didn't give a flying fig about rules.

"Maybe rules were made to be broken." She searched his eyes for a moment and then leaned in and kissed him.

She felt his hesitation and heard him make a sound that was somewhere between a groan and a curse. Suddenly, he was kissing her back, touching her everywhere, and she was tugging the shirt from his waistband. All she could think about was getting closer. The sound of their ragged breathing filled the small space.

"Damn it. I don't have protection." Frustration snapped in his voice.

"It's okay," she whispered. "I'm on the pill."

"Oh, thank God."

He slid her dress up to her waist then yanked his shirt off and lowered his jeans. She couldn't believe that he wanted her as much as she did him. Still, it seemed they'd been heading toward this since the moment he'd scooped her into his arms earlier. Never taking his mouth from hers, he gently lowered her to the mattress and slid her panties off. He ran his hand down her side, letting his fingers graze her breast. Everywhere he touched she caught fire, but it wasn't nearly enough.

"Lani, I want you." The words were hardly more than a breath against her lips.

All she could say was yes and that was all he needed to hear. When he tenderly and carefully entered her, she wrapped her legs around his waist. With every stroke he took her higher until pleasure exploded through her and she cried out from the sheer power of the feelings.

"Lani—" A groan cut off his words, and he went still then found his own release.

Their breathing slowed and returned to normal, the only sound in the small cell. Cuddled up to Russ, being held in his strong arms, made Lani decide that getting arrested wasn't so bad, after all. She wasn't sure what she'd been drinking at the wedding reception, but something had lowered her inhibitions and let her go for it.

And suddenly she was really sleepy and found her eyes sliding shut.

She wasn't sure how long she dozed, but sometime later she felt him move.

"My arm is numb."

Lani blinked her eyes open at the sound of the deep voice. It took her several moments to realize where she was. And what she'd done. What *they'd* done, right here in the cell. And he'd let her sleep, long enough for his arm to go numb. That was awfully sweet.

"We better get dressed." Without waiting for a response, Russ rolled away from her and off the bunk. He picked up her panties and handed them to her. Then turned his back while she righted her clothes.

"Thanks." Although he was correct that they should dress, she missed the warmth of his arms around her, his body pressed to hers. And he'd gone back to the good-looking guy who didn't notice her.

A little while ago they'd been as intimate as a man and woman could be, but now he wouldn't even look at her, and you could cut the awkwardness with a dull knife. She straightened her dress then stared at the bars. If they weren't locked in, she could quietly slip away, but any walk of shame was limited to a six-by-eight-foot cell.

"I feel as if I should say that this isn't something I normally do." Russ met her gaze.

"Me, either."

"Are you okay?" he asked. "You look kind of—I don't know." His mouth thinned to a straight line, clearly regretting what happened. "I'm sorry."

"Don't be." She shook her head. An apology implied what they'd done was wrong, and she refused to believe that. The responsibility for them being in this situation was hers, and she had to confess. “Look, I need to tell you something—”

He held up his hand to stop her. “I know what you’re going to say. I guess technically it’s morning and you hate yourself.”

“No, I—”

The outer door opened and slammed closed. “Russ? You in here?”

“Back here,” he called. There was a grim look on his face. Probably because he was about to face his boss and explain how he got locked in here.

Gage appeared in the doorway and did a double take when he saw them in the cell. “What the hell?”

“Boy, am I glad to see you.” Russ dragged his fingers through his hair.

“You want to explain to me what’s going on here?” the sheriff asked.

“Not really. But I guess you should know, since you’re the boss.” Russ took a deep breath. “I lost the key.”

A wry look settled on Gage’s face. “I’m not a detective like you, but I sort of figured that out. It’s the part where you’re in the cell with Lani Dalton that could use some kind of explanation.”

“I arrested her for creating a public disturbance.”

“It’s true,” said Lani, looking as apologetic as possible—and truthfully, she felt pretty bad at the moment. At least, about nearly getting caught doing the deed with Russ. She’d only meant to stop him from arresting her brother, not get him in trouble altogether! “I was dancing in the park fountain. And I pulled him in. I swear I didn’t have liquor. Not really. They’d said that punch was only sparkling wine, but *punch* was sure the right word for the wallop it gave me—”

“This is my responsibility—” Russ’s voice was clipped.

She felt the least she could do was come to his defense,

since this was all her fault. But he gave her a don't-do-me-any-favors glare that kept her silent.

"Be that as it may," Gage said, "Russ, I'd like to know why you were on that side of the barred door when it automatically closed."

"Lani—the prisoner—was anxious about being left alone. And argumentative."

"You couldn't have calmed her down and argued with her while standing over here?" Shaking his head, Gage put a hand on the barred door in question. "Rookie mistake."

"How long before I live this down?" Russ asked.

"Hard to say. Could take on legend status," the sheriff told him, grinning. He inserted the key, and the lock opened with a loud click. "Good thing I have another set of keys or you'd be stuck in there a whole lot longer."

Lani was okay with that, but one look at Russ told her that one minute more than necessary in here with her was about as appealing as brain surgery with a chain saw. When the door slid wide, Russ walked out and Lani started to follow him. He stopped, and she ran into his broad back.

"Not so fast." He turned and looked down at her. "In case it slipped your mind, I arrested you."

It kind of *had* slipped her mind, what with having sex in the slammer. She may have locked them in, but he'd started *that*. All things considered, the park incident felt like years instead of hours ago, and her head was starting to pound.

"Let her go, Russ." Gage rested his hands on his hips. "Given the way this night has gone, her behavior is small potatoes. Sometimes you can pick and choose which hill to die on, and this is one of those times. She's not a hardened criminal, and it was nothing more than mischief. You and I have more important things to deal with right now."

Russ looked at the sheriff for several moments then nodded. "Whatever you say."

"Do you need a ride home, Lani?" Gage asked.

"No." She was already feeling guilty for taking up law enforcement time on false pretenses.

"Okay, then. Don't get into any more trouble and make me regret cutting you some slack." Gage gave her the intimidating lawman look that was becoming familiar tonight.

She saluted. "Yes, sir."

Gage grinned again then turned and walked out, leaving them alone on the free side of the cell door. Lani was feeling equally happy to be sprung and guilty for what she'd done. Even though protecting her brother was a sound enough reason as far as she was concerned. But all of a sudden it seemed very important that Russ not think too badly of her.

She cleared her throat. "Russ, I just want to say—"

"Not now, Lani. I've got work to do. And first I have to make sure you get home okay."

He walked her to the door of the sheriff's office then opened it and waited for her to go outside. When she did, he let the automatic locking door close behind them then moved to the sheriff's cruiser parked at the curb and opened the rear door. She had no choice but to get in.

Shouldn't she feel better about this reprieve? About this get-out-of-jail-free card? She probably would except that she felt guilty, and Russ refused to even look at her.

So nothing had changed. He was back to ignoring her.

Chapter Three

When Russ pulled the sheriff's department cruiser to a stop in front of her house, Lani opened the rear door. It was a short ride from the office, but he hadn't said a word to her the whole time. The overhead light revealed the tension tightening his jaw.

"Can you get inside by yourself?" he asked.

She almost winced at the curt, cold tone. "Of course. Why wouldn't I?"

"There might not be anyone home. You don't have a purse and that means no keys."

Guilt swept through her, and she wished for another cup of wedding reception punch and whatever magical ingredient had made her bold and fearless. She didn't feel that way now.

"I can get in. Thanks." She met his gaze. "Look, Russ, let me just say—"

"Please close the door, Lani."

"Okay. I'm sorry. Good night." Empty words because

she knew his night had already been anything but good. Thanks to her. But the next time she saw him at the Ace in the Hole, she would buy him a beer and not let him ignore her. "I appreciate you bringing me home."

She got out, shut the cruiser door then watched until the red taillights disappeared when he turned the corner. One glance at the house's dark windows told her that her parents and sister were in bed, which was a big relief. There might just be a chance that her fountain performance would slide by under the Dalton family radar.

Her parents kept an emergency house key hidden in the backyard under one of the bricks that lined the patio. She retrieved it and let herself in the French door to the family room. Moving quietly through the shadowy interior toward the kitchen, she saw the microwave's green digital readout of the time. Holy cow, how did it get to be so late?

Apparently, time really did fly when one was having fun. And she really had been—between the time she'd gotten Russ talking about himself and the moment he'd frozen her out after making love to her. Probably she should feel remorse about being "easy" but couldn't muster it. What happened had really meant something to her but now, thinking about being in his arms, the experience seemed surreal, as if she'd been dreaming.

It was good she wouldn't have to face her family right now. She'd have time for her head to clear and sort out what went down before seeing anyone.

Suddenly, she heard the click of a light switch and lights blazed on.

"Where in the world have you been?" Her sister, Lindsay, was standing at the bottom of the stairs where the kitchen, family room and front hall all came together.

Startled, Lani let out a screech. "Dear God, you scared the crap out of me."

"Sorry." Her sister didn't sound sorry. She sounded

irritated and anxious. “I heard noises and came down to check it out.”

“Why are you still up?”

“Couldn’t sleep. I was worried. In the park I looked everywhere for you. We were supposed to meet after the fireworks and come home together.”

“Unless one of us hooked up, remember?” When they’d discussed the plan, Lani had added that but was joking. She wasn’t psychic and never in the world could have predicted she would hook up with Russ.

“I guess that means you were with a guy?” Lindsay’s brown hair was pulled into a messy ponytail on top of her head. She was wearing boxer-style sleep shorts with SpongeBob SquarePants printed on them and a pink, spaghetti-strapped tank top.

“Define *with*,” Lani hedged.

“Look, I saw you get out of the sheriff’s car just now. Why did he drive you home? Something is up, and I want to know what it is.”

Her sister’s voice was a little louder, and Lani glanced at the stairs leading to the second floor, where her parents were sleeping. “Shh. You’ll wake Mom and Dad.”

“I’m okay with that.” Lindsay folded her arms over her chest. “What in the world has gotten into everyone tonight? You disappeared. Travis and Anderson got into it with Skip Webster in the park—”

After what happened with Russ in jail, Lani had forgotten about her brother. “Is he okay?”

“Skip is fine. He has a fat lip, but with that temper of his it’s not the first time.”

“Not Skip! Anderson. And Travis,” she added.

“The boys are fine. Upstairs sleeping it off. Anderson had too much to drink to drive himself back to his place and bunked in his old room for the night. But it’s not like them to drink that much.” Lindsay gave her an accusing look. "I could have used your help. Where were you? Are you okay? And why did the sheriff bring you home?"

"Technically it wasn't the sheriff," she said cautiously.

"That's not the point." But then she said, "So who was it?"

"Russ Campbell."

"Who?"

"I've told you about him. The detective from Kalispell PD who comes in to the Ace in the Hole." *And acts as if* I'm *invisible*, she thought.

Lindsay looked puzzled for a moment, then the confusion cleared. "Yeah. The really cute cop who doesn't know you're alive?"

He does now, Lani thought. After what they did, he would have a hard time ignoring her from now on. But she only said, "That's the one. He was working a shift for Gage Christensen because of the holiday and wedding reception in the park."

"Smart," Lindsay said. "It was crazy out there. I still can't believe I had the guts to get between our brothers and Skip Webster. It's weird. And all I had to drink was the punch from the reception."

"Weird, all right," Lani agreed.

"And you still haven't explained where *you* were tonight."

"Oh, you know—"

"Not really. And that's why I'm asking." Lindsay's blue eyes narrowed.

Lani wasn't up for this. "Look, just because you're in law school and working in Dad's office this summer doesn't mean you can cross-examine me."

"And just because I'm the baby of the family doesn't mean I'm not entitled to know what's going on. If you won't tell me where you were, I'm sure Dad can get it out of you. We both know how good he is."

Her sister half turned, as if to head upstairs and make

good on her threat. "Wait," Lani said. "Don't wake him. It's late."

"Okay, then, spill."

She took a deep breath and said, "I was arrested."

"What?"

"I was dancing in the park fountain. Singing, too. When Russ Campbell tried to pull me out, I pulled him in." Lani shrugged. "I forced him to take me to jail."

"Why would you do that?" Lindsay blinked, completely at a loss.

"Seemed like a good way to keep Detective Campbell from arresting Anderson for assault and battery."

"So you took one for Team Dalton?" The younger sister shook her head. "That fight was no big deal."

"But Skip Webster was demanding someone be arrested, and Russ seemed more than happy to oblige."

"But there was no real harm done. Surely Dad would have gotten Anderson out of jail and smoothed it over."

"I figured it would go easier for me. Being a woman. And being a public nuisance is less serious than punching someone."

"You do realize," Lindsay started, "that Dad would say you should have let our intoxicated brothers suffer the consequences of their actions?"

That sounded about right for Ben Dalton, Lani thought. But she couldn't reveal the real reason it was necessary to keep Anderson's record spotless. When their brother was ready, he would tell the rest of the family.

"At the time, it seemed like a good idea to keep Russ distracted."

"Russ? Sounds like you got pretty chummy with him in the clink." Lindsay stared her down. "You're not saying anything, and I know that look on your face."

"I don't know what you mean." She knew exactly what

her sister meant. They were close enough that the sisters knew if one wasn't telling the whole truth.

"Then I'll put a finer point on it." Lindsay moved closer. "You just said you had to keep Russ distracted. That sounds premeditated to me. And you're on a first-name basis with him. Just what did you do to keep him distracted?"

Lani felt heat creep up her neck and settle in her cheeks. If only she could have put a bag over her head.

Lindsay's eyes grew wide even though Lani hadn't said a word. "You didn't."

"Of course I didn't sleep with him."

"I didn't *say* you slept with him. What makes you think that's what I meant? Why is that the first thing that popped into your head?"

"Good gravy, Lindsay." Lani had no doubt her sister would be a very good lawyer someday. "You sound like a prosecutor."

"I'll take that as a compliment." There was a pleased expression on her pretty face just before her eyes narrowed. "But I'm not stupid, sis. Something happened between you and Russ. You were gone for hours, and I'd like an explanation."

"It's not a big deal." Liar, she thought. She would throw her sister a bone and get her off that line of questioning. "We were in the locked cell together. I managed to take his keys and hide them. And before you start, I didn't want him to dump me there just so he could go back to the park and arrest Anderson."

"This just gets better and better." Lindsay shook her head. "I'm speechless."

"That's a first."

"How did you finally get out?"

"Gage came looking for Russ. He let us out. When Russ wanted to keep me in jail, the sheriff talked him out of it and said there were bigger problems to deal with."

"That's true," her sister said. "But I can't believe how underhanded you are."

"You say underhanded, I say resourceful. The good news is that Anderson is in the clear."

Lindsay met her gaze. "You're the one I'm worried about. He didn't get arrested. I hope Russ doesn't change his mind and press charges."

Lani hoped so, too.

When her alarm clock went off at zero-dark-thirty, Lani felt as if she'd just closed her eyes. But the holiday was over and she had to work at the ranch today. The cows and horses still got hungry and needed attention even if their humans got only a couple hours of sleep. As motivational speeches went it wasn't great, but she didn't have the energy to kick herself in the ass.

She dragged on jeans, shirt and boots. Pulled her hair into a ponytail, brushed her teeth, washed her face and put on sunscreen. On her way downstairs she smelled coffee, and her attitude perked up a little, no pun intended. No one in this house but her was ever up this early and brewed coffee, so there must be a God.

She walked into the kitchen and saw Anderson grabbing the bottle of Tylenol from the cupboard above the coffeepot. She was happy that he was here and not in a jail cell.

"Can I have a couple of those, too?" she asked.

He held out the bottle. "You look terrible."

"Thanks. So do you." Lani shook some of the white caplets into her palm. "I feel as if there are teeny, tiny elves hammering a Sousa march on the inside of my skull."

"Me, too." He poured coffee into a mug and held it out. "Can you give me a ride to my truck? It's at the park."

"Sure. How did you get home last night?"

"I'm not exactly sure." He dragged his fingers through his brown hair. "It's all a blur. And I don't even know why.

I feel hungover, but all I had to drink was that punch at Braden and Jennifer's wedding reception."

She blew on her coffee. "So you don't remember giving Skip Webster a fat lip?"

There was a frown in his blue eyes as he flexed the fingers on his right hand. "Yeah, that would explain the bruised knuckles, but it's all a blur."

"Hitting someone isn't your style at all, Anderson." She'd always looked up to her brother and knew what a good man he was. He's the one who told her Jase Harvey was a sweet-talking charmer who would crush her heart then held her while she cried when he turned out to be right. If only she'd listened to him.

"Dad raised us boys to never start a fight. But he always said that if anyone else did, don't run away from it." He rubbed a calloused thumb over the thick handle of his mug.

"If it's any consolation, I saw what happened. Skip swung at Travis when he wasn't looking, and you stepped in. He hit you first."

"Okay, then." He nodded grimly and met her gaze. "If you were a spectator to that, I guess that means you stayed out of trouble."

"Define *trouble*."

Those big-brother blue eyes of his zeroed in on her. "What happened, Lani?"

She figured he had a right to know and was the only person she could tell the whole truth. "Russ Campbell was going to arrest you for assault and battery on Skip Webster, so I created a diversion."

"What did you do?"

"It was hot." She had been feeling no fear and wasn't sure why. And just before the incident she'd thought about someone jumping into the fountain but hadn't expected that person to be her. "I took a dip in the park fountain, and there might have been some singing and dancing involved."

His gaze narrowed. "That's not all, is it?"

Lani figured he had a right to know this, too, and was the only one who would understand why she did it. "I pretty much forced Russ to arrest me to keep him from carting you off to jail."

"He actually took you in?"

"Yup."

"Why would you do that? Lani, you should have let him come after me."

"I couldn't. Not with the legal challenge you're facing. If it wasn't about custody and visitation rights regarding your child, I would have stayed out of it. But you can't afford any black marks, or even gray ones, on your record."

His mouth thinned to an angry line. "I'm the one being judged even though Ginnie never saw fit to inform me that I was going to be a father."

"No one ever said life would be fair." That was all Lani could think to say. It wasn't fair that Russ was going to hate her when—if—he figured out she'd taken his keys. And it really wasn't fair that he'd kissed her and she'd responded and both of them lost control when they were locked up together.

"You okay, Lani?" Anderson gave her a funny look. "All of a sudden you went pale as a ghost."

"Fine. Part of the hangover that for no apparent reason is shaping up to be epidemic." She couldn't think about the *what-ifs* or *if onlys* right now. Her brother was going through a crisis. "Surely the court will take everything into consideration. It should matter that your child's mother didn't tell you she was pregnant."

"I was cheated out of that moment, which was bad enough. But she kept this child's existence from me for ten years."

Lani couldn't begin to understand how he felt. But it was the weight of carrying this burden alone that had finally compelled him to confide in her when she caught him at a vulnerable moment. She would help him through it as best she could. Whatever he needed she would do, no questions asked.

"It's not right, Anderson, what happened to you. But it's done. All you can do now is fight for your rights. To do that you can't afford anything but a spotless record."

"You've got a point." He sighed. "But I hate that you're in trouble on account of me."

"Not really. I think I'm in the clear. After Gage let us out of the cell—"

"Us? You weren't alone?"

"That's not important." It was too early and she was too tired to go into it. "Gage pretty much gave me a free pass because he was too busy dealing with other stuff."

"Like what?"

"Not sure. But I think a lot of people in town are feeling the same mysterious hangover that we are this morning." She shrugged. "The sheriff just told me to keep my nose clean. I don't think there will be any charges."

"If that changes, Dad can probably help."

"He could help you, too, if you'd let him," she pointed out.

"I have my reasons." Anderson shook his head. "I'm just glad you're in the clear. I don't want you taking a fall for me."

"That's not your call," she said. "You'd do it for me or anyone else you love. Just like me, you'd protect your family and have their back."

"You're right." His eyes glittered fiercely. "It's what Daltons do. And that's why I don't want anyone else to know about this legal stuff. You can't say a word to anyone in the family."

"But, Anderson—"

"No." He raised his voice then glanced toward the stairs, clearly concerned he'd wake someone. "Child custody cases aren't Dad's field of expertise. If Mom found out, she'd get attached to the idea. You know how much she wants more grandkids. And if I lose, not seeing her grandchild would break her heart. I can't do that to them, Lani, not unless it goes my way and I get visitation rights. You promised not to say anything."

"And I won't." She put her hand on his arm and met his gaze. "No one is going to find out from me."

"Okay." He nodded. "I really appreciate this. And I owe you one."

"I think you're on the hook for more than one," she teased. "Going to jail for you should count more than that. I'm thinking you should give me whatever I want for the rest of my life."

He grinned. "Don't push your luck, little sister."

"I'd never dream of it."

"Seriously, kid, I hope spending the night in the slammer wasn't too bad."

"It was really hideous. I don't care what they say about orange being the new black, it's just not my color. And don't even get me started on the food and those mattresses—"

He reached over and yanked her ponytail. "You definitely have a flair for the dramatic. And while it's very entertaining, we need to get to the ranch."

"Right."

Why did she have to go and bring up the mattress where she'd slept with Russ Campbell? Kissing him was a highlight. Being in his arms had a very high degree of awesomeness. She almost wished he would decide to press charges. That would mean he'd have to speak to her again.

The chances were slim to none that he would drop by

the Ace in the Hole while she was working, so her best hope of seeing Detective Dreamy again was to break the law.

And she *really* wanted to see him again…

Chapter Four

September 1

Russ Campbell pulled his truck to a stop in front of the Rust Creek Falls sheriff's office. It was impossible to step foot in this building without remembering the night he'd held Lani Dalton in his arms. He'd broken so many rules to have her and, God help him, it had been everything he'd dreamed about. Then he'd found out that she'd stolen his keys, deliberately locking them both in.

The next morning when the sheriff's office dispatcher had cleaned up the cell, she'd found them under the mattress. It was clear and irrefutable evidence that she'd made a fool of him. It wasn't the first time a woman had done that, but he vowed it would be the last.

Unfortunately, Lani was still keeping him up nights. He told himself it was because of trying to figure out what she'd really been up to the night of the Fourth. The truth ran more along the lines of he ached to touch her again.

He hated himself for it, but every time something brought him to Rust Creek Falls, he had a devil of a time resisting the urge to stop by the Ace in the Hole to see her. For him it came under the heading of borrowing trouble, and that was never smart.

He got out of the truck and went into the building. Since Gage was still trying to fill the deputy position and the dispatcher had gone home at five, no one was in the main room. He walked over to the office Gage used and saw the door was open. The sheriff was behind his desk, poring over paperwork.

"Knock, knock." Russ rapped his knuckles on the open door.

The other man looked up. "Russ. Thanks for coming by."

"No problem. You said it was important."

"That's right." Gage tossed his pen on top of the papers. "Have a seat."

He grabbed a metal chair from against the wall and pulled it over. "What's up?"

"Folks here in town are still unnerved about what happened on the Fourth of July. Everyone I talked to swears they weren't drinking hard liquor that night but ended up drunk as a skunk."

"Yeah. Not long after that night, Will Clifton paid me a visit while I was at the precinct in Kalispell. He knows I fill in here and wanted to talk to me, said he believed that someone had spiked his wife's punch. But lots of people were three sheets to the wind that night, and he asked if I believed something was put right in the punch bowl."

"What did you tell him?" Gage asked.

"That I hadn't come to any conclusion yet." Russ rubbed a hand across his neck. "But when I'm here, folks still bring it up. I also spoke with Claire Wyatt and her husband, Levi. Both said they were acting out of character after drinking the punch. What you just said is pretty much the same thing I keep hearing."

It's what Lani had told him that night, but he'd assumed she was lying. That hadn't made a bit of difference to him in how much he'd wanted her. How dumb did that make him? Definitely not using his head.

"Yeah, I read your reports. Very thorough."

"The only common denominator I can see is the wedding punch. It was most likely spiked."

Gage nodded. "That's what I think, too. But we can't prove it. By the time the dust settled, all the evidence was poured out and washed up. There was no point in taking samples from people affected because it was out of their system by then. So we've got zero to go on."

"And the more time that passes, the harder it is to get at the truth." Russ knew from working numerous cases that the sooner a crime scene was cordoned off and investigated, the better chance there was of finding evidence and solving the case.

"You're right about that. In two months I've made no progress on the investigation. But Labor Day is next week. Halloween is coming. There will be kids' parties and adult get-togethers, usually some kind of a community event. People are worried that it could happen again."

"I can see why folks are skittish," Russ agreed.

"The thing is, I'm still short a deputy since the last one left to take a job in Helena."

"Big city has bigger problems."

Gage's gaze narrowed on him. "Is that the voice of experience?"

"Yeah."

"Want to talk about it?"

"No." Russ wanted to forget about the fact that he'd worked with some really good cops, but not one of them had his back when he needed it most.

"Okay, then." Gage leaned back in his chair. "In case you were wondering, I didn't call you here just to vent about this mess."

"Didn't think so."

Russ had known this man since high school. His parents grew and sold hay to ranches in the areas surrounding Boulder Junction and Rust Creek Falls. Russ had helped deliver it. At the Christensen ranch, Gage always helped him unload the bales and they'd hit it off. Ever since, he'd considered the sheriff a good friend.

There was worry in the other man's eyes. It wasn't unusual because he tended to be serious by nature, but the depth of the unease was reserved for really serious situations. Like the flood that had nearly destroyed Rust Creek Falls a couple years ago. And now this.

"I keep the peace here," Gage said. "I settle disputes, break up fights and make sure folks are safe. Right now they don't feel safe and are coming to me for answers. I don't have any, but I damned sure intend to get some."

"How?"

"I need your help on this, Russ. You're a detective and you were working on the night in question. You know how to conduct an investigation and piece information together to get the full picture." Gage's mouth pulled into a grim line for a moment. "I'm asking you to do that now. Part-time isn't enough but there's no choice, what with your job in Kalispell, but I'd really appreciate all you can give."

Russ didn't have to think it over very long. He quit his job in Denver after blowing the whistle on a dirty cop there, and then it became too dangerous to stay. So he'd come back to Montana and applied for a position with Kalispell PD. Gage had given him a glowing recommendation and since he was in the law enforcement field, his opinion carried a lot of weight.

Russ had a career thanks to this man, who gave him

a hand up at a low point in his life. He would always be grateful for that.

"I'm in," he said simply. "I haven't taken a vacation for at least two years, not since starting in Kalispell. Between that and personal days, I can give you a month of full-time work." He thought for a moment. "If I stay here in town, folks might open up to me more easily than if I come and go."

Gage nodded thoughtfully. "Strickland's Boarding House might have a room, and if not, Lissa and I would be happy to put you up."

"I'll try Strickland's." Russ was reluctant to impose on the couple who hadn't been married all that long.

"Good. Thanks, Russ. I owe you."

"No. This might put us somewhere in the neighborhood of even for what you did to help me." He cleared his throat. "So the working theory is that someone spiked the punch. That would suggest this person wanted to make a public statement to a good portion of the population. It's personal, but not focused on a single individual."

"Yeah." Gage nodded.

"We have to consider whether or not someone has a grudge against the whole town."

"Makes sense," the sheriff agreed.

"A lot of different people drank that punch." Russ was thinking out loud. He kept the reference general even though a picture of Lani Dalton popped into his mind, sassy and sexy and tipsy in her soaked sundress. "Business types. Ranchers. Young parents." He was thinking about Claire and Levi Wyatt. "Finding a common thread between them all could be a challenge."

"Especially for someone who isn't familiar with the quirks and personalities of folks in this town."

Russ knew that was directed at him and remembered Lani saying he was an outsider, although looking back, some of the nature of that talk could have been due to the effects of the spiked punch.

"Maybe it's not a good idea for me to be the investigator on this. What if I handle the routine calls and you do the footwork, ask the questions? We can collaborate on what you find out."

Gage thought for a moment then shook his head. "Some day-to-day situations here can get delicate, and knowing history and temperament can keep a small dustup from turning into a full-blown feud. I need a guy like you asking the questions. You're trained to read between the lines, to look for connections that aren't obvious. Not knowing people could be a plus. You might see things I'd miss."

"Okay. I'll do my best, poke around and find out what people saw. Surely not everyone was drunk off their butt that night. Who knows what they might have witnessed? And I have the impression that in this town, no one keeps anything to themselves for long."

He remembered Lani saying as much to him when they were stuck in the cell. Well, not stuck so much as her making a fool out of him. She could have given him back the key at any time.

What was her game? Why did she sleep with him? Because she wanted to—or was there an ulterior motive?

"I just had an idea." Gage snapped his fingers. "People do talk, and they do a good portion of that talking at the Ace in the Hole."

"Okay." Russ nodded. "I'll chat up Rosey Traven. She's the owner of the place."

The sheriff didn't look convinced. "Because she *is* the owner, she's not necessarily interacting with the clientele. Someone who primarily works with the customers is a better option."

"Good point. I've been in there from time to time, so

I know a couple of the waitresses. Annie Kellerman and Liza Bradley."

Russ had struck up conversations with both women. Each was pretty enough but they weren't Lani. He deliberately stayed clear of her and that was smart, as it turned out. One conversation with her and they couldn't keep their hands off each other.

Gage shook his head. "Neither of them has been in town that long. I think you should start with Lani Dalton. She knows everyone and might have overheard something."

Color Russ surprised. "Do I have to remind you that her behavior on the night in question was suspicious? You're aware that she deliberately took my keys and hid them to take me out of commission."

Gage laughed. "There were an awful lot of good, upstanding people who did weird things that night because of the spiked punch. She was a victim, too, don't forget. Whatever her reasons, I'd bet my badge her intentions were not about breaking the law. She's salt of the earth." A gleam stole into the other man's eyes. "Maybe she just had the hots for you, Russ, and wanted to get you alone to have her way with you."

That was right on the mark, and Russ had to wonder which of them was the better detective. And, for the record, Lani didn't have her way with him. He'd actually started it and was a willing and eager participant.

Russ couldn't quite meet the other man's gaze when he said, "She's a piece of work."

"Like the rest of her family," Gage said. "But I can tell you that she's never been in trouble."

"I'll have to take your word for that, Sheriff."

"Then take it on this, too. Talk to Lani. Start the investigation with her."

Russ stood up. "Is that an order?"

"It can be. But let's call it gut instinct."

"Okay, then. It's your town. We'll do it your way."

And wasn't this a fine mess. The moment he'd laid eyes on Lani he knew getting close to her would be borrowing trouble. The time had come to look trouble in her big, brown eyes and hope it didn't expect to be paid back.

So, after months of avoiding her, his job was to talk to the woman he had no reason to trust. The hell of it was that the person he mistrusted the most was himself.

It was just about quitting time for most people in and around Rust Creek Falls, and sometimes they stopped by the Ace in the Hole. But it was Tuesday and Lani never knew how busy her shift would be. She was getting ready for whoever showed up, filling napkin holders and saltshakers at the booths and tables.

Glancing out the window she saw the hitching post, where cowboys could tie up their horses when they rode in. Lighted beer signs in the window signaled the type of establishment this was as did the oversize ace-of-hearts playing card that blinked in red neon.

The screen door had rusty hinges and screeched every time it was opened and worked just fine as a signal for alerting them that a customer had arrived. Behind her the bar ran the length of the wall and had stools in front of it. Anyone sitting there looked into a mirror mounted on the wall, where the bottles of liquor lined up in front of it were reflected. Booths ringed the outer wall and circular tables big enough for six surrounded the dance floor in the middle of the room. In a couple of hours the place could be jammed with people ready to shake off the stress of the workday. Or not.

There were a few people in the place already. A couple lingering over a late lunch, holding hands and giving each other adoring—and annoying—smiles. There were a few guys nursing beers at the bar, but Lani focused in on Wes

Eggleston, recently split from his wife. He was looking at his beer as if wishing he could dive in headfirst. Rosey, her boss, was in the back with her husband, supposedly taking inventory, but Lani guessed they were taking inventory of each other. More than once she'd caught them making out like a couple of teenagers. She envied the bond they had—both business and personal.

Lani was handling bartending and waitressing duties until Annie Kellerman arrived to take care of drink orders. The bartender had called in and said she was going to be a little late tonight. Glancing at Wes again, Lani felt kind of sorry for him and walked behind the bar, stopping in front of where he was slumped.

"Hey, Wes, can I get you some water?"

His eyes were sad and bloodshot. "No, thanks."

"How are things with you and Kathy?"

"Separation's not doing it for her. She wants a divorce. Told me today."

That explained a lot. "I'm sorry," she said. The couple had a three-year-old daughter. "Any chance you two can work things out?"

He shrugged. "She wanted me to go to counseling. But I said no."

"Why is that?" Lani saw stubborn slide into his expression and held up her hand. "Sorry. It's none of my business. You don't have to talk about it if you don't want to."

"Nah. It's okay." He shrugged again. "I just don't see how telling a stranger our problems is going to solve 'em."

The screen door behind her screeched and slammed shut, but whoever it was could wait just a minute.

"I don't know, either," she said to Wes. "But what can it hurt to talk to someone? An objective stranger could give you some things to think about."

"Seems like nonsense to me," he said stubbornly.

She scooped ice into a glass then squirted soda water

into it. After dropping a lime into the bubbly liquid, she set it on the bar beside his beer bottle.

"If you don't do anything, it's over, right? So you've got nothing to lose by trying it Kathy's way. And if it turns out to be nonsense like you say, no harm, no foul. At least someday you can tell your little girl you tried everything to keep her family together."

He stared at her for several moments then nodded. "Never thought about it like that."

"See?" She smiled. "Talking to someone can change your perspective, get you to see things differently. Can't fix a problem you don't know about."

"I'll consider it. Thanks, Lani."

"Don't mention it." She set a paper-wrapped straw beside his soda water. "Let me know if you need anything else."

She half turned to the new arrival and said, "Sorry to keep you waiting, I—"

The words stuck in her throat when she saw Russ Campbell in all his worn-jeans, snug-T-shirt and leather-jacket-wearing glory. Last time she'd seen him, the town was all dressed up in red, white and blue, in the full swing of summer. Now Labor Day was a week away and fall just around the corner. She might not have seen him since *that* night, but she'd thought about him plenty.

At first when she worked a shift, every time that squeaky screen door opened, her stomach dropped as if she was riding the jackhammer at the county fair. But he never showed. After a few weeks of that adrenaline roller coaster, disappointment settled in and she was torn between wondering what might have been and relief that it turned out to be nothing.

Now *nothing* was sitting at the bar in front of her.

"Hi, Lani." That voice was smooth as dark chocolate

mixed with expensive Scotch. Those hazel eyes studied her intently.

She couldn't believe he was really here, had convinced herself that he would never darken her doorway again. Let alone voluntarily speak to her. He wasn't ignoring her. "It's been a while."

"I'm here on official business."

So, his talking to her wasn't voluntary; he was here as a cop. "Just when I thought I'd beaten the rap, you talked Gage into filing charges against me for my fountain dance. Isn't there a statute of limitations on that?"

"This isn't about the fountain." One corner of his mouth curved up. "But I am here about what happened on the Fourth of July."

Her heart pounded. Maybe he'd been thinking about her, too. Heat filled her when she glanced at his wide chest, and memories of him holding her came rushing back. "Oh?"

"A lot of folks have reported drinking the wedding reception punch and getting drunk then doing things that were out of character."

"Like me?" She couldn't manage to keep a little bit of I-told-you-so out of her voice.

"Yeah," he said. "Like you. We're pretty sure someone put something right in the punch."

"That's a sobering thought, no pun intended. Who would do that?" Chills prickled through her. "Why?"

"Don't know. But Gage hired me as an investigator to find out."

"Don't you have another job?" She knew he did. He was a detective. She almost winced, remembering when she'd called him Detective Dreamy. Out loud. It was the truth, but still…

"I'm taking a month's leave to handle this."

"Now you're scaring me. The sheriff's really that concerned?"

Russ nodded. "The who and why are important. If someone has a grudge against Rust Creek Falls, there could be another incident. Labor Day is coming up. There will be picnics and public celebrations. If someone wants to cause harm, it's another opportunity."

"Oh, my gosh—"

"Then there are more holidays—Halloween. Thanksgiving. Christmas. All of them traditionally have community events attached. I'm going to get to the bottom of this before then." His expression was determined. "And I'm starting with you."

"Me?" She blinked at him. "You don't seriously believe I was responsible for that?"

"I don't know for sure who did it, but it's not like you didn't stir up trouble that night."

It was the first time ever, but that was splitting hairs. "You say trouble, I say…mischief. I had some of that spiked punch and was experiencing a sensation of…happy."

And feeling no fear.

"You call stealing the keys to the jail cell and locking me in while I was on duty *mischief*?"

"Me?" Maybe she could bluff. "Someone else could have—"

"Don't." He held up a hand. "They were under the mattress."

It didn't seem as if he was in the mood to be teased out of being mad about this. She'd wondered if that's what had kept him from coming back to the Ace in the Hole. The suspicion on his face told her she might be onto something.

"I'm sorry, Russ."

"Really?" He didn't sound convinced. "Anyone else would have used them to get out of jail, not hidden them to stay locked *in*. The question is why you would do that? What were you up to?"

That night she'd had her brother's back, but she couldn't

tell him. "I would never do anything to hurt anyone, especially the people here in Rust Creek Falls. They're my friends and neighbors."

He looked at her for several moments, assessing her sincerity, no doubt. She really hoped those eyes of his didn't miss anything, because she was being absolutely straight about this.

"Gage vouched for you." He rested his forearms on the edge of the scarred bar. "But I've learned not to take anything or anyone at face value."

Needing something to do with her hands, she grabbed a damp rag and used it to wipe the already clean wooden surface in front of him. "That sounds really cynical."

"I've got my reasons."

A girl didn't deal with the public as much as Lani without picking up instincts about people. Some of what happened that night was fuzzy, but other things were crystal clear. She remembered how he'd guessed about her bad relationship experience, and she was going to return the favor. "Spoken like a man who's been dumped. Want to talk about it?"

The tough cop facade slipped for a second, then he recovered. And ignored the offer. "My job is all about dealing with people who break the law then lie through their teeth. If that doesn't entitle a guy to be wary, I don't know what does."

"I suppose."

"Look, Gage sent me here to talk to you. He says you know pretty much everyone in town, and you're an astute judge of character. That you might be able to shed some light on what went on that day. Maybe someone had a little too much to drink and started bragging. Maybe you've overheard something that would give us a lead."

Lani thought for a moment, but knew something like

that would have stuck in her mind. She shook her head. "If I had, I'd have brought it to Gage's attention right away."

"Okay, then." He slid off the stool, apparently anxious to get away from her.

"But Gage is right. I do know everyone. And I can read people pretty well, unless romantic feelings are involved," she said ruefully. She'd completely misread the guy who walked out on her.

"So I was right about you getting dumped." His gaze held hers. "Want to talk about it?"

"Wow, a man willing to listen. That's a surprise." She folded her arms over her chest. "But, as you said, it's part of your job description."

"Pretty much."

"Well, you're off the hook, Detective. I don't want to talk about it except to say that my romantic life consists of listening to the sad stories of folks who come into the bar here."

"Yeah. I heard you talking to that guy on the end."

She glanced over her shoulder and saw Wes finishing off his water. "It's even sadder when kids are caught in the middle."

"I know what you mean." He rested his palm flat on the bar. "Okay, then. If you do hear anything, can I count on you to pass it along to someone in law enforcement?"

"Of course. But I really want to help find whoever did this."

"Get in line."

"Seriously. Like I said, I know nearly everyone in town. I have information about things that happened way back when. Feuds, fights, disagreements. Someone who might have a reason to do harm. I could be of help."

"That's okay—"

"Look, Russ, I understand why you don't trust me, but Gage assured you that I'm on the up and up. Don't blow off a potential resource because of what happened." Heat burned up her neck and into her cheeks because the list of sins under the heading of *what happened* included sleeping with him. She couldn't go there.

"This is my town," she continued, "and I have a personal stake in helping to protect the people here that I care deeply about. You know you'd never forgive yourself if someone got hurt and you didn't do everything possible. I know I wouldn't."

"I understand what you're saying, Lani, but—"

She held up her hand to stop him from saying no. "In the spirit of fair disclosure, you should know that I'm going to do it anyway. I'll keep my ears open and ask questions. So you can either let me work with you or I'll just go rogue."

"Go rogue?" Suddenly, he smiled and looked completely adorable.

"Yes." All her girlie places tingled, and she wanted to flirt like crazy. Too bad she'd burned that bridge in a jail cell. "It's up to you."

He looked at her for a long, assessing moment. Finally, reluctantly, he said, "Okay."

"Great. We need to talk about—"

"Not here." He looked around. "Anyone could overhear."

"Right. This is too public. So we need to find a place where no one can eavesdrop." She thought for a moment. "Can you ride a horse?"

"Yes. I'm a farm boy, remember?"

She nodded. "Okay. Meet me at the ranch tomorrow. Around noon. I guarantee I can find a place where no one can listen in."

"Okay. If you need me, I'm staying at Strickland's Boarding House for the next month. I'll see you tomorrow."

Lani couldn't wait.

Chapter Five

Damn his protective instincts, Russ thought, as the horse he was riding kept pace with Lani's. If not for that, he would be at the sheriff's office in Rust Creek Falls mapping out an investigation strategy on his own. But he'd seen her bullheaded single-mindedness for himself and couldn't let her go rogue on this. Until they knew who was responsible for spiking the wedding punch, the motive was a mystery. He couldn't risk Lani working on her own and getting hurt.

So, at the appointed time, he'd met her at the Dalton ranch, where she'd had two horses saddled and waiting for their ride.

"It's awfully quiet over there."

Russ looked at her and waited for the thump in his chest that always happened when he looked at her. He felt it and sincerely wished he hadn't.

"I'm using all my powers of concentration to stay in the saddle."

"Oh, please," she scoffed. "You sit a horse as well as my brothers do, and that's their job."

"You're not so bad yourself."

She looked sexy all the time but, for some reason, even more so on the black-and-white pinto pony named Valentino. Worn jeans covered her legs, but there was something even more tempting about what he couldn't see. Her hair was in a French braid that hung down her back, and a brown Stetson protected her head and face from the sun.

She met his gaze. "Riding a horse is my job, too."

So she'd told him while they shared a jail cell where they'd done a whole lot more than talk. The problem was he really wanted to do a whole lot more again. He'd come back to Montana to kick-start his stalled career. Spending time with Lani had distracted him just as he'd suspected it would the first time he laid eyes on her. Now he was forced to interact with her—which gave him greater incentive to solve this case quickly.

Russ realized they were heading for the local waterfall when he heard the sound of rushing water. They crossed a wooden bridge and rounded a bend in the mountain trail. After lazily moving through a stand of trees, he saw the clearing and the waterfall for which Rust Creek Falls had been named. At the base there was a pool ringed by rocks. It would be a romantic spot with the right person. That was a dangerous thought in itself, since he'd been unable to resist this woman in a jail cell, which was the polar opposite of romantic.

"No one will overhear us here," Lani said.

In a grassy area she stopped her horse and slid off then led Valentino over to the pool for a drink of water. Russ followed her lead.

He patted the neck of his mahogany horse. "Coming all the way out here might be an overabundance of caution."

"Maybe. But it's a spectacular day, and I never get tired

of looking at the falls. I call that a win-win." She looked around and breathed deeply of the clean air.

His gaze settled on the chest of her plaid, snap-front shirt and the way it perfectly fit her full breasts and trim waist. Another spectacular view and a definite win-win.

But that wasn't why they'd come here.

After the horses finished drinking, they ground-tied the animals near the grass so they could graze.

"Okay," he said, "about the investigation—"

"Hold on." She grabbed a cloth bag and a blanket roll tied to the back of her saddle. "I packed lunch. Don't know about you, but I'm starving, and I can't think on an empty stomach."

Russ was hungry, too, and not just for food. Deliberately avoiding her since that night in jail hadn't done anything to diminish his wanting her, and seeing her last night had only made things worse. But it had been thoughtful of her to pack lunch for them.

"Thanks, that would be great." He took the blanket from her and spread it out under a shady tree.

Lani sat cross-legged then handed him an apple, a small bag of chips and a sandwich, then she took hers out of the plastic bag. "Hope you like ham. And if you're a mayonnaise hater, you're not going to be a happy camper."

"I'm good with it." He pulled one of the sandwich triangles out of the bag. The fact that she'd cut it in half struck him as a womanly touch, not something he, or any guy he knew for that matter, would do. It was nice.

"Okay, then." She took a bite of hers and they ate in silence, the only sounds in the clearing coming from the waterfall rushing over the rocks on the side of the mountain. Or the occasional chirp of a bird.

"I've come up with a list of suspects," she said, after chewing the last of her sandwich.

"What criteria did you use?"

"Incidents from that night." She held up three fingers and ticked them off. "A couple got married. Another split up. And a ranch was won in a poker game. That's just for starters."

"I'm aware of the first two," he said. "A week or so after they got married during the reception, Will Clifton approached me about the possibility that his wife, Jordyn Leigh, was drugged at the wedding."

"Did *he* act guilty?"

"No." In Russ's opinion, he'd behaved like a man who was looking out for the woman he loved. "And I talked to Claire Wyatt about the fight she had with her husband."

"And?" Lani took a bite of the apple.

Russ couldn't seem to take his eyes off her mouth and the small bit of apple juice on her lower lip. The urge to lick that drop was almost irresistible.

"Russ?"

"Hmm?"

"You started to tell me what Claire had to say," she prompted.

"Right." If he didn't keep his head in the game, this investigation was going to take three times as long. "She didn't tell me anything that would shed light on who might have doctored the punch."

He'd taken notes during each interview and added them to his own observations from that night. Will and Claire both said that their partners'—and their own—behavior had been out of character and consistent with being drunk even though they hadn't consumed any hard alcohol. Russ had noticed an awful lot of people were feeling no pain that night even before he'd arrested Lani.

"I think the Cliftons and the Wyatts were victims. Like you," he added before she could say anything. She was innocent as far as how she'd become intoxicated, but stealing the cell keys to detain him was not so easily explained.

"It doesn't make sense that Claire or Levi Wyatt would have anything to gain by getting the whole town drunk. He's just feeling the pressure of providing for his family. A wife and baby is a lot of responsibility."

"Being young parents doesn't automatically make them innocent," he pointed out.

"True. But I just don't see either of them doing something like that. What possible motive could they have?"

He agreed, but couldn't resist needling her. "I don't think your gut instinct would exonerate them in a court of law. Hard evidence is the only thing that matters."

"If you had any evidence, hard or otherwise, we wouldn't be here now."

"True enough." And as much as he wanted to mind being here with her, he couldn't seem to manage it.

"We have to look at who had something to gain by getting everyone drunk." Lani leaned back against the tree trunk and stretched her legs out in front of her.

"So, let's talk about that poker game."

She put her apple core in the empty plastic bag and started on the chips. "Old Boyd Sullivan gambled away his property to Brad Crawford in a really high-stakes game that was apparently going on at the Ace in the Hole."

"That's definitely motive." He met her gaze. "Anything else?"

"Jordyn Leigh Cates married Will Clifton that night. Rust Creek Ramblings got a lot of mileage out of that story."

"What is Rust Creek Ramblings?" This is where a local could really help.

"It's a gossip column in the *Rust Creek Falls Gazette*, written by someone who apparently wishes to remain anonymous, because there's no name on the articles." There was a gleam in her eyes that had nothing to do with the sun peeking through overhead tree branches. "Whoever it is has gotten a lot of juicy stuff from what happened at that wedding reception."

"That's also motive," he pointed out, carefully watching her.

"I guess so."

"You know everyone in town and their business. Could it be that you're the one who writes Rust Creek Ramblings?"

"You're not serious," she scoffed.

"Dead serious."

She looked at him for several moments then laughed. "Let me point out the holes in that theory. A lot of stuff in those columns was about things that happened while I was in jail with you." The shadow of her hat couldn't hide the pink that stained her cheeks.

"Let me point out the hole in that alibi. You could have gotten information to write about from anyone you talked to at the bar."

"True. But I didn't." She shrugged. "When would I have time to write it down? I'm up before God to work on the ranch and I have the other job."

"Part-time." He leaned back on his hands and stretched his legs out. His boots nearly touched hers, making this more intimate than he wanted. "When you have the gossip, how long could it take to knock out the column?"

"Hmm." She nodded thoughtfully. "I can see how you'd come to that conclusion, but I don't write it."

"If that's not a lie," he said, giving her a pointed look, "then I would really like to know who does. They seem to have a whole lot of facts about what happened that night. It could save a lot of time on this investigation."

"So you're anxious to have it over and be rid of me?"

"I didn't say that." Didn't mean she wasn't right, though. "But solving this would put people's minds at ease."

"Right." She nodded. "Okay. Be skeptical. It's probably mandatory for a detective. And, for the record, I don't blame you for suspecting me, but I didn't do it. So don't waste too much time looking in the wrong direction. Now, back to the case… It's common knowledge that hairstylists and bartenders know everyone's business."

A good deal of Russ's detective work was done by observing people. In his experienced opinion, Lani wasn't at all concerned about being a suspect. Either she was innocent or she was a very accomplished liar.

"Moving on," she said. "Let's go back to Jordyn and Will. They got married."

"And here's where your knowledge of the key players comes in handy. Do you think she would drug an entire town to get a man to marry her?"

"It wasn't a secret that she moved to Rust Creek Falls hoping to meet someone and get married. But she already knew Will from Thunder Canyon." She was thinking out loud then shook her head. "Since she works with children at Country Kids Day Care, I'd like to think she would never do something like that."

"But you can't be sure?"

"No."

"It's not a good idea to let it slide, then. I'll talk to her."

"That would be best," she agreed.

"And I think you should be there when I do." He was trying really hard to believe he'd said that for the good of the investigation and not personal reasons. "Since people seem to feel comfortable spilling their guts to you."

He'd seen it for himself when he went to the Ace in the Hole last night. That cowboy at the bar was talking to her about marriage counseling, and he admired the way she'd gotten through to him.

"Okay. I can do that," she agreed.

"And what about Brad Crawford? Do you think he's capable of something that underhanded?"

"Good question." She tapped her lip thoughtfully.

"Where real estate is involved, the Crawfords can get intense, but..."

"Okay. He can't be ruled out, either."

"No," she agreed.

She had to go and tap her lips, distracting him again. He'd had about as much of this brainstorming session as his willpower could take.

"I need to get back to the sheriff's office," he said abruptly.

"Okay. Yeah—" She stood up and started gathering their trash. "Me, too. Back to work, I mean. I have stuff to do this afternoon."

After Russ rolled to his feet, he had the damnedest urge to pull her into his arms and kiss the living daylights out of her. If only his protective streak extended to protecting her from him or saving him from himself.

He'd included her in his investigation to keep her out of trouble, but spending time with her was its own kind of danger. Wasn't that the classic definition of a catch-22?

"Did you have any trouble getting the evening off?" Russ kept his eyes on the road.

"Since I wasn't scheduled at the bar tonight, it wasn't a problem." Lani glanced over at him, sitting in the driver's seat of his truck.

He'd picked her up at home, and they were on the way to Jordyn Leigh and Will Clifton's ranch, which was located east of Rust Creek Falls. She was fascinated by his hands on the steering wheel—so competent, in control, strong.

The memory of those hands touching her bare skin was vivid and had desire curling through her. The sensations he'd coaxed from her that night seemed a lifetime ago, and she craved them for a second time. But since he'd turned up in her life again, he'd given no indication that he even remembered the passion that had so easily flared between them. Maybe it was best that she try to forget, too.

"Does Jordyn Leigh know we're coming?" she asked.

He nodded. "I called her and explained that there are still questions about what happened that night. She mentioned that Will was busy with work and wouldn't be there, so I told her you would be with me. I thought that would put her more at ease."

"Did you tell her that I'm helping with the investigation?"

"No. For two reasons. First, if word gets out that you're narcing, the flow of potentially helpful information will dry up. And second—again if word gets out—you could be in danger from whoever is responsible for what happened."

"So what did you tell her?" She looked at him. "About why I'm here, I mean."

"Nothing."

"Really?"

He glanced at her, and his expression was seriously annoyed. "She didn't ask."

Lani shook her head. "Here's the thing—Jordyn Leigh is a woman, and unless she's a quart low on estrogen, she's going to wonder what the heck I'm doing on this ride-along. There's a reason people are talking about that gossip columnist and buying the *Gazette* to read the columns. This is a small town, Russ, and they're curious about what's going on with everyone else."

"Okay, you have a point." A muscle jerked in his jaw. "Then I guess we should have a cover story in case she asks."

"She's going to ask," Lani assured him.

"Any suggestions?"

"It has to be personal, otherwise I'm on official business, and then the word would be out that I'm a narc, as you put it."

The corners of his mouth curved up and for just a moment there was the possibility of a smile that would blossom into adorableness. Then he turned serious again.

"Can't fault your logic. So, on the off chance she asks—" he gave her a quick, pointed look "—I stopped by the Ace in the Hole, saw you and asked you to dinner. We're going right after I interview her."

Lani was more than a little annoyed at his selective memory. Considering he'd been showing up where she worked for months and barely talked to her, then suddenly lightning strikes? That story was pathetic. At least from her point of view.

"She'll have more questions."

"Like what?"

"I'm not psychic." Maybe Lani was projecting because *she* had a lot of questions. Like during all these months, had he been more aware of her than he'd let on? Had he thought about asking her out and just never did? If so, why not? But she couldn't ask any of that. "It's just that she's had a lot of time since your phone call to think about what you told her and wonder about the two of us."

"We'll have to cross that bridge when we come to it because we're almost there."

They'd been driving on a road with acres of rolling green land dotted here and there by stands of cottonwood, pine and oak. The sun was low in the sky, just above Fall Mountain and the snowcapped peaks of the Rockies. The ranch compound came into view and included the main house, foreman's cottage, a bunkhouse, barn and corrals. There were a series of fenced pastures close by.

He drove through the open gate, underneath an arch that said "Flying C." Beyond that Lani spotted the two-story, white-sided, blue-shuttered farmhouse with a wraparound porch. There were lights glowing in the windows. It was after six o'clock, and the sun finally disappeared behind the mountains, bathing everything in shadow.

Russ parked the truck in front of the place. "Remember, don't say too much. Let her do the talking."

"Trust me. I've had a lot of experience with that." Of all people, he should know that sometimes a person just didn't say much of anything. That was his standard operating procedure with Lani at the Ace in the Hole.

Side by side they walked up the newly repaired steps to the door, which had a shiny new coat of paint and a fan-shaped window set into the wall above it. Russ knocked lightly, and Jordyn Leigh answered moments later. She was a pretty blonde who looked as if she didn't have a deceptive bone in her body.

"Hi, Detective Campbell. Come in."

The door opened to a small foyer with stairs in the center that led to the upper floor. There was a living room to the left and dining room on the right. The floor was wide-planked hardwood that looked freshly refinished, and the old-fashioned sash windows would let in lots of sunlight.

Jordyn Leigh stood back and let them by. "Can I get you something to drink? Coffee? Iced tea?"

"Appreciate it, but no," Russ told her. "This won't take long. We don't want to keep you."

"It's very sweet of you to help," Lani added.

Jordyn Leigh smiled warmly. "Lani, I haven't seen you in a while."

Lani looked around. Word on the street in Rust Creek Falls was that this place had been a mess when they moved in, but the two of them had worked hard to fix it up fast. The inside looked brand-new now and incredibly homey. She envied the newlyweds, finding each other and building a future together.

"I guess you've been pretty busy settling into married life," Lani said.

"That's for sure. I've been taking online classes for my degree in early childhood development on top of cleaning, repairing and upgrading this house." Jordyn Leigh's blue eyes sparkled with happiness. "I was surprised when the detective said you'd be here, Lani. How long have you two known each other?"

Lani knew that was a polite way of asking how long they'd been dating. But since she'd been instructed not to say much, she looked at Russ, indicating he should field the question.

"Well," he said, "it's a small town. You know how that is."

He could have said they weren't dating but that would make her presence here more curious. Probably he was hoping to avoid any finer points to explain her tagging along, but no way that was going to fly, Lani thought. She decided to embellish.

"We officially met at the big wedding reception, when he arrested me for dancing in the fountain."

"I heard about that." Curiosity was obvious in the other woman's eyes.

"Technically I took her in for resisting arrest." The look on Russ's face indicated he still wondered why she'd done that.

Jordyn Leigh smiled. "Sounds like there's an interesting story there."

"You don't know the half of it," Lani said. "We've gotten to know each other pretty well since then."

She felt Russ's disapproval and realized that his body language did not scream of his attraction to her. Either he was lousy at undercover assignments or he just didn't like her. Too bad. There was more at stake here than his delicate sensibilities. They needed to look as if they at least liked each other. And she couldn't resist messing with him a little.

She moved closer and leaned her head against his

shoulder. "You'd be surprised how romantic a jail cell can be. Right, Russ?"

His eyes narrowed, but he turned into Detective Adorable and smiled that special smile as he slid an arm around her waist. "Don't spread that around."

"I wouldn't dream of it."

"So, this is an official visit?" Jordyn Leigh asked. "You wanted to ask me about the night of the Traub-MacCallum wedding?"

"That's right," Russ said.

"You didn't really have to drag Lani along for this. I feel completely comfortable with anyone Sheriff Christensen trusts."

Lani knew there was a question buried in that statement and sent him an I-told-you-so look. She was going to cross that bridge he'd mentioned, and this would probably not make him happy.

"We're heading out to dinner after this. And it's so sweet. He wanted me to ride along with him. Keep him company."

"That's right." His voice had a slight edge to it.

"Very sweet." The other woman smiled. "What did you want to ask?"

Russ removed his arm from Lani's waist. "Sounds like you and your husband just moved in."

"We did. Right after we got married on the Fourth."

"By all accounts, that was sudden. Did you know Will was buying property when you married him?"

"Yes. We talked about it when I bumped into him at the wedding reception." She frowned. "Why do you ask?"

"It's a nice spread, and he's got plans to really make something of it." Russ stopped and looked at the new bride.

Lani recognized that this was his interrogation style and knew he was getting at a motive for spiking the punch. She knew this tough detective tactic was the fastest way to alienate Jordyn Leigh and shut off the free flow of information.

Lani made a stab at damage control. "You moved here from Thunder Canyon a couple years ago, right? Didn't you and Will know each other there?"

"We grew up together. I had a crush on him for a while, but he always treated me like a kid sister." Her eyes sparkled at the memory.

"So, when he showed up here in town for the wedding, did you think about giving him a push in a direction you wanted him to go?" Russ asked.

Lani wanted to elbow him in the ribs. He was about as subtle as a sledgehammer. Probably this approach worked with a hardened criminal in the precinct interrogation room while half the force was watching from the other side of the two-way window. But on someone as sweet and innocent as Jordyn Leigh Cates—now Clifton—it was going to backfire. She needed a lighter touch.

"What Russ means is, something must have shifted for Will, because it's all over town how much in love the two of you are," Lani said. "Talk about romantic. Since you two knew each other before, it can't be love at first sight. More like being struck by lightning?"

"Good question," Jordyn Leigh admitted. "I remember Will taking my punch away and implying that I was tipsy. But that was impossible because it's a public park and there's no hard liquor allowed."

"That didn't stop some folks," Russ interjected.

"Will said the same thing. But I was miffed and just got up and got another cup for myself. I poured him some, too, and we hung out the rest of the night."

"And what happened?" Lani asked.

"It's fuzzy after that. My next clear memory is waking up in the morning. With a monster hangover and a marriage license."

Russ nodded and his cop face relaxed. "The sheriff and I think the punch was spiked."

"Will thought mine was. I remember that from the reception. Before I don't remember anything," Jordyn Leigh said ruefully.

"Do you have any idea who might have wanted to get half the town wasted?" Lani asked.

The other woman shook her head. "But I have to say…"

"What?" Russ asked.

"I know you've been hired to find out what happened, and that folks are nervous, thinking someone is up to no good. I truly hope no one was seriously hurt that night, but Will and I would like to thank whoever did it. We found each other, thanks to that punch. It got us together, and he's the love of my life. We feel very blessed."

"Okay." Russ nodded politely. "I appreciate your time."

"If I can be of any further help, let me know," she said.

"Tell Will I said hello," Lani told her as they walked out the door.

"Absolutely. You two have a nice dinner." Jordyn Leigh smiled and waved.

Russ handed her into the truck then walked around to the driver's side and got in. "Just as I suspected. There's no way she's responsible."

"I agree." But something Jordyn Leigh said stuck with Lani. "Was anyone badly injured that night?"

"Not that we know of. Why?"

"Because it could just be a onetime prank. Or a case could be made that because there were no major consequences, another incident might be in the works."

"Gage and I had the same thought," Russ acknowledged.

"You could have said something."

"That theory could panic folks and is better not made public," he said.

"I see your point. What a mess."

At least Jordyn Leigh and Will found love and got a happy ending out of that night. They got together. Lani and Russ did, too, but love had nothing to do with it, and now he acted as if nothing had happened. She didn't know what to make of that.

If she were a man maybe she could pretend nothing of consequence took place. But she wasn't a man and was irritated that he didn't seem the least bit interested in her.

Still, there was no doubt in her mind that word would spread about their going out to dinner. She got more than a little satisfaction from the fact that to maintain this cover while working on his case, he would have to deal with her. Up close and personal.

Chapter Six

Russ opened the squeaky screen door at the Ace in the Hole and walked inside. He scanned the dimly lit interior for Lani as he always did, as he couldn't seem to avoid doing. If there was a way to keep himself from looking for her, he hadn't found it yet. But tonight he needed to talk to her. It had been a couple of days since the interview with Jordyn Leigh Clifton, and so far he hadn't come up with anything new. He was really hoping Lani had picked up something here at her job that would give him a lead to go on.

It was Saturday night of Labor Day weekend, and the place was more crowded than normal. The upcoming holiday gave him a sense of urgency in solving this mystery. He and Gage would be vigilant for the public community picnic in the park, but they couldn't be everywhere.

He finally spotted Lani delivering baskets of fries and burgers to a table where four cowboys were seated. She chatted with them for a few moments, laughing and smiling at whatever was said. If he didn't miss his guess, there was some major-league flirting on both sides.

She was single; Russ had no claim on her. But that didn't stop something dark and dangerous from coiling in his gut.

He walked through the place on his way to the bar and could tell exactly when most of the people inside knew the lawman had arrived. Conversation nearly stopped, and the noise level dropped noticeably. Everyone looked at him suspiciously. He was conscious of the change because that's the way the guys at his precinct in Denver had looked at him after he'd ratted out a dirty cop.

The circumstances were different, but obviously word had spread in Rust Creek Falls that he was working for Sheriff Christensen and asking questions in an official capacity.

He nodded to Lani on the way by and gave each of those overexcited cowboys a look with a message every guy understood: back off. Then he walked over to the bar and took the stool on the end that was all by itself. He wasn't sure when being a loner had started coming naturally, but that's the way he was now.

Moments later Lani walked up, a menu in her hand. "Hi."

He nodded. "How's it going?"

"That depends. In the last two days, more than one person has said they heard that you and I went out to dinner."

"But we didn't," he pointed out.

"I know and you know. But that's what we told Jordyn Leigh. Apparently, the Rust Creek Falls rumor mill is firing on all cylinders."

"Does it ever not?"

She thought for a moment. "When the power was out after the flood a couple years ago, it slowed down a lot because we didn't have phone service—cell or landline.

Other than that it always performs equal to or better than our expectations."

"So, folks in town think we're..."

"Dating." Her brown eyes were wary, waiting for a reaction.

A man could easily get caught up in those eyes, and Russ was trying his damnedest not to. But this temporary assignment required him to talk to her and word on the street was that they were going out, meaning he was interested. Just because he wasn't happy about that, it didn't make the conclusion wrong.

He studied her. "You don't look upset. Why is that?"

"We don't have to be covert about talking to each other. We can share information, and everyone will just think you're courting me."

"Do I look like the kind of guy who courts?" But he couldn't help smiling. She came out with some of the darnedest things, and it was getting harder to overlook the way her sunshine lit up the darkest corners of his soul.

"Call it what you want," she said. "Courting. Flirting. Set your cap for. Woo. Cozy up to. *Date.* I'm your ticket to not being an outsider. If people think you've got the hots for me, they'll let down their guard with you."

There was no *thinking* about it. He definitely had the hots for her. He'd proved that in a jail cell because he couldn't seem to help himself. And he hadn't been able to forget about her since. But she was right.

"Okay, then," he said. "Let's do something that will set the town rumor mill on fire."

Russ settled his hands on her hips and moved her between his legs. Those big brown eyes went wide with surprise, and her mouth formed an O. He just didn't have the reserves of willpower to keep himself from kissing her, just a soft touch of his lips to hers. It was barely contact, but set him on fire just the same.

"Well, color me fuchsia," she said against his mouth. There was a hitch in her breathing. "One picture is worth a thousand gossip-filled phone calls."

"Roger that." His own breathing was more unsteady than he would have liked. And he hoped the four guys who'd flirted with her were watching. "But you're working. I don't want to get you fired and lose a potential information stream."

"Right." With what looked an awful lot like real reluctance, she moved away and used the menu still in her hand to fan herself. "Speaking of that, have you found out anything?"

There was no one close enough to them to overhear, what with the noise level on a busy night. He didn't think a short exchange was a problem now that everyone thought they had a good reason for chatting.

"I was hoping you had something," he said.

"No. Does that mean you don't, either?"

He linked his fingers with hers and set their joined hands on his thigh. Just to maintain their cover, of course. "I've talked to the couple who got married that day and hosted the reception, their family and friends. I interviewed Bob and Ellie Traub, parents of the groom, who mixed up the punch. Just fruit juice and mixers and a little sparkling wine, that's all. They gave me no reason to think they're not telling the truth about the harmless ingredients used in making it."

"So we're back to square one?"

"Looks that way. Unless you overheard something here."

"Nothing." Her eyes turned darker and more troubled. "I can't think of anyone who would do something like this."

Her hand was starting to feel too natural in his, too good. He removed his fingers from hers and folded his arms over his chest. "My list of suspects hasn't changed."

She searched his face and came to a conclusion that made her mouth thin to a grim line. "And I'm on it."

The betrayal in her voice made him feel as if he'd kicked a kitten. He didn't like the feeling, and it brought out his defensive streak.

"Look at it from my point of view," he said. "I still don't know why you deliberately stole my keys to the jail cell and kept me locked up. Are you an accomplice? Working with someone else to keep the law busy? If I'd been out there where I should have been, maybe I'd have seen something, and whoever did this would be off the streets."

"We'll never know," she said, as the sparkle in her eyes flickered and went dark. "You have no reason to believe me, but I didn't do anything to the punch and I have no idea who did. For what it's worth, I do understand why you're skeptical about me."

"Generous of you." Russ hated that doubt about anyone he met was his go-to emotion now. It might be an asset for law enforcement but not the rest of his life. He'd never regretted it more than he did right this second. "But here's the thing that keeps tripping me up. Detective work is logical, and with you things just don't add up. It's that simple. If you want to come clean, that could change my mind."

She caught her bottom lip between her teeth then shook her head. "You have no idea how much I wish I could, but I made a promise. I have to honor that."

So she did have an ulterior motive, and it was about someone else. Under normal circumstances her loyalty might have impressed him, but nothing about this was ordinary. Someone had endangered people in this town, and he'd been hired to find out who. He had a promise to honor, too. From where he was sitting this looked an awful lot like a stalemate.

"I'll take that menu now," he said. "And could I get a beer?"

"Coming right up." It obviously wasn't easy, but she gave him a flirty smile.

Russ realized that she was pretty good at pretending. Although there was no denying the sparks between them. But he had to be skeptical of her motives and the sparks between them that refused to go away.

Lani returned and put a cocktail napkin on the scarred bar then set a bottle of beer on it. She smiled brightly, but the expression didn't match her words. "I really don't understand how you can use me in this investigation and still believe that I might be responsible for doing that to my friends and neighbors. My family was there, too."

Before he could tell her she had a point, she walked away. But that saying about keeping your friends close and your enemies closer kept running through his mind. Still, there was a part of him that didn't buy Lani Dalton as an enemy. He trusted Gage Christensen, and the man had urged Russ to use her as a reliable source.

In spite of his respect for Gage, he held tight to his skepticism. Russ had a sneaking suspicion that his doubts about Lani were all that stood between him and breaking his promise not to let another woman make a fool of him.

"Thanks for inviting me to dinner." Russ was sitting in the backyard at Gage Christensen's ranch house, not far from the heart of town.

"No problem," the sheriff answered. "Consider this a celebration for getting through the long Labor Day weekend without a repeat of the crisis on the Fourth of July."

"Definitely something to drink to." They clinked the long necks of their beer bottles.

Russ was enjoying this and the mild September air at the same time he was missing the friendly atmosphere of the Ace in the Hole. Or maybe the feeling was more about going three days without seeing the pretty brown-eyed brunette who worked there. But the last time he'd talked to her, she'd been pretty ticked off at him. Hell, he couldn't blame her. If someone accused him of getting the whole town drunk, he'd be mad, too.

The sun had just slipped past the mountains, and the yard was bathed in shade. On the patio, four Adirondack chairs with thick cushions formed a conversation area with a round table in the center. Gage had ribs and chicken in the smoker and his wife, Lissa, had set out appetizers: cheese, crackers, toasted French bread and some creamy vegetable dip.

"Eat up, Russ." After arranging everything on the table to her satisfaction, Lissa sat down beside him. She was a beautiful blue-eyed redhead, outgoing and friendly.

Russ put down his beer and took one of the small plates she'd set out. "If my appetite is spoiled, I'm blaming you."

"I'll send you home with leftovers if you can't eat dinner."

"You do know I'm staying at Strickland's Boarding House and there are no room refrigerators?"

"Then you'll just have to clean your plate. We thought it was time to have you over for a home-cooked meal. Right, Gage?"

"Right." The sheriff pointed to his wife and mouthed, *it was her idea.* Then he put the lid back on the smoker and joined them. "Lissa was worried about you being a lonely bachelor."

"*Worried* is a little strong." She picked up her glass of white wine and sipped. "But you uprooted your life to try to figure out who committed a crime here in our town. The least we can do is make you feel at home just a little."

Russ almost wished the couple had just let him be. Not that he didn't appreciate the gesture. They were friendly and entertaining, and the smells coming from that smoker made his mouth water. But from the second Lissa had opened the door and settled him out here on the patio, a feeling of dissatisfaction bordering on emptiness spread through him. Feminine touches were everywhere, from flowers and pictures to pillows and a hanging rack in the kitchen for pots and pans. This place felt like wedded-bliss central, and he envied these two people. If anything, being here made him feel more like a lonely bachelor than bunking at the boardinghouse. It was like being on the outside looking in.

"Speaking of feeling at home…" He looked at Lissa. "How do you like living in Rust Creek Falls after living in the city?"

"It's different," she said.

Following the flood that nearly destroyed Rust Creek Falls, she'd come here representing an organization called Bootstraps. Her mission was to help people rebuild their lives after losing homes and businesses. While she'd worked with Gage coordinating relief efforts, the two had fallen in love.

Russ had gone to Denver and understood how different a small town and big city were. None of his reasons for coming back to Montana were positive. That made him wonder about Lissa's response.

"Define *different*," he said.

"It's a slower pace. A lot less stress. People know your business." She sipped her wine, a thoughtful look on her face. "But I saw firsthand how everyone pulled together and helped each other. I love this place, where a person can count on their neighbors when the chips are down." She smiled and held out her hand to her husband, who was sitting beside her. When he took it and squeezed her fingers she said, "Plus, then I fell in love with this man. That sealed the deal for me because he wouldn't live anywhere else. And I couldn't live without him."

An image popped into Russ's mind of Lani, lying in his arms with her hair a mess and her dress all wrinkled. But she still managed to look more beautiful than any woman he'd ever met. That night, locked in the jail cell, she'd said almost the same thing about this town.

Russ looked at his friend. "What do you love about this place, Gage?"

"I have the best of all possible worlds." The sheriff, a muscular guy with brown hair and eyes, shifted in his chair. "There's this little piece of land that's mine. I have a few cattle and horses. And I really like being the sheriff of Rust Creek Falls. Helping folks and making sure everything in town runs like a well-oiled machine is satisfying in a way that I can't even put into words."

"Balance," Russ said.

"Exactly. And when something isn't in balance it bothers me." He sipped from his bottle of beer. "That's why I really want to know how and why so many people who are normally solid and steady ended up acting so out of their heads at that wedding. It's my responsibility to make sure it doesn't happen again."

"*Our* job," Russ said.

"Is there anything new on the investigation?" Lissa asked.

"Not yet. Everyone I talked to claims to have seen nothing. Although even if they had, most of them were in no condition to remember anything useful."

"There's at least one person who remembers an awful lot of details," Lissa commented.

"The gossip columnist," Russ said.

"Right." Lissa looked at each of them. "The person who writes the pieces in Sunday's edition of the *Rust Creek Falls Gazette* seems to have a whole lot of details from that night."

"How much confidence do you have in gossip?" Russ had read the back issues but wondered what the sheriff's wife thought.

"Well, I can't say that anything was a lie. Will and Jordyn Leigh *did* get married suddenly."

"But they're in love." When both of them gave him funny looks Russ said, "I talked to her, and she admitted that the effects of the punch lowered their inhibitions, but it all worked out and they're glad to have found each other."

Lissa nodded. "It's also true that Levi and Claire Wyatt had a falling-out that night. But their relationship seems stronger now that differences have been aired out so publicly. That happened because of being under the influence of whatever was in that punch." She snapped her fingers. "And don't forget that poker game where Brad Crawford won Old Man Sullivan's ranch. So whoever wrote those columns saw things."

"And I would give anything to know the identity of that person." Russ set his empty appetizer plate on the table and grabbed his beer bottle. "So, Lissa, any idea who's writing Rust Creek Ramblings?"

"How would I know?" Her blue eyes were blank for several moments then sparkled with humor when she caught his drift. "Because I'm a blogger you think I might have some psychic connection with another writer?"

"Long shot," he admitted. "But worth a try."

"I know it's a guilty pleasure, but I can't wait for the Sunday paper. Reading that column to find out what's going on with people is just too much fun."

"Whatever floats your boat." Russ shrugged.

"It does. And speaking of that…" Her eyes sparkled in a way that made him nervous. "I'm curious about something that wasn't in the paper."

"What?" Russ asked warily.

"You arrested Lani Dalton that night." She glanced at her husband. "And I have a reliable source who says the two of you were locked up together for a few hours."

"Really?" He looked at the sheriff.

"Sorry." Gage didn't look sorry. "She has her ways."

"I do." Lissa gave Russ her I'll-get-it-out-of-you look. "And I would really like to know what the two of you did to occupy yourselves for so long in jail."

He shrugged. "Oh, you know…"

She tilted her head and gave him a pitying look. "You seriously believe that's going to get you off the hook with me?"

"A guy can hope." When she shook her head, Russ sighed. Wild horses couldn't drag the whole truth out of him, but he could throw her a bone. "Okay. You win."

"And don't forget it. Now spill your secrets, Detective."

"Lani and I talked." At her look he added, "It was her idea."

"Now, there's a big surprise." Her tone was wry. "No one would accuse you of talking their ear off of your own free will."

"It's part of my charm." When Lissa laughed he thought his distraction had worked.

"So you expect me to believe you spent *hours* alone with a pretty girl like Lani and nothing happened besides conversation?"

"Like what?" He gave his friend a help-me-out-here look.

Gage stood and headed for the smoker. "I'm going to check the ribs."

Whatever happened to male solidarity? Russ wondered. Apparently, things changed when a man got married.

"Did you kiss her?" Lissa asked.

That was a loaded question, and he knew where it would lead. Russ decided on a flanking maneuver. "Did Gage tell you that she stole the keys to the cell to keep me locked in?"

"He did. What's your point?"

"People with nothing to hide, who have done nothing

wrong, don't do things like that." He shifted in his chair. "That means she can't be ruled out as a suspect."

"Lani Dalton? Seriously?" Lissa shook her head and looked at her husband, who had rejoined them. "What do you think?"

"I've known that girl and her family all my life. She's open, honest, loyal. Never been in trouble. If she's guilty, I'd take a dip in Badger Creek in the dead of winter."

"I'd like pictures of that," his wife teased.

"There won't be any because there's no way Lani did anything to that punch," Gage said emphatically.

Russ wanted to believe him but refused to let go of his doubts. Maybe that was an overabundance of caution, but he tended to think it was more about keeping her at a distance. Letting down his guard was the first step in trusting, and he wouldn't do that again.

Chapter Seven

After riding fences all day, Lani watched the sun sink lower in the sky as she headed back to Anderson's house on the Dalton ranch compound. She was hungry, dirty and tired, really looking forward to getting home to her parents' house in town for a hot shower and her mother's meatloaf. She rode into the barn and dismounted then led Valentino over to the water trough for a drink. She gave him a good rubdown and a generous portion of oats before walking to the house to see Anderson.

But as soon as she saw the familiar truck parked out front beside her own, it was clear that her plan for a hot shower and dinner was going to have to wait.

"Damn it, Russ," she muttered. "You better not be here to arrest Anderson."

Or accuse him of doctoring the punch. She was still annoyed about the other night when he'd insinuated she'd been responsible for getting the whole town drunk. The funny thing was that she didn't get the feeling his heart was all in on suspecting her. It was only after kissing her in front of everyone at the Ace in the Hole that he brought up the suspect list then aired his doubts about her. As if he was reinforcing his reasons for pushing her away. But everyone was a suspect, and the investigation could be the reason he was here at the ranch. She needed to find out what was going on.

She walked inside without knocking and found her brothers in the living room with the detective. His back was to her and she couldn't see his expression, but that body language didn't say relaxed.

"He threw the first punch when Travis wasn't looking, so I stepped in," Anderson was calmly explaining. "Skip Webster is a jealous hothead. Anyone in town will confirm that if you ask them."

Lani had slammed the door, and the wood floor didn't muffle the noise from her boots. It appeared no one had heard her come in, and she chalked that up to a surplus of testosterone making these three men deaf.

She didn't wait to be asked. "Skip Webster *is* a jealous hothead. That's exactly what went through my mind when I saw what happened."

At the sound of her voice, Russ turned. "Hi, Lani."

"Detective." She met his gaze, trying to decipher what was in his. She couldn't and decided she didn't much like the cop face that hid what he was thinking. "What brings you out here?"

"As I was just explaining to your brothers, I'm investigating all of the incidents that occurred after the Traub-MacCallum wedding. And that the sheriff and I believe the only reasonable explanation for why folks who are normally easygoing and law-abiding started acting crazy after drinking the punch is that it was spiked."

"What does that have to do with my brothers?" She walked past him to stand with Anderson and Travis. Her body language was telling Russ that this was three against one if he was going after Anderson for assault and battery when it so obviously had been self-defense.

"It's okay, Lani. No need for you to get involved," Anderson said. *Any more than you already are*, his look told her.

"I'm not here to single anyone out." Russ rubbed a hand across the back of his neck. "I'm interviewing everyone who was in the park that day, which is pretty much the whole town. Someone I spoke to remembered Travis and Anderson being there because of the altercation."

"It was stupid what happened," Anderson said. "Although that's just an impression, since the whole thing is kind of hazy. And you're right about people being rowdy, but Skip Webster throwing a punch is pretty much how he operates on a routine basis. He never pressed charges, by the way."

"I know."

Lani felt the heat and sharp accusation in Russ's hazel eyes when he looked at her. She knew he was thinking about being locked up that night instead of arresting her brother. He wouldn't forgive her for taking his keys, so it probably wasn't wise to point out that she'd saved him a pile of paperwork. Not to mention rescuing an indeterminate number of trees. The goal had been to keep her brother out of jail. Whatever was in that punch had given her the guts to do what she had to. And she was sworn to secrecy about her motive.

"Have you made any progress on the case?" she asked.

"None. I was just getting to that when you came in." His eyes narrowed first on Travis then Anderson. "Did either of you see or hear anything suspicious that night?"

"Besides the fact that you arrested my sister?" Travis said.

Lani felt Anderson tense and wished Travis hadn't

brought that up. She couldn't explain because it would lead to more questions she wasn't at liberty to answer. She had to do damage control.

"Like Russ said—" she met his gaze "—along with everyone else, I was acting weird, and it was getting pretty disorderly."

"I arrested her because she was going to hurt herself in that fountain. So I took her in for her own protection."

"He was there to maintain the peace," she confirmed.

"Maintaining the peace must have been a challenge when you were locked up in a jail cell with my sister." Travis had the angry, defensive big-brother thing down to a T.

Lani loved him for it, but barreling down this road wouldn't do Anderson any favors. "If it's all the same to you, Travis, that wasn't my finest hour, and I'd rather not talk about it. Except to say the whole thing was my fault, not Russ's."

The detective looked surprised that she'd backed him up. It bothered her that he would never know she had a good reason for doing the wrong thing.

Russ looked at her brothers. "The sheriff and I figure someone spiked the punch, and the subsequent individual behavior is a direct result of that illegal act, so no one will be held accountable. We're only interested in finding out who's responsible for drugging everyone and why."

"So it doesn't happen again, right, Detective?" she clarified.

"Exactly." He looked at her, and his eyes went smoky hot for a second before he shuttered the emotions.

"I'm not buying it." Travis still looked angry. "He's got a funny way of asking a question, making it sound more like an accusation."

"Easy, Trav—" Anderson put a steadying hand on his brother's arm. "I don't like it any more than you do, but he's the law."

It was so like Anderson to be the voice of reason, calming everyone around him. Now that she thought about it, Russ did the same thing. Maybe it had something to do with being the oldest sibling.

"He doesn't work for the Rust Creek Falls Sheriff's Department." Travis's gaze was full of suspicion. "Kalispell is his jurisdiction. And from what I hear, he's there because he couldn't hack it when he was with the Denver Police Department."

Lani was looking at Russ and saw the muscle jerk in his jaw. Clearly there was a story there, and she would give anything to hear what happened because it had obviously changed him—and she wanted to know everything about it. But this wasn't the time or place to discuss the matter.

"Look, you guys," she said to her brothers. "Maybe you've been spending too much time on the ranch, but here's the scoop. The sheriff hired Russ to investigate, and he's taken time from his life to do that. The least we can do is cooperate in order to get to the bottom of what happened."

"Be that as it may, he's an outsider," Travis commented. "If Gage Christensen asked me anything, I'd be happy to answer."

"That's the thing." Lani glanced up at her brother then back to Russ. "He's standing in for Gage, and we have an obligation to help. The fact that he isn't from around here makes him perfect for this. His objectivity won't be in question because he has no emotional investment in the outcome of the investigation."

Although Lani was wishing more and more that he had an emotional investment in *her*. She'd tried to stay mad at him for refusing to cross her off the suspect list. But as soon as she'd seen him here standing up to her brothers, her anger deserted her. And she really missed it.

"I heard that you're going out with him." Travis angled

his head toward Russ then gave her a challenging look. "What's up with that?"

It was too much to hope that gossip regarding their public kiss at the bar wouldn't get to her brothers. Normally, they didn't meddle in her relationships, but being questioned about that day in the park had pushed Travis's buttons.

"It's not serious. Russ and I are just getting to know each other," she said.

"That's right," he confirmed, but something flickered in his eyes.

"Are you sure about this?" Travis asked. "About him?"

"No one gets a guarantee about a person," she snapped. "That's why it's called becoming acquainted. And really, it's no one's business but mine."

"Understood," her brother said, but there was disapproval in the dark stare he leveled at her.

"Look, I'm only asking questions." Russ faced the other two men squarely, feet braced wide, looking them straight in the eyes. "Even though your memories of the night in question aren't clear, you might know something and not even realize it."

"You're asking if we saw anyone suspicious hanging around," Anderson guessed.

"Pretty much," Russ agreed.

"Look." Travis's voice had less of an edge, but the sarcasm was ratcheted up. "Everyone in town was at the reception. Everyone was getting something to drink. It was a hot day."

"Was there anyone you didn't recognize? A stranger? Someone who looked suspicious? Anything out of the ordinary?"

The two brothers looked at each other, clearly trying to remember, then shook their heads. Anderson spoke for both of them. “Community events are held in that park all the time, and I didn’t see anything different about this one.”

“Okay. I appreciate your help.” Russ nodded.

“Are we done here?” Travis asked.

“For now.” Russ glanced at each of them.

“Okay,” Lani said. “I’ll see you out. I’m heading back to town.” She looked at Travis, who’d driven his own truck to work today from their parents’ house. “See you at home. Bye, Anderson. See you in the morning.”

“Drive carefully,” he said.

She nodded then headed to the door with Russ behind her, certain that his gaze was on her back. Now that the tension was gone, she thought about her appearance. Spending the day on horseback didn’t lend itself to looking cover-girl gorgeous. She was dusty and sweaty, and if she took off her Stetson there would be serious hat hair. Not to mention no makeup and grime all over her face. He was probably thanking his lucky stars that they weren’t actually dating.

Walking down the porch steps, she felt the need to say something. “Travis and Anderson aren’t normally so prickly.”

“I didn’t think they were.” His expression was cop face again.

“No one is at their best when being questioned about a crime.”

Duh. He already knew that better than she ever could. She’d defended him to her brothers and was now doing the same for her brothers. For reasons she didn’t quite get, it was important that Russ didn’t think the worst of her family.

“My brothers are good men. Not perfect. They have flaws, but would never do anything dishonorable.”

“I get that, Lani.” He walked over to her truck and

opened the driver's-side door. "I'll follow you back to town."

"Okay. Thanks." Lani wasn't ready to say goodbye, but after she climbed in he closed the door, indicating that he wanted to be done. "See you."

"Right." He turned his back and walked to his truck.

If he hadn't cut this short, she knew she would have babbled on and defended herself. Told him again that she wasn't in the habit of throwing herself at handsome cops in a jail cell, but he didn't give her the chance. All business, all the time for Detective Russ Campbell.

That was probably for the best, she told herself. Otherwise he might confirm that the intimate moment they'd shared in that jail cell meant nothing to him.

"Lani, I need to talk to you."

Starting a conversation like that never meant anything good, Lani thought. She hadn't even closed the front door before hearing her father's voice from the kitchen. When Ben Dalton was waiting for her, she knew her shower and dinner were going to have to wait a little longer.

"Hi, Dad." She walked into the room, and the good smells coming from the oven made her stomach growl. "Where's Mom?"

"She had to run to Crawford's. Something about making gravy."

"Mmm." She was barely back in control after seeing Russ at the ranch, and now this. What the heck was going on? The last time her father said he needed to talk to her she'd been a teenager, and he took away her cell phone until her geometry grade improved. "What's up, Dad?"

Her father was a tall man, about six foot two, with some silver running through his brown hair. It was a family joke that his kids had turned him gray. And he was looking so serious right now, it was a wonder his hair didn't turn white on the spot. The man had no belly fat and didn't make a habit of imbibing, so it was a surprise when he pulled a beer out of the refrigerator, twisted the cap off and took a long swallow. Good Lord, she'd driven him to drink!

He set the longneck bottle on the granite-topped island beside him. "Anderson just called."

"Oh?" She figured it had something to do with Russ's visit, but as a lawyer's daughter she'd learned not to say much before knowing the full scope of the situation.

"He said Detective Campbell was at the ranch asking questions about a fight at the July Fourth wedding."

"That's true."

"Did you know that Anderson decked Skip Webster that day?" Ben was wearing a white dress shirt with sleeves rolled up and his red tie loosened, not the way he would appear in court. But that authoritative voice firing the question made it feel as if she was in the witness box with judge and jury looking on.

In her mind she heard the words: swear to tell the truth, the whole truth and nothing but the truth. So help you God.

"I'm waiting, Lani."

"Yes, sir. I knew Anderson hit Skip. For the record, the jerk had it coming. He threw a punch, the first one, at Travis. When he wasn't looking. Anderson did what he had to do."

"You saw what happened?"

"Yes."

Ben took another pull on his beer. "I'd heard that Gage Christensen hired Detective Campbell to find out why everyone went off the rails that night."

"I heard that, too." Because Russ had told her himself.

"It's a good idea. And folks will rest easier knowing that something is being done." But her father was frowning. "I just never expected my family to be accused of spiking that punch."

"Russ wasn't accusing, just asking questions, Dad. Gathering information. It put Travis on the defensive. You of all people should know that Russ can't play favorites if he's going to get to the bottom of this."

"I do know. That doesn't mean I like it." He toyed with the bottle sitting on the island, turning it in his fingers.

"He's talking to everyone who was in the park that night." She leaned her back against the cupboards across from him and folded her arms over her breasts.

"Have you spoken with Detective Campbell about this before today?"

"I was the first one questioned." Possibly because of her behavior in the jail cell that night.

"Why?"

What she did wasn't something she could share with her father. "Because Gage told him that my access to the public could be useful, and Russ must have agreed."

"Why?" her father asked again.

She wished it was because he liked, respected and wanted her with an intensity that burned bright and hot but that wasn't the case.

"Why not start with me?" she said instead. "It's as good a place as any, what with the flow of customers in and out of the Ace in the Hole on any given day. People tend to say too much when they're drinking. I might have inadvertently come across information to help him in the investigation."

"Did you?"

"No."

"I don't mind telling you that I'm very concerned, Lani." Her father's expression was grave.

"I can see why. In a town that prides itself on community and fellowship, it would be a shame to cancel public celebrations because of what happened."

"That's true. But I actually meant that I'm concerned about you."

Back to not embellishing at the risk of giving away something she didn't intend to. "Oh?"

"I know what you're doing." Her father's look was wry. "I taught you."

"What?"

"Answer everything with a one-word question when you're trying to hide something."

"Why would I?" That was a three-word answer. "I have nothing to hide." Liar, liar, pants on fire. If there was a deception buzzer, it would have sounded just then.

"Okay." Her dad looked at the floor for several moments then met her gaze. "Then tell me this. Why did Russ Campbell arrest you that night?"

"You know why. All of Rust Creek Falls knows why. It was in the *Gazette*, in that gossip column."

"Tell me again." He was in full lawyer mode now.

"I drank the punch. Along with everyone else, I was completely unaware that it was spiked and made me drunk and do things I wouldn't ordinarily do. I jumped into the fountain at the park. It was hot and the water was refreshing."

Some of the heat she'd experienced was less about summer weather and more about her close proximity to Russ Campbell. Again, not something she planned to share with her father, of all people!

"I think there's more to it than that." He gave her the dad stare, which intensified exponentially when he threw in some attorney-on-the-attack technique. "If I have the timeline right, Anderson was involved in that altercation just before you took your act into the water."

"So?"

"Really?" He looked at her. "That's not going to work."

"I object."

"You don't get to. This isn't a court of law. But points for trying." His grin was fleeting.

"I'm not sure what you want me to say, Dad."

"The truth would be good." He dragged his fingers through his hair. "You're involved in something."

"What do you mean?" A four-word response. Proof that he was gaining the upper hand.

Their father was an exceptional lawyer; Anderson should let him help with his legal problem. But they'd gone over that and he refused then swore her to secrecy. She'd never realized how truly awful it was to be caught in the middle.

"What I mean is that Anderson told me," her father said.

This was where she couldn't afford to get trapped and involuntarily spill something. "What did he tell you?"

"He said Detective Campbell was going to arrest him for assaulting Skip, and you created a diversion in the fountain."

"He told you that when he called a little bit ago?"

Her father shook his head. "It was a day or two after the fact."

"Then why are you asking me about it now?"

"Because now there's a police investigation into the park incident that endangered folks who unknowingly got drunk. And you were arrested during that incident. This has taken a serious turn. A detective is asking questions, and if I'm going to protect my kids, I need to know the truth."

"You know it already, Dad. Like Anderson said, I created a distraction to keep him from being arrested."

Lani knew her father was only trying to help, but the truth she'd been entrusted with weighed heavily on her. That put a defensive note in her voice. This interrogation was headed to a place where she'd have to draw a line in the sand, and she hated doing that. Ben Dalton was the most honest and loyal man she knew, and he set a high bar for his children. She looked up to him and tried to be like him. By that standard, she needed to guard the secret entrusted to her.

"What I don't understand is why you got involved. Anderson can take care of himself."

Not this time, she wanted to say. Her big brother had always been there for her. Taught her how to drive; and when she dinged the bumper of his new truck, instead of yelling at her, he made her get back in and drive it until her confidence was restored. When Lani and a couple friends toilet-papered the house of a popular boy who bullied some of the weaker kids, her brother took the blame to keep her from a grounding that would've made her miss the Homecoming dance. He was like their father, loyal and strong. And she wanted to be that for him.

She met her father's gaze without flinching. "He was protecting Travis, and I protected him. It's what Daltons do."

"I know." But her father was looking at her as if he could see into her soul.

She really hoped he couldn't because she would never willingly betray Anderson's trust.

"The problem is," he continued, "Russ Campbell spent some time locked in that cell along with you. That was also in Rust Creek Ramblings. I know it's gossip and so left it alone. Until now. But as I said, things have taken a turn, and we have more questions than answers."

"I know, Daddy." The worried look in his eyes made her move closer and put her arms around him. She pulled back and met his gaze, willing him to understand and not judge even though she couldn't give him all the facts. "I can only say that I had a very good reason for spending the night in jail. Fortunately, there were no legal consequences. Besides, in my own defense it has to be said that I was a victim of the spiked punch, too."

"Yes, but you made the conscious choice to intervene for your brother."

"I did. And you're not going to like this, but I can't tell you why."

"You're right. I don't like it." Was it a trick of the overhead lighting, or did he have more gray hair than a few minutes ago?

"I won't say I've never given you reason to worry," she started.

"Good. Because I'd take issue if you did." He smiled. "A father will always worry most about his daughters. It's part of the job description."

"Let me rephrase. I can say that I've never given you reason not to trust me."

He nodded. "That's the truth. You're a good girl."

"You and Mom taught us to put family first. I'm asking you to keep trusting me without all the facts. I know what I'm doing, Dad."

He studied her for a long moment and finally nodded. "Okay."

She kissed his cheek. "I'm going to take a long, hot shower."

"Good. I was going to say something—" The teasing expression was back on his face and, knowing him, that wasn't easy to pull off.

Lani headed upstairs feeling both better and worse. It was technically true that there were no legal consequences from her actions that night. But the personal ones were unsettling and ongoing. She hated that she was keeping the truth from the best parents on the planet, but awed that they trusted her in spite of it.

If only Detective Dreamy would give her the benefit

of the doubt. Even the sheriff vouched for her, but Russ refused to be swayed.

Maybe skepticism was a by-product of being a cop. Or the reason was something more personal. Something that caused him to leave Denver and come back to Montana.

It was time to find out which.

Chapter Eight

Russ had Lani's cell number on speed dial and had been fighting the urge to use it. Two days ago she'd defended him to her brothers, and he didn't know what to make of that. And her.

Now it was Sunday. He'd been working seven days a week since starting the investigation, and Gage insisted he take the day off and clear his head. Now the prospect of a very long day stretched in front of him.

And before he could stop himself, Russ hit the call button. Now he'd done it. Maybe she wouldn't pick up.

"Hello?"

And there was the sugar-and-spice-with-a-splash-of-sexy voice that took his breath away. "Hi, Lani."

"Russ. What's up?"

Damned if he knew, but now he was on the spot. "I know Friday and Saturday are busy at the bar. Just wondered if you've heard anything."

"Not so far."

He looked around the room he'd been renting at Strickland's Boarding House. It was neat as a pin and lonely as a space walk. The bed was covered by a quilted spread without a single wrinkle, and that made him think about twisted sheets and tangled legs. The problem with hearing her voice was that it gave him a powerful need to see her.

"Maybe it's time to shake up the investigation," he suggested.

"How?"

"Good question." He blew out a long breath. "Maybe we should get together and brainstorm."

"Well, I—"

"You've got plans." The depth of his disappointment was surprising. "Another time."

"Not so fast. The thing is, my mom cooks dinner for the family every Sunday, and expects us all to be there. Very few excuses get sanctioned. I'll have to figure out what to tell her."

"You're not planning to say anything about being involved in the investigation?" He didn't like the idea of not having that excuse to see her.

"Of course not. I just meant it's important for me to come up with an acceptable reason for not being here. Since I'm not bleeding, on fire or just had a baby, I need to get creative."

"What about meeting my family?"

"Well," she said thoughtfully, "they think we're going out, so it's a logical next step. As lies go it would probably work because one of the ironclad Dalton rules is family first."

"It wouldn't be a lie if we actually go to the farm." In for a penny, in for a pound, he thought. "I'll pick you up in an hour."

"Okay."

Russ didn't want it to be the truth, but suddenly his day off looked a whole lot more exciting.

It was late in the afternoon when Lani sat in the passenger seat of Russ's truck as he drove toward Boulder Junction, the small town halfway between Rust Creek Falls and Kalispell. Her parents happened to be together when she broke the news about not being there for Sunday dinner. She knew her dad told her mom everything, including the conversation they'd had after Russ interviewed her brothers. And she could see the curiosity in her parents' eyes, but they were on their best behavior when Russ came to the door to get her. There was no interrogation and she appreciated that they trusted her.

"Your parents are very nice." It was as if Russ was reading her mind.

"I know. And now they're very curious about us."

"Oh?"

"When I told them you were taking me to meet your family, I was questioned relentlessly about how serious we are."

His mouth curved up, but aviator sunglasses hid the expression in his eyes. "Then you've already had a preview of what to expect from my family. Just maintain your cover and follow my lead."

"Yes, sir. Understood, sir."

He laughed and she felt an unexpected sense of satisfaction because that didn't happen often. Sometimes being with him felt easy and natural, not an act. A peek into what it could be like if they hadn't started out on the wrong foot. Best not to think about what might have been and concentrate on what was happening now.

During the drive, Lani waited for him to bring up the investigation, but by the time they reached the Campbell farm he hadn't mentioned it. Just over a rise she could see a two-story yellow clapboard house with white trim. Behind it there was land as far as she could see, planted with different crops that formed a sort of natural patchwork.

Russ pulled into the curved drive and parked his truck in front of the house. Beyond it, down a dirt road, there were outbuildings that no doubt contained tools and equipment. She could see a green tractor and another huge machine. No idea what it did for a living. Trees shaded the house, and the grass in the yard was neatly trimmed. Shrubs and flowers lined the walkway up to the solid oak front door.

"This is very charming," she said.

"Yeah." He took off his sunglasses and set them on the dashboard. "Let's go get the interrogation over with, then I'll give you a tour of the place and we can talk about the case."

"Okay."

After exiting the vehicle, they walked up two steps to the front door, where Russ knocked. Moments later a pretty young woman answered.

"Hi, Addie."

"Russ." The green-eyed redhead grinned then gave him a big hug. "I didn't know you were coming."

"Surprise."

Addie looked at her, one auburn eyebrow lifting. "And who's this?"

"Lani Dalton. A friend." He put his hand at her waist, apparently remembering their cover. "Lani, this is my little sister, Adeline."

"Russell, you know I hate that name." She winced. "Addie will do."

Lani shook her hand. "It's lovely and old-fashioned."

"That's what Mom says and exactly what I don't like about it." She pulled the door wide. "She'll be happy to see you, big brother. And to meet your friend. Everyone is here for dinner. Don't be afraid, Lani."

"I've got three brothers and two sisters. I'm not easily intimidated." But now that they were actually here, she *was* a little nervous.

Just inside was a formal dining room where the large table was set for dinner. The wood-plank floor of the entry led to the kitchen with stainless-steel appliances, double ovens and cooktop. Very modern and not quite what Lani had pictured in a farmhouse. This place could be in a photo shoot for *Better Homes and Gardens* magazine.

"Look who's here," Addie announced.

A woman who looked to be in her fifties turned from stirring something. She had short, stylishly cut brown hair and hazel eyes. Russ's eyes. She smiled and, like her son, it transformed her appearance.

"You should have told me you were coming." She looked at Lani. "And that you were bringing someone."

Russ looked down at her. "Lani, this is my mother, Teresa Campbell. Mom, Lani Dalton."

"It's nice to meet you," Teresa said.

"Same here," Lani answered.

"Everyone come meet Russ's friend," his mom ordered.

Three men were standing in the spacious adjoining family room, their attention focused on a wall-mounted flat-screen TV and the football game that was on. They took one last glance then did as directed and walked into the kitchen.

Russ shook hands with all three then made introductions. "This is my father, John," he said, indicating the older man with dark, silver-streaked hair. "My brothers, Micah and Carson."

When he moved closer to shake her hand, she noticed Micah's expression was just this side of wary, and he had a limp. She couldn't help wondering about it. The twinkle in

Carson's brown eyes reminded her of Travis's mischievous streak, and she pegged him as the youngest of the boys.

"It's a pleasure to meet all of you." Lani smiled.

"Tell me you're staying for dinner. Both of you," Teresa said.

Lani looked at Russ, giving him a look that said it was time for him to take the lead. "I don't know—"

"It's been a long time since you were here for Sunday dinner, Russell James."

"Uh-oh," Lani said. "It's never good when your mom uses both names. When I hear Lani Elizabeth it makes me want to put myself in time-out."

Everyone laughed, including Russ, and the tension she'd sensed in him eased.

"Yeah, Mom, we can stay. I'd like that if it's not too much trouble," he said.

"Of course not. I always make too much food."

A little while later, after extra places had been set and drinks handed out, they were sitting around the dining room table, passing fried chicken, mashed potatoes, salad and corn. When plates were filled they started eating, and the interrogation commenced.

"So, how did you and Russ meet?" Teresa asked.

Lani probably would have choked if she'd been chewing food. She should have expected the question. Her bad. But now she had to wing it, no pun intended to the chicken.

"It was on the Fourth of July. There was a wedding reception going on in the park, and Russ was on duty." That was the truth, but not the whole truth.

"You all know I fill in when needed," he said. "Gage Christensen has been my friend for a long time, and he's the sheriff of Rust Creek Falls. With one deputy short, he asked for my help."

"Gage is a nice young man. I bet he's as glad to have you back from Colorado as we are," his mom said. "And it's about time you brought a young lady to Sunday dinner." She turned to Lani and whispered, "He's been lonely since things ended with Alexis."

Lani saw his mouth pull tight. She wanted to hear about this probably way more than he wanted to talk about it.

"That woman was a witch," Addie said. "Probably still is."

At the head of the table John was nodding. "You dodged a bullet there, son. And leaving Denver was probably a blessing in disguise. Colorado's loss is our gain."

Russ shifted in his chair. "Dad, I—"

"Aren't you conducting a special investigation in Rust Creek Falls?" Micah asked, bailing out his brother.

"Yeah." Russ sent him a grateful look.

Lani figured that level of gratitude over changing the subject meant Russ would rather take a sharp stick in the eye than talk about either of those subjects. That made her curious and even extra determined to find out the details, maybe discover what made Russ Campbell tick. But he was off and running with an explanation of spiked punch and small-town anxiety. This wasn't the time to question him.

After the table was cleared, dishes cleaned up and leftovers put away, Teresa suggested Russ take Lani for a walk—show her around the property—and he jumped at the chance. It might have been about being alone with her, but she figured he just wanted to steer clear of their references to his past.

Side by side they walked up the road leading to the outbuildings, and he showed her the equipment and machinery that made farming on such a large scale possible. He pointed out where the different crops were planted, but that was only what they could see from this vantage point. Not too far from the house he stopped beside Boulder Creek, a valuable water source for the farm.

It was also a pretty spot with spruce and pine trees on

either side. The water cheerfully gurgled over rocks, and Lani sighed as she took in the peaceful surroundings.

She had a feeling what she was about to say was just the opposite of peaceful, but she was compelled to ask anyway. "Who's Alexis, and why did you leave the Denver Police Department?"

A dark look slid into his eyes and a muscle tightened in his jaw.

"You don't beat around the bush, do you?"

"No point. I'd be lying if I said I wasn't curious." She stared at him. "So what brought you back to Montana?"

"Let's just call it irreconcilable differences."

"The reason most often given for a divorce and just as empty of personal details." She shook her head. "Come on, Russ. Something happened. What made you leave—"

He reached out a finger and traced it over her mouth, a smoldering look in his eyes. Before she could regroup and finish asking her question, his mouth was on hers. The contact was like a zap of electricity and just as effective in frying her thoughts. Heat poured through her, pooling in her belly. His arms came around her, snuggling her closer, pressing her breasts against his chest.

He threaded his fingers into her hair, cupping the back of her head, holding her still while his tongue caressed the inside of her mouth and dueled with hers. He kissed her for a long time, sweetly, tenderly, gently, thoroughly, completely messing up her head.

Finally, he pulled back and fortunately didn't remove his arms, because she was fairly certain her weak legs wouldn't support her weight. The only sounds were their ragged breathing mingled with the babbling stream rushing past them.

Lani blinked up at him, and rational thought slowly returned. "So… As a distraction technique, that was pretty effective."

The corner of his mouth curved up nearly to adorable territory. "Did it work?"

"I got the message, if that's what you're asking. You don't want to talk about it."

"Smart girl."

"At least this time you picked a decent setting to kiss me. This is leaps and bounds better than the Ace in the Hole or a jail cell."

"I aim to please."

"No, you don't." If only. "Your goal was to avoid opening up about your past."

"There's no point." It was a surprise that he didn't deny the accusation. He let her go and stared at the gurgling stream. "Water under the bridge."

"I get the feeling it's a dark and twisty story." She saw his mouth thin and held up a hand. "I won't push. Don't worry."

"I appreciate that."

"You're welcome."

It cost her a lot to hold back the questions. If she wasn't starting to care about him, she would have asked whatever she wanted and damn the consequences. But she was starting to care about him a lot and didn't want to rock the boat. At least not yet.

He'd lied to Lani.

Russ had kissed her because he couldn't resist. He hadn't done it to distract her from asking about his past, but couldn't argue that stopping the questions was a happy by-product of his actions.

It was now Friday night, almost a week since taking her to the farm. Every day they'd chatted on the phone to compare notes about the investigation, and he always managed to keep her on longer because she made him laugh.

He liked her. More than he wanted to.

For the weekend he was taking a break from the investigation and patrolling the annual carnival for Rust Creek Falls Elementary School. Traditionally, this fund-raiser was held soon after Labor Day, when classes started up again. This year was no different, although the mayor and town council had urged the sheriff to be more vigilant after what happened on the Fourth of July. This was another public gathering, and there would be food and drinks, which put everyone on edge.

So here he was in the park. He stopped by the infamous fountain where he and Lani first clashed and saw her not far away in the bake-sale booth. Stalls were lined up parallel with the parking lot and contained various games and activities designed to make money that would fund school supplies, computers and extracurricular programs.

Lani was wearing a red apron that said Rust Creek Falls Elementary School in white letters, and her hair was pulled back in a sassy ponytail. She took a bill then smiled and gave a woman a plastic bag containing sugar cookies. That smile went straight through him, cranking up the tension already coiled tightly inside him every time he saw her or thought about her.

Through everything that happened in Denver, his professionalism had never slipped, but it was now when all he could think about was kissing Lani Dalton. As much as he would like to trust her, he had to focus on rebuilding his career, making up for the time he'd lost. He couldn't afford a distraction, to blindly put his faith in another woman—especially a woman with a secret.

Checking his watch, he realized it was time to put his cop skills back to work, because he wasn't being paid to look at Lani. It was getting late, and tonight's activities were almost over. Only a few people were milling around, and most of them were shutting down the booths until tomorrow morning.

The food was closed up and secured. Most of it was prepackaged, making tampering difficult. Everything else was being supervised by the school principal. If anyone started acting weird, he would know who to question.

Lani was counting money and didn't notice him right away. When she glanced up, the automatic smile that normally came so easily to her disappeared.

"Hi," she said.

"Evening." He slid his fingertips into the pockets of his jeans. "Everything quiet?"

"If you mean has anyone spiked the cupcake icing, the answer is no."

Her voice was a little cool, and he could understand why. Taking her to meet his family sent a certain message, one he hadn't meant to send. Everyone had told him how much they liked her, but he wasn't after their approval. He didn't need it, since there wasn't now and never would be anything serious between him and Lani. But then he'd kissed her and claimed it was nothing more than a distraction. As mixed messages went that was a doozy.

"Good. Nothing out of the ordinary." He nodded. "After what happened on the Fourth, we can't be too careful."

"Do you really think it could happen again?"

"My gut says no, but until we find the creep who did it, there's no way to know for sure." Shadows lurked in her dark eyes and made Russ want to protect her from whoever had messed with the punch that July day. It was a given that guarding everyone in town was part of his job, but with Lani the feeling was very different. Intense. And more personal than he cared to admit. "Are you finished for the night?"

She nodded. "I just have to give this money to Carol Watson, the parent coordinator in charge of this whole thing."

Just then an attractive brunette walked up beside him.

"Hi, Russ. It's so reassuring to have a law enforcement presence."

"Carol." Russ had met her during a final logistics meeting for this fund-raiser. Like everyone else in town, she was nervous about any community event since the wedding. "Everything is quiet."

The woman nodded. "Lani, how was business?"

"Good. Almost everything sold out." She handed over a blue zippered cash bag.

"Excellent. I've got volunteers lined up for Saturday and Sunday to donate more baked goods. Fingers crossed that the volume of customers keeps up."

"I'm pretty sure it will," Lani said. "Takes more than a little spiked punch to scare off the people of this town. Traditionally, folks in Rust Creek Falls support their school."

"From your mouth to God's ear," Carol said. "What happened on the Fourth was shocking and could scare even our resilient citizens off."

"We've been spreading the word that the sheriff's office has an increased presence," Russ said. "Everything possible is being done to make sure this fund-raiser goes smoothly."

"I know. And your vigilance is appreciated." She smiled but it was tense around the edges. "Lani, thanks for pitching in."

"No problem," Lani said. "My sister Paige teaches at the school and can be very persuasive in encouraging Dalton family volunteerism."

"Still…thank you." She nodded at both of them. "Good night."

Russ watched Lani put the few remaining cookies, cupcakes and brownies into a pink bakery box before grabbing her purse. She looked at him. "Good night, Russ."

He wasn't ready to say good-night. "I'll walk you to your car."

"I left it at home. Didn't want to deprive a paying customer of a parking space, since my house isn't that far from here."

"Then I'll give you a ride home," he said.

"That's all right." She exited the rear of the booth and came around to where he was standing. "See you around."

"Just a second." He loosely curled his fingers around her upper arm to stop her. "You've been on your feet all night. Might feel good to sit."

"I'm used to standing."

The outdoor park lights illuminated her tight expression. "What's bugging you, Lani?"

"Other than someone who gets their kicks from watching a whole town get drunk? That's not enough for you?" Her mouth pulled tight. "That really bugs me. People were trying not to be, but they were on edge tonight. This is supposed to be a fun and carefree event. It wasn't, and that's frustrating. Even working together we can't figure out who did it."

Her clipped tone and the pinched look on her face were evidence that she'd been feeling the pressure of watching out for suspicious behavior. She wasn't used to that, and it had taken a toll. Gently, he took the bakery box out of her hands.

"I'm taking you home."

There was a moment of hesitation before she nodded. "Okay."

Side by side they walked across the grass to the parking lot, where his truck was one of the few vehicles left. Gage's cruiser was still there, so he knew his friend was on alert. He opened the door for Lani and waited until she'd climbed inside. Then he went around to the driver's side and deposited the box of baked goods on the rear seat before getting behind the wheel.

Russ could practically feel the waves of anxiety rolling through her. "Talk to me, Lani."

"Everything is different since that day," she said. "This carnival used to be fun for the kids and parents, but now it's a big headache." She glanced over at him. "How do I know I'm not selling a child a cupcake that will make them sick?"

There was no way to be sure, but he wouldn't tell her that. He put the key in the ignition, started the car and backed out of the space. Then he exited the lot and turned right toward her house.

"Every precaution has been taken," he said. "The sign-ups were completely controlled. Items delivered were checked off a master list. Nothing was accepted without being on that list. All of the names were run by Gage and the school's administrative staff. We know who baked what and can cross-reference if anyone reports a problem. No one would try anything because the odds of getting caught are pretty high."

"But it's not impossible."

"True." He thought for a moment. "But the incident with the punch was different. No one expected it. No one was prepared. Now we're watching. If there's a tainted batch of cupcakes, it would be small-scale and easy to identify who did it. No one would take the risk."

"That makes sense." She sighed. "But I hate this. One person is ruining things for everyone."

"Yeah."

"I can't believe our investigation hasn't turned up a darn thing. We're no closer to finding out the truth."

"Not yet." If she'd noticed that he used their investigation as an excuse to see her Sunday then never brought the subject up, she didn't mention it.

"I'm not so sure anymore."

It bothered him that her fundamental trust in the goodness of people was shaken, and he wanted badly to reassure her. "I've been a detective for a long time. You never know when you'll get a lead that will break a case wide-open."

"Maybe sometimes it's necessary to do something to make things break your way."

Russ didn't like the sound of that. "What does that mean?"

"It's time to shake things up and see what happens." Those words were laced with a whole lot of stubborn.

"Never underestimate the value of pounding the pavement and the interview process from a law enforcement perspective."

"That's not working for me," she said.

He pulled the truck to a stop in front of her house, and the overhead light went on when she opened the door. Determination was written all over her face, and he had a bad feeling. "Whatever you're planning to do...don't."

"Brad Crawford won Old Man Sullivan's ranch in a poker game that night. I believe you would call that motivation." She met his gaze. "I'm going to get Brad to ask me out on a date, and then I'll find out what he knows."

"No, Lani. It could be dangerous and—"

She slammed the door and hurried into the house, effectively cutting off his protest. Frustration rolled through him, and he hit the steering wheel with the flat of his palm. Pain radiated up his arm but also cut through his irritation and let in a dose of reality.

It wasn't his detective instincts that were objecting to her going out with Brad Crawford. He didn't want her alone with another guy.

He was jealous.

Chapter Nine

Lani refused to give in to the yearning to turn and look at Russ driving away. She walked into the house, closed the door behind her then leaned her forehead against it. It occurred to her that he might be jealous at the idea of her going out with Brad Crawford, then she realized that was crazy and possibly a little pathetic. Darn him anyway. She swore he wouldn't get to her, but somehow he always did. There was something about the confident way he walked, the cocky tilt of his head, that adorable smile—when he chose to use it.

Things with him changed direction so fast a girl had no idea where she stood. One minute he was kissing her senseless, the next he treated her as a suspect in his case.

"Lani?"

Her sister's voice came from the kitchen. Lindsay must be home for the weekend. Busy with her last semester of law school before she'd study for the bar exam, she didn't have a lot of time to spare, though she tried to get back home as often as possible. But this visit was unexpected, and Lani wondered what was up. She headed in that direction and found her sister opening a bottle of Chardonnay. There were two wineglasses sitting on the island.

"How did you know I needed this?" Lani asked.

"Mom said you were working the carnival." There was a "duh" in her sister's voice as she poured the wine. "And I couldn't help noticing that the very hot and sexy Detective Campbell dropped you off. Again."

Lani didn't want to talk about that. She just took the glass her sister handed over and said, "You know me too well, sis. Thanks."

"And you know me." She held her wineglass up. "Let's drink to sisters before men."

"Right on." They clinked glasses and sipped. Lani thought her sister looked troubled. "Everything okay?"

"Oh, you know how it is. Men suck."

"Barry didn't meet your expectations?"

Lindsay's expression was wry. "I have an expectation of fidelity when a man suggests we be exclusive. Apparently, his interpretation of being faithful was different." She sighed, and the miserable look was back. "I caught him with his secretary. On the desk."

"Ouch." Lani winced. "But seriously, could that be any more clichéd?"

"I know, right? Absolutely no creativity." Her sister toyed with the end of her ponytail. There was a frown in her blue eyes. "Except that what they were doing on that desk showed quite a bit of imagination—and passion that I never experienced with him."

Lani's heart hurt for her sister. She gave her a quick, hard hug. "You know, I could tell you he's not worth crying over. There's someone out there for you who's ten times the man Barry is. That he'll get what's coming to him. But I'm not going to."

"Really?" Lindsay's eyebrows rose.

"Nope. Not going to go there," she confirmed. "Instead, I say we get Anderson, Travis and Caleb to pay him a visit."

"That's like putting out a hit on him. If I'm going to be a lawyer and an officer of the court, I can't condone that kind of behavior." But she grinned, and her unhappiness faded for a few moments.

"But it's not a hit," Lani insisted. "If the three of them simply walk into his office, Barry will start to sweat. Our brothers don't have to do anything but stand there and look like the avengers they could be. They're a pretty imposing threesome."

"The plan does have a certain appeal." Thoughtfully, she tapped her lips then shook her head. "Going to that much trouble would make him think I care."

"You do," Lani reminded her.

"Sadly. But ignoring him will put a dent in that ego of his. That's where he's vulnerable." Lindsay looked fierce for a moment before her eyes turned dark and tragic. "We talked about plans for the future. I was going to join his law practice and help him take on high-profile property development. That's not going to happen now."

"Better to find out before jumping into the deep end of the pool." Lani was aware that her sister already knew that. She also knew that right this minute the truth of the statement wouldn't make Lindsay feel any better. Only time would do that. "You'll find someone, Linds."

"I used to believe that once upon a time. Naively, I used to have hope. Then I got cheated on. Not once. Not twice." She held up three fingers. "Third time's the charm."

"What does that mean?"

"Isn't it obvious? I give off some kind of vibe that makes men think they can cheat on me. Or—" if possible her expression grew even more bleak "—I'm just a placeholder. Someone to be used until a better prospect comes along."

Now Lani was getting worried. Her sister tended to look at life as not being fair. It was one of the reasons she'd wanted to be an attorney, to sort of even the odds for folks who didn't have faith. But this hopeless attitude seemed deeply entrenched and reinforced, a core belief that would be difficult to shake.

It was time for some tough love, and that meant not playing her game. "That's just ridiculous. You're a hot, beautiful woman who has a lot to offer. In high school you were voted the girl most likely to break men's hearts."

"That's when the curse began," she countered, her voice full of conviction.

"Oh, please. Don't be a martyr. This isn't about you. There's nothing wrong with you except for your judgment in men. Try swearing off them for a while. Clear your head. A different perspective and all that."

"You're onto something, sis." Lindsay drained the rest of the wine in her glass. "I'm done with men and not temporarily, either. This is permanent."

"That's the spirit." No point in trying to change her mind right now when the wound was still raw and bleeding, Lani thought.

"They'll call me the bachelorette barrister. Don't you just love alliteration?"

"It has a certain ring." A little reverse psychology. "Maybe we should spin off a group from the Newcomers Club and call it the Wallflowers Club."

"It should be singular, since I would be the only member."

"I'm joining with you," Lani explained.

"You can't. What would Detective Dreamy say?"

"He doesn't get to say anything about what I do." Lani meant the words even though part of her wanted him to have a say.

"That's not the way I see it." Lindsay rested her elbows on the island countertop.

"Then it's time to get your eyes checked because that's the way it is."

"You're seriously trying to convince me that you don't have feelings for Russ Campbell?" her sister asked.

"Oh, I have feelings all right, but not what you're implying."

"So nothing has changed between the two of you since the Fourth of July when you gave the impression that he was one step up from a Neanderthal?"

"You could say that." Lani wouldn't say it but didn't mind if her sister put the thought out there.

"Then I rest my case."

"Good." She hated that her sister was a lawyer. It was like talking to their father, being cross-examined, every little thing she said analyzed and dissected.

Lindsay pointed at her, indicating she had more to say. Apparently, resting her case was too much to hope for.

"This is what you always do, Lani. Proclaim that you don't like some guy, which is a big clue that you feel just the opposite."

"That's so far off the mark," she scoffed, even though there was a ring of truth in the words.

"Oh? Then I give you exhibit A—blowing off the Dalton Sunday dinner to meet the Campbell clan. Yeah, Mom told me. Then there's exhibit B—kissing him at the Ace in the Hole. That's all over town. And exhibit C—defending him to Anderson and Travis."

"Wow. Where'd you hear all of this?"

Her sister grinned. "Travis and I are close."

Lani couldn't argue any of that. Her only excuse was working with Russ on the case, but they were keeping the association quiet. She was at a loss to explain why he'd never once brought up brainstorming their strategy during the trip to his family's farm. Or that out-of-the-blue kiss by the stream. But just now when he'd dropped her off she'd been prepared, and he didn't make a move. What was she supposed to think?

Finally, she said, "None of that means anything."

"Right." Lindsay sighed. "Look, sis, I'm only saying this because I'm concerned. Don't make the same mistakes I have."

Lani refilled her glass. "There's nothing between Russ and me, so cheating isn't an issue."

"I meant don't choose an inappropriate man." She held up her hand to stop the words when Lani opened her mouth to argue. "Don't waste your breath. I know the signs, and it's clear you're falling for him. But keep this in mind, Lani. He's an outsider. When his work here in Rust Creek Falls is done, he'll be gone."

Or at least go back to the way it was before—when he'd come into the Ace in the Hole and ignored her.

Lani really wished that this conversation had unfolded in a different way or that her sister hadn't been betrayed one too many times, because having someone to talk to would be helpful. Her feelings for Russ were muddled and confused, and bouncing them off the person she was closest to in the world would really be awesome. But Lindsay was too cynical right now to be objective.

"Okay, then," she said. "It's official. You and I will be charter members of the newly formed Rust Creek Falls Wallflowers Club."

Lindsay grinned and held up her hand. "Pinkie swear?"

"I solemnly vow." Lani hooked fingers and made the promise sacred, binding and official.

They hugged, and her sister said good-night before going upstairs to bed. Lani stayed in the kitchen to finish her wine, mull things over.

And the more she did, the more convinced she was that no way Russ was jealous about her dating Brad Crawford. It was just foolish, wishful thinking on her part. It was also the right move. She'd promised to help Russ find the culprit, and she wouldn't go back on her word. But the sooner this investigation came to a conclusion, the better.

With any luck, that would happen before Detective Dreamy captured her heart completely.

After the school carnival closed down on Saturday night, Russ went to the Ace in the Hole. Alone in the crowd here was better than another evening staring at the walls of his room at Strickland's Boarding House. It wasn't all that different from hanging out at his house in Boulder Junction, but it sure felt lonelier. Somehow, he knew Lani was responsible for the attitude shift but couldn't put his finger on exactly why that was. It didn't matter, really. He just knew that one more night alone with his suspect list and interview notes might drive him nuts.

About a year ago, he'd discovered the bar after working a shift for Gage, and the two of them had come in for a beer. It was a good place to hang out, especially on busy nights like tonight. No one noticed you unless you wanted to be noticed, and if they didn't it was no big deal.

Rosey Traven was behind the bar, talking to one of the other waitresses, Annie Kellerman, who was serving beers and making drinks for customers. And then the hair on the back of his neck stood up and he glanced to his right, where Lani was delivering an order of food at a booth by the window.

Relief slammed through him that she was here and not with Brad Crawford. That was something he needed to talk to her about, but it would have to wait. After setting baskets of burgers and fries in front of the middle-aged couple, she smiled. Although from across the room he couldn't hear her, Russ knew she was telling them to flag her down if they needed anything else.

She glanced around the room, checking her customers,

and spotted him. An instant smile turned up the corners of her mouth, as if she was glad to see him. Then it shut down. Her body language said she wanted to turn her back and head in the other direction, but she must have remembered they had a cover to maintain.

Smiling a big, fat, phony smile, she headed straight for him and threw her arms around his neck. Whispering in his ear she said, "Just to be clear, this is because everyone thinks we're dating."

"Understood."

And he really did. Reading between the lines, that was her letting him know she didn't appreciate his mixed signals. And he wasn't proud of himself for it. That was just what happened when a man was mixed up. Lani messed with his head, scrambled the messages about focusing on his career and the necessity of fighting the longing to have her in his arms.

He put his hands at her waist and smiled. Then he asked the question he would ask if they really were a couple. "When do you get off?"

"Pretty soon."

"Okay. I'll wait for you." He said it loud enough for everyone around them to hear.

Her eyes took on that look they got when she turned stubborn. "You don't have—"

He touched his lips to hers and murmured against her mouth, "It's our cover."

"Right." She smiled and pulled back. "Have a seat at the bar. I'll be as quick as I can."

"Take your time."

She nodded then moved to a table where four women were seated and whipped out her order pad. Russ walked over to the bar and took the empty stool on the end. Annie appeared in front of him. "Hey, Russ. What can I get you? The usual?"

"Yeah."

The usual would be a longneck bottle of beer, and it appeared in front of him. Since he'd started dropping by the bar, more often than not he'd chat with whoever was serving drinks here. Unless that person happened to be Lani. From the first moment he'd seen her, he'd known she was trouble, the kind of woman who could make a fool out of him if he wasn't careful. Now here they were, pretending to be a couple. Fate had a warped sense of humor, because he had the feeling he wasn't pretending anymore.

"Hey, Detective." Rosey Shaw Traven was suddenly in front of him on the other side of the bar. "You look lost in thought."

"Yeah." He hadn't noticed her approach, which wasn't like him. "Got a lot on my mind."

"I imagine you do." She rested her hands on curvy hips, and the movement pulled her peasant blouse down just enough to reveal a hint of ample cleavage. "Any progress on finding out who spiked the punch at the wedding this summer?"

"No."

"You being a hotshot detective and all, that must be frustrating."

In more ways than he'd ever been frustrated before. "You could say that."

"I heard the school carnival has been quiet so far."

"That's right." It closed up a little while ago without incident. But the pressure was still on. "One more day and then we're home free. For now."

"Sunday's traditionally a big day. After church a lot of folks stop by with their families."

"Gage briefed me. We just have to make it until everything shuts down at four tomorrow." He met her gaze. "There's a part of me hoping whoever it is tries something and then we'll have him. Put an end to it." And his time with Lani would end, too. At least under the current rules.

Rosey picked up a tumbler and started to polish the glass with the rag in her hand. "So, I hear you and Lani have been hanging out together."

"You heard right." He took a sip of his beer.

"Why is that?"

"Why's what?" he hedged.

The older woman smiled shrewdly, as if she knew he'd dodged the question deliberately. "It's like this. You come into the Ace for months and never give a pretty girl like Lani a tumble. Then the two of you are stuck in a jail cell for hours while everyone at that wedding reception was three sheets to the wind."

"That can be explained," he protested. Although he still didn't know why she'd taken his keys to the cell.

"No doubt." She put the glass down then picked up another one and started polishing. "But I haven't made my point yet."

"Okay." Whatever it was he knew he wouldn't like it, so the longer it took to get there, the better. "Please continue."

"Thanks. Where was I?" She thought for a moment then nodded. "Right. Locked in a jail cell together. Then two months go by, the sheriff still doesn't know who doctored the punch that day and you haven't shown your face here at the bar. But he hires you to investigate."

"That's true," he agreed.

"Suddenly, you and Lani are hanging out, spending a lot of time together." She met his gaze again. "Why is that, exactly?"

"We're getting to know each other."

"So I heard. Dating." She sounded skeptical, which was actually very perceptive of her.

"Do you have a problem with that?"

"It all depends on how you define *problem*."

"Why don't you tell me how you define it," he suggested.

"I intend to." She put down the glass and the rag then rested her hands on the scarred wood of the bar. "I've known Lani for a few years now. She's a good girl, and I'm very fond of her. I've watched her go out with different men. I've seen her in love or infatuated, even smitten a time or two. Whatever you want to call it when a woman falls for a guy."

Russ didn't like the flare of jealousy that streaked through him at the mention of Lani with other guys. "I'm still waiting for you to get to the point."

There was an odd smile on her face, as if she knew what he was feeling and approved. A moment later it was gone, and all that remained was a warning. "I've seen her in various stages of a relationship, but I've never seen her acting the way she is now with you."

"Maybe that's good."

"Or maybe it isn't." She drilled him with a fiercely protective look. "Lani got her heart stomped on once, and I won't stand by and do nothing while it happens again. *That's* my point."

"Got it."

"So, we're clear?" she demanded.

"Yes, ma'am."

"Good. Nice talking with you. Enjoy your beer." Rosey turned and walked away, hips swaying.

Russ figured that woman had missed her calling and could have had a brilliant career in law enforcement. It wasn't often he knew how it felt to be interrogated, but he did now. And the experience was illuminating but not in the way he would have expected.

First the sheriff had stood up for Lani, and now her boss had made her allegiance clear. Neither of those two could be labeled a fool, which meant that Lani Dalton inspired loyalty in the people around her, not just her family. That would be impossible to pull off if she wasn't trustworthy. So he had to take her off the suspect list even if she was only on it in his head.

But something unexpected happened to him after Rosey's revelation about Lani's love life. Russ knew she'd been dumped—she'd told him when they were in the jail cell that she'd sworn off men. Now, though, he wanted to know more about the jerk who had stomped on her heart.

And he was going to ask when she got off work.

Chapter Ten

It turned out that Lani didn't get off work as soon as she'd expected. The bar got busy, and Rosey asked her to stay. She passed that on to Russ and told him he should leave, but he didn't. That made her feel pretty good before she reminded herself it was dangerous when he was nice to her.

She liked him a lot and desperately wanted to be in his arms again. The thing was, he was attracted to her, too. The kiss at the farm was proof because there hadn't been anyone else around to put on an act for. But he didn't want to want her, and that didn't bode well for anything long-term. An affair didn't interest her. Well, she was *interested*, but giving in to the temptation didn't make it any less stupid an idea.

She grabbed her purse out of the office in the back room, said good-night to her boss then walked out into the main bar area, stopping beside the stool where Russ was sitting.

"I'm heading home." She glanced around the room,

where only a couple of customers remained. "There aren't enough people here to make a difference in maintaining our cover. You really didn't have to stay."

"My alternative was an empty room at the boardinghouse."

"Wow, I was the lesser of two evils," she teased, but was secretly touched that he'd admitted being lonely. It tugged at her heart. "Way to make a girl feel special."

"I didn't mean it that way." He stood and put his hand at the small of her back, urging her toward the door. "And you are special."

His voice lowered to a sexy drawl and made her tingle all over. *Don't take it seriously. Danger, Lani Dalton*, she warned herself.

"There you go being nice to me, Detective. That could turn a girl's head."

"Not yours. You're too smart for that."

"Don't bet on it."

Russ opened the door and let her precede him outside. The cool air felt good on her hot cheeks. On nights when it was wall-to-wall people in the bar, it got pretty warm in there. Looking up, she dragged in a breath and let it out slowly. The night sky was clear, and stars sparkled like fairy dust. It was spectacular, and she reminded herself not to take it for granted.

"Montana is really beautiful in September."

"Unpredictable, too. The weather can turn suddenly."

Not just the weather, she thought. A girl never knew what to expect from Detective Campbell. He'd stuck it out and waited for her to get off work when both of them knew this wasn't a relationship. So why had he done that? Was he going to kiss her good-night this time? Should she kiss him? She hoped he would make a move, and so much for trying to stay mad at him for running hot and cold. But she couldn't manage it after he'd admitted being lonely.

Besides, playing games wasn't her style. She just wasn't wired that way.

"My truck is parked around that side of the building," she said, pointing to the right. "I need to get going."

"Before you do, can I ask you a question?"

"About what?"

"The guy who broke your heart."

The chill in the air penetrated her thin sweater, and she shivered. Without a word, Russ slipped off his battered brown leather jacket and dragged it around her shoulders. It felt good, warm from his body. Like being wrapped in his arms. Safe.

"What did Rosey say to you?" She pulled the edges of the jacket closer around her.

He leaned his elbows on the hitching rail in front of the bar. "For one thing, she's suspicious of what's going on with you and me. Your boss is a very observant woman."

"Suspicious how?"

He shrugged. "She noticed me coming in for a while, but you and I didn't get friendly until recently, when Gage hired me to work on the case full-time."

"Is that why you stayed tonight? To prove something to her?"

"Partly." He glanced at her. "But she warned me not to stomp on your heart like the last guy. Now I'm curious about him."

"Rosey is protective of all her girls. Don't worry about her."

"I'm not. But you once told me that a woman doesn't need a man to be happy and fulfilled. That sounds like a disillusioned woman to me."

The subtext was that he was concerned about her, and that sent warm fuzzy feelings sliding through her. "Don't lose any sleep over it."

"That's not why I asked," he said. "But what she told

me is motivation for that remark of yours, and I'd like to know what he did to you."

There was no point in refusing to talk about it. Anyone in town could tell him her sad story.

She leaned back against the hitching rail and met his gaze. "Jason Harvey was a good-looking cowboy who sweet-talked me until hell wouldn't have it. He had me at *darlin'*."

"What happened?"

"He told me he'd come to Rust Creek Falls to buy up land. After the flood two years ago some folks just didn't have it in them to rebuild and walked away from their property. Jase talked a good game about developing it."

"I sce."

"I was really interested in him. And as we've already established, I know a lot of people in town. I introduced him to anyone who might be able to get his dream off the ground."

"What happened?"

"Someone who didn't have stars in their eyes asked the sheriff to run a background check on him, and bad stuff turned up. He conned people out of money in a phony real estate scheme. When the heat was on here in town, he disappeared without a word to me." He not only broke her heart, she felt as if he'd damaged her reputation. Some people trusted him because she did. Now she felt stupid, felt as if she'd let her friends down. "Is it weird that his not saying goodbye, not facing me at all, is what bothered me most?"

"Maybe that was simpler and easier for you to grab on to and deal with."

"As opposed to the fact that he made a fool of me, used me," she said.

"Lani, I—" Russ dragged his fingers through his hair. "In a way, I'm using you. I feel guilty about that."

"Completely different. You're not after something and pretending to care about me to get it." She thought about that. "Well, I guess you are, but I'm in on it. By mutual consent we're putting on an act to achieve a common goal. For the greater good."

He didn't look convinced. "Still, I want you to know that your help is appreciated."

"Are you 'breaking up' with me?" she teased. "That sounds an awful lot like things are over. If it would be easier, you could text me."

He flashed a smile and fortunately the moon was bright enough to highlight how adorable he looked. "What kind of guy do you take me for?"

"A good guy." She tapped her lip. "At the very least, we should have a fight. Otherwise how would it look when I go out with Brad Crawford to pump him for information?"

"I thought we agreed you were going to wait on that," he said sharply.

The smile disappeared and she missed it. "We didn't agree on anything. You just said it wasn't a good idea."

"I stand by that." He looked down at her. "And I think you should let that strategy go."

"I disagree. So far, he's the one who seemed to have the most to gain from getting the town drunk. What's the big deal if I talk to him? Butter him up a little to make him let down his guard."

"The big deal is that a date with him could be dangerous if he's guilty and suspects that you're onto him."

"What if I do it in a very public place? The bar, for instance?"

"I still don't like it. You have no experience with this sort of thing, and in my opinion, holding off for now would be best."

"You're the professional," she said, shrugging. "I'll defer

to your judgment. But if we don't get a break soon, I'm going to contact Brad."

"Let's talk it over first."

"Okay. As long as an opportunity doesn't present itself before I can do that."

"Please don't go rogue." His voice was wry.

"I make no promises," she said. "Now I really have to go."

"Okay."

She turned to the right and walked around the building to where her truck sat all by itself. After she unlocked the driver's door with her key fob, Russ opened it for her. This was where one of them usually said something about a plan to meet and compare notes. Right now there was nothing to compare, but she really wanted to know when she would see him again. And his remark about an empty room at the boardinghouse had struck a nerve.

"Would you like to come to Sunday dinner at my house tomorrow?" The words came out before she could think them through and she held her breath, bracing for rejection.

He hesitated. "Are you sure your family would be okay with that?"

She knew he meant Anderson and Travis because Russ hadn't rubbed anyone else the wrong way. "They'll be fine."

He hesitated a moment then said, "I'd like that."

"Good. Come by the house around four."

"I have to wrap up the school carnival, so..."

"Okay. Dinner is around five-thirty."

"Shouldn't be a problem." He leaned down and touched his mouth to hers in a sweet, swift kiss. "Good night."

"'Night." Reluctantly, she handed over his jacket then got in and put the window down. "See you tomorrow."

"I'll be there."

She truly hoped Anderson and Travis didn't hold a

grudge. Otherwise the Dalton family dinner was going to be more exciting than usual.

Lani was nervous. She'd been watching out the front window, waiting for Russ to arrive and be the one to answer the door. It felt as if she'd been waiting forever but the clock only said four-thirty. Technically he wasn't late, but she was still anxious.

Finally, the familiar truck pulled up out front, and her heart started pounding. She brushed her sweaty palms down the sides of her jeans and hurried into the family room. Travis and Anderson were sitting on the couch, watching a football game.

Leaning on the back of the sofa she said, "Russ is here. Remember what I said. Be nice to him. He was only doing his job."

Travis gave her an irritated glare. "We get it. Geez, Lani. We're not idiots."

Anderson grinned. "Don't worry, sis. We'll be good. Do you want to talk about why our behavior is so important to you?"

No, she thought, it was the last thing she wanted to discuss. Before she could say that, the doorbell rang.

"I'll get it." She shrugged at them then hurried down the hall.

After stopping in front of the door, she released a deep, cleansing breath before opening it. Russ stood there in all his masculine splendor: jeans, boots and leather jacket. The word *handsome* didn't do him justice, and the whole package made her girl parts quiver with excitement.

"Hi," she said in a voice that was hardly more than a whisper.

"Hey. Hope I'm not late. The carnival breakdown took longer than I figured."

"Everything okay?" That was when she realized a part

of her was holding a breath, uneasy about the possibility of another incident.

"Fine." He came inside. "Quiet."

"Well, brace yourself. That's about to change." She angled her head toward the kitchen-family room, which was the heart of this home—and where everyone was waiting for them. "On the upside, you only have to meet four of my siblings. My sister Lindsay is away, at law school."

"Walking in her father's footsteps?" he said.

"Yes." Obviously, he'd remembered her telling him that she wouldn't be in jail long because her father was an attorney and would get her out. Not something she wanted to discuss further right now. "Are you ready for this?" she asked.

"I'm a cop. Ready for anything."

"It's a good motto. Let's see if it holds up." Lani led the way down the hall and stopped in the doorway. "Everyone, this is Russ Campbell." The announcement was followed by a chorus of greetings from the group. "Some of you already know him—Travis and Anderson—and we'll make the rounds for the rest of you."

They started with her parents, who were in the kitchen working together on preparing dinner. "Russ, this is my dad, Ben, and my mom, Mary."

"Nice to meet you, Russ." Her father shook his hand.

"We're glad you could join us for dinner," her mother said. "Lani says you have a big family."

"Yes, ma'am. Two brothers and a sister. But you and Mr. Dalton have my parents beat."

Ben glanced at everyone in the family room. "Wouldn't trade any one of them."

"Maybe Travis," Lani teased.

"He would say the same about his annoying little sister," her mother pointed out.

"True," she admitted. "And I take great pride in whatever I can do to make him feel that way."

"I have to get these potatoes mashed," Mary said. "Please excuse me."

"Can I help, Mom?"

"Not this time, sweetie. You make introductions and when you're finished, dinner will probably be ready."

"Okay. Follow me," she said to Russ. In the family room she stopped by the large corner group in front of the TV. "You know Travis and Anderson."

Both men stood and politely shook hands.

"Nice to see you again." Travis smiled, and it didn't look forced.

"Same here." In spite of the casual words, Russ looked wary. He held out his hand to Anderson. "How's it going?"

"Good. You? Any progress on the investigation?"

"No, but I wish. Rust Creek Falls really needs closure on what happened. Everyone is paranoid."

"And that's not how the people of this town are used to feeling," Anderson commented. "About the last time we talked… We might have given you the wrong impression. The thing is, everyone is grateful for your focus on this."

"I second that," Travis said. "You just kind of caught the two of us off guard, and we got a little defensive. Didn't mean anything by it."

"I appreciate that."

Russ seemed to relax, and Lani wanted to give both of her brothers a big hug. They gave her a hard time, but that was their job as her siblings. They would do anything for her, and she felt the same about them.

She sent each of them an appreciative look. "Sorry to interrupt the game."

"You should be." But Anderson's grin telegraphed his teasing.

She took Russ's hand, and they walked over to a corner

of the family room where her mom kept a toy box for her one-year-old grandson. Her sister and brother-in-law were sitting on the carpet, supervising the little guy.

"This is my sister Paige, her handsome husband, Sutter, and their adorable baby, Carter Benjamin."

The little boy had fairly recently started walking, and at the sound of his name he looked way up at the stranger then promptly fell on his tush.

"Hey, buddy." Russ went down on one knee and held out a hand to the child. "You okay?"

"He's used to it, poor baby. I take comfort from the fact that he won't remember." Paige was a sixth-grade teacher at Rust Creek Falls Elementary School. She was looking at Russ. "I've heard a lot about you."

"Don't believe everything—unless it's good."

When he smiled, Lani swore the world stopped turning on its axis, or maybe her heart spinning out of control just made it feel that way.

"I hear you've got a tough job." Sutter had light brown hair and blue eyes. He made his living training horses.

Russ shrugged noncommittally. "Just wish there was progress to report." He smiled when the baby slapped a tiny hand in his big palm. "High five, pal. Or should I say low five?"

The baby grinned and did it again.

"He's got teeth," Lani said to her sister, admiring her nephew's two on top and a matching set on the bottom.

"Funny how that happens on his way to eating solid food," her sister responded wryly.

Lani leaned down and brushed baby-fine strands of hair off his forehead. "He's growing up too fast. Please tell me you're not going to cut his hair."

"Ever?" Sutter and Russ said together in matching tones of male disapproval.

"Well-done, sis," Paige said, supporting the effort to get a rise out of the two men.

"It was too easy."

Carter had used Russ's hand to pull himself to a standing position then grunted and indicated he wanted to be picked up. That was unusual, since the kid was normally shy with strangers. But Russ obliged, proving that he'd been telling the truth when he claimed to be ready for anything.

The baby touched his nose, made a funny face after brushing his small palm over the slight stubble on Russ's jaw then studied his hand while flexing his fingers. The big man patiently waited while the little guy scratched the leather collar of his jacket and slapped at his shoulder. He seemed to know when Carter was bored and gently set him on his feet, protectively holding him until he was steady.

"You're good with kids," Paige observed.

Lani's heart melted a little more. "You're a man of many unexpected talents."

"Kids are easy," he answered. "It's adults who get complicated."

She couldn't argue with that. "I'm still on introduction detail. Where are Caleb and Mallory?"

"They took Lily outside. She's playing soccer this year and wanted to practice her ball skills," Paige explained.

"Okay." She looked at Russ. "This is the last one, I promise. But again I say brace yourself. Lily is really something. Very precocious. There's just no way to prepare for her."

He didn't look the least bit intimidated, which was impressive. "Lead on."

They walked out the French door leading to the backyard and a brick-lined patio. There was an expanse of grass and a gazebo in the far corner of the enclosed area. Her brother Caleb, his wife, Mallory, and their nine-year-old daughter, Lily, were standing on the grass, kicking the black-and-white ball back and forth.

"Hi, Aunt Lani," the little girl said. "Grandma told us your boyfriend was coming over. Is that him?"

"This is Russ." She wasn't quite sure how to address the *boyfriend* comment.

"I'm Mallory," her auburn-haired sister-in-law said. "And this is our daughter, Lily. Sweetie, your grandma said that Aunt Lani's *friend* was going to be here."

The adorable black-haired, almond-eyed child had been adopted by Mallory's sister and her husband. After they died in a car accident, her aunt took on guardianship. She and Caleb had finalized the adoption after they were married.

The little girl lived up to her billing as precocious. "He's her friend and he's a boy. Doesn't that make him her boyfriend?"

That was a literal assessment, and Lani was trying to figure out how to address the personal nuances of what her niece had said.

Her brother, bless him, stuck out his hand and said, "I'm Caleb."

"Nice to meet you."

"You're a policeman," Lily commented.

"Yes. A detective."

"Do you arrest bad people?" she wanted to know.

"If they're caught breaking the law."

"Do you put them in jail?"

Russ looked at her, and the expression in his eyes said he was thinking about that night they'd spent together in the cell. Lani didn't think she was a bad person, but what she'd done was filed under wrong thing, right reason.

Russ met the little girl's gaze. "Sometimes."

"How come not all the time?" the little interrogator wanted to know.

"Okay, Lily," her mother said. "You're going to make Russ's ears tired."

The child looked up with a puzzled expression on her pretty face. "Ears don't get tired."

"Trust me," Mal said, "they do."

Lily shrugged. "I'm going inside to see baby Carter."

"And I'm going to see if your grandmother needs any help getting dinner on the table," her mother said.

Caleb picked up the ball. "Nice to meet you, Russ. I hope my daughter's questions didn't bother you."

"Not at all," he said. "But it wouldn't surprise me to see her become an investigator someday."

Her brother grinned. "No kidding."

The rest of the evening went just as smoothly as the introductions. Russ got along with everyone, including the children. He seemed to fit in really well, and Lani realized a part of her wished he hadn't. She'd been anticipating a reason to cross him off as incompatible with her family, which would definitely be a relationship deal breaker.

She was looking for a flaw in him because her feelings were growing deeper, but she had no clue how he really felt. He gave her a kiss here, a compliment there. Saying she was special. What did that mean? And why did he refuse to open up about himself?

But she knew one thing for sure. Until the spiked punch mystery was solved, she wouldn't know whether he was just seeing her because of the investigation. If so, he would disappear when it was over, and she needed to know one way or the other.

It was time to speed things up on the case. That meant chatting up Brad Crawford even if Russ didn't like the idea.

Chapter Eleven

When opportunity taps you on the shoulder, you don't just walk away. Not when it was important to Russ's investigation. The day after Lani decided it was time to go for broke and talk to Brad Crawford opportunity presented itself and she wasn't going to miss it.

Oddly enough, her chance came on Monday, traditionally the least busy day of the week at the Ace in the Hole. She'd just finished her shift when the guy in question came in. Of all the gin joints in all the world, Brad had to walk into hers, right? Except gin joints in Rust Creek Falls were limited.

She said hello to him because they had a passing acquaintance, and he said hello back. It was now or never, so she asked him if he'd like to have a beer with her. When she said she was buying, he agreed.

After texting Russ to let him know about this lucky break and a vow to fill him in later about what she learned, she grabbed a couple of longnecks and joined Brad in a quiet corner booth. Her cell phone buzzed before she could sit down across from him, but she ignored it.

She held up her bottle. “What should we drink to?”

“Why do we have to drink to anything?”

“We don’t,” she said.

Hopefully, that wasn’t a sign that he was going to be difficult. Brad was about as tall as Russ and too handsome for his own good. He had brown hair, green eyes and was really built, as in broad shoulders, wide chest and muscular legs inside those worn jeans.

He was six years older than Lani and she hadn’t gone to school with him but had heard talk. And like every unattached woman in town, she was aware of his story and his reputation. He’d been über popular in high school and had never been without a girlfriend. It was common knowledge that he was in no hurry to settle down, so it had been a big surprise when he married Janie Delane seven years ago.

They divorced three years later because, rumor had it, she was fed up with him only wanting someone to cook, clean and do laundry. Apparently, she’d told him he should have just hired a housekeeper. That would have been cheaper and easier for both of them.

“I was just trying to start a conversation,” Lani said. Her cell phone buzzed again, and she ignored it again. “How’ve you been?”

“Since when?” He leaned back in the booth and sipped his beer.

“I don’t know. How about today?”

“I’m fine.”

“Anything new with you?” she asked.

“Like what?”

Wow, he was being difficult. “Are you seeing anyone? Is there anyone special in your life?”

“Are you offering?” His smile was charming but didn’t

hide the slightest bit of wariness in his eyes. "I heard you and that Kalispell detective hooked up."

Though in the current colloquial definition of that phrase, Brad heard right, she didn't consider the two of them a romantic item. But since they'd been acting that way for the sake of this investigation, the rumor needed to be addressed for purposes of this conversation.

"Russ and I are friends. Kind of." She thought for a moment. "We're just having fun."

"Let's drink to that." Brad held up his beer bottle. "To having fun. Nothing complicated. And no demands."

"To that." Lani touched the neck of her bottle to his and tried to be enthusiastic, but wasn't sure she pulled it off. He was one cynical son of a gun. If she had to guess, the edge of bitterness he conveyed probably had something to do with his divorce. Then she realized he'd bobbed and weaved and avoided answering her question.

"How about you?" she asked. "Hooked up with anyone?"

"Hooked up? Yeah." He toyed with the bottle on the table between them. "Serious about? No way."

"You sound determined about that."

"Because I am. Like I said—all fun, all the time. No strings. No drama."

Lani didn't know if that was a warning or an invitation. She wasn't the least bit interested, though. Even if she was attracted to his charm and good looks, that lone-wolf-Lothario thing he had going on was a total turnoff. Although it occurred to her that Russ was something of a loner, too, and that man turned her on just by walking in the door. Go figure.

She didn't have to be attracted to Brad to get information out of him and would play any game he wanted in order to do just that.

"Okay, so personally you're not tied down and have no

intentions of ever committing. But professionally it seems you're doing all right."

"Oh?" His green eyes narrowed on her.

"Yeah. I heard about that poker game on the Fourth of July. The word is that you did pretty well."

"You mean because I took Old Man Sullivan's ranch." It wasn't a question.

"That's what I mean," she said, trying to assess his emotions. Angry? Guilty? Ashamed? She couldn't decide.

"Have you ever played cards, Lani? I mean for real money?"

"No," she admitted.

"That's what I thought." He took a long swallow of beer. "Rule number one—never wager anything you can't afford to lose."

"Even so…it's the man's home," Lani pointed out.

He met her gaze squarely. "I can't help it if I'm a more skilled player. I couldn't swear to it, but it's as if the old man wanted to lose."

"Too bad we can't ask him. He's disappeared," she said. "No one has heard from him for a while."

Brad shrugged. Lani wasn't sure what she'd expected, although a written confession from Brad that he'd slipped a mickey to the whole town so that he could win at poker would have been awfully tidy. Most people would have been ambivalent about winning and taking a man's property. But this guy didn't show any sign of letting his conscience get in the way of raking in his poker winnings.

She'd never actually believed he was the perpetrator. After all, despite the feud between the Crawfords and the Traubs that was so old, no one could clearly remember how it started, he was part of a nice family. They were upstanding citizens and, as far as she knew, had never been in trouble with the law.

But every barrel had a bad apple, and it could be that

she was looking right at him, Lani thought. Maybe it was time to mention how everyone got drunk that night and gauge his reaction.

"Isn't it crazy what happened after the wedding? How so many people you'd never expect got drunk and began behaving out of character?" Including herself, she thought, hoping he wouldn't point that out.

"Wasn't your boyfriend hired to find out who spiked that punch?" It was hard to tell whether his tone leaned more toward suspicion or curiosity.

"The sheriff thought his skill as a detective would come in handy, since his own investigation wasn't getting anywhere. People are squirrelly. Worried that there could be a repeat of what happened. Or even worse. Did you have any of the punch?"

"Yeah."

She wanted to ask if he'd had enough to get drunk but didn't want to come off as an interrogator even though she was. "Doesn't it creep you out that someone put something in that punch and most of the town ended up acting weird? What if someone had gotten hurt because of it?"

"It's…unsettling," he allowed.

"Not to mention a crime," she said.

"After all this time and from what I hear not a single clue, does your boyfriend really think he can find out who did it?"

Was there a deliberate challenge in those words? Could it be he was toying with her because he was responsible for getting everyone drunk? Or just messing with her because he was mad at the world? Now was the time to ask.

As she was formulating the question, some part of her mind registered the fact that the bar's screen door had just opened and closed, admitting a customer even though it was getting pretty late.

"I wouldn't call Russ my boyfriend," Lani started. "We're just—"

At that exact moment Detective Russ Campbell walked up to the booth and leaned down for a quick kiss. "Hi, babe. Got here as quick as I could."

Lani slid over to make room because he was obviously planning to sit down beside her. It took her a few moments to form a coherent response because her brain was short-circuited from the sizzle of that unexpected kiss.

"You made good time."

"Helps when you're the law." Brad eyed the newcomer skeptically.

"I don't think we've met. Russ Campbell," he said, holding his hand out across the table.

The other man shook it. "Brad Crawford. Nice to meet you, Detective."

Russ stared at him, and even though she could only see his profile, Lani noticed tension in his jaw and felt the hostility. Then he looked at her and she also felt the heat of his irritation and disapproval. "So, what were you two talking about?"

"Oh, you know," she said. "This and that. It was no big deal."

"Yeah," Brad agreed. "Small talk. Like who spiked the punch after the wedding."

"Did you come up with any suspects?" Russ asked, his eyes narrowing on her.

"No. I guess Brad and I still can't believe that someone who is our friend and possibly a neighbor would do something like that." She looked at the man sitting across from them.

"I was just telling Lani that it seems unlikely you'll find the perp, since so much time has gone by."

"Not if that person slips up and tries it again," Russ said. "We're ready for that."

"Okay, then." Brad pressed his lips together and nodded. "I've got to get going. A lot to do tomorrow on the ranch."

"And the land you won in the poker game gives you even more responsibility," Lani said.

"Yeah." Brad slid out of the booth and looked at each of them. "Thanks for the beer, Lani. See you around, Detective."

Then he walked straight to that noisy, rusty Ace in the Hole screen door, opened it and headed out into the night. Lani and Russ sat side by side, alone and still no closer to finding out who had gotten the whole town drunk.

It was several moments before Russ said anything and when he did, she wished he hadn't.

"What the hell were you thinking, Lani?"

"I was thinking a lot of things. You might want to be more specific."

"Confronting Brad Crawford by yourself. Is that specific enough for you?" he demanded.

She shifted on the booth seat, and her shoulder brushed against his. It wasn't clear if the sparks she felt were her attraction or his irritation. If she'd been straight across from him, she would have made a point of direct eye contact, so she was pretty glad they were side by side. That way she didn't have to see the expression on his face confirming that he couldn't stand the sight of her.

"I was thinking that the investigation was stalled, and Brad Crawford won a ranch in a poker game. That's strong motive." She glanced at his profile and saw the muscle jerk in his jaw. "And you forgot to say thank you."

"What the hell for? Putting yourself in a potentially dangerous situation?" He didn't sound angry as much as concerned for her safety. "You promised to talk to me first."

"Brad came in just as I was getting off work, and I took that as a sign."

"Of what? That you should play detective?" He gave

her a sideways look. "There are any number of ways that a solo interrogation could have gone south if he's the guy we're looking for."

"This is a public place. I thought about that."

"Public but practically empty." He glanced around. "Whoever is tending bar went in the back for something. That would give a suspect the perfect opportunity to overpower you."

"I'd scream for help. It's not like this place is a deserted alley," she scoffed.

"What if he had a weapon and told you not to make a sound?"

"Oh." She hadn't thought about that.

"Yeah. Oh."

"But he didn't do anything," she pointed out. "I'm fine."

"Because I got here in time to stop you from—"

She waited but he didn't finish the statement. "To stop me from what?"

"Never mind."

Now it was her turn to be irritated. The way he shut down like that was really starting to bug her. If he wanted a fight, she'd be happy to oblige and maybe clear the air. But he wouldn't fight fair. Or at all. "If there's nothing else, I'd like to go home now."

She waited for him to slide out of the booth and let her leave, but he didn't budge. And he was too big for her to push him out of her way.

"Please move so I can get out of here."

"Tell me what Brad said."

"You're welcome." His grunt made her smile. "He said a lot of things and for the record, he seems like kind of an arrogant jerk. I asked him how he could take away someone's land and home and he said Sullivan was asking for it."

"How?"

"By wagering something he couldn't afford to lose and

not being a very good poker player." She shrugged. "That sounds a lot like motive to me."

"As much as I don't like that guy, and make no mistake—" he looked at her sideways "—I don't like him a lot, there are a couple of holes in your theory."

"What?"

He rubbed his chin thoughtfully. "That was a pickup poker game, meaning there was nothing arranged ahead of time. If Brad did spike the punch, it would only have given him an advantage in that the other guys would be drunk and sloppy players. He couldn't know who those players would be or how much they would bet on a hand."

"I see what you mean. Still," she said, "that reasoning doesn't let him off the hook, either."

"How so?"

"He seemed edgy to me. Sort of cynical and bitter. He might have a grudge against someone."

"Do you know anything about his personal life?" Speaking of edgy, Russ's voice had a tinge of tension. "Is he dating anyone?"

"He dates everyone. In fact, he wanted to drink to having fun with no strings attached." She was remembering his exact words. "I asked if he was seeing anyone special and he asked if I was offering."

"Son of a—" Russ's fingers curled into a fist.

"Don't go all macho." The words came out of her mouth but inside she was cheering his tense reaction. It meant something. She was almost sure of it. "I was the one who offered to buy him a beer."

"Don't remind me." He looked thoughtful. "You said he's divorced? Could be he wants to get even with someone for that."

"I got the impression that he's just lonely. And doesn't even know it."

"Interesting assessment when he's playing the field. Lonely in a crowd?" he asked wryly.

"Sure. Quantity doesn't make up for quality. Guys won't admit that publicly. It's a very closely guarded manly secret."

"What is?"

"That men want to settle down. Have someone special to share their life with."

Come to think of it, men weren't the only ones who felt that way. Lani was lonely. If she admitted that out loud, Russ would laugh, especially after having dinner with a crowd of Daltons.

She was grateful for her family and knew they'd be there for her always. But it was different from having a guy there when she woke up in the morning and someone to come home to at night. With Jase she'd had a glimpse of what making a home together might have looked like, which is why there was such a big hole in her life when he left. Since then she'd never let anyone become that important. Then Russ came along and scooped her out of the fountain.

"If it's a manly secret, how do you know about it?" Russ asked.

"I have brothers. There's talk. Sometimes they don't know I'm listening."

"Last time I checked, that was known as eavesdropping."

There was a teasing tone in his voice and even from the side she could see his mouth curve up in a smile. And even from this vantage point the adorable factor in that smile was plenty powerful.

"I like to think of it more as research into the male point of view. This may come as a shock to you, Detective, but guys are not easy to understand."

He laughed out loud, and the sound was magic to her heart. How she wished to hear him like this more often.

"Compared to women," he said, "understanding guys is as easy as falling off a log."

"So why was he on that log in the first place?" she mused. "Did he get pushed off or jump? And how did the log feel about a two-hundred-pound guy standing there?"

"I rest my case. When a woman plays the feelings card, there goes all rational thought."

"So you're a just-the-facts-ma'am kind of guy?"

"I'm a detective. You can't make a case against the bad guys based on feelings and supposition."

And that brought her down to earth with a gigantic thud. For just a few minutes she'd been able to pretend that they were just any guy and girl sitting in a bar and flirting. But that was an illusion. He was a detective hired to solve the town mystery and was only giving her the time of day because she had a job that gave her unique access to the general public. And tonight she was pretty sure she'd eliminated one of the prime suspects.

Her work there was done.

"Speaking of making cases, it seems there's not one to be made against Brad Crawford. At least not from what he and I talked about tonight."

"And speaking of that, there's something I've been wondering about."

"Oh?" She must have left out a detail in her recounting of the conversation with the poker-playing cowboy.

"When I walked up a little while ago you were denying that I was your boyfriend. You were just about to define what we are."

"Thanks to your timely arrival I didn't have to. So I guess you saved me tonight, after all." Her boyfriend. If only. Getting a glimpse of something she couldn't have was a real mood breaker, and she was ready to be gone. "And now, if you'll excuse me, you have my report. I need to go."

Again he didn't budge. "What would you have told Brad about us? What are we, Lani?"

"I don't know. Co-investigators?" She shrugged. "I told him we were getting to know each other. Just friends." Chancing a look at him, she asked, "Are we?"

"That's not quite right."

Exasperating man. What did that mean? She thought about what he'd started to say earlier. That he'd come here to stop her from doing…something. He hadn't finished the sentence, and now she wanted to know what he'd been about to say.

"Why did you really come here tonight, Russ? We both know I wasn't in any danger from Brad. He's not an idiot or a psychopath. Even if he's guilty there's no way he would have hurt me, especially here. What did you come here to stop me from doing?"

He looked at her, and his hazel eyes glittered, making them more green than brown. Intensity rolled off him so thick she could almost touch it.

"I was going to stop you from leaving with Brad," he finally said.

"I wouldn't have done that," she protested. "Sure, I bought him a beer, but that didn't mean anything. I could have told him there was no spark. You didn't have to bother coming over."

"Yeah, I did."

"Why? I had him right where I wanted him."

"I came because there's somewhere I want you, Lani. And it isn't here at the Ace in the Hole."

The truth was beginning to dawn on her. "Are you jealous of Brad?"

"Yes." The single word was almost a hiss.

"There's no reason to be. Telling him there's no spark would have been the honest-to-God truth. I wouldn't go anywhere with him—"

His finger on her lips stopped the words. “Will you go with me?”

“Where?” she whispered.

“My room. My bed.” Just like that, there was more brown in his eyes than green, highlighting the heat, want and need he couldn’t hide. “Say yes, Lani.”

All she could do was nod.

Chapter Twelve

His room and his bed were temporarily located at Strickland's Boarding House.

Lani would love to see his house in Boulder Junction, but was really glad they didn't have to go that far right now. The drive from the bar didn't take long, and soon they made it to his room on the second floor. As far as they knew, no one had seen them. Not that it would be a problem, since word was all over town that they were a couple. But Melba Strickland had standards at her boardinghouse that didn't include tolerance for a man and woman cozying up too intimately before taking marriage vows.

Russ closed the door behind him and blew out a breath. "We made it."

Lani laughed quietly. "Is Melba in the habit of patrolling the halls?"

"I wouldn't put it past her," he said. "In the morning at breakfast she looks everyone over, and I swear she knows who broke the rules."

"That's just your imagination. There's no way she could tell just by looking."

"I'm not so sure. After a once-over, she has this subtle way of letting us know that what happens in the marriage bed is sacred."

Lani grinned. "If that woman isn't eighty years old, she's darn close. And her husband, Gene, thinks a woman's place is in the home raising babies. Times have changed."

"But those two haven't," he swore. "And let's just say I'd rather be involved in a high-speed car chase than face Melba in the hall while you're in my room."

She looked around. "And a lovely room it is."

The bedside lamp illuminated the comfortable interior including a bed with brass head- and footboards. It was big and covered by a wedding-ring quilt. There was an oak armoire and matching dresser with a ceramic pitcher and washbasin on top. One modern touch was the flat-screen TV mounted on the wall across from the bed.

"This is nice. Homey," she said. "An improvement from the jail cell."

All these weeks he'd pretended nothing had happened that night, forcing her to pretend, too. Now here they were, and she had Brad Crawford to thank for it. She had a feeling if Russ hadn't seen them talking, he wouldn't have brought her here. Seeing her with another man had flipped a switch in him, and she was finally where she wanted to be.

He carefully removed the decorative throw pillows from the bed and set them on the ottoman that matched the red, floral-print chair in the corner.

When he was finished, he stood in front of her at the foot of the bed. "I'm going to make that up to you."

"What?"

"The jail."

"Ah." She shrugged. "There's nothing to make up for. That was pretty awesome."

"You'll get no argument from me, but the ambience left something to be desired." He cupped her face in his big hands. "This time it's private."

She knew what he meant. No danger of anyone walking in on them. That night when they were locked up together and Russ kissed her, all she could think about was being with him. There was no space in her passion-filled mind to think about the fact that they were in a public place.

That time she'd been wearing a sundress, but now she had on a blouse and jeans. Since there was no fear of discovery and they could take their time…

She started unbuttoning her cotton shirt and was working on the last one before glancing up at Russ. He was holding his breath, anticipation stamped on his features. The intensity of his gaze made her knees go all wobbly.

He leaned down and lightly kissed the spot where her neck and shoulder met. "You're killing me here."

"I can speed this up if—"

He touched his tongue to her earlobe then softly blew on it. "I know it didn't sound that way, but I wasn't complaining."

"So I'm getting mixed messages here. Are you in a hurry, or—"

"I'm just so damn glad to be here with you. So damn glad you didn't leave with Brad." He met her gaze, and there was fire in his. He pulled her close and buried his face in her hair. "I've thought about you this way so many times, and it's been driving me crazy. You smell like flowers and sunshine. Just the way you did before. I tried to forget, to get you out of my mind, but you just wouldn't stay put."

So she hadn't been the only one affected by what happened that night. It hadn't been just a fluke, a fling, a one-night thing. Her heart swelled at his words and beat even harder than it already was.

"And would you like to know what I've thought about the most?" he asked.

"What?" The single word was hardly louder than the sound of a sigh.

"Undressing you and taking my time."

"Oh, my."

"Any objections?" One corner of his mouth curved up.

"No."

His smile was completely adorable as he brushed her hands away and undid the last button on her shirt. Then he slid it off her shoulders and unhooked her bra. He dropped it on the floor and stared at her as if he couldn't look hard enough. "Beautiful," he breathed.

As he released the button at the waist of her jeans, she toed off her sneakers and kicked them away so he could take off the rest of her clothes. His gaze slowly moved over her, and there was no mistaking the approval in his eyes.

"Wow," he said.

The removal of his clothes went a lot quicker, and before you could say boo there they were, neither of them wearing a stitch. She had to admit slow and deliberate had its advantages over doing the deed behind bars. This time she could really look at him, the wide shoulders and contour of his chest with its dusting of hair. She'd read magazine articles with pictures of actors and models with a six-pack, but had never seen one up close and personal before. The temptation to touch was simply too strong to resist.

She put her palms on his chest, letting the hair tickle her fingers before sliding down to his taut abdomen. "Very impressive, Detective Campbell."

"Glad you think so, Miss Dalton." When she traced a finger down his side to his waist, he sucked in a breath. "Now you're playing with fire."

"Am I?"

"Yes. But two can play that game," he said.

He cupped her breasts in his palms and lightly rubbed the tips with his thumbs. The touch sent shock waves vibrating through her. For the first time she knew what "putty in his hands" actually meant. Her body felt boneless, as if she could collapse in a puddle at his feet.

Just the excuse she needed. "We're wasting that perfectly good bed."

Without another word she grabbed his hand, walked to the side of it and climbed in then moved over to make room. The mattress dipped from his weight, and just before he pulled her into his arms, she had the fleeting thought that the sheets were cold. Then he slid his arms around her and drew her close to him, and all she could think about was heat.

When he touched his lips to hers she couldn't think at all. The man was nothing if not a good kisser. That was probably the reason she hadn't been able to resist him the first time. But now she knew him better and had the privacy to really appreciate that the man knew what he was doing.

He took his time, leisurely kissing her lips, cheek, jaw and neck. She was already having trouble catching her breath when he took her mouth again, and there was nothing leisurely about it.

He traced her lips with his tongue then dipped inside when she opened to him. At the same time he brushed his hand down her side and over her hip. Her flesh was sensitized and seemed to catch fire everywhere he touched.

While he was kissing the living daylights out of her, Lani let her fingers roam over his shoulders and arms. The muscles and sheer masculinity delighted and amazed her. He was so strong yet deliciously gentle. Feelings that she'd been so careful to hold back seemed to spill over, like lava from a volcano. It was beautiful and dangerous.

He seemed to feel the shift in her mood, and his kisses grew more intense. The sound of their ragged breathing filled the room, and touching became more frantic. He nudged her to her back, and she rested her hands at his waist, urging him toward her. After settling between her legs, he entered her.

At first his movements were slow, as they got used to the feel of each other. Then he picked up the pace and intensity. Lani's body moved easily with his, remembering the rhythm from that night when it was hot outside and he'd unexpectedly kissed her. She couldn't hold back now any more than she could then.

Breathing became a definite challenge. He thrust harder, driving her higher, until finally pleasure exploded through her and rocked her world. She cried out and he kissed her, absorbing all the sounds of her overwhelming reaction that she couldn't hold back.

And then he started to move inside her again. She clutched his hips and met him thrust for thrust. Seconds later he groaned, and she wrapped her arms around his shoulders, and her legs circled his waist. He held her tight until the shudders of satisfaction stopped rolling through him.

It was late when Russ watched Lani roll out of bed. This was the first time since he'd started his official investigation that this warm country-themed room hadn't felt lonely and empty.

He couldn't help admiring her shapely backside even as he wanted to pull her back into his arms and make love to her again. All that soft skin and those feminine curves were really something.

But she had to be at the ranch early, and he had to take

her back to the Ace in the Hole, where her truck was still parked. So they dressed quickly then stood a whisper apart at the foot of the bed with the tangled sheets just inches away.

They smiled at each other as satisfaction hummed between them. Her shiny brown hair was tousled and sexy, just the way it should be after fantastic sex. He reached out and touched a finger to her bottom lip, slightly swollen from his kisses. Her cheeks were pink and her eyes sparkled—in other words, she looked beautiful.

It was time to admit the truth to himself—he had feelings for Lani Dalton. If that wasn't the case, no way would he have given in to temptation again. First being that night in jail.

The problem was that she had secrets. Not knowing what they were made it impossible to trust her, so getting more deeply involved was a bad idea.

"You're awfully quiet," she said. "Do you hate yourself?"

Not quite, but he was in unfamiliar territory here. "Is there some reason I should?"

"Isn't that what people say when they try to resist doing what we just did? That you'll hate yourself in the morning?"

"Right." Russ got it now. "No, I don't hate myself. Do you?"

"It's after midnight, so technically morning has arrived, but I don't hate myself." She smiled and linked her fingers with his. "I just wish I didn't have to go."

"So don't. Stay." He was a little surprised at how much he meant that. A fiercely intense longing tightened in his chest.

"I can't. We might not hate ourselves now, but if we get caught in your room, Melba Strickland could change that. Besides, I have to get my truck."

"I'll take you. Later." He couldn't help feeling they only had now, and he wanted to put off saying good-night.

"You'll get more sleep if we do this now. There's no point in both of us being exhausted."

She was right, but he didn't care about sleep. And that wasn't good. It was time to find out what she was hiding before he got in any deeper than he already was. Maybe she felt the same way about him. She'd been curious about why he left the police force in Denver. He wanted to tell her about it, get that weight off his shoulders. Let her know that keeping secrets inside made them more powerful than they had any right to be. Quid pro quo.

He would tell his story, then she could share hers. "There's something I want to talk to you about."

"Okay."

And that was one of the things he found so irresistible about her. It was late. She had to be tired after working at the ranch then a couple hours at the bar. And she had to be at work again at dawn and was already facing the prospect of very little sleep. But he wanted to say something, and she agreed without question or hesitation.

He took her hand and led her over to the floral-patterned chair in the corner, sitting her in it after he moved the throw pillows to the bed. He lowered himself to the ottoman in front of her and leaned forward, elbows on his knees.

"About why I left the Denver PD..."

When several moments went by she said, "You don't have to tell me. You know that, right?"

"Yes. But I want you to know." Because when you felt a pull as strong as he did for Lani, she had a right to his past. And he had a right to hers. "I found out my partner was on the take."

Her eyes grew wide. "What?"

"He was being paid for information about undercover drug operations, raids, imminent arrests, evidence for trial and even perjuring himself in court."

"How did you find out?" she asked.

"Little things at first. He wasn't where he said he was going to be. A big new house that seemed too much for a cop's salary. Expensive car. Bits of phone conversations. I got suspicious, followed him. Got pics of him meeting with a known drug dealer and cash changing hands."

"Oh, Russ. What happened?" She reached out and linked her fingers with his.

"I went to the watch commander with what I had."

Lani's clear brown eyes were full of sympathy and concern. "What did he say? Something bad happened or you wouldn't have left Denver."

"I guess you don't have to be a detective to figure that out." He smiled but knew it was grim. "He told me to leave it to him."

"And?"

"When nothing happened I tried again. He said I should just stay out of it. My job was to uphold the law so I went over his head to Internal Affairs. But they could never make a case against him. He got careful and no evidence was found. And that's when it all went to hell."

"I don't understand," she said. "You did the right thing. How could that be bad?"

"Cops have a code. You watch each other's back. No matter what." He blew out a breath. "I broke the code. Ratted him out."

"He was a bad cop, breaking the law." She was adamant, on his side. "He's the one who did wrong."

"But all of them had been together for years. I was the newcomer. An upstart. Going for the big score, a promotion at the expense of a brother. I was downgraded in rank and took a pay cut. A subtle way of trying to force me out, but I refused to go. So the precinct cops circled the wagons. They closed ranks, refused to partner with me and, if forced to, slanted incident reports to make me look dirty."

"Oh, my God. That's awful, Russ."

"The thing is most of those guys are good cops. But the mind-set of supporting a brother in arms is more sacred than finding out the truth. In the beginning I backed them up in tough spots and they did the same for me. I thought I'd built up trust, made friends, but it turned out the truth wasn't the most important thing to them."

"But it is to you." She nodded. "It must have been hard being shut out like that. I can't even imagine."

"I could deal with that. But the situation became dangerous. Damned if I did, damned if I didn't. The trust was gone on both sides, which put people at risk. No one had faith in me to watch their back and based on what happened, I didn't believe they had mine. I responded to a domestic violence situation, and a woman and child were endangered because I was alone. No backup. And you never know what you're walking into. I was lucky on that one. It resolved safely."

"So you resigned," she guessed.

He nodded. "If I hadn't, someone could have been hurt—or worse."

"You sacrificed your career for the sake of fellow officers and the public." She squeezed his hands. "That's pretty heroic."

"My fiancée didn't think so."

"You were engaged?" She looked surprised. "Alexis?"

"Yes." He stood and started pacing the room. "Alexis Davidson."

"Pretty name."

"It fit her. She was beautiful." He stopped walking and looked down at her. "I needed a job. When I told her about the one on the force in Kalispell, she said no way she was moving to a two-bit town in backwoods Montana."

"If she loved you, she would have gone anywhere just to be with you."

"Then I guess she didn't." Some detective he was that

he hadn't seen the truth. "It never crossed my mind that I'd lose the career I'd worked my ass off for and the woman I loved because I did the right thing."

Lani shook her head. "I'm sorry she hurt you, but it seems to me you dodged a bullet there."

"How so?"

"That woman was, probably still is, shallow as a cookie sheet if she couldn't see that you're a good man, with character and the courage of his convictions. Then there's that little thing in the marriage vows—for better or worse. The going got tough and she got going." Lani's eyes blazed with anger and disapproval. "She didn't know what she had and didn't deserve you. You're better off without her."

"You think so?" Russ wondered if Lani was as loyal as she seemed.

"I know so. And I'm not sure which is worse—her leaving you or good men who take pride in supporting each other but didn't support one of their own."

"Yeah. I learned the hard way that having someone's back doesn't mean it's okay to lie for them."

Lani went still for just a second then looked up at him. There was a plea in her eyes that said she knew what he was getting at. "Sometimes having someone's back means you can't say anything at all."

The words opened up a hollow feeling in his gut. She wasn't going to tell him why she made him arrest her, or kept him locked up and off the street. Damn it. Now the line was drawn—and Russ had to figure out whether or not he could risk crossing it.

Even for Lani.

Chapter Thirteen

Three days later Lani was working at the Ace in the Hole and fretting because she hadn't seen Russ since he'd dropped her off to pick up her truck. It had been the best of nights and the worst.

She'd felt all gooey and warm and intimate and *close.* For just a little while the attraction between them was something more. Something special that had a chance of being more. But then he opened up about the horrible way he was treated while working for the Denver PD. Outrage didn't begin to describe how she felt for him. And he'd endured a double whammy when the woman he loved had dumped him. Alexis. She was an idiot, and there was nothing left to say about her.

Lani knew from personal experience that honest men didn't grow on trees and Russ was that, and so much more. That night he'd taken her to his room at the boardinghouse he'd wanted her as much as she wanted him. Then the other shoe dropped. He'd said having someone's back didn't mean it was okay to lie for them.

She knew he was asking why she'd forced him to arrest her. She couldn't even explain that she'd done it so Anderson wouldn't be hauled off to jail and end up with a police record. That would lead to questions that she couldn't answer and would make her look even worse.

Telling the truth would break her promise to her brother. Refusing to answer would fuel Russ's doubts about her. As he'd said the other night—damned if she did, damned if she didn't.

She'd seen the look in his eyes when she hadn't taken the hint to tell all about her arrest that night. She knew that answers were important to him. Heck, he was a detective, and a case could be made for answers being his life. But this one she had to keep to herself. When he drove her to her truck, they didn't say anything, which kind of said everything.

So here she was, working at the bar and getting her hopes dashed every time the rusty screen door opened and Russ didn't walk in. It was slow right now, the time of the day after the lunch crowd and before the dinner rush. She stacked the few burger baskets and eating utensils in a big plastic tote and dropped them off in the kitchen. Busing tables was busy work and just what she needed if there was even the slightest chance of getting Russ off her mind.

To get ready for the dinner crowd she put napkin-wrapped silverware in booths and on tables. Filling saltshakers and napkin holders also needed to be done. Behind her she heard the screen door open and gave herself a stern warning not to look. Herself didn't pay the least bit of attention and looked anyway, just in time to see Russ walk in with Gage Christensen. The two men took a booth by the front window.

Alrighty, then, she thought. He would have to talk to

her now. It was her job to take his order. So she walked over and did her best to look normal, as if her heart wasn't hammering hard enough to be heard.

She smiled at both men. "Hi, Gage. Russ. How's it going?"

The sheriff took off his hat and set it on the booth bench beside him. "Good."

"Glad to hear that."

"It would be better if you and Russ could find out who spiked that wedding punch."

"Yeah." She looked at the detective. "It's pretty hard to figure out who's responsible when there are zero clues. So you shouldn't feel bad." About the case, she thought.

"I don't. Sometimes you get what you need." He met her gaze, and there was a disappointed look in his eyes. "And sometimes you don't."

Right now she wished he would cut her a little slack. More than anything she needed to talk to him, but not in front of Gage.

"So what can I get you two?" She pulled a pad and pencil out of her jeans pocket."

"Burger and coffee for me," Gage said.

"Isn't it a little late for lunch?"

"We've been busy. Going over all the information Russ gathered in the investigation."

Something squeezed in her chest at the reminder that Russ was temporary, and his allotted time was soon coming to an end. "Do you want fries or a side salad with your burger?"

Gage's expression was wry. "Salad? Seriously? Have you been talking to my wife? She thinks I need to eat more healthy food, and salad is at the top of her list. How can a man do a hard day's work when he eats the equivalent of grass?"

"This is where I point out that cows and horses kind of

do that, and they work pretty hard." Lani tapped her pencil against the pad.

"It's a conspiracy, right?" Gage teased. "All you women stick together."

"Darn right." She glanced at Russ, who'd been really quiet. "You're going to leave him blowing in the wind on this?"

One corner of his mouth curved up. "At the risk of mixing metaphors, he dug the hole. All he had to say was 'I'll take fries.'"

"He's got you there, Gage."

"Two against one. And I thought you were my friend, Russ." He sighed. "Fries it is. But don't rat me out to Lissa."

"It's not carved in stone, but I think discretion in this job is sort of client privilege. Your secret is safe with me." She looked at Russ. "What'll you have?"

"The same."

"Okay. So, I've got two burgers, fries and coffee." When both men nodded she said, "I'll get this going and be back with the coffee."

She took the order to the kitchen, where Rosey was doing the cooking, filling in during this slow time until someone came in to work the evening rush. Lani handed her the piece of paper.

"This is for the sheriff and Russ Campbell." Her boss gave seriously generous portions to law enforcement and US military veterans, so the information was important.

"Coming right up," Rosey said, tossing a couple of thick beef patties on the industrial-sized stove top. She lowered a basket of sliced potatoes into the hot grease then looked over her shoulder and frowned. "You okay, Lani?"

"Yeah."

"Now that I think about it, you've been kind of down the last few days. Not yourself. Are you really okay?"

"Fine."

"That's the code word for man trouble."

"No, it's just—"

"Save it." Rosey flipped the burgers and pulled two red plastic baskets from the shelf above the stove. "I know when a woman is unhappy, and it's all about a man."

She couldn't tell her boss about the problem because it involved Anderson's issue, and he'd said not to talk about it to anyone. But there were concerns that she *could* talk about. "Russ's time here in Rust Creek Falls is almost over."

"Not the end of the world." The other woman grabbed the long handle of the fry basket and pulled it up, hooking the contraption above the grease to drain. "He lives in Boulder Junction, and it's not that far away."

And that's when Lani voiced another something else that had thrown her. "He didn't want to give up his career in Denver and come back to Montana."

"Then why did he?"

"He exposed a corrupt cop on the Denver force, and no one backed him up. Without officer support it became dangerous for him and the general public if he stayed on." She watched Rosey put tomato, lettuce, onion and pickle in the baskets beside the open buns. "So he came home. But what if he decides small-town life doesn't appeal to him after living and working in the big city?"

"Then you go with him if he decides to make a change." Rosey's tone said "duh" but when she looked over, there was sympathy in her eyes. "Life is full of choices. Not all of them are no-brainers."

"Yeah." Lani had voiced the concern because it would break her heart if he moved away. There wasn't a doubt in her mind that if Russ asked, she would follow him anywhere. "I have to get their coffee, then I'll be back for the hamburgers."

"Okay. And, honey?"

She looked over her shoulder. “Yeah?”

“For what it’s worth, all those months Russ was coming here? Let’s just say it wasn’t about the beer.”

“Then what?” Lani asked.

“You. It’s obvious.”

“Not to me. Respectfully, you’re wrong, Rosey. He never talked to me.”

“I’m not saying it was easy for him to come in. Maybe he didn’t want to, but he couldn’t help himself. Couldn’t stay away from you. And—” Rosey pointed the spatula in Lani’s direction “—he couldn’t take his eyes off you.”

That was before she’d gotten herself arrested then took his keys to keep him from arresting her brother. If only she could tell him why she’d done it. Then he might understand. “Thanks for trying to make me feel better, Rosey.”

“Anytime. Hang in there, honey. The course of true love is never smooth sailing. That’s what Sam always says. He likes to talk in navy SEAL metaphors.”

Lani really hoped this wasn’t love. She didn’t know what to call it, but she didn’t want to even think the L-word.

She poured coffee into two mugs and delivered them to the lawmen. Both took it black. A few minutes later she brought their food and said, “Let me know if you need anything else.”

Then she turned her back and occupied herself with busy work while stealing looks at Russ. A couple of times she was almost sure he was looking at her, too. That was all she needed to make up her mind to talk to him alone if she got the chance.

Just after finishing his food, Gage pulled out his cell phone and answered it. She was too far away to hear what he said, but he grabbed his hat and slid out of the booth before ending the call. He reached into the pocket of his uniform pants to pull out money, but Russ put up his hand. Lani didn’t have to hear what they were saying. This was men dealing with who would get the check. Women usually split it however many ways down to the half cent. The guys were more macho and straightforward, and that wasn't altogether a bad thing.

She waited until Gage was gone to bring over the bill and set it on the table. "No rush on that. Can I get you more coffee?"

"No, thanks." That was his cop voice, the one without a drop of emotion and designed to make a person believe God gave him extraordinary good looks at the expense of a sense of humor. "I have to get going."

"Back to the sheriff's office?"

"Things to catch up on." That didn't answer the question.

"Well, things will just have to wait a few minutes." The place was practically empty, and this was as good a time as any to talk, so Lani sat in the space Gage had vacated moments before. "I have a question."

"Okay."

His expression wasn't as agreeable as his response. A woman couldn't have three brothers and not know when a man would rather eat glass than have a conversation. Tough.

Lani folded her hands together and settled them in her lap. "What's bugging you? And don't pretend you don't know what I mean. You acted weird the other night when we left the boardinghouse, and I'm pretty sure it had nothing to do with Melba Strickland's house rules. You've got the same look on your face now, so it's a good bet that nothing's changed."

"You don't want to have this conversation, Lani."

"If I didn't, I wouldn't have asked." Her heart was pounding hard. "So, what's wrong?"

"Okay." He toyed with the handle on his coffee mug. "I keep going back to that night. The Fourth of July. You made it impossible for me not to arrest you. I need to know why."

"And I told you that I can't tell you. But it has nothing to do with—"

He reached for the check. "We're done here."

"Wait, Russ. Please try to understand. I have a very good reason for what I did. Ask anyone and they'll tell you that I'm an upstanding person who follows the rules." She thought for a moment. "Except maybe at the boarding-house."

He didn't smile. "I know all of that. But honesty is the cornerstone of trust, and I can't overlook the fact that there's something you're not telling me."

"This thing isn't mine to tell. Haven't you ever made a promise to someone? A vow to keep something to yourself?"

"Yes. And my word is important to me. But when laws are broken, everything changes."

She remembered the look on his face when he told her about the woman he'd loved not supporting him at probably the lowest point in his life. A violation of his trust that left a mark. It was making him dig in and not give an inch now.

"This isn't entirely about obeying the law or honesty, is it, Russ?"

His mouth pulled tight, and a muscle jerked in his jaw. "I was blindsided once. It's not a feeling I ever want to experience again. That cost me my career. Now I have a second chance, and I'm not going to blow it."

Before she could collect her thoughts and tell him she was nothing like his ex, he'd tossed some bills on the table.

"Keep the change," he said. Without another word, he stood up and walked out the door without looking back even once.

Well, she had more to say. And if Russ thought that was the end of this, he didn't really know her at all.

* * *

After leaving Lani at the bar, Russ went back to the sheriff's office to go over his eyewitness interviews for the investigation. Maybe there was something he'd missed, a slip of the tongue to warrant another conversation. To the best of his knowledge, he'd talked to everyone who was at the park that night, except Old Man Sullivan, who disappeared from town after losing his ranch to Brad Crawford during the poker game at the Ace in the Hole. Without a lead, there was nothing left to go on, and Russ was damned frustrated. So he went back to Strickland's Boarding House.

After pacing his room for a while, he yanked his duffel out of the closet and set it on the bed then pulled jeans and shirts from the dresser. His assignment wasn't over for a couple of days yet but since he had the evening ahead of him, he might as well pack. He had nowhere to go, nothing to do and no one to do it with. Getting ready to leave Rust Creek Falls might take his mind off Lani and how much he wanted to see her, take her to bed again. If only he could trust her…

There was a knock on the door, and the sound was almost as startling as a gunshot. He hated himself for it, but couldn't help hoping Lani had changed her mind about holding back her secret.

He opened the door and was almost as surprised by who was there—Melba and Old Gene Strickland, the boarding-house owners.

"Hi," he said.

"Hello, Mr. Campbell." Melba was somewhere in her late seventies or early eighties, but didn't look a day over sixty-five.

"I thought you were going to call me Russ."

"If it's all the same to you, we prefer to address our

boarders more formally." Old Gene cleared his throat. "Friendly but not friends, if you know what I mean."

Not really, Russ thought. But he'd handled characters more eccentric than these two. "I'm okay with that."

"Good. Sensible. Young folks today have no boundaries. They walk around with those dang machines in their hands and don't look either way before crossing the street."

"My husband doesn't like smartphones," Melba shared.

"Stupid name," the old man grumbled. "If you ask me, the world would be better off without everyone sharing everything they do and think with everyone else on the planet."

"Change isn't easy," his wife sympathized.

"That's for sure," Gene agreed. "Computer nerds call it updates. Keep trying to make things better and just confuse the dickens out of folks. Should just leave well enough alone."

"He's still mad about Words with Friends. Gene loves to play Scrabble. Keeps his mind sharp," Melba explained. "So one of our granddaughters set him up and got him started. Then some genius decided it needed to be updated. The contraption wouldn't let him play until it was."

"The thing is," Gene said, "I couldn't figure out how to do it and got so aggravated I nearly chucked that machine from here to Kalispell."

"Finally, I started fiddling with it and somehow got a phone call from a nice young man who helped. Now Gene is playing again."

"Until the next time they want to make it better." The older man shook his head.

"Let's not borrow trouble," Melba advised.

"All this virtual stuff… There was nothing virtual about anything in the old days. You could see it, touch it, smell it. Hard work was hard work. Men were men, not telephone operators. And women had babies and took care of their families. They didn't have a badge and a gun and drive a fire truck."

"You're a bit of a chauvinist, dear," his wife told him affectionately.

Russ was beginning to wonder if they needed him and if not, why they'd come to see him at all.

"Was there something you wanted?" he asked. "Maybe you'd like to come in?"

"No, Mr. Campbell. We don't want to invade your privacy. This won't take long." Melba's voice took on a stern quality. "It's come to my attention that you had a visitor in your room the other night." She raised an eyebrow, waiting for him to confirm what she obviously already knew.

But how did she know? Was the room bugged? Did they have video surveillance? She continued to wait for him to fill the silence, and he wondered if she'd ever done criminal interrogations. But he wasn't a rookie and stared right back at her without saying anything.

Melba cleared her throat. "This is a boardinghouse, not a brothel, Mr. Campbell. I don't approve of premarital sex. If Lani Dalton visits you in this room, she best have your ring on her finger when she does it."

"Lani? How did you—" Damn. Melba was good. Drop a name, make it personal, emotions took over and something slips out.

Satisfaction sliced through the older woman's eyes. "I have a business reputation to maintain. It's my job to know what goes on under my roof."

"You do know that my stay here is almost over," he said, neither confirming nor denying.

"Of course. It's my responsibility to know," she said. "That still doesn't make it all right to break the rules. If we look the other way for you, standards go out the window. You're a policeman, Mr. Campbell. You know about enforcing rules."

"She's pretty set on this," Gene said.

Russ swore there was man-to-man sympathy in the old guy's eyes, but not enough to take on the little woman. There was no point in protesting, since he would be gone soon. And judging by the anger and hurt in Lani's eyes earlier, there was no chance she would step foot in this room again. He missed her already.

"I understand," he lied. "I guarantee no woman will be in this room while I still occupy it."

"I'm glad to hear that." Melba smiled. "Thank you for your understanding, Mr. Campbell."

Funny, Russ thought, how she could go from stubborn to sweet in a heartbeat. He would bet she was a formidable mother, loving and warm unless forced to take a hard line with her children.

"You're welcome," he said. "Don't worry about me—"

"Mrs. Strickland. Mr. Strickland." The voice in the hall sounded just like Lani. She appeared in the doorway and smiled at the older couple. "How are you?"

"Hello, Lani, dear," Melba said. "Gene and I are fine. How are you?"

"Good." She glanced at him, and the shadows visible in her eyes said that she wasn't fine at all. "I'm here to see Russ. Just to talk."

"If a pretty girl came to see me, I wouldn't be thinking about talking," Gene mumbled.

"Be that as it may," Melba said to Lani, "we know you were here the other night and were just discussing the situation with Mr. Campbell. Remember that respectability and reputation are important."

"Yes, ma'am. I'm the soul of propriety. Honest and true blue." She gave him a pointed look.

"All right, then. Can't do any more. It isn't against the law, so no one can be arrested." But the older woman gave each of them a look then settled her gaze on Lani. “You’re on your honor. Remember us to your parents, dear.”

“Yes, ma’am.”

“If I were you,” Gene said to Russ, “I’d give her a ring.”

“Come along,” Melba said to her husband. They started to walk away but she turned back and asked, “Any progress on your investigation into that unfortunate spiked punch incident on the Fourth of July?”

“No, ma’am. I’ve followed every lead, questioned everyone there that night who’s still in town. Didn’t turn up anything.”

“Too bad.” The older woman moved down the hall with Old Gene following.

And then he was alone with Lani.

“What did they say?” she asked.

“That they didn’t want to invade my privacy,” he answered wryly. “Just before invading it.”

“They mean well.” She shrugged.

He was still standing in the doorway, looking at her in the hall. “I’m surprised to see you.”

“I took a shot.”

Russ wanted to hold her so bad it hurt deep down inside. He wanted to kiss her and break Melba Strickland’s ridiculous rule. But he held back. “A shot at what?”

She tucked a long shiny strand of hair behind her ear. “Coming to talk to you. It felt like there was more to say.”

“That’s up to you.” And there it was. The elephant in the room. The secret she wouldn’t give up.

“Can I come in?”

“Sure.” He stepped aside and she walked past, the scent of her burrowing inside to warm his blood. He closed the door then turned and saw her staring at the bed, more specifically, the duffel with clothes beside it.

“You’re leaving?”

It sounded like an accusation, a breach of trust. Coming

from her that was ironic and got his defenses up. "I was only ever staying for a couple of weeks."

"But your time isn't up yet," she protested.

"It will be soon."

"So you're packing early." Her tone was flat. "I guess that means you can't wait to get back to your regularly scheduled life."

Truthfully, his life was a mess. He'd tried so hard to not let Lani matter to him, and now he knew it was going to rip him up to say goodbye. When he walked away from this assignment and this woman, all he'd have would be his job with Kalispell PD and it was safer to focus on that, on his career. But dammit, right this second, while he was close enough to feel the heat of her body, smell the scent of her skin, he couldn't imagine being alone, and the thought gave him a hollow feeling in the pit of his stomach. He'd better get used to it.

"Cases in Kalispell have probably been piling up on my desk while I've been gone. I'm going to be busy when I go back."

"So you're telling me you won't be coming to Rust Creek Falls? To fill in when the sheriff asks?"

"No." Because seeing her with no way to bridge the divide between them would probably kill him. But she'd come here to say something, and the least he could do was hear her out. "What did you want to talk about?"

"Are you even going to say goodbye?" There was a world of hurt in her eyes. "Never mind. It's not important now. Sorry I bothered you. Hope I didn't get you in trouble with the Stricklands."

"You didn't bother me. Lani, I—" He stopped when she opened the door.

"Bye, Russ," she said without turning around.

And then he was alone, and not even the fragrance of

her perfume lingering in the room could stop the empty feeling from widening inside him.

He kicked himself for not being able to get past his past. Lani said she wasn't at liberty to explain her behavior that night, and if he hadn't been sucker punched at the worst time in his life, her refusal probably wouldn't matter. He could overlook it. But even though all his instincts were telling him that Lani was as loyal and honest as she was beautiful, he kept tripping over his doubts. And as much as he wanted to go after her, Lani's secret was standing in the way.

Chapter Fourteen

On the way to the ranch the next morning Lani was tired. It tended to happen when you couldn't sleep, and that was Russ Campbell's fault. If he hadn't told her last night that he wouldn't be back to Rust Creek Falls, she'd have slept like a baby. But he did tell her, and he meant it. Tears she'd been fighting since walking away from the boarding-house filled her eyes. And that made her mad. He wouldn't take another chance on a relationship, and she wanted five minutes alone with his ex. It would feel good to give that woman a piece of her mind and a stern lecture about loyalty and support. She certainly hadn't loved him.

Not in Lani's book anyway. You couldn't be in love with someone and abandon them when they needed you most. She was pretty sure it wasn't her Russ distrusted as much as it was love. He was just looking for an excuse to push her away.

She parked her truck in front of Anderson's house and went inside to make coffee. The pot was already brewing, and she peeked into the living room and remembered the day she'd defended Russ when he took on Travis and Anderson. The room blurred as moisture filled her eyes.

"Morning, Lani." Anderson walked into his kitchen.

"Hey." She hadn't heard him approach and needed a minute to compose herself. She didn't want him to see her upset. "How are you?"

"Good." He moved closer and reached past her into the cupboard to get a mug. "We have to check the fences on the south edge of the ranch. Winter's coming."

In so many ways, she thought, a cold feeling settling around her heart. She brushed a rogue tear from her cheek and cleared her throat. "Okay. I'll take care of it."

"I've got Travis riding fence on the north side of the property."

"Right." She sniffled and still didn't look at her brother. She couldn't because he would know she was upset and grill her for answers she didn't want to give him.

"Are you okay, Lani?" There was concern in his voice.

"Sure." She went to the refrigerator and got out the cream then pulled the box of sweetener that he kept there for her out of the cupboard. "Why?"

"You're acting weird."

"So what else is new?" She was trying to act as if nothing was wrong, and it took a lot of energy she didn't have.

"You keep sniffling. Are you catching a cold?"

"Allergies," she said.

"Since when? I've known you all your life, and you never had allergies before."

"I've read that a person can develop them later in life. It happens." She was going to lose it and didn't want him to be here when she did. "You should go saddle up and get to work."

"Since when are you the boss?"

"It's getting late. You should go."

"Yeah, you're right. And I'll do that as soon as you turn around and look at me."

Damn. Why couldn't he be like most men and not notice that her attitude was off? No way she could get out of it, so she plastered on a smile and faced him. Anderson looked suspicious as he studied her for a moment.

A muscle jerked in his jaw. "You've been crying."

"I'm not a crier. You know that—" Of all people he knew that wasn't true. He'd held her the last time she cried over a man.

"Trust me on this, Lani. You're not a very good liar."

It was the sympathetic look in his eyes that finally did her in. She put her hands over her face and started to cry for real.

"Come here, kid." Anderson pulled her into his arms. "What's wrong? Whoever it is, whatever it is, I'll beat them up for you."

Dear God, his white-knight complex was what got her into this in the first place. He'd hit Skip Webster for punching Travis when he wasn't looking. "I…I don't want to talk about it."

"Don't care what you want, sis." He patted her back. "If you don't tell me what's going on, I'll have to find out on my own. And I'll start with Russ Campbell."

"No!" She pulled away and brushed at the wetness on her cheeks. "Why would you talk to him?"

"Because you haven't blubbered like this since that no-good, sweet-talking liar Jason broke your heart. This is man trouble, and he's the man you've been seeing."

"That doesn't mean this is about him. I don't want to talk about this, Anderson. It's not important."

"It's important if you're upset." His expression was hard, firm. "I know you, little sister, and you don't feel sorry for yourself as a rule. You'll feel better if you talk about what's bothering you."

Not if it made him feel bad. And he would. Because the secret she was keeping belonged to him. She knew he had his reasons for wanting it this way, and she respected whatever they were. Russ Campbell wasn't his problem, he was hers.

"I'll get over it." She sniffled, rubbed her eyes then did her best to smile. "See? All gone."

"In a pig's eye." Anderson's blue eyes flashed with anger. "Okay. That does it. I think I'll just go over to Strickland's Boarding House and find out what the heck is going on between the two of you." He turned toward the doorway that would lead him outside where his truck was parked.

Lani couldn't afford to call his bluff. If he really did see Russ, there might be punches thrown, and everything she'd gone through the night of the Fourth of July would be for nothing. And she'd have a broken heart on top of it.

"Wait. I'll tell you."

He turned around and poured himself a cup of coffee then leaned back against the countertop. "Start talking."

"I fell for Russ Campbell, and he's leaving town."

"That's not unexpected. His assignment was temporary."

"I know. See? I told you it was nothing."

Anderson took a sip of coffee from his heavy mug. "There's more, right? There has to be. You're not one to overreact like this."

"He's gone for good."

"He works in Kalispell and has a house in Boulder Junction. It's not like that's on the moon. You can go see him." Her brother had the look of a man who was sorry he'd started this conversation. "And the sheriff hasn't hired a new deputy yet, so he'll be back to help out just like before."

"He told me his workload has been piling up and he won't be back. Translation—he's just not that into me. Going after him would make me look just as pathetic as begging him to stay. It's déjà vu. Apparently, I'm not the kind of woman a man sticks around for."

Anderson set his mug on the counter then rubbed a hand across his neck. "I don't get it. Word all over town is that you've got him hooked."

"Not so much." She didn't say more. No need to tell him their relationship had been up and down. That it started with sex in a jail cell, turned into a cover for working on the investigation then ended with sex in his boarding-house room.

Anderson stared at her for several moments, and then the light went on in his eyes. "This is about that night in the park. When he arrested you."

"Yes." She should have known eventually he would put two and two together. "I'm not very good at pretending. He knows I had a reason for getting him to take me in."

"A distraction," Anderson said grimly. "So he wouldn't arrest me."

She nodded. "He doesn't trust me."

"You should have just told him you did it to keep me out of jail and left it at that."

"He's a detective, Anderson. He wouldn't have bought the family-loyalty thing. He'd dig deeper to find out why it was so important that you not be arrested and have a black mark on your record." She sighed. "With your custody issue pending, it wasn't a chance you could afford to take."

"I love you for what you did." He smiled, but it faded fast. "But the promise you made to me is costing you the happiness you deserve." Her brother made a fist and slammed it on the counter.

"It's complicated. And one way to look at it is if he can't trust me, believe that I had a good reason for not telling him, and that I'm not breaking any laws, maybe I dodged a bullet and this is for the best."

"You don't really believe that," he said.

"I might after a while."

He closed his eyes for a moment and shook his head. "This is my fault. I never should have made you promise. Better yet, I never should have told you about my personal problem in the first place."

"No. I'm glad you did." She sniffled and put her hand on his arm. "It's a heavy burden to carry alone. I just wish—"

"What?" He frowned when a tear rolled down her cheek.

"I wish Russ didn't have baggage that makes him not want to take a chance on me, on us."

The tears started up again, and Anderson pulled her in for a hug. "I'm so sorry, Lani."

"Me, too."

"It will be all right."

"I know." She grabbed a tissue from the box sitting on his counter and blew her nose. "I'm made of stern stuff. It takes a lot more than this to get me down."

"We'll figure out something."

How she loved her big brother for wanting to fix what was wrong with her life. But there was nothing he could do. His child was involved, and that had to be his priority.

"I can take care of myself," she assured him. "I'll be fine."

But she didn't believe that. Not really. She was in love with Russ, and it had taken losing him to bring that realization into sharp focus. She had a feeling nothing would be all right ever again.

Several days after Lani had come to see him in his room Russ was at the sheriff's office late into the evening on his last day of the spiked punch assignment. There were loose ends and paperwork to tie up before he left Rust Creek Falls for good. He was writing his final report on the investigation, and it was taking a lot longer than reports usually did. Everything in the account of his findings reminded him of Lani.

Riding with her to the falls for strategy planning. The interview with Jordyn Leigh Cates Clifton that resulted in their dating cover story to explain spending time together. When she went rogue and had a beer with Brad Crawford before she ruled him out as a suspect but ended up in Russ's bed. That hadn't moved the investigation forward, but it was a night he would never forget.

He'd known better than to make love to her but hadn't been able to help himself. But that was no excuse. It was selfish to keep seeing her when he couldn't take a chance and had no intention of committing. He didn't trust any woman to be there for him, so what was the point?

Still, he kept seeing the look in Lani's eyes when he'd said he wouldn't be coming back to Rust Creek Falls. She'd felt used, and he couldn't blame her. He hated himself for hurting her, and it was all he could do to stop himself from going to her.

But she deserved better than that.

The front door opened and the sheriff walked in. "I thought you might still be here."

"I didn't expect to see you. Thought you'd gone home to your wife." Russ envied his friend. Gage was good at his job, and there was no question that the man was devoted to the town. But Russ always got the feeling that a part of him was only filling time until he could be with the woman he loved. "Why did you come back?"

"This is your last night. I thought we might go get a beer at the Ace in the Hole."

"I have to finish this report." Russ was stalling because the thing was finally done. The truth was that if he saw Lani, his resolve to put Rust Creek Falls in his rearview mirror might weaken. He refused to be made a fool of again, and the only way to be sure it wouldn't happen was to keep her out. And speaking of the investigation report… "I'm sorry I let you down."

"You didn't." Gage obviously understood what he was referring to. He moved closer and rested a hip on the edge of the desk. "Why would you say that?"

"We still don't know who spiked the punch." He shrugged. "That's a complete failure to achieve the objective for which I was hired."

"Not from my perspective," Gage said. "Your interviews ruled out pretty much everyone who lives here in Rust Creek Falls, so we know who didn't do it. On top of that, there hasn't been another incident. My theory is that this was random mischief, probably by someone who was passing through town. Folks are starting to breathe easier now. Not so skittish. And that's thanks to you."

"Still, not knowing who did it is like a rock in my boot. I really wanted to catch the person responsible."

"Whoever did it was smart. They covered their tracks and got lucky that no one witnessed it. But the exhaustive investigation sent a warning that misconduct won't be tolerated. My gut is telling me there's no further threat."

"I agree." Russ printed out a hard copy of the report for the file along with his notes. Then he saved everything on the hard drive and shut down the computer he'd been using.

"So, about that beer…" There was a definite challenge in Gage's eyes.

"I'm all packed up. Ready to head out." Russ let the thought hang between them.

"I've never known you to turn down a beer."

"Always a first time. Been here in Rust Creek Falls a long time. I really should get back." Back to an empty house and a life that was nothing but work. No Lani. No sassy lady with a quick wit and sunny smile waiting for him at the end of a hard day. He was going to miss her. But he'd been lonely before and could learn to deal with it again.

"I think you're avoiding her." Gage folded his arms over his chest. A challenge if there ever was one.

"You're wrong." Russ didn't need to clarify who *her* was.

"I don't think so. You're the detective, but I keep the peace here in Rust Creek. I'm an officer of the law, too, and powers of observation go with the territory."

"What's your point?"

"A blind man could see there's something simmering between you and Lani. And there has been ever since that night you were locked up together."

Because she stole my keys, Russ thought. Funny, he didn't mind so much anymore that she had. What happened after that was another fine memory he could take with him.

Gage looked thoughtful. "Come to think of it, even before that night there was something. More than once I was at the bar with you. I saw the way you looked at her, and she was looking back just as hard. I was always surprised that you never did anything about it."

"I got burned once."

"Figured as much. But still… You didn't make a move."

"Like what?"

"Like asking her out, Sherlock," Gage said.

Russ thought he'd covered his feelings pretty well, but now Gage's detective senses were apparently tingling. "Is that why you suggested Lani could help with the investigation? Were you playing matchmaker?"

"Wish I'd thought of it." But there was a self-satisfied look in Gage's eyes. "But she really does know everyone in town."

"You were playing Cupid? Trust me, it's not a good look for you," he snapped.

Russ could have refused to work with her, but took the suggestion because this was Gage's town, and he understood it. Maybe part of him jumped at it for an excuse to see her. But after spending so much time with Lani, leaving her was going to rip his heart out.

"What the hell were you thinking, Gage?"

His friend's eyes narrowed. Instead of answering the question, he asked, "What the hell did you do that night in the cell?"

Russ recognized the brotherly protectiveness in the sheriff's attitude and respected it. But before he could frame a response, Lani's actual big brother walked into the office.

Anderson Dalton stopped in front of the desk. "Gage."

"Nice to see you, Anderson. What brings you in here?"

"I need to talk to Detective Campbell." He looked at both of them before his steely-eyed gaze settled on Russ. "Alone, if that's all right."

"No problem. I've got paperwork." He straightened then went into his private office and closed the door.

The angry look on the other man's face made Russ stand, ready for anything. He figured Gage had seen it, too, and that's why he didn't leave the office.

"Nice to see you, Anderson."

"I doubt that. We need to talk."

There was only one thing they had in common. "About Lani."

"You made my sister cry. She doesn't do that very often, and it makes me want to tear you apart."

Russ wouldn't mind mixing it up. The other man was about his weight and height but didn't have the kind of training a cop gets. But he understood where Anderson was coming from. Having a sister was a responsibility, and Russ *had* hurt Lani.

"So what's stopping you?"

"For one thing, my sister wouldn't like it." Anderson almost smiled.

"What else?"

"I want all the facts out in the open."

"What might those be?" Russ asked.

"This misunderstanding between you and Lani is my fault."

That was a surprise. Russ stared at him. "Go on."

"The night of the wedding reception I was drunk from whatever was in that damn punch."

"You and most of the town," Russ said. "What's your point?"

"I decked Skip Webster because he sucker punched my brother. It was pretty obvious that you were headed over to slap cuffs on me. Lani saw what was going on and jumped in the fountain to distract you from arresting me."

"Why would she risk going to jail?" Russ demanded. "Charges would probably have been dropped, especially when it turned out that the punch was tampered with."

"In the moment no one knew that or was thinking about it." The other man's expression hardened. "Lani was only thinking about me, about the fact that it would put a black mark on my record."

"So what if there was an arrest? It wouldn't be that big a deal."

"It could be for me." Anderson let out a long breath then met his gaze. "Recently I learned I have a child I never knew about. I'm going to file for custody, and we both know the family court system favors mothers, so any ding on my record would affect my chances of prevailing in court."

"So why didn't Lani just tell me that?"

"I made her promise not to tell anyone." His blue eyes blazed, evidence that he was angry and frustrated with himself and the whole situation.

"Not even your family? Your father's an attorney." A good one, according to Lani. She'd made that clear to Russ when they'd spent the night behind bars.

"The last thing I want is to involve my family." Anderson rubbed a hand over his face and suddenly looked tired. "It would just hurt them to know there's a grandchild out there and they never knew. It's my problem, and I'll deal with it. I'll give them the facts when the case is resolved."

"And Lani is the only one who knows?"

He nodded. "And now you."

"Why are you telling me?"

"Because when Lani makes a promise, she keeps it. End of story. She's so loyal, she would jeopardize her own future in order to keep a vow she made to me. I couldn't live with myself if I was to blame for her unhappiness."

Russ felt as if he was in a shoot-out, with bullets coming from every direction. He was having trouble wrapping his brain around all this. "What are you saying?"

"God knows why, but Lani loves you, and this secret is coming between you. She says you've got your reasons. But personally I think it's an excuse to play around then duck and run when things get complicated. An easy way out."

"You're wrong." Anger pulsed through Russ. "I know what it feels like when a woman you thought you knew throws you under the bus when the going gets tough. Your career is going full-speed backward and just when you think things can't get worse, she hands back the ring and proves you wrong."

"So you got dumped." Anderson clenched his jaw and a muscle jerked. "Detective, you don't know what personal betrayal is until you find out a woman had your baby and for years never bothered to let you know."

He was right. Holy crap, Russ thought. That was pretty low. With absolute certainty he knew that Lani would never do that. With that realization came another one. He'd acted like an ass.

"Okay, Anderson. You win."

"Believe me, I'd give anything not to come out on top in this situation. But it got to me," he said. "And I needed to tell someone. Lani was there for me, and I don't know if I could get through this without her. But there's no way I'm going to let my problem cost her."

"I appreciate you telling me." Russ felt a weight lift from his shoulders and realized those weren't just words. He really meant what he said.

Anderson nodded. "I'd appreciate it if you'd keep what I just told you confidential."

"No one will hear it from me." Russ held out his hand, and Anderson took it.

He respected what this man was going through and his overriding concern to protect his family. And Lani was helping him. She was so committed to keeping her word and having her brother's back that she was willing to let Russ think the worst of her.

That's what the pain in her eyes was all about, and he hated himself even more for putting it there. He knew now what she'd meant about not saying anything also being a way to have someone's back. He was too blinded by bitterness from his past to see her pure heart. There must be a way to fix what he'd done.

"Thanks, Russ."

"No problem." He watched Anderson walk outside and get in his truck parked at the curb.

Gage must have heard him leave because he came out of his office. "So what was that all about?"

"I could tell you, but then I'd have to kill you." Russ dragged a hand through his hair.

"Lani." Gage's tone said *gotcha.* He rested his hands on his hips. "And before you risk your detective shield by asking why I would say that, I'll just give you the facts."

"Please do." Russ folded his arms over his chest and waited.

"If Anderson was here to report stolen cattle or inform us that a crime was committed, you would have happily shared that information. But he's Lani's brother, so the logical conclusion is that he came to confront you about your relationship with his sister." Gage stopped and made a great show of examining Russ's face.

"What?"

"I was just wondering where the black eye is. The fat lip."

"And why would that be?"

"Because you courted his sister, and now you're running out on her."

Russ opened his mouth to dispute that assessment then realized there was a lot of truth in it. And it was pointless to ask how he knew all this. Rust Creek Falls had a gossip mill that was second to none.

"Let's just say that Anderson is a very civilized man."

"So you're really not going to tell me what he said?"

"It's classified." Russ grinned at his friend's obvious frustration. "Lissa will just have to find something else to blog about."

"I thought we were friends," Gage commented.

"We are."

"Good. Then in the spirit of friendship I'm going to let you know that Lani is working tonight." Gage met his gaze. "Go to the Ace in the Hole and buy your own damn beer."

"Understood."

Russ grabbed his leather jacket off the chair and headed out the door. It was always good when a friend's advice coincided with your own plan of action.

Chapter Fifteen

"Hey, Lani, can I get a glass of wine for Kathy?"

"Sure thing, Wes. What'll you have?"

"Beer."

She opened a bottle of Chardonnay and poured some into a wineglass, got a longneck from the small refrigerator below the bar then set both on cocktail napkins in front of Wes Eggleston and his pretty brunette wife.

"Thanks," they both said together.

"It's nice to see you two in here. Where's that adorable little girl of yours?"

"My mom is keeping Chloe overnight." Kathy smiled at her husband. "This is date night."

"Oh?"

"We went to counseling," Wes explained.

Lani remembered talking to him about it just a few weeks ago, the day Russ had come in to ask for her help in solving the town mystery. Fortunately, things worked out better for this couple than they had for her.

"How did that go?" she asked. "Since you're here I'm guessing it was positive?"

"It wasn't as bad as I expected." He glanced at his wife. "We have some things to work through. Make our relationship stronger."

"And she suggested we make an effort to do something alone at least once or twice a month." Kathy took a sip of wine. "And I have to say it's working for me."

"That's great," Lani said.

"I love my daughter so much," she said, "but it sure is nice to have a break. Quiet time just for Wes and me."

"I never knew she felt that way," her husband said. He looked at the woman beside him with a lot of love in his eyes. "Communication is one of the things we're going to work on. Sometimes that means just listening."

"Makes sense," Lani said. "I'm so glad for you guys. This is really wonderful."

"Hey, Lani—"

She glanced over her shoulder and saw a cowboy at the far end of the bar, his arm around a tiny blonde. He was trying to get her attention. Holding up a hand, she signaled that she'd heard then said to the young couple, "Congrats. I'll ring up your drinks when I get a few minutes. Gotta go."

Annie had picked the wrong night to call in sick, Lani thought. The Ace in the Hole was always hopping on Fridays. The dinner rush had slowed but a lot of people were coming in for drinks. And by people she meant couples. They were smiling, laughing and cuddling. The PDAs going on were enough to make her wish they'd all get a room. Fate seemed determined to rub her nose in the fact that she was alone. She'd lost Russ. Although technically she'd never had him, which meant she couldn't really lose him.

Her attitude sucked, but there was no way to take a

timeout and adjust it. *Sue me*, she thought. It was hard to watch couples in love when the night before you'd had your heart handed back with a firm no-thank-you.

She grabbed two beers and handed them to the cowboy and his lady. He gave her a bill and told her to keep the change, so that's what she did. Standing beside the cash register, she surveyed the bar. Almost every stool was taken, and she couldn't see the tables in the main dining area. Just as well. It was probably full of more happy couples for her to envy.

A twosome right in front of her got up after leaving money with their bill. Before she could say boo, the empty stools were taken by her brothers.

"What do you want?" she said.

"Wow." Anderson's eyebrow rose. "If that's the best you can do, your people skills could use some work."

"My skills are just fine, thanks. I don't have to be nice to you."

"Says who?" Travis's eyes twinkled. "I'm telling Rosey."

"Seriously? You'd rat me out?"

"In a hot minute," he said cheerfully. "What are brothers for?"

She put a hand on her hip. "Somewhere I read that brothers teach us you can love someone even though they irritate the crap out of you. Why are you here?"

Lani glanced at Anderson, and he nodded slightly, letting her know that Travis was aware of what happened between her and Russ. So this was a show of family support. It was all she could do not to cover her face and blubber like a baby. Along with so many other wonderful purposes, brothers were there to cheer you up when a man broke your heart.

"You guys are the best." She pointed at each of them. "Don't let that go to your heads, or I'll deny I ever said such a thing."

"My lips are sealed." Travis gave her an evil grin. "Until the next time you get me in trouble with Mom. Then all bets are off."

"We'll see about that. It will go badly for you." She dragged the side of her hand across her neck, the universal sign for cutting his own throat. "What can I get for you troublemakers?"

"Beer," they said together.

"Okay." Lani retrieved two from the fridge and noticed the supply was getting low. She made a mental note to restock as soon as business slowed down a bit. Twisting off the caps, she set the drinks down in front of her brothers. "Cheers."

Travis took a sip. "Speaking of troublemakers… I had no idea you were really sweet on that detective."

"I'll get over it." She knew this was his last night in town, and her heart was breaking.

Rosey chose that moment to join them. Of course she'd heard everything. "I knew there was something bothering you. If these two clueless cowpokes are here to cheer you up, it must be bad. What happened with you and Detective Dreamy?"

There were customers sitting to the right and left of her brothers, and people with drinks in hand filling the open area behind them. All of a sudden it got very quiet, as if everyone in the bar was waiting to hear her answer.

"Well," she started, "things didn't work out."

"That tells me exactly nothing," Rosey informed her. "It didn't work out for you? Or was it him? It makes a difference who the not-working-out part came from."

If there was a God in heaven, Lani thought, the earth would open and swallow her now. She waited, but nothing happened, and her boss was looking as if she expected a response.

She leaned over and whispered, "You know, Rosey, I don't really want to talk about this right now."

"It's all right, honey. This is the best time to get it out. No one is listening."

"What'd you say, Rosey? I can't hear you from back here."

Lani couldn't see who'd said it, but the voice was male. She gave her boss a "really?" look.

"Everyone cares about you, Lani."

"She's right about that," Anderson chimed in.

Lani pressed her lips together and again fought the urge to cry. People being nice to her was both a blessing and curse. If they were mean, she could get mad. For a little while, anger would fill up the empty place inside her. But all this caring threatened to reduce her to a puddle of goo, and that wouldn't be good, since she was trying to keep a low profile over this whole thing. And she knew if she started talking about it, she would cry.

"Please, Rosey, about Russ and me? Let's just call it a draw."

Russ wasn't the bad guy. She wasn't enough for him. She wasn't the one he wanted enough to take a chance with. And her heart cracked a little more when she thought about him being alone.

"That means it was him," Rosey said.

"No. It's just one of those things," Lani answered.

There was a murmur from the crowd, and Anderson glanced over his shoulder at someone. There was an odd expression on his face when he said, "Stop protecting him, Lani. He doesn't deserve it."

"It's not about being deserving." She stared at her brother, who'd gone all negative and intense, which wasn't like Anderson at all. "A person is entitled to their feelings. You can't force something that isn't there."

"You're too good for Russ Campbell," Anderson continued. "He's a fool to let you get away. Someday he'll regret his bonehead move."

Lani blinked at him. Something was wrong. She knew he'd come to the bar during her shift in a show of family solidarity and support. But it wasn't like him to trash-talk publicly like this. She glanced at Rosey, who was staring out into the crowd around the bar.

"You're one of the most open-minded people I know. And a good judge of character. Will you please talk some sense into my brother?"

"Can't," her boss said.

"Why not?"

"He's right. I never knew what you saw in that outsider anyway."

"Right on," someone said. "Didn't trust him at all."

"Travis? A little help." Lani was hoping for backup.

"Don't look at me. I can't say Anderson is wrong. The sheriff hired him, but I was never all in on that." Her brother shrugged.

"I can't believe this," she said.

"He's a snoop and a spy." That was Skip Webster, aka the sucker-punching weasel. "Asking questions. Insinuating a guy's guilty when he's not."

Lani thought he had some nerve criticizing Russ. After all, he was the one who'd started the fight on the Fourth of July. That guy was the reason she'd gotten herself arrested in the first place. Part of her wanted to thank him because otherwise she wouldn't have some wonderful memories of Russ. The other part wanted to call him out for being a hypocritical jerk. The other part won and she snapped.

"Stop it, all of you. I can't believe what I'm hearing. Did someone spike your drinks again? Because this isn't the way Rust Creek Falls folks act. How ungrateful you are! The only thing he's guilty of is trying to keep you all safe. And this is the thanks he gets." She glared at everyone in general and Skip Webster in particular. "You could take a lesson from Russ Campbell, you Neanderthal twit. That man is good and kind. Loyal and upstanding. He deserves your thanks for putting his life on hold. And the only thing he wanted was to help this town. You should be ashamed of yourselves. God knows I'm ashamed of you."

"And you're in love with him," Rosey said as if she'd known it all along.

The time for discretion had passed, Lani realized. She didn't care who was there, who knew how she felt. She stared at her boss and said, "Yes. I'm in love with him. So there. Now the whole town knows, and I don't give a flying fig."

There was movement in the crowd near the bar, and everyone was whispering as they parted to let someone through. When she looked to see what was going on, Russ was standing in front of her.

"Hi, Lani."

Her heart stuttered. "Russ… I didn't see you there."

Russ wanted to jump over the bar and pull her into his arms and never let her go. He'd almost been stupid enough to walk away from her, from the best thing that ever happened to him, without trying. Without telling her how he felt.

"I know you didn't see me," he said to her. "But Anderson did. That's why he was dumping on me."

"Anderson?" Her eyes went wide as she snapped a look at her brother.

"It's true," he admitted. "Rosey, too."

"That's right," the older woman said.

Lani looked at first one then the other, clearly astonished that they would publicly put him down. "But why?"

Russ knew the answer to that one but let her brother respond.

"Even though you're ticked off at him right now, I

knew you'd defend him. Because you always do the right thing, no matter what. That's just the way you roll." Anderson looked at Russ, daring him not to blow this opportunity. "I thought you should know just how special my sister is."

"I knew it before I walked in the door." Russ nodded his thanks. "Someday I hope you meet a woman even half as remarkable."

"I'm done looking." Anderson's vow was laced with the bitterness of his betrayal.

"I thought I was done, too." Russ figured it was a waste of breath to try to change the other man's mind. No one could have convinced him that he would ever meet a woman as beautiful on the inside as she was on the outside.

A woman he could count on.

Travis was watching the exchange with an expression that was equal parts amusement and confusion. "Well, chap my hide and slap me silly."

"Maybe later." Russ looked at Lani, hoping he could undo the damage he'd done. "Lani, we need to talk—"

She shook her head and backed away from the edge of the bar. "Rosey, I'm taking a break now."

"Take as long as you need, honey," her boss said. "I've got this."

As an officer of the law, Russ couldn't say that he always got his man, but he'd be damned if he was going to lose this woman. Lani quickly moved to the end of the bar and flipped back the top to make her escape. But Russ was waiting for her. Blocking her exit. She tried to pass but he didn't move.

"Let me pass," she ordered.

"Not until you hear me out."

"You've already said more than I want to hear." She tried to maneuver around him, but he sidestepped and checked her.

"It can't be overstated that I admire your loyalty, but this stubborn streak of yours is kind of annoying." But cute, he thought. As long as she used it for good, and by that he meant being on his side. Somehow he had to get her there.

"Isn't it lucky that you're leaving Rust Creek Falls and won't have to deal with me any longer, Detective?"

"I'm not going anywhere until we clarify some things." Now he was getting frustrated. And everyone in the crowded bar was watching and listening to what they were saying. Probably taking notes for the gossip column. It didn't escape his notice that some of the spectators were pointing, whispering, and money was changing hands. If he didn't miss his guess, they were betting on the outcome of this standoff.

What Russ had to say should be said in private, and he knew just the place. He reached for her hand and said, "Come with me."

She pulled away. "I don't think so."

"Wrong answer." Russ scooped her into his arms.

Lani made a surprised little sound, but he ignored her and turned toward the door. A man on a mission. It must have shown on his face because the customers standing around the bar with drinks in their hands parted like the Red Sea. He moved to the screen door and someone opened it for him. Russ appreciated that, since his arms were full of wiggly woman.

"Let me go," she said angrily.

"No."

"This is humiliating. Obviously, you haven't finished making me a joke in this town, one that I can never live down."

"This isn't a joke to me. All I want is for you to listen to what I have to say." He turned left and carried her down

Sawmill Street, past the Rust Creek garage and gas station. "So I'm taking you somewhere you can't run away."

Apparently, she was getting a clue about what he had in mind because she asked, "Are you arresting me?"

"Yes."

"What for?"

"Failure to yield."

"Oh, please. Don't pretend you're not relieved that I turned you down." Her tone dripped sarcasm even as her arms sneaked around his neck.

"If I was relieved, would I be carrying you through town?" Their faces were inches apart. "I mean this in the nicest possible way, Lani, but you're not a feather."

"Well, excuse me for not losing five pounds on the off chance that you were going to trump up charges and arrest me again. If I'm so heavy, just put me down."

"Nope."

Russ carried her to the door of the sheriff's office, and Gage opened it. Thank God he was still there.

"Got a citizen's tip from the Ace in the Hole," he explained.

"Here's another one for you," Russ said. "Go home."

"Understood."

"Wait," Lani said. "This is false arrest."

Grinning from ear to ear, the sheriff let himself out and closed the door behind him.

Russ carried her through the office and stopped in front of the empty cell they'd occupied the last time she was here. He used one hand to slide the barred door open then walked inside as it shut and automatically locked with the two of them inside.

He set her on the bunk. "Now you're a captive audience."

Lani blinked up at him, and suddenly all the sass and spirit were gone. She looked uncertain and vulnerable. "I don't understand. Why would you do this? It will be all over town soon, if it's not already. People will think we're… That you and I are…"

She was his life, that's what she was. She'd been there for her brother, for her family. There was no doubt in his mind that she would do the same for anyone she loved, and he hoped with everything he had that she cared about him.

"I love you, Lani."

"Since when?" She sat up straight, folded her arms over her chest and refused to look at him.

"Since the first time I saw you."

Her gaze jerked to his. "What?"

"I walked into the Ace in the Hole after working a shift for Gage. You were carrying a heavy tray full of beers, and I wondered how you didn't drop it. Surely the power of the lightning that hit me would knock you off balance."

"But you barely said a word to me." Her eyes were wide and so beautiful a man could drown in them and go down smiling.

"I couldn't. I knew if I did, resistance would be futile." He shrugged. "And I was right."

He looked around the cell, remembering the night he'd arrested her, in that wet yellow sundress that was practically transparent. It hadn't taken long for her to break him down, annihilate his defenses. He'd kissed her and was lost. The rest was history.

He sighed. "Even after the night you deliberately locked me in here and I fought against trusting you, I tried to ignore what I felt. My history had been nothing but a horrible warning."

"You and me both," she said.

"My instincts were telling me that you were exactly what you seemed—beautiful, loyal, someone who put her family first. Everything I ever wanted. But I couldn't trust that. My judgment was so far off I didn't have any faith in what my gut was telling me."

"What changed your mind?" There was the tiniest bit of skepticism in her voice.

"Two things." He blew out a breath. "When I faced the reality of leaving town and not seeing you every day, it felt wrong, empty. I've gotten used to seeing that pretty face, and leaving you was the last thing I wanted to do."

"What was the other thing?"

"Anderson told me about his legal battle and said that's why you deliberately got my attention the night he hit Skip Webster. That he couldn't afford to be arrested. And how he made you promise not to tell anyone."

"I can't believe he did that."

"Just so you know, he swore me to secrecy, too. And I plan to honor that promise just like you have. You set a high bar, Miss Dalton."

A small smile curved up the corners of her mouth. "So at the bar, Anderson was playing matchmaker."

"Yeah. And he's not the only one." At her questioning gaze he said, "Gage was at the sheriff's office when Anderson came in. After your brother left, he suggested I go to the Ace in the Hole and talk to you."

She smiled mysteriously.

"What's so funny?"

"I'm just trying to picture the two of them dressed as Cupid—tights, wings, the whole nine yards. Oh, wait. Cupid wears a diaper. Either way, not pretty," she said.

"Yeah." He dragged his fingers through his hair. "So, in front of everyone tonight, you defended my honor and said you love me."

"Yup, everyone heard," she agreed.

"Then there's only one thing left to do to close this

case." He moved in front of her and went down on one knee. "Marry me."

"Yes!" She grinned then threw herself into his arms and said, "I give myself up."

Epilogue

Lani snuggled up to Russ in the big king-size bed at his house in Boulder Junction. After the night he'd proposed in the jail cell, she'd all but moved in with him. He was back to work as a detective for Kalispell PD, working a shift for Gage now and then when he had time, to keep up the investigation into the wedding punch situation.

Every night after work they ended up in the bedroom, and sometimes they even watched TV. It turned out both of them liked crime dramas and trying to figure out whodunit. She took great pride in the fact that she guessed right as often as he did.

She fluffed the big pillows behind her then moved back in beside his big, warm body. He pulled her closer, and she rested her cheek on his chest, listening to the steady beat of his heart. He didn't know it yet but she had big plans to get that Kalispell PD T-shirt off him. Not that she didn't love the way it hugged all his delicious muscles, but she'd rather see and touch his bare skin.

Right now she was going to be smug and superior and rub in the fact that in the show they'd just finished watching, he had deduced wrong. "I told you it was the angry coworker."

He made a scoffing sound. "That was way too obvious. I was sure it was the nauseatingly sweet employer of the undocumented workers."

"You underestimate my investigative skills and powers of observation."

When he laughed, the sound vibrated through her. "I have never underestimated any of your powers, brainy Lani. Especially the power you have over me. You are one smart lady."

"Not smart enough to figure out who spiked that punch at the wedding."

"Yeah. It really bugs me that we couldn't solve the case." He shook his head. "All the shenanigans that went on that night, and no one saw anything."

Lani tapped her lip. "That's not entirely true, Russ. Whoever writes the gossip in Rust Creek Ramblings for the paper saw quite a bit. There were stories for weeks."

"Never could get an ID on the writer, either," he grumbled. "But I have an idea."

"Is it necessary to remind you that you're not on the case anymore?"

"Not full-time. But Gage asks me to follow up every once in a while. Besides, I can't stop thinking about it." He shrugged. "Occupational hazard."

"So what's your idea?" she asked.

"I think I'll send a note to the paper addressed to this anonymous columnist and ask whoever it is to come up with his or her own theory about the mystery. I think that will be irresistible to this person and could stir the waters. Maybe flush out the perp."

"It's worth a shot." She leaned back a little and looked

up at him. "You know that at some point you might have to put this in the unsolved file?"

"Yeah, but I hope not." There was an amazingly tender expression in his eyes when he looked at her. "And it's not about justice."

"Really?"

"Do you remember when we talked to Jordyn Leigh Clifton? When she said that she and Will are grateful for what happened. If they hadn't unknowingly gotten drunk that night and married, happiness might have passed them by."

"Yeah," she said. "Now I know what she meant. If that punch hadn't been spiked, my brothers wouldn't have mixed it up, and I wouldn't have danced in the fountain to save Anderson."

"And I wouldn't have arrested you."

She grinned happily. "Getting arrested wasn't nearly as bad as I thought. Both times it was kind of amazing, each in its own way."

"Yeah. As weird as it sounds, I'd really like to thank whoever messed with the punch at that wedding."

"I know what you mean." That day would always have a special place in her heart. "But I have to say when we get married, I'm a no vote on having an open punch bowl. I don't want my groom to be in detective mode on our big day."

"Where's your sense of adventure?" he teased.

"Alive and well." She caught the corner of her bottom lip between her teeth then decided to share something she'd been thinking about. "I really liked working the mystery with you. We make a good team.

"No argument there." He ran his finger along the side of her neck, over her chest, and stopped at the swell of her breast. "What's going on in that creative mind of yours?"

"This might sound a little crazy, but…" *Just spit it out.*

"We could open a detective agency, be like those husband-and-wife private investigators on TV."

"Hmm." His mouth was on her neck, and the single syllable vibrated through her.

"I have another idea." She reached for the bottom of his shirt. "Let's get this off."

"I'm a yes vote on that." His look was wicked as he whipped it off over his head then tossed it away. When he stared into her eyes, his expression was completely serious. "I love you, Lani."

"I know." There wasn't a doubt in her mind. "And I love you."

He wrapped her in his arms, and they were lost in each other for a long time. She was grateful for everything that happened. The park. The punch. A mystery ingredient. All of it had brought her to this moment and a lifetime of magic with her very own maverick.

* * * * *

MILLS & BOON®

If you loved this book, you will love the other books in this fantastic The Vineyards of Calanetti mini-series.

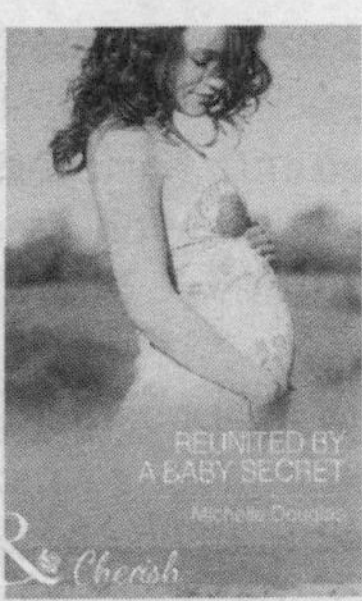

A Bride for the Italian Boss – Susan Meier
(July 2015)

Return of the Italian Tycoon – Jennifer Faye
(August 2015)

Reunited by a Baby Secret – Michelle Douglas
(September 2015)

Soldier, Hero...Husband? – Cara Colter
(October 2015)

His Lost-and-Found Bride – Scarlet Wilson
(November 2015)

The Best Man & The Wedding Planner – Teresa Carpenter
(December 2015)

His Princess of Convenience – Rebecca Winters
(January 2016)

Saved by the CEO – Barbara Wallace
(February 2016)

Visit www.millsandboon.co.uk/calanetti

0815_23_MB514

MILLS & BOON®

Buy A Regency Collection today and receive FOUR BOOKS FREE!

Transport yourself to the seductive world of Regency with this magnificent twelve-book collection. Indulge in scandal and gossip with these 2-in-1 romances from top Historical authors

Order your complete collection today at **www.millsandboon.co.uk/regencycollection**